WATCHED

"I agree," Sheriff Tyler said evenly. "If this is about money, though, I can think of others around Irv who had even greater need. What I can't figure out is just why you've always been so certain it *is* murder. If we hadn't sent the body out for an autopsy with a genuine forensic pathologist, old Doc Harmon would have signed off on this as an accident and we would never know that murder had been done."

I looked him in the eye. "So, it is murder."

"Yes, blunt force trauma. One killing blow to the head. Probably from a fireplace poker, which is still missing. You were right about that, too."

I nodded, not surprised. "That was quick work."

"It's the only suspicious death in the county. Irv got moved to the head of the line." Those probing eyes were back on my face. Those beautiful, probing blue eyes.

"I feel like you've been watching me, Sheriff. Constantly. Why? Do you think it likely that I killed Irv and am trying to blame someone else for my wicked deeds?" I asked bluntly, and watched with satisfaction when Tyler blinked.

"Hadn't crossed my mind." But he was lying.

"It better have," I said, "or you're in the wrong line of work."

Other books by Melanie Jackson:

MELANIE JACKSON

A
Curious
Affair

LOVE SPELL NEW YORK CITY

LOVE SPELL®

June 2008

Published by

Dorchester Publishing Co., Inc.
200 Madison Avenue
New York, NY 10016

ISBN 10: 0-505-52738-3
ISBN 13: 978-0-505-52738-7

The name "Love Spell" and its logo are trademarks of Dorchester Publishing Co., Inc.

Printed in the United States of America.

10 9 8 7 6 5 4 3 2 1

Visit us on the web at www.dorchesterpub.com.

For my husband, who almost wasn't here.
And also for the many wonderful employees and volunteers
who make the animal shelter a home for the dogs and cats
until they can find new families of their own.

A
Curious
Affair

FOREWORD

My name isn't Jillian Marsh. I don't live in Irish Camp.
I don't have a friend named Crystal, a lover called Tyler,
or a cat named Atherton.

But that doesn't mean that this story isn't true. The
details have been changed to protect the innocent, because I have to live with my neighbors. And a few laws
were broken. But the gist of the story is true. Cross my
heart and hope to die.

When a Cat adopts you there is nothing to be done about it except to put up with it until the wind changes.

—*T. S. Eliot*

CHAPTER ONE

It was raining. This isn't unusual for March in the Sierras, but it had rained without let-up for the last seventeen days. That wasn't the only reason that I was on my third Seconal and fourth Drambuie, but it sure had something to do with it.

Suicide wasn't my goal that night, but I hadn't ruled it out either. The TMJ—temporomandibular joint disorder, if you want the full medical term—wasn't getting better and I was tired of sucking on soup and mumbling at my concerned neighbors through clenched teeth. I also felt guilty, and without means of making reparation to the one I'd wronged. After all, how do you apologize to the dead?

Winter had rushed the calendar and arrived weeks ahead of schedule, in early November. It was the kind of season where the cold actually leans on you until you're ready to buckle under the weight, your frozen bones snapping when you hit the unforgiving ground. We'd set new records for cold and snow for the first six weeks of the season, and then it warmed up marginally and started raining. I didn't think it was an improvement.

It wasn't the dark or cold that was bothering me, though. The fact was, I was more alone than I had ever been in my life. Calvin was barely a memory to everyone else, but not to me. In spite of the usual assurances of time healing all wounds, my heart was still a space filled with dull aching, and there was no one to talk to about it. We'd spent eleven years together—pretty happy ones. And then he'd gotten this nasty cough. He was a smoker, and the surgeon general had been proven right; the carcinogens had caught up with him. I couldn't face what was happening, so we never spoke about it. It seemed to me that he hadn't lived long enough to be dying, but it turns out he had, and our silent avoidance of the subject and two rounds of chemotherapy didn't keep Death away. How I regretted that silence now when there was so much of it! I should have let him talk, admit his fears, allowed him to say anything he needed to say. But I hadn't let him talk to me. I had never told him how much I would miss him, either, and regret was my constant companion. That was three autumns ago. And that morning I had finally cleaned out his bedroom closet, erasing yet another part of him. Cal was an orphan who had no siblings or other relatives that we knew of. When he was gone from my life, he would be gone from everywhere.

I don't know why I chose that morning to erase him. The sad odor of loss hadn't yet begun to eddy about his clothes. The closet wasn't stale or musty. But it didn't smell like him anymore, either, and in a moment of bravery I had decided to clean it out. I did it, too—cleaned it down to its damned dust bunnies cowering behind the cowboy boots. All the His and Hers things went into boxes as well: the champagne flutes from our wedding etched with our names, the Himself and Herself towels, the twin sets of luggage monogrammed with our initials. They all seemed to mock my loneliness. *I am Grief—I am Legion*, they sneered from every room in the house. And every time I thought I was done I found something else, some fresh cruelty: unused season tickets to the opera; the new gas grill still sitting in its box in the garage because, by the time warm weather had rolled back around, Cal had felt too ill to use it.

My intention was to have a yard sale on the first clear weekend, but with the rivers of mud and downed limbs from the ancient oak trees, the front yard looked more like a beach after a shipwreck than a formal garden. I knew I'd have to hire a cleaning crew before I let anyone on the property or risk a personal injury lawsuit. It was all too much. I gave up on the plan. My loneliness had been honed to surgical sharpness on the strop of guilt and grief, and now it was slicing at my heart—a heart that already, in the days after Cal's death, had gained an incision as long and deep as itself. I didn't understand why it went on beating then, and I didn't know why it was beating now. All those midnight hours I'd put between me and his death hadn't been enough. No matter how many things I boxed or bagged, the mercy of forgetfulness was denied me.

I'm not ready to sell Cal's things anyway, I thought, tossing back the last of the Drambuie. Why had I emptied the closet? I could have just as easily sawed my wounded heart out with the rusty blade from Cal's abandoned toolbox. It would have been less painful than packing my love away in black garbage bags.

But none of this was the worst. The worst of all my tribulations—hands down—was that getting hit by lightning thing. It had happened last October, on Halloween in fact, and ever since then the cats had been talking to me.

How sweet! you're thinking. *She talks to cats.* But that isn't it at all. I wasn't talking to the cats. The cats talked to *me*.

And this isn't something sweet. Not at all—not even now that I'm more used to it. The implications are rather horrifying. Think about it. First, there was the little matter of this peculiarity making me question my sanity, especially when I was out in public and no one else seemed to hear what I was hearing. Leaving questions of my rationality aside, it wasn't like the cats and I were discussing Descartes, politics or fashion. Why would we? We didn't even have species in common. They crap in bushes and eat carrion and wash themselves with their tongues. They're not . . . well, human. Personally, I wouldn't dream of relieving myself in a bush, and am a very picky eater. Conversations with felines tend to run to demands for food and observations about how I smell. They follow me around, whining in voices that grate the nerves, repeating themselves incessantly. And by that night I was sick of it—the sly feline voices pouncing on me every time I went outside; the cold, the rain, the pain. Sick enough to take way too many pills and chase them down with the last of Cal's favorite liqueur. It was sink-or-swim time, and I still didn't know which I wanted to do; so I thought I'd let the pills decide. If I lived to see morning, then I would start swimming again.

Anyhow, that's what I was doing the night Atherton arrived. I didn't know his name was Atherton then. At first I didn't even know he was a cat. He was just a shadow hovering in my window, slightly more solid than the wet night behind him and the phantoms in my brain. It took him a few minutes and lots of name-calling to finally get my attention, but once he did get it, I was all ears. This cat actually had something interesting to say.

Admittedly my impressions of our first meeting are

confused, being filtered through a river of amber liqueur and floating on the rafts of my little red pills. It took me a while to understand what he wanted—and to throw up the last of the drugs and alcohol in my abused stomach—while Atherton perched on the edge of the bathtub and looked on like Virtue reproving Vice. As hard as it was to imagine, death had come calling in our small mountain town. The agent of death had been male, worn a sodden denim jacket, and smelled like butt—as in, unhygienic ass; not cigarette ends. And as soon as I could get my head out of the toilet, Atherton would take me to see his handiwork for myself.

It shows you how bad I was feeling that, when I stopped vomiting, I actually pulled on my boots and a parka and followed that talking cat into the rainy night. But I had to see if Irving Thibodaux was, in point of fact, dead.

If animals could speak, the dog would be a blundering outspoken fellow; but the cat would have the rare grace of never saying a word too much.

—Mark Twain

(Author's note: Mr. Twain clearly never heard cats talking)

CHAPTER TWO

The night was cold and wet, just as I expected it to be. I must admit to having been a little frightened by Atherton's grim summons, so I armed myself with a knife, which I don't normally do when I go for an evening perambulation. I was unnerved, and not because I was following a talking cat, though I'm betting that's the part of the story that most bothers you, since I assume you're sensible and sane. I don't blame you, either. It strains the credulity. But, no, I was nervous because cats didn't play practical jokes in my recent experience, and I truly believed that someone had killed my neighbor. And since the most likely person to have done that was a junkie looking for the stash from Irv's marijuana patch, they might still be out there looking around for it.

Not for the first time, I found myself reconsidering my stance on firearms in the home. Sometimes there is just no substitute for what my brother calls "a fistful of boom-stick."

Atherton tried to lead me straight up the hill, over the fallen log that had lain there rotting on the deer path for the last five years and past the stand of cedars whose whispering branches were scabbed with graying lichen and sagging as though they carried the weight of the world. I wouldn't have minded a scramble in daylight, but the mountain was also thick with poison oak and I'm quite allergic. So I called to the cat and insisted we take the road, even if the water and gravel flowing down the mountain made it more of a stream than a street.

I ended up carrying Atherton, who didn't want to get his paws any wetter. It could have been a comforting experience, but he was heavy—the cat is really more of a puma than a domestic feline—and he was too tense to trust me not to drop him. We did a sort of push-pull isometric exercise all the way up the hill with both of us squinting against the greasy rain that filtered through the oaks and arrived in fat drops that felt as bitter as tears. Wind sang in the power lines beside us and the remorseless, wounded sound in the wires set my jaw to sympathetic thrumming. Ever since I was hit by lightning, my jaws lock when I get cold. I wished I'd thought to grab my hunting cap with its long fur earflaps before leaving the house.

If you've never lived in the country, then you'll have no idea how dark a moonless night can be. We had a moon, but just barely, and the tiny lunar sliver at the corner of the sky wouldn't have provided much light even if the heavens hadn't upended themselves over the town in an impenetrable barrier of wet that would have blocked out the sun at high noon. As it was, the night that pressed in on us was as black as the color black can be. Perhaps Atherton could navigate it unaided, but the flashlight was necessary for me, since I had no desire to fall down the mountain, whose face sheered away from the ever-shrinking road now crumbling away under the rain's relentless onslaught.

I looked back once and saw the lights of Lincoln

Street winking through the bare tree limbs. It looked beautiful, even in the rain, a watercolor in amber that reminded me of a painting by Avi Thaw. I could hear the faint strains of bass-heavy music riding the damp air. In my slightly nauseous state, I still found the scene magically charming, even though I knew the glow was due to smoke from the fireplaces that had been burning nonstop for weeks, probably causing acid rain.

My late husband Cal and I had always had a nostalgic—and mostly book-and-television-manufactured—wistfulness for a life in the era that preceded the one we were born into. That was why we ended up living in the Gold Country of the Sierra Nevada foothills. It was sort of the land that time forgot. In the 1850s, it had somehow been encased, preserved, frozen at the apex of its charm. Some days, I thought Irish Camp the best of all possible worlds: straddling the line between my desire for life in another era, and being plain old boring or even dangerously third-world. This was a small town of few cell phones. Poor reception in the mountains kept them away, though if Nature hadn't provided a deterrent, the town council might have passed an ordinance. We didn't have strip malls downtown, but did have a few doctors and access to antibiotics and X-ray machines. Basic cable was available right in the town proper, if it didn't have the mind-numbing number of stations obtainable in the Silicon Valley. Few kids owned iPods; instead most had bikes. The town wasn't rich, but it wasn't grindingly poor either—until you got to the very edges, where the forest and the secrets got thicker and older. That's where the multigenerational families lived—usually all together in cabins that have never seen a building inspector, and where one could only dream of indoor plumbing.

As a rule, the higher up the mountain you go in Irish Camp, the rougher the pavement grows—assuming that the roads were ever paved in the first place, which is a

chancy hypothesis. In many places, the growing pot-
holes are filled with gravel every spring when the winter's vengeance becomes apparent and even the Jeeps
can't cope without taking some damage. After a few years
of neglect, the macadam completely disappears. Some
of us find this rustic and appealing. That's because we
have four-wheel drive and aren't too particular about
the state of our paint jobs.

The lack of paving also keeps out all but the most in-
trepid tourists.

Don't get me wrong, our town loves tourism and
thrives on the money it brings. But we want to keep our
visitors on the picturesque main streets where the
shops and restaurants are, and not have them falling
into the many abandoned—and not so abandoned—
mine shafts and coyote holes that litter the countryside. Which was yet another reason to travel by road on
this dark night: our hill has more than its share of
death traps.

In spite of the sky's endless drooling, stinging rain, I
slowed as we neared Irv's shack, feeling reluctant to take
the next step. The cabin was a shake-sided affair whose
dessicated shingles were an invitation to the gods of
fire. It had no insulation and its heating was provided
solely by wood-burning stove. Because it was in a bower
of trees, the constant smolder coming from the stove-
pipe chimney tended to keep the cabin in a constant
haze. But not that night. The shack was dark and no fire
was burning in the potbelly. More telling still, the four
pie tins Irv filled with crunchies for the neighborhood's
stray cats were all empty.

I set Atherton down at the bottom of the three
wooden steps that led to the shack's only door. The cat
immediately set about smoothing the fur I had ruffled.

"Are we alone?" I whispered, as best I could through
clenched jaws. I have no idea if I actually need to speak

out loud for cats to hear me. If I don't, they tend to ignore me unless I get their full attention.

Yes. Except for food man. Atherton's eyes were wide and unblinking.

"And he's really dead?" I mumbled.

Really, really dead. Atherton's mewl sounded mournful, but his meaning was getting clearer.

"You saw Irv die?"

Yes. Atherton hesitated. *Irv sent us away. He does when humans come. But I didn't leave. I stayed by the window. Smelly-butt man was wrong. He smelled . . . dangerous.*

"I don't know what dangerous smells like."

Bad. It smells bad.

"But smelly-butt's gone?" I wanted to be sure.

All gone. He ran away.

I walked slowly up the stairs, testing them as I went. When I'd visited Irv last September, I'd had one break under me and scraped up an ankle pretty badly. He'd replaced that step—probably with lumber he'd salvaged from somewhere else on the property—and assured me it was now safe, but I still didn't trust the stairs.

The door stood ajar. Since I was wearing thick gloves, I didn't hesitate to reach inside the room and flip on the lights. Or, I should say, light. The cabin was a one-room affair with one corner blocked off by a short wall to form a rudimentary bathroom. Being a thrifty soul—or perhaps fearing to overload the ancient wiring he'd rigged up on his own—Irv had a single, twenty-five-watt bulb screwed into the ceiling-mounted fixture in the center of the room.

The light was dim but sufficient to show us Irv, who was lying sprawled on the floor with his head resting on the sandstone hearth he'd laid under the stove. It was too narrow to be a real hindrance to shooting sparks, and definitely not up to code, but then neither was the wiring, or the cabin itself—which I doubted was even on the county tax rolls—so this wasn't a surprising violation.

I viewed the floor with trepidation. Irv had joked once that the foundation consisted mainly of old car jacks and prayer, and since he wasn't on the best of terms with The Lord, it paid to be a bit cautious when visiting. Fortunately, I didn't need to get any closer. By leaning to my right I could see all of the body. It was apparent that Irv was, as Atherton insisted, really, really dead. The milky eyes were fixed and staring in two directions, one knocked out of place by the blow that had dented in the side of his head. More disturbing was the half-smile on his blue lips. It suggested a residue of unsuitable emotion, an inappropriate degree of humor from someone dead by misadventure.

"Damn."

There is nothing so horrible as the moment when you realize that you will never see someone again. Not ever. They will always be gone, forever and ever. There is a *then* when you had them and a *now* when you don't. The two are segregated, divided by an insurmountable barrier: death. And even when death brings an end to pain for someone who is suffering—and a horrible kind of relief to the ones who have had to watch the agony—it is still rather like having a vampire swoop down and give you a hateful, draining kiss. This is part of death's—or life's, I've never been clear which—ritual. As the old saying goes, life is a slow way of dying. From the moment we are born we are heading for the final demise.

It's true, we deny this vehemently. This is because it is impossible to live happily while in mortal dread of disintegration. And while the experience of loss doesn't kill you outright, once the leech of fear and grief takes hold, you never know—or I never have—quite how much of your soul or will it will suck out before it moves on. One's anguish at a loss is a sort of protection money that you have to pay for the privilege of going on living. Few of us die without first paying this tax of grief and failure. Most of us get charged a bit at a time; first a parent, perhaps a friend and then another, a spouse. God help us, a child. John Donne had it right— "Any man's death diminishes me." At least the death of anyone I ever cared about.

Death, however, wasn't going to be getting much out of me this time. I was anemic, down a quart on emotion since Cal died. The vampire had taken too much, and I hadn't enough left to mourn Irv properly.

That didn't mean I was indifferent. Seeing him made my heart twist, and butterflies with razor-sharp wings began to flutter in my stomach. Irv was a hermit who lived alone . . . like me. Our cases were too similar for me not to have a brief moment of *There but for the grace of God go I*. How long might I lie dead on my kitchen floor before someone found me?

I gave a sigh that was as much weariness as mourning, and looked at the rest of the room. Muddy tracks criss-crossed the sagging floor. I wasn't a Girl Scout in good standing, but anyone could see that the top layer of prints came from a pair of what we used to call waffle-stompers. Large ones, too. I looked at the worn soles of Irv's smallish cowboy boots and felt my already found-ering spirits sink. This definitely seemed to suggest that he wasn't just dead; he had been murdered. Irv didn't have visitors to the cabin, excepting his sometime girl-friend, Molly Gerran, who had petite feet. And, once in a while, me. The big-footed stranger hadn't come be-cause of some long-standing invitation.

"Well, hell." It came out more as *ell-ell*.

I wasn't drunk anymore, but I wasn't in the best phys-ical shape of my life either. My stomach felt like the aftermath of a tornado, and depth charges of my ap-proaching hangover were beginning to go off behind my eyes. And—oh God—I was going to have to call the sheriff. The thought made me uncomfortable, because this situation presented me with a bit of a conundrum. First off, I had to hope that the relatively new sheriff would know who I was—a respectable writer—and who I was talking about—Irving—and where the cabin was located. Sheriff Hartford—of the Hartford Foundry, Hartford Quarry, Hartford Inn and the Hartford Shoes Hartfords—had retired in September and, in a move that was so revolutionary as to be thought damn near socialist, the town council had hired someone from Southern California to replace him. Someone who actually had a background in law enforcement.

There was also the matter of what I was going to say, and how I would say it. Clear speech was excruciating when I was cold, and right now I was pretty much stuck with locked jaws. I also reeked of booze. I'd have to talk, though, liquor-breath or no. This wasn't a case where one could just write a note and slip it under the door, or send an e-mail.

Understand, I'm not bug-eating crazy, so I look normal enough, but the termites in my mental attic had been eating away at the supports of reason for the last several months. I'd been hearing voices—ones that belonged to cats—at inconvenient moments, and that's enough to draw the interest of any lawman or head-shrinker. This kind of interest was something I wanted to avoid, especially with a murdered body at hand. Who better to blame for a death than the local psycho?

"Damn it, Irv. Why me?" It actually sounded more like *Tham-ith-Irvvvv-iiii-ee*, but Atherton understood. He had no answer, though, beyond the obvious one. The cat told me: Because I was the only one who would understand.

"Swell," I responded. "But what are we going to do?" *We must find smelly-butt man and punish him.*

I didn't try to explain that this was only one of our problems. I figured the workings of the criminal justice system might be beyond kitty-cat comprehension. Certainly it was beyond me to explain when my face hurt so much.

"Something is wrong here," I said instead. I meant wrong beyond Irv lying dead on the floor.

Poor food man. Atherton sounded sadder than I did, and perhaps he was.

Irving was a friendly enough guy, but few of the newer people—mainly the Bay Area refugees, who were refurbishing the old craftsman bungalows and Victorians on our hill with an eye to living in them during their golden years—knew that. You see, Irv had a few off-putting habits, like spitting constantly and smiling broadly, showing uneven, chaw-stained teeth that belong only in the past, or in a postapocalyptic world where they have no dental care. Or, more to the point, where people do a lot of drugs and forget about oral hygiene. Yeah, drugs. We weren't entirely stuck in the 1850s. Stills and moonshine had been partially replaced with backwoods pot patches, and at least one methamphetamine lab had been discovered last April by federal agents. Pot was a more reliable source of money than panning for gold—which Irv also did, in the summer. I knew about this because Irv had kept Cal supplied with marijuana while he was doing chemotherapy, and he had assured me that it was pesticide-free because he grew it himself.

I exhaled slowly, looking at the black mold that was growing up the cabin walls, sensing the general air of filth and neglect, and found the place to be the most overall depressing home I'd ever been in. The air was worse than musty, worse than moldy. Thank heavens the stove wasn't lit, the place would have smelled like the world's most repulsive barbecue.

The sheriff would probably recall Irv. Irving had had a habit of getting pinched on drunk-and-disorderlies at the roadhouse in Charlestown or The Three-Legged Mule on any Saturday when the temperature got to be over ninety degrees and irritated his heat rash and his temper. Surely the new sheriff, Tyler Murphy, would have arrested him at least once. Actually, I was sure he had. One of the brawls even made the local newspaper. There had been a small fire at The Three-Legged Mule early in October: stupidity in burning candles in unstable wine bottles, the fire chief ruled, not deliberate arson, and not bad enough to close the place for good. A coughing and smudged Irving had been there, front and center, with a set of busted knuckles and the bar's gasping cat sitting at his feet. Irv had broken off the fight to go back in and save the cat when he'd realized it was trapped in the storeroom. The poor thing died three weeks later, in spite of Irv's heroics. I recall Irv being more upset about the cat than having to pay the court-ordered fine for brawling.

"Irv." I shook my head. I was pissed off at being the one to find him, but I also felt sad. No one should die alone. Or with a murderer shuffling you off this mortal coil before you were ready.

Some of his clients would miss him, and maybe his ex-girlfriend, Barfly Molly, though she had once told me in a fit of drunken honesty that Irving was the worst possible result of a one-night stand between the town floozy and an itinerant gold prospector, so maybe not. Mostly his passing would be mourned by the town's feral and stray cats. Irving was the patron saint of strays, which he used to say he liked a whole lot better than people. He'd spent a lot of time talking to those cats ever since his accident. Oddly enough, Irv had also been hit by lightning and survived. We had that in common.

Now, given my recent experiences, I had to wonder if they ever talked back to him.

Atherton patted my leg above the ankle. He was careful to keep his claws sheathed.

"Yeah. I know. Give me a minute," I mumbled, but the cat had no trouble understanding my slurred diction. "Something just isn't . . . Something is . . ."

Not right.

Something was wrong, but I wasn't able to figure out what and time was ticking by. I should either go in and close Irv's staring eyes, which were unnerving me, or else I should shut off the light and head back down the hill and make the call to the sheriff. Instead, I just stood there, freezing water running down my neck, this time really looking hard and feeling uncomfortable in a way I'd rather not have experienced.

Irv's cabin looked like I felt. And the more I saw, the more disheartened I was. First of all, because Irv was dead and staring off at nothing, but also because the cabin itself was so utterly forlorn. Molly had left a year ago, but she also seemed to be hanging around the place as a gingham ghost. Her style of decorating had always made me claustrophobic. The new owners of Molly's Eats hadn't bothered to redecorate when they bought her diner, so it remained as a testimonial and warning of what happened when domesticity ran amok. Irv's place looked like a smaller, dirtier—much dirtier—facsimile of Molly's Eats. Dusty checked curtains with too many rows of eyelet ruffles hid the only two windows in the cabin. A small, claw-footed table was smothered under a filthy tablecloth sewn out of red and blue bandanas, also trimmed in eyelet, and buried under mounds of dirty cups and dishes. There was a vase of flowers on the sill that was too old and cobwebbed to be poignant. I'd had some bad days after Cal died—who cared about dishes or laundry when your insides had been emotionally gutted?—but this wasn't something recent, some momentary domestic despair. It looked like the work of someone who was certain that his shack would never be visited and therefore would never need to know cleanliness again.

I felt a sharp pang of guilt. I hadn't come to visit Irv in weeks. The cold and wet—and yes, my own despair—had kept me indoors.

I looked left. Tacked to the walls were dozens of Polaroids of cats. Some people take pictures of their family, Irv took pictures of his obsession: felines. Or maybe the cats were his family. I didn't know of anyone else who would claim him as kin, though it was likely he had some, and the old-timers at The Mule would know who and where they were. The upside of small-town life is the intimacy you share with your neighbors. The downside is the inbreeding and nepotism that created mini-dynasties like the aforementioned Hartfords and Andersens (of Andersen Insurance, Andersen Automotive, and Andersen Lumber). And the inability to keep any secret for long.

A gust of wind blew by me, stirring the skirt of the dirty tablecloth and making dust and ash from the cold hearth dance in the air. Atherton sneezed. I shook my head and stepped back, hoping it was laziness and not soul-shattering despair at losing Molly that had kept Irv from changing things when she broke it off between them.

Atherton patted me again and looked pointedly at the empty pie tins. As I stared out into the wet night, I became aware that we were no longer alone. A number of thin felines had crowded in around the base of the stairs and were staring at me with fixed gazes.

"I can't feed you, guys. Not here. If Atherton is right, then this is a crime scene. I can't go in and get the food."

The cats mewled. *Hungry*. It was a Greek chorus that

grew steadily louder, making my head echo with painful sound. *Food man hasn't fed us since morning. Cold! We need food.*

"Stop!" It was more plea than order. Like Atherton, the cats seemed to understand me even though my diction was terrible.

I looked back into the cabin and the telltale prints on the floor. The giant sack of cat food that Irv bought—or maybe stole—from the feed store was right where it always was, sitting on the floor right next to the door. Knowing I shouldn't, I picked it up and started pouring kibble into the dented tins. A dozen lean shadows crowded in, purring thanks as I put the sack back in its place and then closed the door.

I told myself that it wouldn't matter. The food would likely be gone before the sheriff got here, and no one would be the wiser. Surely no one would notice the raindrops that had collected on the glossy face of the purebred Persian that adorned the bag.

The sheriff. My nagging feeling of unease returned, but this time I squarely faced the problem that awaited me. What was I going to say—or slur—to the sheriff? That Irv was dead certainly; but murdered? That he had been killed by a man in a denim coat and waffle-stompers who "smelled like butt"? And I knew this because while drunk and considering ending my life, a stray cat had come to my window and told me so? Yeah, that would all go over real well.

I shivered, feeling cold, wet and frightened. Just as I had since October.

"Thit, thit, thit," I said, but only because I was having trouble with my sh's. Then I reached into my pocket, found the tube of Rolaids I always carried and forced one between my teeth and began tonguing it. It would be bad if I threw up because I wasn't sure I could actually get my jaws open.

"Okay, let's go," I thought and slurred.

As I started down the hill, I could almost feel Atherton slinking after me like my shadow, a reminder that I had to do the right thing and not just go home to my warm bed. He needn't have bothered. Seeing Irv lying up there dead and all alone had shaken me. I had to ask myself again: If I died, how long might I lie on my kitchen floor before someone found me? And when they did find me, would they care? Or would they just feel inconvenienced by the discovery of the hermit lady who seemed to spend her days talking to cats instead of humans?

My eyes began to sting. I hate to admit that it was at least half self-pity that put the tears there.

Again I thought, *There but for the grace of God go I.*

The city of cats and the city of men exist one inside the other, but they are not the same city.

—*Italo Calvino*

CHAPTER THREE

There were lights in town, but segments of the old streets near the sheriff's department were still drenched in darkness that, for the first time to me, felt ominous. I spent a lot of that walk looking behind me for things that weren't there. Perhaps I would have been braver if Atherton had come with me, but I was alone. Atherton had elected to stay at my place since it was wet and there was nothing he could tell the sheriff that he hadn't told me. And bringing him along might seem downright weird. After all, it wasn't like he was a dog who would want to go for a walk no matter what the weather.

The sky's normal nighttime black-and-white color scheme was distorted by more than winter clouds. Small fires, though mostly neutered and contained inside tidy houses where they devoured only small bits of trees, remembered enough of what it was to conspire together and become a forest fire. They vomited smoke together, painting the air above town with smoldering ash until the sky was as darkened by this as it would be by a more terrifying, summertime conflagration. The suspended soot in the air had turned the town into a place as dank and dark as an old miner's lung. The rain tried, but it couldn't clean the air fast enough to outpace the chimneys' steady output. It was worst in the narrow streets where the wind never ventured. Eventually, the town was going to have to give in and pass an ordinance forcing the use of clean-burning stoves. I thought about this as I pushed open the door to the sheriff's office, eyes stinging and nose protesting the smoky assault.

The door had a cowbell that rang out like the knell on doomsday. Lucky me, the man himself was on duty. I had been hoping that maybe I would catch one of the deputies who had been friendly with Cal.

I'm not stupid or masochistic. I had tried phoning the sheriff's office before walking into town through the mud river that used to be the road. But I had been so cold and the connection so bad that the sheriff or whoever answered hadn't been able to understand me. My choices were to forget Irv until morning, or slog down the hill to the station.

So I'd slogged. And grumbled, though I knew whoever was on duty would grumble more going back up the hill. We are a small county and the sheriff, along with his two deputies and a secretary/dispatcher, was responsible for all of it. In an emergency like a forest fire, the sheriff could ask for help from other agencies like the highway patrol, but for little things like homicide, he was on his own. I knew he'd be thrilled to hear he'd need to take a midnight stroll.

In the Central Valley, the farmland has been tamed and even trained to do man's bidding. The foothills and the Sierras themselves are less biddable; it's the geography. Once the mountains were whole, but in some long ago cataclysm, the Sierras had shrugged during one of the great earthquakes and clefts appeared. Water, ever the opportunist, had done the rest. The land was fissured.

Sure, it's beautiful here, but hard, and the land does not suffer fools. Killing heat in summer, murderous cold in winter, rock slides, flash floods, avalanches—both seasons lay traps for unwary hikers and skiers who come from more moderate climes. The poor fools don't even know to be afraid.

Part of the sheriff's unofficial job is to see that visitors don't blunder into danger, and if they do, that they are rescued right away. For this reason, I was given to understand, he had embraced the geological version of know-thy-enemy. Which is a long way of saying that he had already hiked some of Viper's Hill and checked out some of the abandoned mineshafts located along what looked like a great cross-country ski trail.

But would his familiarity get me off the hook for a return trip to Irv's cabin? No. Neither would my protest that I was cold, tired, scared and in pain. Any lawman would wrestle with my guilty conscience and easily overpower it. I was in for a long, painful night.

Sheriff Murphy is handsome enough to look at. He's one of what my mother would have called the Black Irish. Some of my friends have even admitted to crossing the room to get a closer look at him. I stood there in the doorway that night and glared at him with eyes that failed to find anything to admire.

The sheriff looked up and smiled pleasantly, not put off by my glower.

"Was that you on the phone earlier, Miss Marsh? I thought maybe it was an obscene phone call. Livened up the still watches of the night."

"Not tonight," I said. My glower deepened, and so did his smile. A hint of a dimple appeared in his left cheek.

"Damn. Well, let me guess—you've seen a UFO, Miss Marsh. That's what brings you in. Please pull up a chair and make yourself comfortable while I get the particulars."

"Miss*us*," I corrected. Actually I said *mithuth*. My jaw was loosening up in the heat of the station, but it was still far from functional. It's a tribute to the sheriff's ear that he could understand me. "And if I say yes and I've ridden in one, will you let me go home and sleep it off as soon as I'm done here?"

"Perhaps." His gray eyes twinkled—they actually twinkled—and I thought of that G. K. Chesterton poem, "The Ballad of the White Horse":

> For the Great Gaels of Ireland
> Are the men that God made mad,
> For all their wars are merry
> And all their songs are sad.

He finally explained when I said nothing more. "Don't get cranky. I just want to know if you've been seeing any of the strange lights folks have been calling in about this evening. I'm going to have to get onto PG&E and find out what's up at the station. There'll be hell to pay if folks lose power again. It's been out three times this week already, and they seem to think that I am personally responsible for it."

In a small town the sheriff was pretty much responsible for everything that couldn't be handled by the priest, the doctor or the undertaker. I felt a moment of sympathy.

"Oh. No, I haven't seen lights or green men or even downed power lines," I said, less grumpily. "I've seen rain and a dead body, though. My friend, Irving Thibodaux, is dead. That's what brings me in. And if you want a guide up the hill to Irv's place then we need to go now. The road is mostly mud and getting worse by the minute—and we can't take the car because the track's barely graded, let alone graveled."

"I see. Well, let me fetch my coat." He reached for

the sheepskin jacket on the back of his chair. It was a large coat. Tyler Murphy isn't a small man. "Are you quite certain that Irv is dead? Might he just be . . . extremely indisposed?"

He meant dead drunk.

"No, he's really, really dead," I said, echoing Atherton's reply to me when I had asked the same question.

The sheriff finally lost his smile. He sighed. "Then we'd best be off at once, while there's a break in the rain. Tell me, Missus Marsh, does it ever stop raining up here?"

"I heard tell that it happened one July."

Murphy was a gentleman after that, holding open doors and taking my arm when the terrain got rough because I kept slipping in the worsening mud. But though he was polite, I couldn't shake the feeling that he somehow didn't believe me about Irv. Maybe it was the cloud of alcohol that clung to me in spite of the antacids I'd been sucking to calm my stomach. Or perhaps it was that I sounded like a ridiculous cross between Daffy Duck and Yosemite Sam. Maybe it was that I had called myself Irv's friend—which I wasn't. Not exactly. But I didn't want Murphy thinking I was buying pot from Irv, and I'd had to have some reason for paying a social call on a dreadful night like this.

I ground my teeth. It was frustration, but it was also being out in the cold again. Why hadn't I put in my bite plate when I could still get my jaws open? It made my lisp worse but it blunted the pain enough that I could think logically.

Tyler was right. The rain stopped during our walk up the hill, which was nice, but the cold and wind came down hard as soon as the clouds began to depart, and it froze our breath. Sheriff Murphy's soft but steady profanity at the state of the road clotting his new boots with mud made miniscule crystals that gathered quickly now that we were still. Moonlight punched a hole through the clouds with a silver fist, but I didn't look up. I felt it would do violence to my eyes if I looked straight at it, and I'd seen enough brutality for one night. Irv's lonely cabin was enough of a visual assault for the time being.

The wind died as we crested the hill, and the sudden quiet pressed against my eardrums. The silence of lone-liness and death is different from the simple cessation of noise. This stillness of the heart and mind is a crea-ture of near-substance, a dank shadow that hovers over my own house even on a sunny day, and now it hung over Irv's. I rarely noticed it anymore, mostly because I'd been using enough pills to stupefy my brain—in part because of the physical pain, but also because I saw the vampire's shadow far too often that reminded me I was alone. Love, I was infuriated to find, had limitations. It might move mountains, but it couldn't stop death when he decided to call, and it couldn't banish his shadow from my heart and mind when he'd decided to linger, feeding on my grief.

Winter. The dead season. I hated it. It didn't care about me or anyone. The short days and long nights rolled by; gray, then black, then gray, then black—the sequence repeating itself for the last nine weeks and more. My eyes had forgotten what the sun looked like and my jaw could no longer recall what it was like to exist without the cold ice-pick pain as its companion. I knew that I had been depressed, but had failed to be sufficiently frightened by my degraded mental condi-tion because I had accepted that this was my new steady state. It took Irv dying, and the sheriff's skepticism at my story, to rouse me enough to feel alarm at my situa-tion.

I realized in that moment I owed the sheriff for keep-ing me away from home and the pills and Drambuie on the coffee table. Because there was still a part of me that found their easy solution an appealing alternative.

Shaken by the realization of what I was thinking, and wanting a distraction, I stood close to the sheriff, trying to see Irv's cabin as he did. It didn't help my mood much. I didn't need anything else to remind me that we are helpless creatures, easily broken by our emotions.

The view wasn't any more inviting, in spite of the new company and emerging moonlight that was kind to the building's flaws. The front porch still sagged like the beer belly on an old drunk. The prolonged wet had made the shingles swell until the rusting nails had come unstuck. Damp had invaded the loosened joints and been held back only by the constant fire in the potbelly stove. But now that fire was out and the wet and cold had crept down the chimney and in through the rotting walls. It didn't seem possible that things could have worsened in the short time I was gone, but somehow they had. This place was one step beyond desolate. It was dead, deserted. Even the cats were gone.

I had a weird and uncomfortable thought: What if the body was gone, too?

Then a much worse one: What if it had never been there at all?

Swallowing hard, I walked gingerly up the stairs, deciding to be nice and warn the sheriff about their possible instability. It wasn't because I had warmed to him any, I told myself, but if he broke an ankle, I'd have to slog down the hill again to get help.

"Be careful. Some of the steps are rotten."

"Some?" He pushed at one of the empty pie tins with a foot. Like Irv, he wore cowboy boots.

I shrugged.

"Irv fed the ferals?" Sheriff Murphy asked.

"Yes. And I know that officially this is discouraged because of the risk of disease. Unofficially, it is done in almost every neighborhood. We have a terrible problem with wild cats. Too many assholes dump their animals when they don't want them anymore—and that means when they're pregnant." My words were garbled but angry. I have always believed that there is a special ring in hell for people who abandon their pets.

"I know. It's heartbreaking," Tyler said, and I believed he meant it. That raised him in my estimation.

I stepped onto the porch and opened the door with my gloved hand, and then reached inside to turn on the light.

"Sorry about the doorknob," I said without thinking as I clicked off my flashlight, "but I probably wiped out any fingerprints when I closed it before. It was open when I arrived. Maybe there are some prints on the inside."

"Was it open?" Murphy repeated, coming up behind me. I stepped left so the sheriff could see into the room. A part of me was relieved that Irv was still there. It's kind of sickening, I guess, that I felt better that Irv be dead than I be crazy. I mean, crazier.

Murphy didn't step inside. Neither did I.

"You noticed the footprints too?" I asked hopefully when he hesitated in the doorway.

He didn't answer, so I turned to look up at him. He was staring at me oddly.

"Are you suggesting that he was murdered?" the sheriff asked. "Why didn't you mention this before?"

Was I? I mean, was I willing to admit out loud what I was thinking—that I actually believed a cat when it told me that Irv had been murdered?

"Well, it just occurred to me that he could have been," I said. "He did sell . . ." I trailed off, not wanting to say what Irv sold, though I don't think he was ever ashamed of the deals he made.

"Yes, he did, didn't he?" Murphy said, and a frown

appeared on his face. He looked at the floor and noted the two sets of very different prints, some of which were scuffed and elongated.

"Not that anything like this has ever happened before," I said, feeling the need to defend what Irv had done. "Irv was not a violent man."

Even as I said this, I knew it sounded absurd. In his own way, Irv had been violent. Brawling was a favorite pastime. But he hadn't associated with people who practiced organized violence—at least I didn't think so. He wasn't a drug kingpin.

"Hm . . . I don't suppose those are yours?" he said, pointing at the waffle-stomper prints.

I turned and lifted a shoe so the dim light would shine on it. Looking over my shoulder I could clearly see the sunflower pattern stamped on my sole. What can I say? I have always had a thing for cute shoes, and even my rain boots are fashionable.

"And if my feet were that big I'd slit my wrists," I said absently as I looked at the room again. Something was different from the last time I'd stopped in to see Irv. What was it that bugged me? I felt like I should be able to see what was different. What was missing?

"What's in those jugs?" Tyler asked, jerking his head at the ceramic pots near the stove.

"Cherry cider. It's worse than prune juice. I had a glass once and found out my colon had more moves than a Chinese acrobat. I truly thought I'd shi—uh, lose my intestines." Then, before I could say anything else so crude, I managed to find the misplaced item in my mental catalogue of Irv's artifacts. "The poker is missing," I said. "He always leaned it up next to the jugs."

"Poker?"

"The one Irv kept by the stove. It was this twisted black wrought-iron thing. Heavy, with a wicked point. It's gone."

"Well, hell." The sheriff pulled out his radio and frowned at it. "I'll have to get Farland Tulloc to bring up my bag and the camera. It looks like we might have a suspicious death. That news will get the mayor's blood pressure up." He didn't sound like this fact distressed him. Maybe he had the good taste to dislike our mayor. I certainly did.

"Sheriff?" I asked tentatively.

"Yes? And please call me Tyler. It's so much friendlier. We may as well be on good terms since it looks like we will have a lot to talk about, at least for the next little while."

Oh goody.

"Your radio won't work up here. You better come down to my place and use the phone." He hesitated, perhaps as surprised at my suggestion as I was. "I'd call for you, but no one can understand me when my jaw is locked."

"Your jaw is actually locked?"

It was my turn to sigh.

"Of course it is. Do you think I always talk like this?"

I must have also sounded really annoyed, because the sheriff blinked at me. He wasn't smiling.

I said slowly, "Haven't you heard anything I've been saying? My jaw is locked. I have TMJ and I am in pain. I want to go home."

Murphy looked contrite.

"I'm sorry, Mrs. Marsh. In truth, I've only under-stood about half of what you've been saying. I thought it was just shock and cold"—and booze, but he didn't say this—"and I didn't like to make you repeat yourself when you are obviously struggling."

"Oh," I said, anger leaving me as quickly as it came. Either I was very tired or Sheriff Murphy had the knack of disarming me. "You can call me Jillian. 'Mrs. Marsh' still makes me think of my mother-in-law whenever I hear someone use it."

"Gilligan?" he asked carefully.

"Jillian," I said slowly, but with no more clarity. I sighed and turned my flashlight back on.

"Okay, we'll get to it later," Murphy answered peaceably, closing the door but leaving on the light. It would make it easier to find the cabin again. "Let's get you home and I'll find Farland and Dexter while you make tea."

Dexter, aka Deputy Dawg, so named for his long jowls and perpetually gloomy disposition. There's a rumor down at Caffeine Jill's in Charleston that he's had hemorrhoid surgery—twice. His ex-wife, Golden Sugarbrown, says they are wasting their time trying to deal with these small things and should just get to the point and remove his head, which was really the unnecessary and painful growth on his body. Goldie was a direct sort of woman. I didn't think of Dexter as a hemorrhoid, but he had struck me as being about as dumb as a sack of nails, only not so potentially useful. It was no wonder they had hired Murphy instead of promoting Dexter, who was next in seniority in the department. Geniality was nice in a sheriff, but not as important as having a measurable IQ.

"Who says I'm making tea?" I asked belatedly.

"Oh, I really think you should. Nothing like tea to help a person get over a shock. We could both use a cup." Murphy sighed and added, "I suppose I'll have to get Animal Control up here to trap the strays before they tear this place down. No way the city will let this death trap stand when they're forced to officially notice it."

"I'll take care of the cats," I said quickly, thinking that things were about to get very complicated. Maybe in time I could convince the cats that they would *like* the animal shelter. It was a really nice one, and they would be out of the cold and wet. "Will they tear it down soon, do you think?"

"I should hope so, at least come spring. It isn't up

to code and I doubt there was ever any building per-
mit issued. Certainly no one inspected this dump after
the wiring went in. I'm amazed it hasn't burned to the
ground and taken the whole mountainside with it. We
need to get rid of it before we have homeless people
move in."

He had a good point. Not everyone would be as con-
scientious about fire as Irv.

"Do you know if Irving had any family?" Murphy
asked. "We should try and contact next of kin. In cases
like this, I always wish we could raise the dead. It would
make things easier for everyone if they could talk."

"I don't know about Irv's family." I looked at Irving's
corpse, wondering if he'd speak to me if I talked to him.
Raising the dead wasn't that hard for me—all I had to
do was remember them. The problem was that the
ghosts who haunted me never answered questions—at
least Cal didn't. He never said if he knew now why he
had died so young, or if he was happy where he'd relo-
cated. He just repeated the same old loving things he'd
always said. I'd learned that such fond memories belong
to the bittersweet world of what-might-have-been, and
I tried not to have them often, not for Cal and certainly
not for Irving.

Anyway, that wasn't what the sheriff meant. He wanted
a corpse that could testify about its own demise. I couldn't
help him there. Atherton could point a paw, but Irv
would never point an accusing finger at his murderer.

I changed the subject, and because I was pretty certain that Irv had been murdered and still had a fair
amount of judgment impairers in my bloodstream, I
asked directly: "Are you thinking murder for gain?"

Again, I got that strange look.

"You think his family bumped him off so they could
move into the ancestral mansion?" He shook his head at
Irv's sorry cabin. "I was just thinking they might want to

know that Irv was dead. Maybe claim the body and spare the city the expense of his burial."

"Sorry. Occupational hazard," I lied. I couldn't explain why, even to myself, but I realized that I had been thinking about murder for gain almost from the moment I saw Irv—and not murder for marijuana. "I guess that all writers have vivid imaginations, and we'd prefer a murder mystery." I didn't add that I wrote mostly nonfiction and had never had any such wild thoughts before that night. Murder didn't happen often in Irish Camp—not these days, at least—and the idea hadn't blossomed until Atherton put it there. And I couldn't admit, even to myself, that suicide, not murder, was more what had been on my mind all evening.

Standing next to Tyler, so alive and so focused on the present, made me feel shame for my weakness and inclination to cling to the past. "Let's go have some tea," I said. If we went in through the garage he'd never see the living room, and the pills and booze all over the coffee table.

A cat's got her own opinion of human beings. She don't say much, but you can tell enough to make you anxious not to hear the whole of it.

—*Jerome K. Jerome*

———————

CHAPTER FOUR

We grieve as we love; deep love, deep grief. How long should a person grieve a death? The healthy consensus—arrived at by people who have obviously never faced devastating loss themselves—is two years. But I think they're wrong. You never really stop. You eventually move on; you have to. But the filter of Cal's death will always color the way I see life, and it's that way for many others too. We know who we are. We are members of a club who ever after suffer from a kind of pleasure-deficit disorder. We know that bad things really do happen, and that being good or having great insurance won't protect you.

Cal's death colors my dreams. I'm not going to take out my collection of nocturnal nightmares and heartbreaks and detail them for you; if you've been there then you already know what I dream about. And if you haven't . . . well, you don't really want to know—unless you've been trained for it and you're getting paid one hundred and twenty-five bucks an hour. I don't have the really bad dreams so much anymore. But that night after finding Irv's body I was worried enough about death dreams coming to call that I left the bathroom light on so I wouldn't wake in darkness.

I did dream of Cal, but it wasn't as bad as I expected—Thank you, dear Morpheus—and I was ready to face another day.

The poets have long insisted men have died and worms have eaten them, but not for love. I disagree. I certainly wanted to die when Cal did—and probably would have, except the shame of what Calvin would say at my cowardice kept me going. And eventually my capacity to heal exceeded my heart's low expectations. The sharpest pain finally blurred and my heart returned to pumping blood instead of slivers of icy fury. I regained much of my lost weight and I got on with a life that looked a great deal like my old one. No one on the outside, nor even I, ever suspected how not alright I really was. We all thought I was doing fine, considering that the glue that held my life together had come unstuck and I no longer had any purpose.

Until October and the lightning, of course. But I'm the only one who knows about the cats, so I have to excuse my few close friends for not guessing my true mental state.

Cal's old mantel clock struck eight A.M. in tones of dignified but gentle gravity, a melodious voice wishing me a good morning. It was comforting to think that it was still standing watch in the midnight hours while I slept alone, and that it was there to greet me.

I slowly opened my eyes. Thick syrupy light filled the bedroom. I stared at the ceiling, bemused by the soft glow, at first not recognizing the sun. I actually turned my head to look out the window, something I didn't normally do because it would banish Cal's phantom presence, which sometimes slept beside me and stayed in the instants while I passed from sleep to wakefulness.

I treasured those bittersweet moments with a power that was probably unhealthy. It was in those moments that I could whisper to Cal the truth about how frightened and lonely I was, and say all the things I hadn't dared to while he was ill.

Sunday is easy to identify because of the many church bells that regale the town, though my favorite of the gongs and rings come from the steam engines at Railtown. They run antique trains on weekends and holidays, weather permitting, from the old train station to an abandoned rock quarry on Red Table Mountain. That was the sound I was hearing on the edge of my fading dreams. Old '97 was riding the rails.

For the first time in many long months, I didn't roll over to check that Cal's picture was keeping guard over me on the nightstand. My first thought that morning was not of him.

My old bathroom mirror has a flaw, a ten-inch band of distortion that makes things look bigger than they are. On me, it hits chest high. On Cal, it had been the stomach. Cal wasn't vain, so we kept the thing around. That morning I actually looked into the mirror and really saw myself for the first time in weeks. Though it was all optical illusion, when I stared at my preposterously enlarged chest I found myself smiling like I used to.

Once dressed, I went downstairs and dutifully fixed breakfast. Lumpy oatmeal chased tasteless frozen blueberries around the bowl until they were both weary of the exercise of avoiding my spoon, but I finally admitted that I just didn't feel like being healthy that morning and I dumped the congealing muck in the trash and headed for town. I hoped the bakery was open. I needed a *pain au chocolat* from Le Bon Ton and some coffee strong enough to bolster me against both the rich pastry and the inclement weather bound to return that afternoon.

I didn't realize it at that moment, but this small intended rebellion against the healthy living we instituted at the onset of Cal's illness was the second sign that I was becoming myself again. As portents go, it was a small one, but I should have noticed.

Once started, my defiance of healthy living continued, and I hadn't rinsed my dirty oatmeal dish or put it in the dishwasher. My mother, who was a product of the 1950s when all you needed for happiness—society said—was the ability to make floors shine while keeping your dress clean and your hair tidy, and to make a creditable meat loaf (assuming you had sensibly married a man who brought home a regular paycheck), would have been appalled at my slovenliness. She had done her level best to raise me right, but had only half succeeded. I could cook and was tidy with my clothing, and had married a respectable man, but even on my best days I cared very little about my floors' glossiness. And I felt better when the regular (okay, semiregular and often meager) paycheck was my own instead of my husband's. A dirty dish in the sink wasn't even on my radar. I hadn't misspent my youth as my contemporaries had, but I suddenly felt hope for my adulthood. I was alive, wasn't I? That meant that there was still time for a spot of rebellion and occasional high-cholesterol food.

As a rule, I don't listen to the radio at home. The only way to get decent reception is to stand on the ottoman next to the stereo and hold a large pewter bowl over my head, acting as a satellite dish. And since the programming was completely predictable—I think the local station was playing the same taped show they had recorded last May—I didn't usually feel it worth the bother. But the morning after Irv's murder I decided to perch on the footstool, bowl aloft, and listen to the morning news.

I could have spared my arms and the ottoman's sagging upholstery the effort. There wasn't a word mentioned about the crime, not even that Irv had died. When they got around to the high school basketball scores, the pewter bowl went back on the table and I grabbed a heavy sweater off the rack by the door. Experience had taught me that winter sun didn't mean warmth.

A large-tailed squirrel was waiting on the doorstep with Irv's cats when I opened the front door, and I blinked at the unexpected spectacle of this feline cast of Noah's Ark on my deck. The fresh smell of winter morning spilled through the door and rushed past me, chasing out the odor of claustrophobic unhappiness that had been trapped inside by new weather stripping and my unwillingness to face the gray days. I can't speak squirrel, but the emboldened freeloader who steals meals from the now empty birdfeeder made known his indignation at the long wait for grub. The cats were more polite but just as insistent. They were hungry, Irv was gone, and what was I going to do about it?

I closed the door behind me and stepped carefully through the agitated animals, looking for Atherton but not finding him.

"Stop! I'm sorry. I don't have any food. But I am going to get some today," I promised. For once the cats stopping yowling and seemed to mull this promise over, and I threaded my way through them. I moved slowly, both out of consideration for their tails and because I was a little afraid. To be honest, I don't have a full-blown cat phobia, but I have never been entirely comfortable around felines.

"Look, you can't wait here," I said. "The neighbors will see you and call . . ." I stopped. I didn't want to make Animal Control sound bad by using them as bogeymen. "Just meet me in the side yard in a couple hours, okay? I'll be back soon—with food. And tell the squirrel to relax. He can have some too if he wants. I hear the kibble is delicious."

I was proud of myself. I was demonstrating commitment and doing different things, and I left without even turning on the computer to see if I had an e-mail from my editor. It wasn't because I forgot to, either. It was because I knew it was probably there and I didn't trust my reckless mood of happy exploration to survive the lure of an actual paying assignment.

I walked slowly, thinking hard but keeping it on the logical surface where there was less emotion. Have you ever noticed that our pasts come after us, sometimes limping or even crawling, but they always come? The choice is: kill or make peace with whatever ails you. Or keep running—but that only works short-term. I'd been trying the running thing since Cal died, but stuck in a hamster wheel of negative emotion, weariness, low-grade anxiety and above all, boredom—the trifecta of old grief that embodies habitual mild depression—I wasn't getting anywhere. I had been stranded in some horrible status quo. I suppose that I had been fighting for mental health in my own feeble way. I'd even seen a shrink—before the cat thing—and he'd convinced me I needed to give myself credit for actually writing every day. I didn't produce a lot, but I showed up at my desk every morning and wrote something. I'd even had the guts to scrap some stories that were just too sick to save, thus sparing myself the embarrassment of having my editor pronounce them DOA—I'd submitted far too many "stop drinking/smoking/eating junk food or you'll get cancer and die" pieces. So, I was semi-okay.

At least professionally. For a while. But I wasn't certain how long the permission slip for screwing off granted by Calvin's death would allow me to stagnate, though. Even if my editor forgave me, my self-esteem was suffering. I couldn't go on living off royalties forever, though I regularly thanked a whole pantheon of publishing gods for the biannual checks from my six-times-reprinted cookbook, *Green Tea & Sympathy: Desserts for the Diabetic.*

My life is hard to explain to anyone who doesn't have Writer's Disease. You are probably wondering why I don't just go out and get another job. It's not that simple. I fell hopelessly in love with the idea of being a writer when I was seven and had a poem published in the school newsletter. The pages were creamy yellow, the ink a dark green—my words had never looked so beautiful. I was infected then with something akin to malaria. I *had* to write, had to see my words in print. There were periods of time when the need would disappear and I would go about acting like a normal person, but sooner or later the intense desire returned. And it didn't matter that the pay was lousy and I was always distracted from what others consider real life.

Cal was likewise a young passion, and I was equally enthused about the idea of being his wife. Fortunately the two things had gone well together, and I knew I'd be great at both. I think it's probably good to conceive your passions young before you know the odds against success. I was both lucky and unlucky that neither passion had faded. Writing isn't what I do, it's what I am. And so was being Cal's wife. It became trickier, of course, with him being dead. Like it or not, unhealthy or not, I still saw myself as Cal's wife.

But I was neither wife nor writer that morning. I had other, more interesting and urgent things to do. Like finding Irv's killer. I was making my debut as an amateur sleuth.

In a big city, this kind of crime might be dismissed as impersonal, random. So much of crime is these days, especially drug-related, which this might prove to be. But things weren't like that in Irish Camp. Like our politics, all crime here was local and personal. If you were killed by someone, it was someone you knew—probably really well. Would the new sheriff, coming from Los Angeles, realize this, though? How much would I, or someone else, have to explain about how our town worked? I didn't think that our short visit over a mug of tea the night before had adequately put him in the picture.

Irish Camp has a lot of hybrid businesses and business people. Some even make sense, since certain jobs are seasonal. Ed's is where you go to hire a canoe and fishing guide in summer, and who you call when you need a snowplow in winter. Others are more curious. We have Rod's Bait & Tackle and Notary Public. There is Mels's Accounting, Storage Lockers & Towing. And my personal favorite, Paula's Taxidermy and Taxes. I've avoided most of these places, but do frequent one: Two In Hand. It is a combination card store and porn shop. I go for the cards, I swear—though I did buy some gummy penises for a party I had for some writer friends a few years back. That ended up being a bit embarrassing. A friend of Calvin's stopped by one afternoon and decided to help himself to the candy dish while he was waiting. Anyone but Lorenzo would have laughed, but he's an old-school shrink and thought my offering guests gummy penises was an act of hostility. He just doesn't understand the publishing business. Or writers. It's probably why he couldn't help me after Cal died. We never really clicked.

Anyhow, one of the town's more famous Jill-of-all-trades lived up the hill from me. She had known Irv well and would—I told myself—want to know about his passing. If she hadn't already heard. It would be amazing if she had not. Crystal knows everything about Irish Camp. She wasn't exactly a hardcore gossip, but rather a central exchange for information for the different social groups that inhabit our town. Many people couldn't get past the surface phenomenon of her beauty, but she was also very smart and had an elephantine memory. If only she could develop a sense of discretion, I'd tell her about the cats.

Cal hadn't liked the way she gossiped, but I forgave her this flaw. Isn't everyone just a little bit nosy sometimes? A bit of a voyeur? I am, my mother's training notwithstanding. It's a lot of why I write. I get to ask and then find answers to lots of unusual questions. And like all writers, I have my favorite resources when I need to do research. Understand, I'm no slouch at the answer game and can chase documents with the best of them, but when I want to know something about Irish Camp, I save myself a lot of effort and just go to Crystal Holmes. She's a fourth-generation Gold Country inhabitant and knows where all the bodies—literal and otherwise—are buried.

Crystal lives at the top of Viper's Hill, where the rocky coil ends in a sort of mesa. I asked her once how Viper's Hill got its name and she told me a story about an old tradition called a rattlesnake roundup. Since I hadn't known her very long, I was inclined to dismiss this tale as a colorful legend invented for the tourists, but I later discovered that the nearby town of Columbia holds an annual poison oak festival, so the lunacy might be true.

Soft chanting led me up the hill: *"Om-Hrum-Adityaya-Namah. Om-Hraim-Savitre-Namah."*

I found Crystal in her yard doing her version of sun salutations, which were about half successful, given that she could not lie prone because of the thick mud. What bits of the sky we could see through the forlorn oaks was clear, but the day remained bitterly cold. Crystal waved as I walked up, but kept folding and breathing. Yoga was her most recent enthusiasm. An exasperated friend had once said that Crystal had been baptized in so many faiths that her skin was starting to prune from the holy water. I liked that she was so open to strange things and had almost—almost—told her about the cats back in October. But Crystal also liked to chitchat about the strange and wonderful, and I couldn't risk even a garbled version of this story getting around. I didn't need to get labeled as the village kook.

"*Oh-Hram-Bhaskaraya-Namah*— Hey, Jillian!" She ended her salutation for creativity and balance. Today she was wearing a bipolar outfit known well to mountain folks in the spring. The manic part was gauze harem pants in hot citrus colors and a lace shirt of lime green. The depressive part featured winter boots and a large wool sweater-coat she had belted at her waist. Her smile was wide. Clearly she was dizzy with the rapture of the sun.

"Hey, yourself," I answered with a smile. Crystal was crowding fifty and not beautiful in any classical sense, but people always described her as lovely and gorgeous. I think what made her so attractive—to anyone grown beyond the hormone-driven fascination with teenage pop stars and supermodels—was the joy she radiated. It suggested a lack of suffering, or a transcendence of the earthly sorrow that wears most of us down eventually. Such bliss hints at the divine, and others want to bask in that reflected happiness while they tell their tales of woe. And to drink her homegrown calendula-mint tea, which was delicious and soothing.

"I'm afraid that I have some unhappy news," I said.

"Then I'd better put on the kettle," she replied, predictably. "Let's go inside where it's warm."

It turns out that this was a red-letter day for me. Crystal hadn't heard about Irv, which told me that the sheriff either wasn't pursuing his death as a murder, or else was being very, very cautious about whom he questioned. Either way, I understood. It was annoying when I wanted answers, but reasonable given that he worked in Irish Camp, where everybody minded everybody else's business and nothing would get done if the town council or the mayor got in the way of an investigation.

Disappointed that my usual source hadn't already called everyone in town and figured out who the murderer was, I decided that I would take a trip down to the coffee shop myself. Not to do anything, really, just to hear what people had to say. And for the coffee and chocolate-orange scones, of course. Calendula-mint tea wasn't enough.

I didn't tell Crystal where I was going. I let her believe that I was heading home to write. Usually I did put my nose to the grindstone in the morning, so this inference passed without challenge. I felt pleasantly guilty for telling a lie—even by omission—and getting away with it. I know that sounds odd, but if you aren't a good liar, there is pleasure in being able to pull off any untruth, however small. It wasn't that I would have minded her company, but I had taken to walking indirect routes through town that kept me away from businesses with cats, and she would have noticed this change of pattern.

The road off Viper's Hill is really more of a tunnel. Ancient oaks have overgrown the street, making it a dark and mysterious place. Even in winter, when they drop their leaves, the parasitic mistletoe still cling to the branches in great falls, casting the lower stretch of the road into a perpetual twilight. Its uncanny nature aside, it is of some danger to a pedestrian because the ancient tree trunks are so thick that there is nowhere to go if cars take the corners wide. Still, the residents always walk into town. It's a matter of pride in our mountain-strong legs. And also because there is almost no parking in the town proper, designed when the only traffic was a weekly stagecoach and the odd mule team or two.

I walked cautiously, ears straining for the sound of cars as I crabbed guardedly down the hill. The road was slick with mud and loose gravel.

Crows cawed suddenly overhead, making me jump.

Aerial vermin, Irv had called them. They were the only creatures he didn't like. He said they were an ill omen, and would throw rocks to drive them away. The rough sound of their voices in the cold air now reminded me of Irv's death and made me shiver with a sort of atavistic dread. The oaks' thick shadows grew even darker as my morbid imagination fought for freedom.

What am I doing? I asked myself. Why did I care what happened to Irv when no one else did? He was a drug-dealing hermit, inarticulate, smelly—repulsive, even. I'd like to tell you I cared because he was a human and I am so spiritually enlightened that I know every man's death diminishes me. But really, it was probably just guilt for never having repaid all the hours of work he'd put in on my house since Cal died. It's almost always guilt that moves me to action these days.

No, Irv wasn't a friend in the normal sense of the word, but of course I'd grown to know him. I'd seen him so many times, even before Cal got sick. He was a neighbor, sort of, someone you waved at but didn't stop to pass the time of day. And once people knew about Cal's cancer, he occasionally dropped around and brought Cal some marijuana, often leaving it in the old wooden message box by the door where one used to leave notes for the milkman in the days when delivery came to the door in glass bottles. He was shy, uncommunicative, and I was happy to have it so. I had no energy for anything except trying to save Cal.

Of course, that changed one very long, frustrating day soon after Calvin's funeral, when I decided that I *had* to fix the front gate that hung so crookedly it dragged on the ground enough to leave a rut. The only tool I could find was a hammer, and I was having little success with my repair efforts. Don't ask me why, but Irv chose that day to stop in, and though I don't know exactly how it happened, he somehow ended up fixing the gate while

I went inside and made scones, brewed tea and dried my swollen eyes on a kitchen towel.

After that, every month or so, Irv would drop by to talk about the weather and incidentally fix a few things for me. I wanted to pay him for his work, but somehow the subject of money never came up. I tried once, but the man was evasive when he wanted to be. He seemed to feel that tea and pastry was sufficient payment, so I let it go. Still, I always felt vaguely indebted to him.

Later, I found out about his collection of feline strays and realized that I was probably just one more lonely creature he had taken under his threadbare wing. The thought was both touching and lowering, the latter because it underlined how pathetic I had become.

"Let it go," I mumbled to myself. Then louder: "Shoo! Go away, you loudmouthed buzzards." I threw the words hard, letting the crows know that I meant them.

It did no good.

I eventually staggered out into the light at the end of the oaken tunnel, shutting my dazzled eyes for a moment at the glare of the sun bouncing off the wet parking lot behind the bank. I breathed deeply, sampling the less damp air, and then opened my eyes very slowly. I was not the only stunned mole out that morning, standing in the half-empty lot. We were all eerily pasty extras from *Night of the Living Dead*, except that we smiled and didn't bite one another. This was not a sight I had ever seen in the Silicon Valley where we used to live. Down there, people were polished and presented themselves with year-round tans. But mountain people are different. We have accepted our startling whiteness as part of what has to be endured in the winter, and do not try and hide it with cosmetics or long sessions in a tanning booth. I'd tried self-tanner before, but orange is just *not* my color, and no one had been fooled into thinking that I'd just come back from a Caribbean vacation. Like smile lines and 34B-sized breasts, some things were best accepted with dignity.

I did a slow turn in the mostly deserted lot, taking in the town, recalling what it looked like without its watery veil; then I began walking slowly. My dream of scones ousted by my appetite-killing memories of Irv, I started for The Mule up on Main. This had been Irv's home away from home. Business before pleasure, I told myself. What would Miss Marple do? Feeling brave, I took the shortest route, heading up Hard Rock Lane, watching my steps on the uneven sidewalk and keeping my eyes averted from the windows of the used bookstore where Oscar was sure to be napping. Oscar was a nice enough animal, but he was extremely vocal as well as hard of hearing and would caterwaul when he saw me.

In common with most gold-country towns, we had a Main Street and a Church Street, a Gold Street and a Lincoln Street. What we didn't have was an Easy Street, real or metaphorical. Nothing had been easy for folks when the forty-niners were naming things in this Gold Rush town, and things weren't all that easy now.

As I mentioned before, Irv frequented one of the town's less tourist-friendly bars, The Three-Legged Mule. Around here, if a bar is historic or charming, it's usually called a pub or a saloon. The Mule wasn't charming. For one thing, people still smoked there— excessively. A little foretaste of Hell, Irv had joked. The bar had grandfathered in some clause that permitted both smoking and the sale of firearms on the premises. You walked by it any time from seven A.M. until three A.M. the next morning and belches of smoke and sweaty air would billow at you from under the swinging door. Yes, seven A.M. The Mule opened early, before anything else in town. It was the perfect place to go when you wanted to hurt yourself at sunrise, and sadly there was always a handful of people who did. Rumor also had it that The Mule sometimes served underaged kids equally underaged scotch that hadn't been brewed by the companies whose names were on the bottle labels. They never had happy hour there trying to attract tourists, either. They were at least realistic about that. Their clientele didn't actually expect to be happy; getting inebriated cheaply was enough. Having happy people around would have just annoyed the regulars.

No one was loitering outside in the cold sun today, though there was a bench. Perhaps the break in the weather had gone unnoticed. More likely the bar's owners and patrons were making an effort to stay out of sight of the mayor, who was getting ready to hold some kind of rally across the street at the courthouse. That didn't mean the place was empty, though. It never was during business hours. On a successful Saturday night, ranks of patrons would drink until the bar closed and then lurch out to Fremont Creek Ranch, using the Victorian ironwork fences around the Mason's graveyard as crutches while they pulled themselves along hand-over-hand. After that they would have to lean together, a shambling human tripod, or else crawl the rest of the way up the hill to their shacks and trailers.

I braced myself and then stepped up to the red door with the small diamond-shaped window now gray with smoke. I was a big girl—I could do this.

I held my breath as I stepped inside. The list of beers on the chalkboard behind the bar was short and boring, but no one went to The Mule because they sought exciting beverages. No one here was seeking excitement of any kind; if anything, they wanted to be numbed as quickly and cheaply as humanly possible. They didn't bother with microbrews here, though there were many good ones in the area.

My first impression when my eyes adjusted to the stygian light levels was that everyone in The Mule was suffering from either liver failure or hepatitis. After a second look, I changed that assessment to only about two-thirds. Nevertheless, I resolved not to touch anything or shake any hands. This was the Sierra Nevada's version of the black hole of Calcutta, and who knew what germs there abideth within.

The day was just dawning, but business was already being done at some of the tables. There were stacks of dirty cash on a table, and once in a while something that might have been a contract, though this was rare.

The barter system is alive and well in Irish Camp, and the underground economy flourishes. It starts in the heart of town where most businesses struggle financially even with the help of the tourists who visit, but the system of barter stretched deep into the forest around the township.

Here's a benign example of how it works: Ranchers send sheep and goats to eat back brush that presents a fire danger to some historic old home that belongs to a historic but impoverished family. In return, that rancher gets firewood from trees downed by a storm on the historic property. Sometimes dental work is traded for plumbing or gardening services. A housepainter gets his kid's broken arm fixed by plying his trade for the doctor.

Then there are the less benevolent forms of barter. Like the trading of marijuana or other drugs for food from the fruit stands or the bakery, or for clothes from the thrift shop, or even for sex or a place to stay when it is snowing.

I don't actively partake in this underground economy, but I see it and mostly approve. It's a system that works in a poor county where there is never enough to go around, and I hadn't personally seen anyone being coerced into participating. But that morning I thought that perhaps it had a dark side I didn't know about, and maybe that was what had gotten Irv killed.

Looking at the motley crew inside the Three-Legged Mule, I had to wonder what they were trading for the swill they drank so freely. None of them had regular jobs, and therefore had little money. Few of them had any skills to trade—Josh had worked as a steamfitter, Dell as a logger, Tim as a stonemason before he lost his left hand—but they showed so little inclination toward sobriety these days that only a crazy person would let them near power tools.

Being a writer, and given a slightly higher than average degree of imagination—and now a corpse on my hill—I couldn't help but speculate if any of them might be doing something illegal for Mosconi, the bar owner and tender. Or were the patrons blackmailing him with some knowledge of an old sin even Irish Camp wouldn't accept? Irv would have known if they were. Irv knew everything.

But would Irv have cared? Would that knowledge be enough to get him killed by one of these people? He was definitely considered to be one of their own.

I didn't know and couldn't guess. I had nothing in common with this strange community except our mutual acquaintance with Irv, and I didn't know their stories in any detail, not even Irving's. Maybe it was the tragedy of broken hearts that had led them to the bar to begin with, but it was broken livers and addiction that got them in The Mule now. There weren't many places where jaundice looks good and is accepted as normal, but you hardly noticed it in the dim light with the orange shag carpet that had gotten a bad haircut back in the days when The Mule still had enough pretensions of class that they had music to dance to on Saturday nights. Back when they occasionally shampooed the vomit out of the rug.

I shook my head. Irv wasn't a tidy man, but this place seemed wrong for him somehow. He liked being outside in the fresh air. Did he perhaps not come here to drink with his ex-girlfriend as he had claimed, but instead to do business? Drug business? Popular songs often insist that love that doesn't kill you makes you crazy, and this is often so. But there are many other ways to go insane, or at least comfortably numb. Some are available to everyone, but others require a middleman. If you had a friendly doctor like I did, you could do it legally. If you didn't, you came to a place like The Mule.

I stepped farther into the room and let my eyes finish adjusting. The clientele looked like they had all just come from a police lineup. I also spotted some large dust bunnies under a juke box that had been dead since the music died in the Easter brawl of '97, when the owner foolishly left Tim in charge while he went to visit his daughter over the holiday. The fight started, I'm told, when one patron took exception to another's contention that it was Jesus who hid the first Easter eggs. And to celebrate the day that the Prince of Peace rose from the dead—and maybe hid boiled eggs—the two men spent the morning trying to beat sense into one another with the furniture.

That could never happen today. Almost everybody involved was either dead or so much older and sicker that brawling held no appeal. The furniture was now bolted down tighter than in a cheap motel. And all the guns and hunting knives were locked in a metal cabinet where there was no casual grabbing. Nevertheless, a low-grade danger rode the smoky air.

I swallowed, and breathed shallowly. *Maybe,* I thought, *having cats talk to me* isn't *so bad a fate after all.*

That reminded me again I had to pick up some cat kibble and bowls. I'd be able to hide them under the steps in the side yard for now. That would give the cats some shelter and conceal them from my neighbor,

Abby, whose house overlooks mine. She is a kind and generous soul, but she had never approved of Irv's feline philanthropy, and I didn't think she'd appreciate having the cats at my place either.

"Jillian!"

I turned in the direction of the surprised voice and saw Molly sitting in a shadowy corner with a half-empty glass of beer. At the sound of my name, Dell got up from his place at the bar and walked over to Molly's table. His posture was protective.

Dell isn't my favorite person, nor am I his. He comes from a family whose gene pool runs deep with DNA designed for violent, drug-addicted men. Aside from being a drunk, he is sly in mean ways. Such as, he has the disconcerting habit of playing with his dentures—which I am quite certain were not originally his own, since they seem too large for his jaw—popping them in and out with his tongue in a disgusting game of oral peekaboo. It makes his Adam's apple bob up and down, and reminds me of a dog trying to lick a glob of peanut butter off the roof of his mouth. He does this on purpose, mostly to tourists, smiling meanly whenever someone looks away in discomfort.

I approached Molly anyway.

"Molly. Dell." They didn't ask me to sit down, but I did anyway. This uncharacteristic action made Molly's eyes get big and a little frightened. I cleared my throat, not sure what to say now that I was there. After a moment I fell back on training. Mother was right—good manners cost nothing. And besides, they give you a cliché for every occasion. Molly would understand the ritual. She had been a businesswoman until she gave up cooking to become a full-time alcoholic.

"Molly, have you heard about Irv?" I waited for the slow shake of her head. I hadn't asked Dell anything, but his head wagged back and forth too. I noticed then that he was wearing a chain, and at the end of it was a raw gold nugget that was almost hidden by his silvering chest hair. The sight surprised me. Dell wasn't the type who adorned himself with jewelry, and I would have thought that anything valuable he came across would have ended up at the Red Hawk pawnshop.

"What . . . what about Irv?"

"I'm sorry." And I *was* sorry, which made the next part easier. "Irv died last night. He . . ." He what? Was murdered? I was pretty sure that one shouldn't blurt out something like that. Especially if one was trying to find out what might have happened to the victim and the people you were dealing with were highly allergic to anything that might bring them into contact with the law.

Fortunately, Molly covered for me. She began to cry. She reached for my hand under the table and clutched at it with chapped fingers. I had been hoping to avoid this contact, but couldn't very well pull away.

"Poor Irv. It was his heart, wasn't it?" She pulled a napkin out of the dispenser with her left hand and wiped at her eyes. Dell began patting her shoulder. Both looked upset, if not surprised. If anything, I would have said that Dell looked chagrined, maybe even annoyed.

Again, since I am not the best liar—at least not in person—I opted for a version of the truth when answering.

"I'm not sure, Molly. I think the sheriff has ordered an autopsy. Maybe they'll find out what happened."

"The sheriff!" As I expected, the tears stopped instantly and her hand withdrew. "Did Murphy hurt Irv?"

"No!" My reaction was immediate and strong. "No, I got the sheriff after I found Irv."

At their continued looks of absolute incomprehension, I felt compelled to explain why I hadn't called them instead.

"You know how my jaw is sometimes." I waited for a

nod from Molly. Practically everyone in town knew about my jaw. "Well, it was terrible last night. I could barely move it at all. I knew I couldn't call anyone on the phone. And I had been drinking. A lot." That was something they would understand. "The sheriff . . . was closest." This wasn't as lame an excuse as it might appear. Molly and Dell lived deep in a ravine on the other side of town, at the end of an unpaved, unlighted road. Given the weather last night, only a madman would have been up for a slog through the dark and mud.

At last I got a nod of understanding, but no comment. This annoyed me. I was looking for answers and getting silence instead. Why couldn't they cooperate and just let the clues come tumbling out of their mouths so I could solve this case and go home where the air was clean?

"Did Irv have any family?" I asked. It seemed a natural question. When someone died you were supposed to contact their kin. "Is there someone we should call?"

"There's a nephew, I think," Molly said at last, after she and Dell had exchanged a look. "Gordon or Jordon. But I'm not sure where he is. Last I heard he was living in Lodi . . . or maybe it was Fresno."

Great. I finally had a lead: Gordon or Jordon, who might still be living in Lodi. Or Fresno. There would only be . . . what, hundreds—thousands—of names to sort through?

Or maybe I would kindly tell the sheriff about this and make him look into it. After all, he'd asked me about it the night before. And this would give me an excuse to talk to him and find out why he was keeping Irv's death so quiet.

I found that I was looking forward to seeing the sheriff again.

A cat is a lion in a jungle of small bushes.
                                    —*Indian saying*

CHAPTER FIVE

Special elections were coming in June and our local political scene is surprisingly byzantine, so, bad weather or not, Mayor Nolan Vickers was out pressing flesh and kissing bundled-up babies. Our mayor is impressive in his own way. He has a weight lifter's body, a too-pink shiny face and a lot of teeth he purchased after he sold off the family demolition, truck rental, and self-defense businesses. He always makes me think of that line from Shakespeare about how a man can smile and smile but still be a villain. Not that Nolan was a villain exactly, but he had a black belt in local politics, flexible morals, only a moderate IQ and a long memory for slights, so it didn't do to cross him unless the cause was important. Some people liked this—many of them women who found him attractive and strong, a happenstance I have always construed as proof that God has a bent sense of humor. I think there is also probably a master plan for Nolan that holds a third divorce, hypertension and at least one heart attack.

He had supposedly been a friend of Cal's when they

were on the city council. Then Cal hadn't agreed with him about blocking construction of a skate park for kids, then about closing the county hospital, and things changed after that. Cal was suddenly labeled as a knee-jerk liberal and Nolan worked hard to get rid of him.

Nolan failed the first time. Cal had good friends who forgave him his political leanings since it was for the children.

Our town used to be staunchly Republican, but the war in Iraq poured some political Visine over the county and a few Democrats managed to get into office, where they worked uneasily. Not everyone went true blue, though. In fact, few did. At heart this town still belongs to the Grand Old Party. The county is an odd mix, though, and that's where things get tricky. Many of the smog-eating refugees from Silicon Valley were already Green, and others outside the mainstream joined them as the evidence proving global warming mounted. Which meant we had lovely organic produce at our farmers' markets, a growing Green Party that actually hung up posters at election time (printed on recycled biodegradable paper), and fewer liberal votes to back our few brave Democratic candidates. This meant that those who were blue and wanted to stay in office had to be fiscally responsible in our conservative town. The skate park matter was finessed by getting everything donated by local businesses and having someone give the city the land. But the battle over whether to close the county hospital had raged for a decade. It was the spendthrift Hattfields versus the heartless McCoys, and those attending the public meetings semi-joked about sending for the National Guard to keep the peace every time it came up on the agenda. People were actually searched at the door for weapons.

Admittedly, the hospital was a money pit, a black hole in the budget, a blot on the council family fiscal escutcheon. But, Cal argued, until there was universal health care for everyone in the county, the indigent needed somewhere to go other than the new for-profit hospital that, for a case of pneumonia or a broken leg, charged the uninsured roughly their entire yearly incomes. Cal had wrestled with this problem for months and tried for compromise and creative funding. But when push had finally come to shove and they had to vote yea or nay, he'd finally come down on the side of compassion rather than profit. Nolan didn't agree, and set about once again blackening his name. This time he was more successful and the hospital closed. Cal was feeling truly ill by then and gave in without a great fight. He forgave Nolan. I didn't. Cal got his treatments at the new hospital that had lots of high-tech and very little care.

It was because of this past that I kept my eyes turned away as I passed on the other side of the street. It meant bypassing the French bakery, but I had a bad feeling that if word got back to Nolan that I was insisting the town drug dealer was murdered—and maybe even got the story in the paper—that I would move to the top of his unpopular list. Of course, he'd probably find out what I thought eventually, one way or another. His brother-in-law ran a company called Good Riddance C.S. Clean Up and Septic. The tourists thought the black-and-red van parked outside the gaudy pink tin-roofed Victorian at the corner of Polk and Jackson cleaned out clogged sump pumps and the like—and Hinkley did do that, if the pump happened to be clogged with body parts. The C.S. in Good Riddance stood for *crime scene*. Hinkley was the man you called if Uncle Toby emptied a shotgun into his head and got his brain matter all over your authentic nineteenth-century paneling and fine Persian rugs. Or if you wanted to get a bloodstain from a triple homicide out of the rough wood flooring in a cabin. And if you didn't call him, he would call you. He was worse than an ambulance chaser. Whoever inherited Irv's cabin would need Hinkley's kind of help—along with a lot of contractors to get it up to code—unless Tyler was right and the city just tore it down.

Not that I was afraid of Nolan, exactly. But I was cautious. I still had to be careful around him. Anger came at odd moments and the words or rage would rush out of my mouth, hurling themselves at people—like Nolan, who hadn't visited Cal even once when he was dying—in a most unattractive form of emotional projectile vomiting. It made me seem, well . . . crazy. And I wouldn't put it past Nolan to try and have me committed if I made him angry enough. He probably wouldn't succeed, but it would be a Pyrrhic victory if I bankrupted myself fighting this battle.

I was walking quickly but, prompted by my stomach, I paused to read the daily slate of fare on the sidewalk outside Blend It. They were offering a Sunrise smoothie (mixed citrus), Old Faithful (lemon ice), and a Prune Typhoon that I heard from previous victims could cause an actually tsunami of the bowels. Shuddering, I backed away until I reached the door of Den of Thebes, our import shop that stocks some very questionable treasures from the Middle and Far East.

Something nudged me from behind, impeding my flight from the home of blended frozen fruit. I turned, already knowing who and what it was that had me hemmed in. There was only one person in town who regularly rear-ended me.

"Hi, Pinky. Nice flowers," I added, nodding at the bicycle basket lashed to her walker. She had decorated it herself with a mix of silk and plastic flowers recovered from trash cans and the Dumpster behind the Best of Times thrift shop. Pinky, so called because of her love of the color, was wearing a hot pink and lime satin jogging suit with high-top sneakers that had once been white but were now rusty brown. The bright colors were a bit lurid but I had to smile anyway. Pinky's obvious happiness demanded it. She has fairly advanced dementia, but rather than succumbing to the usual fear and anger that afflicts its victims, Pinky's mental deterioration has left her in a state of almost perpetual joyfulness. She probably belonged in a home for the permanently befuddled, but her kids refused to confine her or curtail her wandering. In any other place this would have been dangerous, but our town had sort of made her into a mascot, and people were generally good about looking out for her.

Pinky thought—God only knows why, perhaps because she once caught me talking to a cat hidden up in a tree—that I was a friendly alien visiting from another world, and she was waiting patiently for the day when my spaceship arrived so that she could go for an intergalactic outing. I was—sort of—sorry that I didn't have a spaceship for her. Talking to aliens was at least something people had heard of around here, where there are frequent UFO sightings. Witness the calls to the sheriff's office the night before and Tyler's laid-back reaction to them.

Pinky had also been a friend of Irv's. I wondered briefly if I should tell her what had happened to him.

"The sun is out. I can see everything," she said, beaming happily.

"The sun is out, but I'm still in the dark," I muttered, trying to match her smile but failing. Those muscles had atrophied. I also realized how much I missed the days of emotional equilibrium when the universe made sense, when I knew exactly what could and could not be. I needed to find that again if I was ever to know peace of mind. And if that meant that cats actually could talk to me . . . well then, so be it. There were more things in heaven and earth and all that. But I had to know if cats actually *were* talking to me, or if I was—well, if I was like Pinky.

"Have you seen Irv?" she asked, as though guessing the direction of my thoughts. "I haven't talked to him in a week." With Pinky everything was a week—last Christmas, next Memorial Day, even her fourth birthday.

"Not today," I said, after deciding not to tell her about Irv being dead. It wasn't my job to spread the unhappy news when clearly the sheriff preferred to keep it quiet, and I wouldn't have volunteered anyway. I have learned firsthand that grief actually steals oxygen from the body. Little by little, it deflates those who are stricken with it, sucking the life right out of them. Pinky would probably forget the unhappy news almost immediately. Then again, maybe she wouldn't, and I wasn't going to be the one who ruined Pinky's sunny day.

A pickup truck rumbled by, the tarmac shivering from both the vibration of the overpowered engine and the rap music pouring from its stereo. Blend It's slate shuddered for a moment and then fell over in a sludge puddle. This was the downside to having a highway pass right through town.

I picked the slate up and then sighed. The sign was smudged and dripping now, but I didn't have the time or inclination to fix it—though I wanted very much to jerk the driver out of his vehicle and dump him in the same puddle. I settled for flipping him the bird. I don't like that the gesture comes so naturally to me. Rage was one of the reasons Cal and I decided to move. I was afraid that my middle finger was going to get stuck in an up-thrust position if we stayed in the Bay Area. As it is, the muscles are still far too developed in the middle finger of my left hand.

Waving good-bye to a puzzled Pinky, I started back up the hill at a brisk stomp as I pretended I was smashing the truck driver's head with my heels. One of the other main reasons Cal and I fled the Silicon Valley was noise pollution and what I can only call a new age of bad manners. The urban din was everywhere down there, the noisy masses not even realizing they offended with their painful music, poured over other commuters who were also stuck in daily gridlocked traffic that happened every morning between six and ten A.M. and every evening from four to seven. Or eight. Or nine. But they did offend, and these otherwise courteous people, who worried about using politically correct language and avoiding bad breath that might bother their co-workers, turned life into an aural arms race between stereos and car engines, horns and cursing: Rush Limbaugh turned up to drown out Britney Spears, who was in turn nudged up another notch so the vegeterian liberal with the preteen in the hybrid car didn't have to listen to the conservative steak-eater in the urban assault vehicle. Rap topped opera until a stand-and-deliver tenor proved that he, boosted by the right electronic equipment, could outsing anyone. The air was fouled with daily commuter aggravation set to digitized syncopation.

Nor could you escape the sound by going to work on foot or bicycle, even supposing the distance to the job was not a bar, which it was in nearly every case. There were millions of people shouting into their cell phones night and day, or just shouting because it was their new "normal" volume level. Shouting at their children, their spouses, their pets, in voices too loud for the shared walls of apartments or even the new "luxury" homes built less than ten feet apart from one another where bathrooms were made of marble but you could still hear your neighbor flush.

Cal and I had done a decade in that endless din and

then opted out. The Silicon Valley was no place for two writers, two lovers of quiet, even if one wrote mainly about computers and the software that ran them. It pissed me off that the noise pollution from the outside was beginning to invade my world. I feared being forced out of it and having nowhere to go.

Being opposed to a lot of so-called progress, it probably goes without saying that I don't have a cell phone. In fact, I keep only one phone in the house now that Cal is gone, and I usually let the answering machine take care of it. This is an act of defiance against the discourteous world that exists outside my little hill in Irish Camp, where ill-mannered but well-meaning people want me to live as an obedient hound to be found at the end of an electronic leash any time they want a last-minute article, a babysitter, or an ear to moan into. This electronic distancing of friends and loved ones is something I do, in spite of the presentiment that I will someday regret not having push-button help close by. In the back of my mind I have always thought that I would bend this rule if I were ever forced into a walker or had a heart attack. Or perhaps when my sibling's larvae have pupated into actual human beings that don't need to be constantly overseen by their aunt when my brother and his wife want a little ski-weekend getaway. Then again, maybe not. It's that old dog learning new tricks thing, and I felt older than Ole Blue. More frustrated, too.

I reluctantly decided it was time to get the car out of the garage and expand my search area for clues. It would be unpleasant, since I dislike being near other cars almost as much as phones, but I had two very compelling reasons for wanting to find Irv's murderer. One, I didn't like the idea of sharing our mountain with a killer. It seemed, at the very least, to be imprudent. And two—which was the more important reason—I needed to prove to myself that I wasn't mad. Because believe me, the idea had crossed my mind more than once that I might be crazier than a shithouse rat. I've done some research and hearing cats talk to you is not a standard neurological condition brought on by lightning strikes. It is, however, rather common in schizophrenics and serial killers like the Son of Sam.

Gritting my teeth—literally—I backed our forest-green Subaru out of the garage and up our driveway, which had a slope like the north face of the Eiger. Triumph over our driveway was never a foregone conclusion in the winter months; ice could easily defeat even the all-wheel drive. That morning, however, the god who looks after fools and people who choose to live on mountains was looking out for me. I made it out of the driveway and onto the road without hitting another car or Abby's moss-covered retaining wall that was already short a few stones from aggressive reversing out of my driveway.

I glanced at my watch. The sheriff wouldn't be on duty yet since he had worked the night shift. That meant I would have to follow other potential leads.

It took nearly ten minutes to get out past the high school, which had been constructed before the advent of the automobile and the need for streets wide enough for two cars to pass abreast. I trickled out of the old town with the other desperate winter shut-ins who were running low on toilet paper and orange juice and wanted to restock at the grocery store before the next storm hit. I had my window cracked open and could smell the delightful odor of greasy sausage and eggs. I don't do fast food; I find it to be the culinary equivalent of elevator music. But that didn't stop me from enjoying the smell as I passed the Tin Roof drive-in.

Have you ever noticed that small towns—and cities, too—are organisms? Some, like Irish Camp, are single-celled; some are more complicated. Some are robust and some are delicate. But we have in common one thing: a need to live, even thrive, in our given environment, which we generally prefer remains unchanged.

Our little hamlet is not pretty, though the downtown area strives for quaint. What we really are is sinewy and hardened, and we know how to survive. That means a certain amount of compromise. Modern life and its conveniences haven't completely passed us by—we aren't that lucky. We have our monster trucks and, at the very base of the mountain, there are a few chain-stores and more fast-food places. They are there for the tourists who go into withdrawal if kept from cheap hamburgers and tacos for more than twenty-four hours. The locals—one of which I now considered myself to be—wince every time we pass these places. I would actually drive miles out of my way to avoid them and the reminders they brought of previous life in the city.

Unless I needed a new ink cartridge for my printer, that is. Then I would conduct commerce with the great Satan. Or if I was headed up the hill on the only road into Sublime—population twenty-seven—because there was only one road up that part of the mountain. I hadn't been up there much since Cal died, and I traveled there slowly on that day, doing no more than a cowardly forty miles per hour, both because the roads might still have ice on them and because I was venturing into a place where Cal's shade might linger.

As I have mentioned before, our part of the world is populated with some strange signs. This bit of forgotten interstate's no different. My favorite: THIS SECTION OF ROAD IS MAINTAINED BY THE LITERARY HITCHHIKERS GUILD. Of course, I've never seen any hitchhikers along here, literary or otherwise—a sheer rock wall on one side of the narrow two-lane road and a steep cliff on the other discourages all but the most suicidal of people—but I must say that the thoroughfare is always very tidy. Perhaps they use a blower slung out of a car window.

There were two other businesses with odd signs prominently displayed in Sublime: DON'S SNOW PLOWS AND 8 FLAVORS OF ICE CREAM!!!! CLEAN RESTROOMS!!! and CAN TANK R US SEPTIC AND SEWER—LAUNDRY, CAR WASH, BAIT AND TACKLE. I was planning on going to both if necessary, since I was looking for an old gold mine that Crystal had shown me last summer, but hadn't a clue where to start searching. The old vein was supposedly played out, and it sounded like it was good for nothing but hiding illegal stills, even more illegal pot patches and possibly a meth lab or two. But Irv had liked to hike up there, in fair weather and foul, and I was running out of things to investigate in town.

I pulled into the Can Tank R Us graveled lot, now carpeted with pine needles and other wind-borne debris, and walked up to the glass door. The hand-painted sign read: SHUT AT 5. Underneath in smaller letters it said: OPEN AT 10. It was well after ten, but I wasn't surprised to find this particular house of commerce empty. These sorts of signs weren't hard and fast guarantees of business hours, but rather optimistic statements of intent. Winter mornings tended to be drowsy times, especially after Christmas. There simply wasn't any benefit to hurrying into the dark and cold when there weren't any customers. I sympathized. The sun would not rise and warm this shady spot until at least noon, and most days the sky would remain an unleavened gray. That was super if you ran a ski resort, but not if you had a non-snow-related business like renting gold pans to tourists who wouldn't arrive until school let out in June. I'd had a bit of trouble adjusting to this lackadaisical way of mountain commerce at first, but eventually learned to adapt to life in a place where the only popular measure of time was geological—and that only if gold and silver were involved.

Shrugging in acceptance, I walked next door, resigned to seeing one of Cal's old friends and hoping for fresh-brewed coffee, though prepared to eat ice cream if I had no other choice. Somehow, I wasn't entirely surprised to reach the end of the short wooden walkway and see the nose of the sheriff's Jeep peeping out from the side of the building. Great minds—or inquisitive ones—really did think alike. Or maybe he just didn't care for Prune Typhoons either, and had remembered that our French bakery is closed on Sundays and Mondays even when Nolan isn't holding rallies right outside the door.

This sign was turned to IN instead of OUT, so I let myself inside, wincing at the jangle of cow bells above the warped door. Not even trying to pretend that I had actually come to town to hire a snowplow, or for any of the eight exciting flavors of ice cream, I sat down at the four-seat counter next to Tyler Murphy and said good morning.

The proprietor, Don Crandall, wore Old Spice, a smell that always reminded me of my grandfather. I inhaled, closing my eyes and allowing myself a moment of nostalgia. It almost compensated for the vague smell of burning coffee that was always in the air.

"Hi, Don," I said at last, eyes still closed. He was used to my sniffing when he was around. I think he found it flattering.

"Hi, Jillian. We haven't seen you for a month of Sundays." It had been longer than that, but I didn't correct him.

"Let me guess. You've had a sudden craving for spumoni," Tyler said. He blew on his coffee, sending an acrid cloud in my direction. This stuff might have been fresh at sunrise, but was long past it now. And Don wouldn't brew another pot until this one was gone—waste not, want not. Cal had never minded the taste of singed brew, but it wasn't my favorite.

"No, the rocky road. One scoop in a dish, please," I answered, opening my eyes and smiling at Don Crandall. Screw the bad coffee; it wasn't any good here, and thinking of Grandpa made me want his favorite ice cream.

"Better choice," Tyler admitted. "So, shall I save you some time and tell you what's up with our little conundrum? By the way, you sound much better this morning."

"Thanks, it's the sun. So, let me guess—you came up here on a whim, maybe to keep an eye on evildoers who are passing through on the way to go skiing," I answered, glancing at Don as he set about digging out the very solid ice cream, which was layered with ice crystals. I hoped the marshmallow wouldn't be too unyielding. I like to squish it against the roof of my mouth, sorting out the nuts from the sweet. I'd started doing that when I began losing my baby teeth to the sticky stuff. I have shallow roots on my teeth and it takes very little to knock them out. As a child, I didn't mind the gap-toothed look, but the tooth fairy only paid up when you had an actual tooth to barter. I had probably been cheated out of maybe a buck twenty-five by unlucky swallowing. That was five weeks' allowance, or one Little House on the Prairie book. Those hard childhood lessons stuck with you, especially when you were now responsible for your own dental bills.

"A whim? Yes, I guess you could say that, though I do try to visit every town in the county at least twice a week."

Uh-huh, a whim of solid steel. Have I mentioned that I can be stubborn? I hadn't mentioned it to Tyler either, but he was a smart cop and I knew he had my number. As I had his. As the old taunt goes: It takes one to know one. We were both mules.

"As long as we're feeling whimsical, let's have some show-and-tell," I suggested.

"Fair enough. Don, would you get me a scoop of strawberry cheesecake while you're at it?"

"Sure, Tyler," Don answered, puzzled but pleased. There hadn't been much call for ice cream during the long, long winter. He added conscientiously: "It might have a bit of freezer burn, though. I haven't restocked lately."

"That's okay. I take my ice cream any way I can get it."

Don smiled gratefully. His business—like so many up here—was barely alive, and he couldn't afford to restock the ice cream in the winter, but that wouldn't stop some people from complaining. The sheriff was catching on quickly, though, and was capable of compassion. I thought it might turn out that I would like him after all.

If only he liked me, too. I wouldn't mind having Tyler twisted around my finger. That would be a useful place for him. However, I suspected that while not unbending, he wasn't flexible enough—or blind enough—to make himself into a pretzel this morning simply because I wanted him to.

Jillian, is that you?

I stiffened involuntarily. A slight scratching came at the door behind the counter. Don and Carol lived above the shop and this was how they reached their living quarters. They had a cat.

"Go away, Clips. You know you can't come in here," Don called. Clips, short for Paperclips and Rubberbands. Clips had been a true gymnast among kittens. None of the drapes had survived his youth. "That darn cat never learns, and I swear he adores Jillian. He rubs on her like she's catnip."

Yeah, go away, Clips. We don't want the sheriff thinking I have cats in my belfry, I thought at the restless feline.

After a second the scratching stopped and we heard

the soft thundering of paws running up a wooden stair. I tried not to react visibly to the reprieve.

"Shall I start? I happened to be in The Mule this morning," I said casually to the sheriff. Then, fearing that the cold ice cream might again lock up my jaw before we were done talking, I added: "Don, could you get me a coffee, too?" I wouldn't drink it, just hold the steaming cup under my chin and keep the joints thawed enough for conversation.

"Did you now? How unusual." Tyler's voice was mild. His gaze was warm, too, not at all sheriff-like. He was inviting me in, willing me to feel safe and confiding. We were just two friends sharing some winter morning ice cream. I wanted to believe that but remained wary.

"Yes, indeed. And I had a short chat with Molly Gerran—that's Irv's old girlfriend." I was being discreet, not mentioning I'd had this discussion with Molly in front of Don.

"Uh-huh." Tyler sipped from his cup, not even flinching as the scorched brew passed his lips. He was a strong man. I thought he was also an interested one.

"She says that Irv has a nephew. His first name is Gordon or Jordon and he lives in Lodi or maybe Fresno." I smiled a little. "I was sure you'd want to know."

"Why, thank you. That will help a great deal." He didn't bother hiding the irony. It wasn't mean-spirited, though, so I didn't get defensive when he added: "I didn't know you had an in with that crowd."

"I don't. Irv is the only common denominator."

Don put my dish of ice cream and a brimming coffee cup on the counter. He seemed inclined to linger and visit with me, but Tyler's clear gaze reminded him of some shipment that needed unpacking in the back room. I was grateful. I didn't want to talk with one of Cal's old buddies about how I was doing these days. Their ongoing concern with my isolation revived my feelings of helplessness, and reminded me of the days when Cal and I had had to wrestle with our own impotence and pity. Yes, pity. Mine, for his facing a horrible death, and he for me because I would have to go on living without him. That we'd never expressed any of this aloud did not mean it was not there.

"Will there be an autopsy?" I asked in a low voice that made allowances for thin walls. I took a tentative bite of my ice cream. It was indeed a bit freezer burned, but I was suddenly hungry enough to enjoy it anyway. When had I last eaten? I couldn't quite recall.

"Yes." Tyler was looking at me straight on now. "It's standard in cases like this. At least it is where I come from. Nolan does not agree. He actually had me on the phone before seven this morning."

"That's too bad. It's really best to be sure about things." I added without looking up: "Makes it easier for the family."

"Yes, I'm sure answers will comfort Gordon. Or Jordan. And anyone else who might be concerned about being killed in their cabins if anyone shares your beliefs about the cause of death." Tyler put his coffee down. He asked straightly: "You weren't thinking of going hiking in the woods today, were you?"

"I might. The sun is a rare sight and I haven't gotten out much lately." And the sunshine was disappearing quickly. Another hour and it could be raining like The End of Days again. I figured that it was now or never.

Tyler looked at his watch and frowned. "I don't suppose you'd like some company on this walk? I haven't seen that much of the countryside."

That hadn't been my plan, having a guest while I searched for Irv's gold mine, but I thought about it while I smashed the last of the marshmallow on the roof of my mouth. On the one hand, I had the feeling that Tyler was suspicious of my intentions because of my friendship with Irving, and maybe he just wanted to make sure that I didn't tamper with any smokable evidence I might find. Or steal it outright. He probably thought that I would be inclined to clean out Irv's pot field before law enforcement found it, to protect Irv's or his friends' not-so-good names. Or just to have some free dope. And he might be right about me, at least about my not telling anyone about what I found. I probably wouldn't call in the law if I found a pot farm, since I'm not a hypocrite and I didn't see anything wrong with occasional recreational drug use, and also understand that some people simply can't endure life without some help—chemo patients being chief among them. If you have insurance or live in a city with liberal drug laws, you get your pain relief from your doctor or a cannabis club. If you don't, then you see someone like Irv, or whoever would take over this philanthropic endeavor now that he was gone—and God bless them.

Of course, all bets were off if I found something that made me think drugs were actually connected to Irv's murder. Then I would report it all. But I didn't think drugs were involved. The conviction had grown in me during the last few hours that this murder had something to do with the other great addiction of Irv's life: gold. All our historic local murders were caused by gold, or the need for water to mine for gold. Irv had grown pot for years without any problems, so why would there be trouble now? What had changed recently was Irv's increasing interest in panning for gold. And maybe in exploring old mines. I think he had come down with a bad case of gold fever, and that could make people very stupid.

On the other hand, perhaps I'd misjudged the sheriff. Tyler might not think I was a potential thief. He might just be concerned about my welfare. There were wild animals out there, mountain lions and bears. He was

probably convinced that there was at least one or two illegal stills out in the woods, too, which could mean
trouble with people who were rigorous about enforc-
ing No Trespassing when it came to their moonshine. I
decided that this was a more likely explanation for his
offer. After all, if he thought that this actually was a
murder or that there was some pot field to be found,
then he would flat-out discourage me from assisting in
his investigation or asking questions on my own. And he
could be right about this being a snipe hunt, which
would make my persistence look foolish—at least to
me—when I found nothing and it turned out I was just
a crazy woman who listened to cats and inner voices.

That last thought argued against telling him why I
was so certain that Irv had been murdered, no matter
how kind the gaze he turned on me. I thought a little
sadly that probably it would be wisest to spend as little
time with him as possible. He wasn't stupid, and he
would be bound to notice that there was something
odd about me if we hung around together for any
length of time.

On the other hand, there was no denying that there
were a lot of illegal businesses up here and druggies
could be dangerous when their livelihoods were threatened by an outsider, which I was, in spite of my friendship with Irv. If I really believed that there was any
possibility of drugs being involved, and that someone
with a denim coat and a smelly butt had murdered Irving, then it might be nice to have the sheriff along on
my explorations. I would just make extra sure to act like
a normal person for the next little while.

"Is it that difficult a question?" he asked. His eyes
were amused. I liked the way he smiled.

"No." I wouldn't mind Tyler's company for its own
sake, I decided. I had been alone for an awfully long
time and that was probably not healthy. I needed to start

living like a normal person again. I'd just be careful around any cats. "Let's get the coffee to go." I raised my voice. "Don! We're going to pour our coffee into paper cups, okay?"

Don reappeared immediately.

"Sure thing, Jillian." He set two Styrofoam cups with plastic lips on the counter. Don was an ex-Republican but he hadn't gone Green enough to practice recycling, or to use biodegradable paper when Styrofoam was cheaper. "You keep warm, you hear? And don't be a stranger. There's always a mug waiting here for you, you know. No, don't pay me. The ice cream is on the house."

"Thank you, Don. Give my best to Carol." I realized that Pinky wasn't the only one people looked after. I needed to remember to count my blessings and bear in mind that other people missed Cal, too.

The sheriff pulled on his sheepskin jacket, put a five-dollar tip on the counter, nodded at Don but said nothing to me until we were outside.

"Okay, Nancy Drew, where to first?" So he didn't buy that I was just going for a walk. That was okay.

"That way. We're looking for a gold mine," I said, deciding to be a bit truthful and see how he reacted to a new idea. I should find out as soon as possible how flexible he was in his thinking.

"A what?" Tyler asked, clearly startled. He really had thought I was looking for a pot field. Well, it was my fault. I'd brought up Irv's extracurricular drug activities myself the night before.

"An old abandoned gold mine. I hear that it may be being used again these days." That was a lie. I'd heard nothing definite. "And, as you have probably figured out, Irv liked to hike up here. All the time." I started for the woods. There was a deer path through the mountain misery on the other side of the road. I hoped passionately that the snow had killed off most of the ticks that lived in the low-growing shrubs. I didn't look at Tyler, though I was aware of him. His aftershave was subtle compared to Don's, but it smelled absolutely delicious. Instead, I concentrated on not turning an ankle and not clenching my jaw as the temperature dropped. It would be a good ten degrees cooler when we got next to the river, and I needed to be prepared.

"So, you think that Irv *was* into drugs and might have been using the mine as a warehouse or a greenhouse?" Tyler asked. He was like a dog with a chew toy. He didn't want to give up his drug theory. I was going to have to offer a very tasty bone if I wanted to pry this idea out of his jaws.

"That's what some people say," I answered shortly.

"But you don't believe it?" The man was perceptive. Of course, I was not great at hiding my thoughts.

"I did at first—sort of. I mean, there's money in drugs and Irv had to get his somewhere. I know he grew marijuana. He gave some to my husband when Cal was sick, but I'm sure he sold, too. It wasn't all philanthropic." I stepped cautiously into the bracken and felt the cold damp reaching for my flesh. I was going to be sopping wet and muddy by the time we got back to the car. "But the more I think about it . . . I don't know if it fits. Winter isn't the usual time to grow dope. And Irv was, in his own way, a rather moral man."

"Moral?"

"He grew marijuana. That's illegal but not immoral—at least, not in my book. If you have ever watched someone going through chemo. . . ." I stopped, unable to go on. "But I don't think he'd do anything else. Nothing that would make anyone around here want to kill him."

"Like cooking up meth?"

"Meth?" It was my turn to be startled. My answer to that was unqualified. "Absolutely not. It's too . . . polluting—of the land and also of people. Irv wasn't into chemicals. Look, he fed stray cats and grew his own vegetables. He dated a woman who never shaved her legs or wore deodorant. Irv was about being organic and natural—and kind. He would never deal in anything that brought living death to people or the land." I hadn't thought of this before, but it felt right as I said it.

Tyler grunted.

"So, we're looking for a greenhouse or maybe a storehouse. Something that would be sheltered in winter."

"Yes, or maybe the remains of one, if someone else knew about it and has been back since Irv died. Or . . ." I took a breath and went ahead and voiced the thought that was nibbling at me, though it was probably fanciful thinking. "Like I said, maybe we're looking for a working gold mine. The man had gold fever like you wouldn't believe. If Irv found something up here he wouldn't be above a bit of high-grading."

"I beg your pardon?"

"Working someone else's mine—if it was abandoned. After all, cold weather wouldn't matter to Irv if he were underground." It wouldn't matter in a greenhouse either, I could hear Tyler thinking. I glanced back to see if he was interested in my trial balloon, or if he was going to shoot it down before I got it aloft. "What if Irv was prospecting for gold near someone else's marijuana patch? Or near someone's meth lab, since you seem sure that there's one about?"

"There is one about. And that might be reason enough to kill someone," Tyler admitted. "But why not kill him on-site? Why follow him home and do it there—assuming that's what happened?"

"I don't know," I admitted. "Maybe so it would look like an accident. Or maybe Irv gave them the slip in the woods and they had to track him down later." The deer trail we followed disappeared in a clearing and I hesitated. I recalled this place from last autumn. Wild grapes had rampaged up the trees all summer and they made a glorious red bower when the leaves turned in the fall. But those leaves were gone now and the vines torn down. Wind and snow had done their brutal work on all the growing things. The snowy glade was strewn with denuded limbs, stripped bare and then broken from their woody torsos. The trunks were also clean of moss and lichen and even much of their bark. They hadn't so much as a fig leaf to hide their nakedness from what remained of the cruel winter. The sight was depressing and confusing without the familiar markers.

I jammed my free hand in my coat pocket. I had gloves but they had gotten wet so many times that winter the leather had lost its suppleness. Having no clear direction to follow, I turned to the right. The land to the left was very stony, and straight ahead was a sheer cliff and then the river. "I just know that prospecting is more in line with what Irv would do than manufacturing drugs. And there is every bit as much money in it— and maybe more."

"Really? Okay. You knew Irv better than I did, so I'm willing to work with this theory." He wasn't discounting other ones, though. And neither was I—not completely. But I preferred that this be about gold than about marijuana, or God forbid, methamphetamines. I didn't want the threat of drug killings as well as noise pollution to impinge on my safe little world.

"You know, you're showing me a side of Irving Thibodaux that I never knew. I feel a bit unobservant," the sheriff said.

"Don't. Irv was an acquired taste, and he didn't make friends easily. It took a long time for me to train my palate to accept him. And I haven't been dwelling on his less attractive points, of which there were many."

There was no noise to warn me, but I was suddenly aware of intense, nonhuman scrutiny. I tried to ignore it since Tyler was there and I was doing my best to be normal, but it grew ever stronger, and after a few more steps I stopped and looked to my right, where the baleful glare was coming from.

Tyler stopped too and began to look around. It took him a moment longer to spot what I knew was there.

"Is that . . . ?"

"Yes. Just stay still." It took an effort to say this, because my jaw had tightened in the cold and because I was terrified.

Are you the woman who talks to cats? That's what I heard. Tyler was only aware of the low growl, and it had him reaching for his pistol. His posture switched from genial to deadly in less than a second.

"No," I said to the sheriff, touching his arm. I was shocked at being addressed by the wild cat, but also relieved. If the cat wanted to talk then it probably didn't want to eat. At least not me.

To the cat I said aloud: "Yes, kitty. What do you want on this fine morning?"

The mountain lion sat down, looking a bit surprised at being answered, or perhaps at being called a kitty. Its posture was more relaxed than it had been. Tyler was still stiff with alarm, so I kept my hand on him.

You're looking for a smelly-butt man who kills his own kind? Its teeth were very large as the cat yawned. He picked up a paw and I swear examined his nails. His lips curled with distaste. The gesture was so human I almost laughed.

Instead, I exhaled slowly. The word of Irv's death might not have gotten out into the human population, but the feline grapevine was obviously fully functional. If this cat could help, I was willing to listen.

"Yes, good kitty. That I am. What do you want me to know?" I could feel Tyler staring first at me, then at the cat, and then back to me again. I couldn't blame him, really. None of the popular hiking guides at the tourist center suggested talking sweet kitten gibberish when confronted with an adult mountain lion. He didn't try to interrupt, though, for which I was grateful.

There are two smelly-butt men near the river in the man-cave. They kill many things and the water is undrinkable now. The cat stared over my left shoulder. A stray beam of sunlight struck his irises and made his eyes gleam gold. His head was huge, larger than mine. *I would like it if you and sheep man made them go away.*

Sheep man? I glanced at Tyler and took in his coat. Sheepskin.

"Pretty kitty," I said, turning back, but I thought, *Thank you! I'll try.* "We're going now. It would be best if you stayed here while we go for our walk. Will you do that for me, kitty cat?"

The cat chuffed and then turned away. In an instant he had disappeared into the trees, making no more sound than a shadow.

"I'll be damned," Tyler said, and I finally dropped my hand. It had begun to shake. I was glad that my coffee had a lid.

"Let's hope not," I answered, again holding the coffee cup against my cheek as I started off in the direction the cat indicated. My pace was brisk but the wind was brisker. There were still some patches of snow on the ground and tangled in the manzanita bushes, which slouched pet-tishly under the cold weight. They were beginning to moan as the currents of cold air passed through them. I wanted to moan, too—damn jaw. It was beginning to feel like some hard-rock miner with blasting caps was trying to blow up my face. Still, I had a lead and I was damned if I was going to ignore it. Especially not when I had the sheriff with me.

"You know where we're headed?" he asked.

"Yes, I have my bearings now. We need to go down

by the river. That's where the mine is." I debated how to explain the next thing I needed to tell him. Tyler didn't seem up on his flora and fauna so I said casually, "There are probably men down there. At least two, and armed. Hunters maybe, but it could be your meth cookers. That's what brought the cat up here. A mountain lion wouldn't have come so close to town unless people had invaded his turf. And if it was just one man, the cat probably would have confronted him and driven him off."

I had no idea if this was true, but it sounded plausible. I hoped a city dweller would think so, too.

"You're a woman of unexpected talents," Tyler said, and I thought he meant it as a compliment. "I would never have suspected you of being such an outdoors woman."

"Sheriff, you have no idea."

"That's true. But I'll figure you out eventually." He said this cheerfully, but I sincerely hoped he was wrong. I didn't want anyone figuring me out, at least not until I understood myself. Tyler added: "I'm betting most people don't get past the surface layer of cute and cuddly, so they never notice the brain underneath. I think it's those big, sad eyes. They're real distracting."

My heart gave an odd kick. Cute and cuddly. That wasn't as good as beautiful and exotic, but I'd take it even if it was a bit of a presumptuous thing to say to a near-stranger.

"So what lured you to Irish Camp, Sheriff? You're not exactly the standard salt of the earth yourself," I said, changing the subject. The gossips in town had been silent on this point. My words weren't as distinct as I would like, but he was getting better at understanding me.

"The fishing." Then he added: "Also a dead partner and a divorce that led me to feel that I wanted a life that held less violence and fewer inventive criminals. A man can only be used as a blunt instrument against the gangs for so long before he starts to lose his humanity. I didn't like what was happening to me."

"We haven't got a lot of criminal masterminds up here," I admitted. I was dying to ask for more personal details, but didn't. I was nosy but not rude. He would have to volunteer the rest of his story, especially about his partner dying. "We do have some good fishing, though, if you like trout."

"I can't wait for some better weather. Maybe you can show me some of the best spots."

Could I? Maybe. If I wasn't living in a home for the seriously delusional by then.

There wasn't time for any more conversation, because we found one of the mountain lion's smelly-butt men. He came staggering toward us, grumbling under his breath. He had a dog with him. And a gun.

Some people are owned, or at least heavily defined, by their most treasured possessions. Prada shoes make a certain statement. So do hats with earflaps. And, of course, so do Dobermans and a shotgun. The man also reeked of alcohol and worse. I learned that day just how bad a methamphetamine lab smells. Taken together, I read his character as mean, paranoid and irresponsible.

And stupid. He actually threatened Tyler with the shotgun. I thought Tyler was going to wrap the thing around his neck. As it was, Tyler settled for taking the rifle away and then whacking him with it, never even breaking a sweat. Maybe after the gangs armed with automatic weapons, mere drunks with shotguns didn't hold the power to terrify.

I was shaken by the encounter, even though the confrontation was over in about ten seconds. I was suddenly very glad that Tyler was with me, though this guy was too wasted to be much of a threat and the dog wasn't as mean as it looked, and wisely refrained from attacking either of us when his master was getting roughed up.

Tyler played it cool and by the book, but I knew he was happy at this unexpected encounter. I shared his happiness, if to a lesser degree. A brief search of the man's pockets showed us that we had found Tyler's drug dealer—Arthur Kingsley, his license said—and maybe I had found Irv's killer, though I would have preferred it if the man had been wearing a denim coat and large waffle-stompers.

We turned and hiked back to the parking lot where the sheriff's Jeep was. I patted my leg and the dog tagged along behind us. I didn't say anything, but studied Arthur Kingsley from the corner of my eye. He wasn't a handsome specimen. All the features of his face were scrunched together in the middle, his upper lip almost touching the tip of his nose, his eyes resting on his cheekbones. This was because he was missing teeth. He looked a bit like headhunters had tried to shrink his head but given up after they finished the face. I wasn't a dermatologist, but his flaccid skin looked like one giant precancerous lesion. Nature had hit this boy with the ugly stick. Twice. And then with the idiot stick to boot. Ugly and stupid—what chance did this guy have? It was probably a kindness to send him to jail before he killed himself.

While Tyler was putting the verbally abusive but now rather subdued drunk into the cruiser, I stole a bandana that fell out of his prisoner's pocket and slipped it into my own. Atherton would know if this was the right man. The dog I tied up to Tyler's rear bumper, with a piece of rope, and then fetched him some water from Don's place. I think the poor abused animal might have been trying to talk to me, but I couldn't understand him. All I

could do was pat his sable-colored head and murmur re-
assurances through clenched teeth that all would be well.
I was certain that the shelter would take him since he was
so gentle. I might have kept him for myself, but with all
the strays that had attached themselves to me, I didn't
think it was the right time to introduce a canine into my
home.

I know Tyler wanted to tell me to be careful around
the mutt. And he was right, of course. But that is one
lesson I will probably never learn this side of the grave.
Cal and I had this in common. We'd been bitten and
scratched more than once while rescuing injured animals, but there you go. In some people, compassion
wins over common sense every time.

The sheriff's cell phone worked fine, and for a wonder he was able to get a signal up on the hill. He ordered
Farland Tulloc to find Dawg, and for both of them to
head for Sublime immediately. I eavesdropped openly
and could hear Farland's usually phlegmatic voice growing animated as he understood that they were making a
genuine drug bust. Maybe it was the bonus he would
receive.

Tyler and I had another cup of ghastly coffee while
we waited for the deputies. I insisted that we remain
outside with the dog even though my jaw was throbbing. I didn't mention that this was because I had the
feeling the mountain lion was close by and I didn't trust
it not to help itself to a doggie snack.

Tyler kindly refrained from conversation. I found the
silence companionable, even though Tyler spent a lot
of time staring at me and the dog with an expression I
can only call speculative.

He was probably thinking that I shouldn't be allowed
along on their search for the meth lab. Not technically.
But I knew the area, and I could tell that Tyler was by
now half-convinced that I was some kind of super nature

guide—which I was, but not because I had ever earned my Girl Scout merit badge. Thanks to the mountain lion, I was the only one who knew—more or less—where the men had been staying, and everyone agreed it would save time if I showed them the way to the mine. The sheriff might have had a procedural qualm or two about including a civilian on a raid, but Dawg and Farland knew Cal's widow and they wouldn't raise any objections to having the search time shortened and getting off the mountain before it rained.

It turns out they could have managed without me. The smell from the old mine shaft was abundant and horrible and all too easy to find. As labs went, it was small and unimpressive. Still, it was a service to the community to shut it down. Methamphetamines are killing America and every battle won is a triumph for our health and life.

The other man mentioned by the mountain lion was missing from camp, but that there were two of them was not in doubt. I had no way of knowing which bedroll was his, so I took dirty socks from the piles of clothes on both sleeping bags. Everyone else was so busy taking pictures and bagging evidence at the back of the caved-in shaft that they didn't notice what I was doing.

The socks reeked, even above the smell of chemicals, but I added them to my coat pockets. Thank God I found no underwear because duty might have compelled me to take it and that would have just been too gross for my increasingly touchy stomach. I finally had to walk some distance away to escape the miasma of odors. It wasn't just the chemicals used, either. The men had been hunting for their meals, and maybe because compounds they used to make their drugs had destroyed their ability to smell, they had taken to dumping the offal just outside the mine opening.

I wasn't too surprised to feel the mountain lion

watching me when I stepped outside. I didn't turn to face it in case Tyler was watching.

"The other man isn't here," I murmured, knowing the cat would hear me.

No, he left. He went in a man machine—a large dark one. The growl was soft.

"We'll keep looking for him," I promised, and walked away. I didn't want to be rude, but what I didn't need was to encourage any thoughts of friendship this mountain lion might have been entertaining. A friendly tabby—even a bevy of strays—hanging about my house could be explained and even ignored by my neighbors; a mountain lion could not.

My jaw had locked solid by the time the job was done, but I managed a smile and thumbs-up for Tyler when we started back for the parking lot, all of us burdened with trash bags stuffed with lab equipment and camping gear confiscated as evidence. Dawg had to carry the portable generator, which was really heavy, but he didn't seem to mind, even though it was beginning to rain. He was talking excitedly about getting a haircut before being on the news. He had a terrible crush on Mary Jane Brighton, our local anchorwoman.

I noticed that at no point did Tyler say anything to the deputies about finding Irv's murderer. Maybe because he was being a thorough investigator and content to wait for forensic evidence before declaring Irv's death a crime. Or maybe because he sensed that I hadn't completely signed off on the idea that we had the right man.

My footsteps slowed slightly as I thought about this. It occurred to me that maybe he still wasn't sure that Irv had actually been murdered. I was getting ahead of myself in thinking he was convinced there had been a crime. Tyler might still believe it was an accident and just be humoring me while he waited for forensic evidence to come in.

I tried not to feel deflated. It seemed likely we did have Irv's killer. Irv could have easily stumbled on their operation while searching out the old gold mine, and the man we arrested was certainly violent enough to have killed someone while sober. But the fact that the cave-in at the site was an old one made me think that Irv wouldn't have bothered with this place. He would be looking for something that a man could work alone—something reasonably safe. And someplace not so well known. Irv would have been watching for something new, some parting on the rock that broke open because of all the rain we'd been having. If I had been thinking, I would have gone looking for mudslides along the river where freshly disgorged nuggets might have slid down into the stream. That was a much more likely place for Irv to work than a mine or some coyote hole. All he'd need is a gold pan and maybe a sluice box.

Also, now that I was watching the path, I noticed again that the tread on the drug dealer's smallish hiking boots didn't match the pattern or size of the ones I'd seen in Irv's cabin. There were other stray prints as well, but they didn't match the ones at Irv's either. There was also the matter of the missing denim coat, though he might have thrown it away if he had gotten blood on it.

Maybe the waffle-stompers and coat belonged to the other man and he never came this way, I thought again, trying to be optimistic about the current state of affairs. And chances were good that he would be found soon. This was a small community and we knew everyone who lived there. The cats were diligently looking for him.

The mountain lion was looking for him, too. Also, I could tell that for all his seeming calm Tyler wanted the other man badly. I just needed to be patient and let the law—and the cats—do their work.

Of all God's creatures, there is only one that cannot be made slave of the leash. That one is the cat. If man could be crossed with the cat it would improve the man, but it would deteriorate the cat.

—Mark Twain

CHAPTER SIX

I kept my word to the cats and got a giant sack of cat kibble at the grocery store. I also threw in a bag of raw peanuts for the squirrel. The clerk on the afternoon shift was new and didn't recognize me, so I was feeling fairly confident of making it home with no one in the neighborhood any the wiser about me inheriting the strays. But of course my luck ran out in my own driveway, not twenty feet from my door. Isn't that always the way?

Abby, my feline-unfriendly neighbor, chose that day to visit on her way back from her volunteer job at the library, and peering through the bare butterfly bush at my opened trunk as I unloaded my telltale groceries, she immediately spotted the heifer-sized bag of economy cat kibble dragged halfway out of the hatchback and left drooping over the bumper while I rested my muscles for a moment. It's nice that they have clerks to help load stuff into your car, but what do they expect to happen when you get these things home?

"Jillian," she called. Hurried footsteps came crunching down the leaf-strewn driveway. I might have imagined it, but there seemed to be a bit of panic in her voice. Abby won't admit to having any phobias, but she doesn't do well with cats, snakes, bees or white dogs.

"In here," I admitted, since she'd seen me anyway. I straightened my spine and turned to face her.

"I just heard about Irv. It's so sad. I hardly know what to say." But she would think of something. She always did.

"Yes." It wasn't just my tightening jaw that kept my answers short. I was hoping that if I looked incredibly busy that Abby would go away. But no such luck. She crow-hopped down the last of the littered drive and stopped at the garage door. She's a stickler for proper social conduct, and she wouldn't step into the garage without an express invitation. It was sheer pettiness, but I didn't make any offers.

"You're feeding Irv's strays?" Abby looked at the sack of kibble laying half over the bumper and had no doubt guessed that I hadn't switched my diet. Then, with a certain amount of hurt at my betrayal: "But why? You don't like cats."

"Compassion." And their promise not to talk to me when anyone else was around, since it made me act a bit crazy. I looked at the huge amount of food I had purchased and said more hopefully than truthfully, "It won't be for long. I'm going to talk to the people at the animal shelter about finding them homes."

Abby nodded dubiously but didn't say anything more. We exchanged the minimal levels of polite chitchat required of neighbors living less than fifty yards from one another, and then she climbed her way back up the drive to her idling car. I waited until I heard the vehicle slip into gear and begin rolling through the gravel before I turned back to my battle with the kibble. I dragged the fifty-pound sack inside the garage while Atherton

perched on the fence Cal built with the optimistic belief
that it would keep the deer out of our vegetable garden.
(Ha! Like it ever worked!) The cat watched my strug-
gles with unblinking eyes and a twitching nose.

I invited Atherton in after I had put out several pie
tins of kibble for the other, now very hungry cats, and a
handful of peanuts for the bossy squirrel. After a short,
surprised look, the cat followed me inside.

I left the groceries on the counter while I caught my
breath, and we went into the living room. We both sat
down on the sofa. I pulled out the things I had collected
in Sublime and laid the socks and bandana on the coffee
table.

"We found a smelly-butt man down by the river today," I began.

With the sheep man.

"Yes. Do you think any of these things belonged to
the person who killed Irving?"

Atherton sniffed, and then sneezed.

*No. These aren't the right men. This one does have very
smelly feet, though*, Atherton said kindly—being understanding about my poor human sense of smell that
would lead me to confuse feet for a butt.

"I noticed that," I answered, thinking I would have
to take my coat for cleaning now that my pocket was
contaminated with foot stink, and hoping that whatever was wrong with this guy's feet wasn't contagious.
I was also feeling a bit discouraged that we hadn't managed to find Irv's killer straight off. I wasn't enjoying
playing sleuth, a job which had so far been everything
from unpleasant to downright painful, but I didn't have
enough money to hire a real detective to do the work
for me. It would have to be someone from out of town.
We had only one private eye in the area. His name was
Graham Belle. He ran a small business that he called

The Curiosity Shoppe. I liked Graham, but he was some sort of distant cousin of Nolan's and I didn't want to go anywhere near our mayor with my theory that Irv had been murdered. He'd find out eventually, but later was better than sooner.

The heater clicked on with a soft *whoosh*. Atherton stared fixedly over my left shoulder. I turned to see what had riveted his gaze, but nothing was there except my long-neglected knitting bag sitting in Grandma Linn's old wing-backed chair.

"Atherton? What are you doing?"

Watching.

"Watching what?" I asked, wondering uneasily if a mouse had gotten inside. I hated catching the things. They always squeaked so distressfully when I caught them in the mop bucket.

The yarn.

"Oh. Um . . . why?"

It moved.

I turned and looked again. Sure enough, a stray blue wisp of mohair was caught in a current of hot air. It swayed slightly.

"You're watching it because it moved." Against my better judgment, I asked again: "Why?"

Because it moved. His green eyes flicked in my direction. *It's a cat thing.*

"Ah." I nodded, pretending to understand. I cleared my throat. "Well, I'm getting hungry for dinner. Would you like . . ." I trailed off, trying to think what a cat might like. Probably not tomato soup with oyster crackers, or Cap'n Crunch cereal. It seemed wrong to serve him kibble when I wasn't going to eat it. I reviewed the slim stock of canned goods at the back of the cupboard. "Would you like some tuna?"

The giant head cocked, and unblinking eyes turned

my way. Atherton reminded me of the helpful mountain lion, and I said another prayer that creature hadn't followed me home from Sublime.

I'm not sure. Would I like some tuna?

Would he? Then, I thought to myself for the hundredth time: Why, of all the creatures on God's green earth, did I have to hear cats? I didn't understand them at all. A dog would have been so much easier to deal with. All you had to do was watch the ears and tail and you knew exactly where you stood.

"I think you would. Most cats do." I hurried to the kitchen, hoping I could find the can opener.

I didn't have any mayonnaise, so I made my tuna sandwich with Italian vinaigrette. It wasn't bad and it helped moisten the rather stale bread that was all I had on hand—unless you counted a very old box of frozen waffles. I know this sounds disgraceful, but my jaw had been so tight for the last few weeks that all I could manage was soup, so I hadn't bothered with anything like proper grocery shopping until today, and I didn't think Atherton would care for grapes or instant coffee.

I paused, tuna sandwich on plastic plate in one hand, Grandma's yellow tea-rose porcelain saucer full of plain tuna in the other. Atherton was eating off the fine china since it was the only kind of saucer I had within easy reach, and a half can of naked tuna would look silly in the middle of a salad plate.

"Where would you like to eat?" I asked. "Would you prefer the floor?"

The green eyes stared at me, probing deeply, asking if I was a species bigot, a rude hostess who treated all her feline guests badly. Or was I so uncivilized that I refused to act like the rest of my species and actually ate off the ground?

"How about on this table? I think you can reach," I suggested, feeling myself flush as I said about my millionth prayer that the cat couldn't actually read my mind unless I willed him to.

I set both plates on the breakfast room table. To my relief, Atherton hopped into a chair but didn't climb on the table itself. He had to stretch a bit, but was very tidy with his meal. In fact, he made less mess than I did. The jaw was a little better, but I had to poke the bread between my teeth and then grind it against them with my tongue until I had a soft paste.

I like tuna, he said later, sitting back to lick a paw.

"Good. It's a kind of large fish that lives in the ocean."

He nodded.

What's wrong with your mouth? Atherton asked, surprising me. In my experience, cats ask for food and comment on your body odor; they don't generally inquire after your health.

"My jaw is locked shut. It's called TMJ. It will get better eventually—the doctors promise. It's worse in the winter when it's cold. I got hit by lightning a while ago and it did something to my face."

Ah. I had a friend who was kicked by a deer. Her jaw wouldn't open either. He paused, then added: *She died.*

"I'm very sorry." And, oddly enough, I was. I reached out to pet Atherton but his body tensed, so I just took his plate and carried it into the kitchen.

I spent a few minutes washing up. Atherton watched from the window ledge, fascinated by the water running from the tap. I didn't know what to do about him. I wanted to keep him near me at least until Irv's murderer was found. He was my only witness and needed to be kept safe, but this was going to be challenging. The cat was a lot like me—worse in some ways of course, and a lot hairier, but I easily saw the similarities. He was a creature so wary, so alone, that he didn't even seek warmth or companionship or the usual things a pet would want. He probably didn't even know he could want them. Or he hadn't. Maybe that was changing, I thought, looking at the saucer I was drying. They said old dogs couldn't learn new tricks, but maybe old cats could. He wouldn't be the first creature corrupted by a soft life.

Of course, that raised the question of whether I wanted him corrupted. Did I want to be the one responsible for keeping him in warm blankets and tuna from here on out? Was I ready for another relationship? With a cat?

Molly called that afternoon and told me that they were holding a wake for Irv at The Mule. I was a bit surprised at the invitation, but pleased since it seemed to mean that Dell and company were going to let me into their group, at least in this marginal way. As little as I wanted to spend any time with them, I knew I would probably have to if I wanted to find Irv's killer.

The idea that I was truly committing myself to the search bothered me a bit, and I realized that I actually felt nervous about doing so. What was I doing playing detective? I was a sheep dressing up in wolf's clothing to hunt a dangerous person, and eventually the real wolf was bound to notice he was being stalked.

And yet . . . damn it! Irv had been murdered. That was wrong. So wrong. And I was the one—unfortunately— who had the best chance of finding out who was responsible.

As I hung up the phone, I noticed that the light was blinking on my answering machine. As always, this made my heart sink. I knew who it was and I couldn't ignore it. I like my editor—really—but I don't like to call New York. It isn't just that the phone is the instrument of Satan, though it is. Along with the general evil of contact, there is some mental time-space difference that happens every time I call the east coast and it leaves me feeling jet-lagged after even the shortest of conversations. There is probably some scientific formula or identified psychological condition that explains this, but I don't understand anything except that in the migration of my thoughts, originating in California and traveling thousands of miles over fiber optics—or satellite relays—and into my editor's ear, if not his brain, leaves me feeling as hungover as the morning after a pub-crawl. Also, the conviction grows yearly that though we were both educated in the English language, we have somehow ended up speaking two different dialects. Normally, I would send an e-mail instead of returning the call, but I had a feeling that things with Irv might take a while and there was a chance I would be a bit late getting my project turned in. There was an etiquette to this, a traditional way of suing for favors. This plea for more time required actual voice messaging.

In the old days, this constant near-miss of deadlines would never have been a problem, but lately my attention and dedication to work had been, at best, intermittent. Deadlines had become like tax payments: something to be handled in the eleventh hour and made by the skin of one's teeth. And, frankly, the subject of my latest work had gone from something already less than gripping to a project I couldn't look at without yawning. Which was my own fault, of course. There are no boring subjects, just boring writers. And there always seemed to be something more important demanding my time—laundry to wash and muddy floors to mop. Ah, the glamour of a writer's life.

Atherton cocked his head at me, sensing my annoyance. I sighed and picked up the phone. It was almost seven in New York, but I knew my editor would still be in his office.

"Work before pleasure," I told Atherton, but his gaze remained blank. I guess this wasn't a concept that translated into Cat.

It turned out that the news was at once better and worse than expected. My boring project was being shelved for the time being. I gave a silent hurrah. I've learned that there aren't enough exciting adjectives—or verbs or nouns—to rescue a story when the author is uninterested, and I think my editor knew I was a few adverbs short of a thrilling piece and was happy to put me on something else. Needless to say, I was pleased to ditch my old project. As it happened, my editor wanted a piece on the perils of feline leukemia in domestic cats. The magazine was doing a special animal edition for April and I was being given the job of convincing people that they needed to inoculate their pets against this invisible killer. The timing was convenient since it reminded me that I was going to need to talk to a vet about the strays. I could kill two birds with one visit.

I hung up the phone with an insulting degree of enthusiasm and turned to Atherton.

What's wrong? he asked warily.

"Atherton? If I asked you to do something for me, would you?"

His wariness increased.

Perhaps. What do you wish me to do?

"I want to make sure that you don't get sick. Would you be willing to see a veterinarian?"

What is a veterinarian?

"It's an animal healer. He would give you some medicine to make sure that you don't get sick."

Oh. Irving did that. A woman in a white coat came to his house and she stabbed us with needles. I didn't like it, but Irving said we must do it to stay well.

"Irving said . . . You mean, Irving could talk to you? Like me?" My voice got a little high-pitched.

Not as clearly as you. He did not understand us so well. But he always listened and tried to comprehend.

I shook my head, trying to adjust my world to this

information. Could it be that I wasn't the first person in Irish Camp to hear cats talking? Then, with a bit of insight that was damn near blinding: Was Irv's insistence on solitude a side effect of having strange cats talking at him whenever he went into town? I had certainly been avoiding town for this reason. Was Irv's feeding the strays his way of bribing them into silence?

Jillian?

Or, was this some new form of delusion I had invented so I felt less of a freak? It wouldn't do any good to ask Atherton if he was an illusion. Obviously, if I was crazy, he would say whatever I needed to hear.

Instead of worrying about it the way I used to, I went to shower. I would need a while to steam my jaw open enough to face a social situation.

Irving's nephew, Peter Jordon Wilkes, had inherited everything. Molly whispered the news to me over a commemorative scotch, preferred to the casseroles some neighbors might have dropped around in lieu of attending the funeral. She uttered this remark in the same tone of hushed outrage as a country vicar finding out his faithless housekeeper had been putting arsenic in his tea. She was taking this matter very personally. That Irv might have had anything of value and not left it to her seemed an insult to her feminine charms. What I wondered at was her belief that Irv had anything of value to leave to anyone.

I nodded and looked concerned, though Molly had dumped Irv long ago and I could see no reason that she should have been chosen to inherit anything from him. And, in spite of my words to the sheriff, I would have been more impressed by the appearance of this will had Irv's *everything* included something of obvious monetary value—perhaps an old family portrait painted by Whistler, or jewels he'd smuggled out of Korea after the war, or a cache of gold ore dug out of that old collapsing mine shaft at the back of his property.

The last thought gave me pause. Could there actually be gold on his own property? Not ore. The mine was played out. But could the recent rain and attendant mudslides have unearthed another golden treasure on our hill? Gold needn't have been discovered on Irv's land—in fact, it most likely wasn't since he was at the top of the mountain and gold, being heavy, washed downward. But might he have found gold somewhere else and backtracked to the source—and when he had, it turned out to conveniently be on his own land?

I would have to talk to Atherton, ask him if he had ever seen Irv digging in the dirt or playing with pretty yellow pebbles.

Avoiding cold drinks and alcohol, I managed to convince someone to give me a plain coffee, which I hid behind as I watched and listened to this strange crowd gathered in Irv's memory. A few of us were there because Irv had helped us in a time of crisis. Cal wasn't the only person to have enjoyed his philanthropy, and I think the others didn't know how else to pay their respects to the man who had helped them or their loved ones through a difficult time. They looked ill at ease, though; and grateful though they were, they didn't stay long in The Mule.

I eavesdropped subtly on the crowd but gained nothing from it. Half of the others in the room sounded like their lives were one long hangover left from the four-year party in high school begun when they still had hopes of achieving some form of greatness. Or at least escape. I had nothing to say to them. I couldn't help them relive their glory days as jocks or cheerleaders, and their inability to face their current reality scared me.

The rest were like Molly and Dell. They had abandoned all hope of a life beyond Irish Camp and were filled with a numb fatalism about the remainder of their days. I wanted desperately to flee from them because they reminded me of my own recent despair, but couldn't leave yet. I had to wait for the nephew.

A ripple eddied through the room and I looked up to see which conversational rock might have been thrown into our midst. It didn't take long to spot him. He was tall, lean and looked an awful lot like Irving, though he lacked Irv's kind eyes. There was something primitive about those eyes, soulless, animal—though that seems wrong to say because I believe that animals have souls and that their eyes are as compassionate as any human's. And there was also—now, don't laugh—an aura about him. I couldn't see it exactly, but I could sense it. *Murderus-lopithecus*, I thought, the modern sociopath's early ancestor. I didn't smile at this joke because, well, it wasn't a joke. I knew I was looking at Irv's killer.

"That's him," Molly all but hissed as the stranger hung up his damp denim jacket on the coatrack by the door. Denim jackets were common enough up here, but this one still gave me what my Scottish grandmother would have called a *cauld grue*. I rubbed my free hand down my arm, trying to smooth the gooseflesh. It took an effort to feign nonchalance as I turned back to Molly. It didn't help my supernatural dread that over her shoulder I could see Atherton perched on the window box, smashing down the dried remains of last autumn's chrysanthemums that hadn't wintered over. His eyes were fixed, too wide and a bit wild. His nostrils were flaring as he drew in fast breaths from the crack in the ill-fitting window.

I exhaled. Atherton had followed me. I had asked him not to, but the cat had a mind of his own.

And now that I thought about it, this was probably a good thing. It shouldn't be hard to get hold of the nephew's jacket and take it outside. The act was a formality, though. I already knew that I was looking at Irving's killer.

I let Dell introduce me to the nephew. It was hard to meet his eyes and I couldn't bring myself to shake his hand, though I still have a hard time explaining why. He didn't look like a killer. His voice was not sinister. It was quiet; not so much soft as utterly inconsequential. Nor was he especially large or threatening, though I could see that there was strength in his bony hand. But within seconds of being introduced it felt like someone with a sledgehammer and homicidal intention was at work inside my skull, frantically trying to beat a way out. I couldn't be near him for more than a second. I could barely breathe.

Part of it might have been because he was wearing Cal's aftershave. On this man it made me feel sick. It was an obscenity, a violation of Cal's memory. I could feel my lips wanting to curl back from my teeth. If I had been a dog, I would have snarled.

I backed away from Wilkes and into Sheriff Murphy. It was a sudden relief to see, or at least feel, the strong presence of the law at my back. I didn't even mind the large hand that settled on my waist for a few seconds longer than was necessary to steady me.

"Tyler, have you met Peter Wilkes?" I asked. I sounded almost normal. My incipient panic had been aborted by his presence. Still, though I had arrested my snarl, I could tell that Tyler was eyeing me with a concerned gaze. Something of the horror and rage that I had been feeling had transferred itself into his awareness. Our Irish sheriff had a bit of the fey about him.

"Yes. We met earlier today. Mister Wilkes, good to see you again."

"Sheriff," the light, inoffensive voice answered. Wilkes didn't seem to notice me huddling away from him, which made me very happy. I never wanted to get near this creature again.

"That's all good, then," I said. I turned away from both men, checking my face in the fly-specked mirror behind the bar. I looked fairly normal. Pale is my natural winter state. For Tyler's benefit I said, "Gentlemen, you'll have to excuse me. It's been a long day and my jaw has had enough of cold and conversation for one night." I managed a quick turn back in their direction and an unfocused half-smile.

I knew that Tyler continued to stare at me, so I made myself walk toward Molly and pulled out some social blither for the ex-girlfriend and Mrs. Jameson, the Baptist minister's wife, whose iron-gray-haired, iron-willed presence in The Mule I couldn't even begin to fathom. Perhaps she had had car trouble and stopped in to phone for a tow truck. Or she had come down with dementia and forgotten that this was the house of iniquity and sin her husband preached against.

Molly didn't want to let me go. She was enjoying herself, playing the near-widow. She began telling me about how Mrs. Jameson had been Irv's grammar school teacher, reaching for sentiment in the old battle-axe that I doubted was there. I nodded politely as Molly chattered, trying to get away but not finding a long enough pause in the conversation to do it gracefully. All I wanted was to get to Peter Wilkes's coat and take it outside to Atherton, but Mrs. Jameson had other plans for me. She had found out that I was a writer and planned to pick my brains clean about a book her nephew was writing.

I think that I was in some kind of shock, because I was unable to focus on the conversation. Instead, Mrs. Jameson's neck fascinated me. It was as wrinkled as an elephant's leg, though a good deal thinner. It was all I could do to pull my eyes away from the loose folds of grayish skin that slipped up and down every time she swallowed or said a word with the letter *p* in it. Instead, I tried staring at the black velvet bow in her steely hair and nodded repeatedly as she told me the excruciating details of what seemed the most ridiculous mystery plot I'd ever heard. In some ways, she reminded me of my maternal grandmother, a righteous woman of Puritan stock whose dead bones were probably still quivering with outrage at my lack of feminine homemaking virtues. Mom had come by her limited world view honestly. Though I wanted to, it was impossible to just walk away from my grandmother's disapproving shade, so instead I looked at the painting over her shoulder, nodded at intervals, and kept saying *Uh-huh, hm, really?*

Finally, feeling desperate enough to do the unthinkable, I reached into my purse and took out a business card. I never do this, since I would rather have my skin removed by a dull potato peeler than give advice to a beginning writer who probably doesn't want anyone telling him the brutal realities of the business, but I pushed the card into her hand and suggested that Mrs. Jameson have her nephew contact me so we could talk about his project. I then made a mental note to change my phone number in the morning just in case he did call.

I leaned toward Molly and performed an air kiss that took her completely by surprise. At last I was ready to escape. I oozed my way toward the door, doing my best to get lost in the clouds of cigarette smoke just in case Tyler was still watching me. I made it to the coatrack by the red door and oh-so-casually lifted down Peter Wilkes's coat. It smelled of Cal's aftershave and I wanted to cry that this memory was being taken from me, forever corrupted by this horrible man. I didn't put the jacket on since it would obviously be too large and I couldn't claim to have made a mistake if anyone saw me with it. Also, the smell made me sick and I'd sooner have wrapped myself in a corpse's shroud.

I stepped outside. It was cold and beginning to rain, but a huge improvement over the atmosphere inside. Atherton had seen me make the switch and was waiting on the bench just outside the door.

"It's him, isn't it?" I asked in a whisper.

Atherton sniffed once and then backed away. His fur began to rise.

Yes, that's smelly-butt man. He can't hide his scent from me with that other stinky smell.

My eyewitness—and nose-witness—had spoken. I looked the coat over, hoping for a blood spatter, something I could show to the sheriff and ask to have tested for Irv's DNA. There wasn't anything that I could see. Perhaps it had already been washed. Could laundry detergent remove all traces of blood? I didn't know.

"His name is Peter Wilkes. He is Irv's nephew," I said. "Wait for me here. I'll just be a second. I have to put this coat back before someone notices it's missing."

Tell the sheep man to take him away. Tell him to put him in a box.

"It's not that easy. The sheep man won't arrest this guy unless we have proof that he's the one."

Proof.

"Proof that a human can understand. Smell isn't enough."

I stepped back inside and swapped coats. My own jacket was denim but of a much lighter shade, and it had a faux fur lining. My hands didn't shake as I made the switch. My attack of nerves were gone. I knew who the killer was. All that remained was to prove that he was the one who had done this heinous deed.

It didn't surprise me any when Tyler appeared at my side. I didn't have to look up at his face to know it was him. Tyler is tall—at least to me—lean and muscled without being freakish. In other words, he has adequate muscle for doing real things and not just exercising in the gym. His badge at eye-level was also a hint to his identity. There was only one man in town whose occupation was stated on his chest in shiny gold.

"Are you alright?" Tyler asked softly. "Frankly, I've seen corpses with better color."

"I'm fine. Just very tired. It was a long day. And the smoke in here is a bit much." I let my words come out indistinctly. I wasn't faking pain, just the degree I felt. I also kept my eyes on another of the bar's bad paintings. This one was really bad, a portrait that any kindergartener could have drawn, but it was hung in an expensive antique frame. I wondered where they got their art. Not the gallery across the street. Hell's bells, Renoir could have scribbled his name on it and still no one of any taste would have touched it.

"Jillian?" Tyler prompted, touching my arm lightly.

"I must be exhausted. I even took the wrong coat." I forced myself to look up at him.

"I saw that. That's the nephew's coat."

He'd seen me. Great.

"Would you like me to walk you up the hill?" he asked.

"No. You stay here and do some detecting," I said without thinking. I opened the red door.

"Detecting of Peter Wilkes?" Tyler asked bluntly, following me outside. I was glad that no one except Atherton was close enough to overhear us, and the cat had had the good sense to climb under the bench. Tyler added: "I'm not blind, Jillian. I know you don't like the man. And I don't think it's because it's like seeing a ghost, though the resemblance is uncanny. There can't be any doubt of him being Irv's kin."

"You're right. I don't like Peter Wilkes—and it isn't because he looks like Irv, though that's obscene in its own way. Everyone should have exclusive rights to their own face." I stopped, unable or at least unwilling to say more. It wasn't that I didn't want Tyler on my side. I did— really badly. But I wasn't sure that the truth was what would put him there, and I wanted some time to think before I said anything more. "Tyler, do you use intuition a lot on the job?"

I willed him to respond affirmatively. He considered my question a moment before answering.

"A certain amount of it, yes. Not that I'd ever admit it in court since we aren't supposed to play hunches in law enforcement," he told me. "Why? Your intuition speaking up about Irv's nephew?"

"Yep. It's loud and clear and ugly. I'm going to go home and have a long bath and a longer think and see if I can't find some reasonable basis for what I know is true. That man is a killer."

Tyler's fine eyes narrowed. "If you find one, call me. Right away. Because right now we have a drug dealer running a meth lab in the area where Irv hiked who looks like a much better suspect—assuming the autopsy proves that Irv's death wasn't an accident, which I don't think it will do. And, Jillian . . ." He paused, probably trying to find a way to be diplomatic. "Look, don't do anything stupid trying to prove your suspicions on your own. She who doesn't fight and runs away, lives to not fight another day. If this guy has anything to do with Irv's death, we'll find it out through the usual channels."

"You'll be the first—and probably only—person I call with any amazing insights," I promised, at least agreeing to the first part of his speech. And it was true. I didn't have anyone else to share my thoughts with except a wary, feral cat. That was a depressing enough thought all by itself. It reminded me again that Cal was gone and that my folks were gone, and there was only my brother,

Garth. We'd been close as kids, but we had both married people with strong and diametrically opposing personalities. Debbie's was self-involved and extremely social—as in upwardly social. Cal was social-minded and involved in mankind. Same word, entirely different meaning. Garth's wife Debbie saw this concern with everyman— and our moving from the city—as being downwardly mobile, and a bad influence on her children.

I should have liked Debbie more than I did since I understood self-absorption all too well these days, but we just didn't get along, even with Cal out of the picture. And I wasn't any too fond of my niece and nephew since they were turning out to be little facsimiles of their label-conscious mother. There was no sign of Garth's easygoing and loveable nature in them. I think sometimes that they were cloned solely from Debbie's DNA.

"I'll see you tomorrow," Tyler said. His voice was again gentle. I was too tired and discouraged to ask why.

As soon as Tyler went back inside, Atherton came out from under the bench.

"Would you like me to carry you back to the house?" I asked him.

He eyed the damp streets, whose gutters were gluey with dissolving leaves, and then looked me over.

No, I shall walk.

I didn't argue. Atherton was heavy and the walk home was all uphill.

There were a few people on the street, huddling in doorways and under awnings as they closed up their shops or hurriedly used their ATM cards at the credit union before scurrying home to a late and well-deserved supper. I found myself looking at them as a stranger might, assessing their vulnerabilities and being horrified at how they simply trusted no one to look over their shoulder and steal their PIN numbers as they entered them into a machine, or that no thief would scoop up the bags of cash the merchants rested on the deep windowsills and ledges as they locked up their old-fashioned and not terribly secure doors, whose locks hadn't been replaced since the turn of the century. They would carry their money in the open, like a purse, taking the day's earnings to the night depository at the bank at the end of the street that was surrounded by oleander bushes where anyone could hide, but feeling no fear of what might be lurking in the shadowy doorways ahead because they hadn't ever needed to be cautious. They would climb into unlocked cars and probably return home to their unlocked houses. Just like I did. Because our town was safe.

My world felt suddenly unfamiliar and dangerous to me, and all because I knew there was a murderer drinking beer back at The Mule, a true wolf among us unwary sheep, and I couldn't prove it, couldn't even spread the alarm. At least not yet.

"Shit."

But at least we know who he is now, Atherton consoled me. *We will get proof for the sheep man.*

"Yes, at least we know." But I wasn't positive that we would be able to get the kind of proof Tyler needed.

The man who carries a cat by the tail learns something that can be learned in no other way.

—*Mark Twain*

CHAPTER SEVEN

Molly insisted on a church funeral in the chapel where Irving had been baptized—and had never stepped foot in since. I couldn't imagine much of anything less appropriate, but every choice of obsequies seemed equally bad, and like everyone else—the long-lost nephew included—I was just attending out of obligation and letting Molly, the only one who cared about such things, play one more day at being the grieving widow.

People entered the old churchyard by twos and threes. This wasn't by choice but rather necessity. The first minister of the Mother Lode Gold Rush Church of Christ the Savior, one Reverend Marvell—formerly a Baptist and gold miner, but one who, late in life, decided to pioneer a new religion for those sinners who worshipped the idol of gold almost as much as God—had specified that the gate be built exactly thirty-six inches wide. He had taken Matthew 7:13 (*Enter by the narrow gate since the road that leads to destruction is wide and spacious*) very much to heart. The door into the now barn-red church was consequently every bit as narrow.

The house of worship was currently presided over by one Reverend Sugarbrown. His stock and trade was decrying the sins of virtue, which fortunately did not include the sin of gossiping. He was Goldie's great uncle and I think that perhaps genetic predestination had arranged for them to be as they are. Like Goldie, Dawg's ex, the reverend had his good points, but he was a bad kind of gossip, someone who didn't trade secrets out of curiosity but rather out of a rabid need to hunt down sinners so he could look good by comparison just in case God graded on a curve. He went around, Monday through Friday, vacuuming up unhappiness from all over town—and well beyond, too, if town life or his small parish proved to be too uneventful that week—until he was so full of dirty secrets that it actually made his face gray and bitter. Then he would sit down on Saturday and write his sermon. I don't think he would have thrived in some happy coastal climate where people were laid-back because of easy living or else happily ambitious and chasing their careers. He needed a place where weather could drive people to desperation and an understandable belief in a vengeful God, and even here, his congregation was sparse. He should have stayed in Maine.

I wandered up the hill and took up a post in the watery shade of the O'Linn mausoleum where it was unpleasantly cold but the acoustics were especially good. It was also a long way from where Cal's urn stood atop a Romanesque pedestal. I should have gone to visit him, I suppose, but the act was beyond me, especially with so many people watching.

The stony angel perched on top of the sepulcher seemed to flutter her wings as clouds passed rapidly overhead—light and shade, light and shade, her face first radiant white and then gray with sorrow. Trying to look inconspicuous, I read the mausoleum plaque with great care while I listened to a dozen conversations floating up the hill. PEGGY, FERNIE, CHARLIE AND NELL. Their young lives had all ended the same year: 1916. What was it that had killed them? One of the pandemic influenzas? Maybe Asiatic cholera. That killed within hours of the victim being infected. Or perhaps it had been a fire. I would have to ask Crystal. The story was bound to be sad, but at least the family could afford a monument, a place for the survivors to come and grieve the lost. Not everyone could pay for such things. In fact, most people had passed out of history without anything to mark their departure. The whole world is an unmarked graveyard. We sit on the pretty topsoil and don't realize we are living on someone or something else's bones. Or maybe we don't care because it isn't yet our turn to feed the worms and therefore can ignore the fact that in life we are still in the midst of death.

I hadn't asked what would happen to Irv's body. I'd assumed it would be cremated once the coroner released it. *Please*, I thought, *let it be cremated*. I didn't want to stare at Irv's restored corpse. My last view had been quite bad enough. I could live with it because it was honest, but I found the sight of the embalmed—made-up and coiffured as they never were in life—to be unutterably horrible.

Someone had left flowers on the tomb steps in the last day or so. HOC FACITE IN MEAM COMMEMORATIONEM—DO THIS IN MY MEMORY, the carving on the threshold said, and so the family had. I didn't bring Cal's urn flowers since he had always thought such things a waste—*Bring me all my flowers while I'm alive*, he'd said—but it still seemed like a nice gesture to me. Perhaps I would visit in the late spring when the wild lupines were out. It was pretty then, and maybe I would feel ready to face his grave.

I wasn't ready that day. The sun was out and doing its best to shine, but the graveyard inspired some less than pleasant thoughts. And why shouldn't it? The cemetery was meant as a reminder that *Thou too shall die*. I enjoy good physical health outside of my stupid jaw, or think that I do since I have no worrisome symptoms of any dreaded disease, and that amounts to the same thing in terms of everyday living. Yet, standing among the dead, I was very aware of my mortality and how few people would miss me when I was gone, and it made me melancholic.

I was aware of other things, too. My dreams, visions of a bright future, weren't dead, but they had been napping long enough to make me ask if they might have slipped into a permanent coma. I needed to find some way to revive them and soon, or I would be dead in all the ways that mattered, just another shadow taking up space until my body was as worn as my soul. But what did I have ambition for? What did I long for? Almost nothing. An end of emotional pain, maybe. To be able to endure human company. That was cause for feeling even sadder. I was lonely, but couldn't bear to be around most people. It's a fine line, the one between being alone and being lonely, and one can cross it so easily. Without realizing it, I had strayed from needed solitude into isolation, peace and quiet metamorphosing into loneliness and despair. Days had been fairly horrible, but I was living my life the same old way because I couldn't think of anything better.

I turned and looked out over the town that I had chosen because I liked it above all others—and I felt nothing. Everything was familiar, but brought no joy. I could plainly see the dark square of cypress near the courthouse. It was one of three cemeteries in town. They were all distinct. The Jews got the cypress trees, the Catholics had white quartz paths and a sea of crosses and Marys that dazzled the eyes on a sunny day, and the Protestants got this place with green lawns and mausoleums. I don't know what Buddhists and Muslims do. Go somewhere else, I guess.

Few tourists knew that the acres of grass I was standing in were kept cropped by a flock of grazing sheep, brought in bimonthly in the spring and summer. They were a sensible choice for a cemetery on a steep slope. The sheep were traditionally pastoral and there was a groundskeeper who made sure that there were no unsightly piles of dung desecrating the graves or visitors' good shoes during daylight hours. At night the flock was watched over by a sheepdog whose job it was to make sure that the coyotes and mountain lions did not enjoy a free lamb-chop dinner.

The churchyard is perched halfway up the side of western hills. From there it is easy to see that the town is really just one long chain of buildings put up a hundred years ago out of handmade bricks, made after they had run out of river rock and learned the futility of building with wood. Repeated fires had convinced folks that rock or brick was the sensible choice in a place where summer wildfires are an inevitability.

What wasn't so easy to see was that those bricks were made as much from blood, sweat and prayers as from local clay and straw. The current occupants of Irish Camp were white—blinding winter white—but what people had forgotten was that a lot of those prayers embedded in the walls where they lived had been said in foreign tongues: Spanish, Chinese, Portuguese, French, Italian, German, Yiddish. They'd all been here, praying for gold, then praying for water, praying to live to see another spring. Gold appealed to all races, and they had come in droves seeking their fortune in the gold-rush of '49. There were many stories and legends of old murders for the nuggets and flakes—many, many, many. I was most afraid of the Chinese ghost who supposedly haunted the old drug store. He had died in the fire that destroyed what used to be Chinatown. The ghost was said to push people down the backroom stairs that led to

one of the numerous underground tunnels that zig-
zagged under the town. The tunnels were all closed to
the public now for safety reasons, but some store owners had failed to board up the entrances. I knew of three
that were still open: one ran from under the art gallery
that had been a bank, one from the music store that
used to be a butcher's shop—I'd been down there and
all the old meat hooks were still embedded in the
walls—and one from a used bookstore that used to be a
bordello to what is now the courthouse. These tunnels
survived because the old merchants found it safer to
travel underground to both the bank and the bordello,
the former because it protected them from robbers, that
latter from their watchful wives who didn't approve of
their spouses visiting the soiled doves.

I'd heard of one other shaft as well. There was supposed to be a tunnel under The Mule. Supposedly it
had collapsed, killing three miners, but I had heard a
rumor that the present owner had opened it back up and
was using it for storage. With how honeycombed our
streets were, it was a wonder we hadn't had more of
them collapse.

I shivered and pushed the thought of ghosts and cave-
ins away. The present day offered tragedy enough. There
was no need to be morbid about old losses and the
number of souls that seemed to get trapped here when
they died.

As I watched, hoop-skirted women and men in duster
coats hurried through the streets, calling out to one another as they organized a posse. A man in black, riding
on an equally black mount, galloped onto Grant Street
and fired a pistol into the air. The men in dusters responded by running for the horses tied up in front of
The Mule. They chased after the bank robbers heading
at a full gallop for the part of Vermillion Creek called
The Red Rapids.

I wasn't seeing specters from the past. These reenactors were my civic-minded neighbors who still enjoyed playing dress-up, and this hubbub meant the rodeo would be coming soon and people were getting ready for the parade, the first big tourist event of the season. It meant we'd be hearing gunshots and general whooping twice a day at eleven and two for the next couple of weeks to bring in spectators who would spend their dollars here.

Irish Camp has always been deliberately—even theatrically—antique. But these days it was closer to thrift-shop goods than anything that belonged in a museum. The people tended to look a bit vintage, too, artifacts dressed in hand-me-downs that didn't fit them all that well. There were exceptions, of course, like Linda who ran the Queendom Come boutique and the natty gentleman who had just bought the art gallery and expanded it to include sculpture and mosaics, and even paintings that didn't have cowboys or miners in them. But by and large, the population wasn't trying to make Blackwell's Best Dressed list. That was one of the few things I missed about living in a city. However, for one week a year, the town dressed in its finest—circa 1880. In addition to the rodeo and parade, there was also a pioneer ball held at the old opera house. Period costumes were mandatory. Cal had adored this tradition and dressed up for it every year.

I swore as something hard bounced off of my head. There's an acorn season, a time of danger when the little missiles escape the parent oaks and achieve a vertical escape velocity great enough to bury themselves in the stony ground. Or a person's scalp. However, acorn season was months away. This particular missile hadn't fallen, but had been hurled at me by another neighborhood squirrel.

I opened my mouth to scold him for his bad manners, but my ear caught a familiar name and tuned back to the conversation carried on between Molly and Dell as they huddled over their cigarettes beside Dell's mother's grave. This combination was like vinegar and waffles. Or peach sauce on lasagna. I didn't get it, but I listened attentively.

Sadly, nothing new was being said at the moment. Bored and frustrated with waiting, I looked beyond the bickering pair at the nearly naked rose that twined about the old wrought-iron fence, studying Irv's pallid nephew. Peter Wilkes, standing alone by a storm-tormented shrub rose, remained a mystery. The recently-active grapevine knew that the sheriff had found him in Lodi, and no one in authority suspected him of anything illegal. In fact, no one suspected him of anything— except me and Atherton.

Which was understandable, I thought with a frustrated sigh I didn't bother to contain. Why would anyone suspect this monkey-looking fellow of anything? He didn't look like the crucible of greed and violence where began a plan for cold-blooded murder. Yet, I believed this primitive-appearing creature, this weak facsimile of Irving with knobby joints and powerful hands, was a murderer. Atherton's certainty aside, you didn't travel a hundred miles in the worst weather in a century to visit an uncle you hardly knew unless there was something in it for you.

I thought about Irv's corpse and how it had worn the faintest of smiles lying there on the floor. It seemed he'd got the joke before he died. I could—barely—imagine the ignorant nephew demanding money from his uncle and then reacting in anger when Irv laughed at him and said there was none to spare. And Irv probably would have laughed. It wasn't anything personal, but the thought of him having any money to give to a near-stranger would have incited his sense of the ridiculous. He'd laugh about it for days. Or he would have done so, if someone hadn't ended his ability to laugh forever.

"What hast though done? Thou thinkest to conceal

it, but thy brother's blood crieth unto Me from the ground," I muttered, thinking of Cain and the murdered Abel. I swallowed once to shove down sudden bile, surprised as always at my abrupt anger. It vibrated in me a nerve strung the length of my throat and chest that was plucked into sudden life at the memory of Irv's wry laughter. I reached in my pocket for my roll of antacids and attempted to think calm thoughts.

"You son of a bitch," I whispered beneath my breath, which I tried to keep slow and even. "I'm going to prove you did it. I swear to God, you will not get away with this."

"You don't like him, then," a voice said behind me. The near-whisper made me jump and drop my antacids. My anger had so distracted me that I hadn't heard anyone approach. Hell, I should have smelled him; he was smoking and smelled like a soggy sidewalk ashtray. His right hand was cupping one of those unfiltered cigarettes that he rolled himself. I'd seen him do his one-handed trick a time or two when he sat outside The Mule on the iron bench that was bolted to the sidewalk with rusting screws. I think he chose to roll his own because of the cool factor, and also because it gave him something to do. Man cannot live by beer guzzling alone.

I wasn't fond of the retired steamfitter, but I liked Josh better than Dell and managed to smile slightly at his concerned face and cheerless eyes, whose uneasy gaze seemed to suggest some lingering shame at falling to society's lowest stratum.

"No," I admitted, trying to look welcoming. I bent and picked up my antacids. "I don't. And I don't think Irv liked him either."

Josh nodded. His neck was so thin that the act looked painful. Poor drunks don't get fat, even if their livers try their best to give them beer bellies.

"Molly doesn't like him at all. Thinks he's up to something. She says Irv was excited about some new thing—wanted to get us together and talk about some business venture the day before he died, but then he called back to say he couldn't come; this nephew was coming for a visit. We thought Irv was blowing smoke about a new business but . . ." Josh looked over my shoulder and then backed away, his lips tightening. His voice was a little louder when he said, "Well, I'll talk to you later. Glad you could make it, Jillian. Irv would be touched. He always spoke well of you and your husband. If you need any help with the yard now that Irv's gone, just let me know."

"Thanks, Josh. I appreciate that." And I meant it. I would need help. The garden had been listless all through the heat of summer and autumn. And winter was especially brutal. But given a few days of sun, I knew from experience that the flora would snap into action and I'd need to whack the wild grass back or it would overrun the propane tank. Another week and the sky would begin raining oak pollen, and opportunistic weeds would become aggressive. I had a weed-whacker, but like my stove it hated me, and it refused to cooperate with my trimming efforts.

Josh nodded and then scuttled away as quickly as his limp would take him. I noticed that he avoided Molly and Dell, and wondered if he thought they would not approve of his talking to me about Irv's business plans.

I didn't turn right away, preferring to take a moment to get my pleasant social face back on. I wasn't surprised, or particularly pleased, to hear Tyler Murphy's voice a moment later. Aside from it scaring Josh away just when the conversation was getting interesting, his presence was beginning to bother me in other ways. I didn't want to admit it, but Tyler Murphy was stirring to life certain feelings—or at least desires—that had been dormant since Cal died. I probably should have been grateful for the proof that I wasn't emotionally beyond the reach of normal sexual wants, but at that point I mostly resented it. Sex, especially the kind that came with any kind of a relationship, wasn't something I wanted to think about. Especially not in the cemetery where Cal's spirit might be watching.

"The nephew has a boilerplate will naming him heir— and it looks legit," the sheriff said without preamble. This wasn't exactly news, but I appreciated his inclination to confide in me. I turned my head finally and wasn't surprised to see that Tyler's face looked rather hard. His eyes were lovely, but his gaze could be as disconcerting as a dentist's above the drill when he's focused on his work. He really didn't want Irv's death to be murder, or for the nephew to have any motive for killing his uncle, but my certainty seemed to have forced him to face the idea that it could be true. And if it was, he wanted to catch the killer. "I don't know why anyone would want Irv's old shack, though. Unless there are some drugs up there that we haven't found yet."

I finished crunching my antacid tablet.

"It could be drugs," I said, keeping my voice pitched low so it wouldn't carry. I didn't believe this theory, but there was no point in dismissing it out of hand— especially if I didn't want him arbitrarily dismissing my thoughts. "But I don't think that's it. Irv never did anything on his own land. I mean, why risk it when you have the Stanislaus Forest to play in? I know you don't like the suggestion, but it was more likely gold. You should look at the deed for the land and see if it includes mineral rights." I didn't say anything about Josh's claim that Irv wanted to talk about a new business venture with his friends. There was no point in it. None of Irv's cronies would talk to the sheriff about anything. And if they thought I was fraternizing with Tyler, Josh might freeze me out too. There had already been an obvious depreciation in goodwill on Dell and Molly's part because of my reporting Irv's death to the sheriff instead of calling them. My gut still said that I needed them on my side if I was going to come up with a reasonable, explainable motive for this murder.

Tyler nodded slowly, glancing at the nephew. I was happy to have his gaze move on to that target.

"Irv didn't have much of anything else, and we haven't found any gold. And we searched that cabin end to end. From what I can tell the marijuana sales were his only income, and the land up the hill isn't worth spit, so mineral rights are probably irrelevant." I nodded back. This was true. The land was mostly sandstone, red dirt and misery—impossible to build on or farm. Even the gold miners had given up on it, abandoning their coyote holes when they hit bedrock. Tyler looked away from Irv's nephew, returning his gaze to my face. "Yet, Mrs. March, in spite of this fact, you think this was a murder for profit—and have from the beginning. I have to ask myself why."

I shrugged. "Logically?"

"I'd prefer that. It looks so much better in my report." His voice was dry.

I'd have preferred that, too. I might be going out on a limb here, but I'm betting that more men had walked on the moon than had been hit by lightning and started hearing cats talk about murder. It just didn't sound plausible, and for sure it could never go in any report.

"Okay, how about this? Irv and Wilkes didn't know each other well enough for it to be a crime of hot blood," I said at last. "From what Molly told me, until last month Irv hadn't seen his nephew since the sister died ten years ago. And before that, he'd only seen the kid twice. I like profit as a motive better in this case. Neither Irv nor the nephew are the type for a crime of passion."

"I agree. If this is about money, though, I can think of others around Irv who had even greater need than Peter Wilkes," Tyler said evenly. I sympathized with his point, but knew he was wrong to suspect Molly and Dell. "What I can't figure out is just why you've always been so certain it *is* murder. If we hadn't sent the body out for an autopsy with a genuine forensic pathologist, old Doc Harmon would have signed off on this as an accident and we would never know that murder had been done."

I looked the sheriff in the eye.

"So it *is* murder."

"Yes, blunt force trauma. One killing blow to the head. Probably from the fireplace poker, which is still missing. You were right about that, too."

I nodded, not surprised. When I questioned him in detail, Atherton had said the man used the old poker by the potbellied stove to kill Irv and had it when he ran away. "That was quick work."

"It's the only suspicious death in the county. Irv got moved to the head of the line." Those probing eyes were back on my face.

"I feel like you've been watching me, Sheriff. Constantly. Why? Do you think it likely that I killed Irv and am trying to blame someone else for my wicked deeds?" I asked bluntly, and watched with satisfaction when Tyler blinked.

"Hadn't crossed my mind." He lied—I could see it in his deep blue eyes.

"It better have crossed your mind, or you're in the wrong line of work." I looked away, smiling grimly. Molly and Dell had cornered Josh, and all three were staring at me and the sheriff. They looked like prisoners, huddling together as they waited to see what the warden would do. They were as pallid and undernourished as junkies, and bowed down either by the grief of their friend's passing or the weights of their unkind lives. I thought it was the latter, and though that burden was mostly self-inflicted it did nothing to make them easier to look at. Would this be me in five years if I didn't get my act together?

"Okay, for maybe half a second the notion flitted through my brain. But why the hell would you drag me into this if you were guilty?" Tyler asked. We were being logical, trying to dress up our gut emotion in respectable reason. We weren't succeeding, though. At least, I wasn't. And Tyler was feeling my anger at Peter Wilkes and it was making his sheriff's antennae twitch.

"Maybe I'm just crazy. Or psychic. Or haunted. Maybe I hear voices from beyond telling me this was murder," I said, gazing at the church as though it was the most fascinating thing in the world. My stomach clenched. *Too close*, it warned me. *You're getting too close to the truth.*

"Maybe," Tyler agreed. I watched as his shadow drew closer and touched mine, mingling our pale shades. I allowed it for a moment and then stepped away. Even that was too much intimacy when I was standing in the cemetery where Cal rested. He added quietly: "But I don't think your madness would have these particular symptoms. From what I hear, writers tend to be quietly eccentric. They wear large hats and have cats and forget to eat. They don't go around bashing their neighbors' heads in because they hear voices. Certainly they don't go to the police afterwards and insist on it being murder."

Cats. I had those, alright—in numbers great enough to make anyone question my sanity. In fact, I'd left the largest one closed up in my bedroom when I came down the hill. I hoped Atherton wasn't too annoyed about that.

I nodded. "Eccentric is fine. I wouldn't want the town's new sheriff thinking I was a homicidal maniac or anything."

Tyler grunted. He was watching as Molly, Dell and Josh put out their cigarettes and went into the church. Josh lagged behind the other two, sending a last glance up at us. I thought he looked guilty, and was betting Tyler thought that, too.

"Well, we'd best go down. People are heading inside. I wouldn't normally go to this funeral but since you're so suspicious of him, I want to keep an eye on the nephew for the next few days. Also, maybe there will be some thaw in the Fremont Creek crowd if I pay my respects. If there is anything to know about Irv, they're the ones who'll know it."

"Hope ever, hope on," I muttered. I didn't think Molly or Dell would thaw for him even under a blowtorch. Tyler wouldn't get anywhere with them.

"Can't hurt any to try," Tyler said. "So, are you coming inside, or will you watch from the sidelines?"

I sighed. I hated funerals and had avoided them since Cal died. There was little chance that I'd actually catch the nephew doing or saying anything incriminating there, especially with the sheriff hanging about. Still, I felt that I had to go. Just in case.

Something stropped at my woolen-clad ankle and it was all I could do not to jump. As it was, I gave a small gasp.

I'm here, the growl announced. *We're all here*.

Speaking of the symptoms of my madness, this was probably what the squirrel had been so upset about. I glanced around quickly. The cats were huddled at the base of the wrought-iron fence at the rear of the cemetery.

"Hello, Atherton," I said. I felt myself pale as I looked into the black cat's enormous eyes. His gaze was hard, predatory, and I was—just a little bit—afraid of the anger I saw in him. "What a surprise. I thought you were having a nice nap in my bedroom."

It can't be a surprise. Not really. Smelly-butt man is here. Is the sheep man going to take him away?

It shouldn't have been surprising after his showing up

at the wake, but I was still taken aback to see the cat here. I had been careful this time. The only way he could have escaped was out the bedroom window, and then only if he had ripped my screen from the frame. And I hadn't said anything to him about where and when the funeral was. That meant he had heard me talking on the phone with Molly. This may sound dumb, but I didn't think the cat could understand my conversations unless I was talking *to* him. Apparently it didn't work that way.

I lifted my head slowly, breaking away from Atherton's gaze without answering him aloud.

"And here is proof of my growing eccentricity. Sheriff, have you met my cat, Atherton? He thinks Wilkes killed Irv, too."

Atherton stared at me.

"I believe I've seen him about. Up at Irv's place. I thought maybe I was being stalked by a panther." I could feel Tyler's puzzled gaze on me and I tried to pull myself together. It was difficult, though, because everywhere I looked now, there were strays ghosting through the shrubs on the churchyard and perching on tombstones. They moved like a restless school of fish— perhaps piranhas. Their eyes were intent, angry; a mob mentality ruled them. I wondered if they would actually attack Irv's nephew if they found him alone.

Then I wondered if I should let them. It could solve a lot of problems and would be just. Let the ones he had most wronged have their vengeance.

Of course, the town would panic when they found the body covered in claw marks, and the stray cats would be rounded up and put down en masse. I couldn't let that happen. There had to be some way to get sufficient proof of Wilkes's wrongdoing.

I turned to face Tyler. "Yes. I inherited him—without a will, even. I hope the nephew doesn't contest ownership. I don't think Atherton would go with him." Talking was getting difficult. I could feel my jaw locking up again. It was partly the cold wind and the disappearing sun, but partly nerves and distraction. The sheriff hadn't noticed the other cats, but he would if he turned around, and even the most rational and unimaginative of men would question what so many mean-looking strays were doing in the churchyard. Cats didn't travel in packs like dogs. This was unnatural behavior.

"You brought the cat to the funeral?" Tyler asked, unable to hide his surprise.

"No, but Atherton tends to follow me around. I think he's lonely." I'm not a good liar, so I knelt down and picked Atherton up, hiding the lower half of my face in his coarse fur. Neither of us was comfortable with this, but he didn't struggle while the sheriff was watching. He even let me check his paws for wounds from the screen. I wondered what we looked like to the others. Me, all in black, holding a dark cat—did we look like a witch and her familiar? "I don't think Irv would mind the cat being here. We'll sit in the back of the church," I added. "No one will see him."

Tyler's eyes grew compassionate as he watched me rub against Atherton. His sympathy wasn't for the orphaned cat, though. He could sense my tension and probably thought that I was feeling fragile, perhaps remembering Cal's funeral and wanting to hold something close so no one would see me cry. Normally I would have done something to banish this concern, which I found so hard to accept in strangers and even friends. But this time I let him believe this was why I held the cat so close and kept my face mostly hidden. It was almost true, anyway.

"Come on," Tyler said again. He reached for my arm, but a hiss from the cat made him step back. "That's a large beastie you've got there. Biggest cat I've ever seen. Seems real . . . protective."

"Manners, Atherton," I said softly. "The sheriff means no harm. He's just trying to help us."

The cat began making a harsh noise that might have been purring. Then again, it might not. I lifted my head and forced a smile for Tyler. I hoped it was more convincing than Atherton's purr.

"He just doesn't like strangers much. He and Irv were loners." My jaw was definitely getting tighter.

What I don't like is the smelly-butt man, Atherton grumbled through his buzz-saw purr. *Take me to him now*.

I didn't like "smelly-butt man" either, but I didn't say so out loud. Just in case the sheriff was serious about thinking I might be something more than eccentric for bringing a cat to a funeral.

I glanced one more time at the shuddering shrubbery. So far, the cats had kept a prudent distance from the church itself. Whether out of piety or fear, I didn't know. I didn't know if it would work, but I sent out a stern mental message: *Stay out of the church. Atherton and I will watch smelly-butt man*.

"That cat isn't the only loner," Tyler said mostly to himself. "Let's get you out of this wind. I can tell your jaw is hurting."

I smiled fleetingly at Tyler and started down the hill, being careful not to step on anyone's grave. Atherton was a bundle of tensed muscle and fur, but he must not have had any true demonic connections because he didn't disappear in a puff of smoke when we entered the sanctuary and slid into the rear pew.

I didn't protest when Tyler slid in beside me. Atherton wasn't thrilled, but he was too busy watching the nephew to pay the sheriff much attention. An asthmatic old organ began playing "Rock of Ages." I bowed my head and tried to look like I belonged in church. I was confident that if Wilkes did anything interesting, Atherton would let me know.

A cat is more intelligent than people believe, and can be taught any crime.

—*Mark Twain* Notebook, 1895

Chapter Eight

Irv's land is posted with NO TRESPASSING signs, but the neighbors have always treated them as a mere request for privacy. The whole *trespassers will be shot* thing didn't make sense when Irv didn't have a gun. None that we knew about, anyway. Perhaps if he'd had one, he'd still be alive.

The next home on the hill was a step down from Irv's place on a stony outcrop that jutted over Stockyard Road. The place was more of a temple than a house. It was called The Parthenon for obvious reasons. The current owners, Elena and Carl Malking, were avid gardeners and apt to be out in the yard at all hours tending to their massive container garden. It was a well-manicured property completely at odds with others on the hill that rather grew like Topsey. Unfortunately, the attentive Malkings were away for the month. The only two residents at The Parthenon were Elena's mother, Miranda, and the day nurse, Justie Fillmore, who left The Parthenon promptly at six P.M. every afternoon. Miranda was an insomniac and might have been a hopeful witness to interview since there was a clear view of Irv's driveway from her bedroom window. However, when God was handing out the afflictions of old age, he had been thorough with Miranda. The eyes may be the conventional windows of the soul, but curtains of cataract had been drawn over these panes years before, and she refused surgery so no one would be peeping in or out of them anymore. Asking her to recall and articulate her thoughts was not a viable option, either. Aside from the missing teeth that had mutinied and abandoned their gummy posts decades ago, her grasp of present-day reality was tenuous at best. Nor would she wear her hearing aid since arthritis had bound her to a walker. Miranda was waiting to die and stubbornly refused all succor.

I sighed. It figured that the one person who might have seen anything on the night Irv died was blind, deaf and dumb. It was the way the luck was running on this very amateurish investigation. It was probably partly my fault that I was making no progress, but it was also par for the course on anything involving Irv. Way down deep, most likely buried in his DNA, Irv was burdened with a kind of ironic bad luck. It had haunted all the males of his family for as far back as he could recall. When Irv had inherited the family farm in Fresno—a piece of land that had been fertile and profitable until Irv's father, a refugee from the Dust Bowl, got hold of it—Irv immediately lost the water rights and found that he couldn't afford the taxes on the place anyway. He'd had to sell at once, and the land hadn't brought in enough to cover the family debts. His parents were dead by then and his sister, sensing there was no future in agriculture or in sticking with her brother, took up with a crop duster and sometimes stunt pilot named Dukie Wilkes. They'd left for the bright lights of Hollywood seeking fame and fortune, or at least regular work. The sister came back alone two years later with a snot-nosed brat in tow. Dukie had moved on to bigger and better—and younger—things.

All alone in the world and unable to find work in Fresno, Irv retreated to the family mining shack in Irish Camp that had been cobbled together at the very end of the nineteenth century. There he decided to fall back on a crop that was always in demand and that he knew how to grow. He planted his first patch of marijuana in the Stanislaus National Forest in a grove where a harsh winter had struck down a number of trees and left a promising sunny glade. From what he'd told me, it would have been a bumper crop, but two days before he planned to harvest, a forest fire swept through that part and he lost everything. Only slightly daunted by this loss, Irv tried again that next spring. Year two had looked to be a little better until there had been an invasion of some kind of hemp-eating beetle from Japan. He'd lost most of that crop, too, and what he salvaged had an odd piquancy that he suspected was beetle dung. Year three, he'd lost more than half of his crop to a mudslide caused by record-breaking summer rainfall that washed out the scarred land now left naked and unprotected by the forest fire.

And so it went on, year after year. He made enough to live on—barely—but like his father, his green thumb was overshadowed by natural disasters.

Then, in the spring of '86, when he was struck by lightning, he had taken up gold panning. Irv wasn't exactly prosperous, but he found the odd nugget here and there and managed to provide himself with slightly better cuisine and clothing, if not a fancier roof over his head.

And now, after twenty-two years, when he'd finally hit the mother lode and was looking at spending his final years in some degree of comfort, if not actual middle-class affluence, his greedy nephew had probably killed him for his find.

I shook my head at Irv's profound bad luck and mentally walked past the Malkings' without stopping until I reached the next house on the map.

On the other side and down the south face of the hill was Crystal, but I already knew that she had no details of the nephew's visit to share with me. And no one else could have seen anything. So, Atherton was still the only witness and he couldn't exactly give a statement to the police. Nor could I come forward at this late date and say, oops, I just recalled that I *did* see everything that night, and Peter Wilkes is a murderer.

So, there we were. I didn't have any witnesses—at least none that could go to the police—but I did have a possible motive that I could investigate if I could figure out how to go about it.

Gold. I kept coming back to it. If the nephew had been after drugs, he would have taken them that night and hightailed it back to Lodi. He would not have stuck around and produced a will naming himself as heir to Irv's squalid little cabin that would be torn down shortly anyway.

It followed that if Irv had found a cache of gold, he either would have sold it or hidden it somewhere safe. Selling it would be wise only if he'd found a stray nugget and there was no hope of discovering more in the same location. No gossip spreads as fast in our town as news of a gold strike. One whiff of fresh gold-bearing ore or cache of nuggets and every Tom, Dick and Peter Wilkes with a gold pan starts following the lucky finder around. There hadn't been any word of a new gold find, so I didn't think Irv had gone to any of the local jewelers he usually sold to. That in turn meant Irv believed he had hit upon a rich vein and wanted time to mine or pan it before others got wind of the sweet spot. That he might have talked to Molly, Dell and Josh about going in with him on a business venture suggested that this could be a mining operation, something underground and dangerous and not just casual surface panning. But then again, it might just be that he had found something along the river—on someone else's property—and he needed a lot of bodies to cover the territory before they were found by the rightful owners and booted out.

This was a whole lot of supposition, but it hung together. For me.

Yes, I figured that the gold was secreted away somewhere on Irv's property. Irv could have hidden it anyplace, but it seemed to me that he would want it someplace both safe and where he could get to it anytime he wanted. That probably meant somewhere in or near the cabin. Which, I thought for the tenth time, would be torn down soon because it was an illegal structure and no one wanted vagrants moving into it.

There was also the matter of the nephew who would be looking for the gold. And he was still looking, of that I was sure. It was like with the pot: If he'd seen the stash of nuggets, he'd have taken what he found and skipped town.

Unless the source of the gold was on Irv's land and the nephew knew there was enough ore to make mining it worthwhile. I hadn't found out for sure, but he likely would have mineral rights if he'd inherited Irv's land—almost all property comes with those rights up here.

Regardless of whether it was drugs or gold, what all this meant was that I needed to make my move, investigate the crime now or forever hold my peace. Even though Tyler had specifically warned me against doing it.

I exhaled slowly and gave myself a count of five to

change my mind about being impulsive and imprudent. When I got to six I went to the garage to fetch a hammer and screwdriver, as well as a strong flashlight. Irv might have hidden his hoard in a cookie jar or spare boots beneath his bed, but I'd read a lot of Nancy Drew, and I was betting it was under the floorboards.

I think that Irv did have a hole in the floor, Atherton said. *I heard him taking up boards sometimes*.

"Then you can come with me," I said, reaching for a jacket. "I'm going to try my hand at cat burglary. You can give me pointers," I joked.

Atherton wasn't enthusiastic about a trip to Irv's, but was still agreeable about coming and acting as lookout while I dismantled the place.

I told myself that I needed to find something concrete to give Tyler so he could make an arrest. Without dope or gold, Irv's death looked like a senseless, random killing by druggies looking for a fix. Of course, it wasn't senseless. People always kill for a reason—a host of reasons sometimes—even if they are ones we don't understand. But Tyler needed something tangible he could take to the DA. And so did I. Because if the law couldn't take care of Irv's nephew, I would have to. Or let the cats do it.

Looking at these words now, I feel queasy. Revenge. That's what I was talking about. I know that's a very Old Testament way to think, but I was only a few days away from having almost killed myself because I couldn't think of any reason to go on living. Getting rid of a cold-blooded murderer didn't seem like such a bad a thing to do, comparatively speaking, supposing I could get over my general squeamishness about breaking the law and fear of blood.

How does cat burglary differ from other kinds of robbery? Atherton asked, after giving the matter a ponder.

"Well, you need to very secretive and stealthy." Atherton winced as I stepped on an acorn cap and it crunched noisily. "I'm better at the secretive part," I admitted. "Mostly cat burglary is about finesse rather than brute force. And it usually involves taking gold or jewelry."

Ah. I didn't think it was about food.

We walked on. I made an effort to be more careful about where I placed my feet. I was a bit nervous, but not actually afraid. Irv's nephew—even should I run into him, which wasn't likely—had no reason to think that I was anything other than a helpful neighbor, stopping by to put out cat food for the strays who were living under his cabin. Of course, Tyler would be annoyed if he found me at Irv's, but he rather owed me for the meth dealer and would probably cut me some slack. So, there was no reason for fear. None.

Still, the woods were very dark and very cold with the sun down, and the trees were filled with stealthy noises. Though the trek up the hill had gotten easier with practice, it was still not enjoyable and I arrived at Irv's winded, my heart shuddering in my chest.

Time hadn't improved the view of Irv's place. The cabin was still so lonely and sparse that even a Spartan would have disdained the accommodations. The mold was getting bad enough, too, that even a coal miner might have moved due to caution for his lungs. I wished that I had brought a dust mask.

Atherton and I crossed the threshold anyway. Clearly I had abdicated all caution and regard for the law. There was no crime-scene tape in evidence, but I certainly could never claim that I was unaware that this was the site where a crime had been committed. And I knew that when Tyler had mentioned expecting a degree of eccentricity in me because I was a writer, he hadn't meant that to include trespass and tampering with evidence. Perhaps he would believe me if I told him I thought I had heard one of the cats trapped under the house.

I flipped on the overhead light, which drove back the dark to a limited degree but did nothing to banish the stealthy shadows where spiders watched with too many eyes. I looked around carefully, but saw no obviously loose or ill-fitting boards near the door. Clearly my disrespect of property was progressing from trespass to vandalism. I decided, after a moment's cogitation, that the most likely spot for a cubbyhole was under the mislaid hearth that Irv had only recently installed.

Atherton jumped up on the table to watch my deconstruction. I pulled my limited tool supply out of my pocket and laid the screwdriver beside him. Reversing the hammer so it was claw-side down, I began pulling up the small sheets of sandstone that had been jigsawed together with loose sand instead of mortar.

Unfortunately for my hands, the most likely spot was not *the* spot. I dropped the last abrasive stone back into place, not being particularly careful of where I let it fall. The nephew might notice that someone had pried up the stones, but that information wouldn't help him any. Wearing a fine and probably not terribly attractive sheen of perspiration flecked with white sand, I started testing the floorboards next, searching for one that was loose.

Again, the view of Irv's cabin did not improve from my position on hands and knees. Down there it was easy to see that not only did the floor sag, but the walls and tired old beams overhead did too. I was hoping that the worst bowing was just an optical illusion brought on because there wasn't one thing in that room that was square or level, but I knew it was just as likely that the inadequate supports were actually buckling under the combined cruelties of old age and termites, whose small piles of sawdust on the floor and furniture were a dead giveaway that they had taken up residence along with the spiders.

You'll need another bath, Atherton said.

I laid the hammer aside and sank back onto my butt. My knees were beginning to holler about all the crawling and squatting.

"I've been over the whole floor and haven't found anything. Are you sure you heard him taking up the floor?"

Atherton considered.

I heard him shifting wood. It might have been low down on one of the walls.

I looked at the room and groaned. There were four walls. That was four more surfaces, and the floorboards had already taken me a painful hour to go over.

"It can't be the walls," I said, realizing that they were only a single board thick. The planks had been nailed to the two-by-four framing and there was no interior paneling. Take down one of these boards and you opened the cabin to the outside—except at the tiny room he had erected for a bathroom when Molly had started visiting. Those walls had been sheathed on both sides.

Scooting across the floor, I began pulling at brittle pine siding and quickly found Irv's cubby. "As we seek, so shall we find," I muttered, feeling vindicated.

Most of his treasures were worthless—an Agnew for President button, an old black and white photo of what I assumed was Irv and his mother, along with his birth certificate and a deed for the land, which was terribly faded and would need to be read in better light. There was no will naming Wilkes as Irv's heir, but that didn't prove anything one way or another.

I opened an envelope from the photo shop on Lincoln Street that was new but smudged with red earth. There were only two prints inside. The quality was poor, like they had been taken by a disposable camera. The pictures were of a familiar gold pan, which now that I thought about it was also missing from the cabin. It was sitting on the bank of some creek, half-buried in Mountain Misery. I couldn't tell what was in the pan. It looked like rocks and water.

The gray hue to the picture suggested the sky was overcast the day the photo was taken. The foliage around the pan was also thick with red dust. That meant the picture was from late summer or early autumn. Late in August the winds start blowing in from the east, a dry hot airstream that carries much of the mountain with it. If there are fires, the mountains get coated in light gray ash. If there are no conflagrations in the desert then everything is covered in red iron-rich dust, and it stays covered until the first rain of autumn. Last year we had been blessedly fire-free, all the serious firebugs and lightning storms having headed for southern California in July and deciding to remain there for the season.

I turned the photo over, seeking confirmation of my suspicion. The date stamp was for October second of last year. That was when the film was developed, not necessarily when it was taken. The date was familiar, though. A surprise snow that night had shut down both the one-oh-eight and the forty-nine, stranding in the high country more than a dozen campers who had needed rescuing. Irv wouldn't have been able to get back up the mountain for the better part of a week, and by then the river would have been in full and violent spate.

I looked through the envelope, hoping for other photos, but found only strips of blank negatives. Irv had only shot two pictures and then taken the film in to be developed. My intuitive radar was blipping like crazy.

I went back to the cubby. The last item was a dirty hankie wrapped around something hard and heavy. I opened it up and found what I was looking for. In it was an irregular-shaped nugget about the size of my thumb. The handkerchief was stained with red earth and showed the imprints of several other stones, leading me to believe that there had been more than one nugget in there.

Something began to tickle the back of my brain. Where had I recently seen a gold nugget like this one? It was somewhere strange . . . out of place. . . .

It was Dell! He was wearing a nugget on a cord that day I went to The Mule. But not on the evening of Irv's wake. His chest had been bare that night. "Why take it off?" I asked, thinking aloud but also hoping Atherton might have some thoughts to share.

To hide it. The cat's voice was practical.

"Right." So that no one—like the sheriff or Irv's nephew—would see. Could Irv have given Dell the nugget as proof of his find and perhaps as earnest money for the new business? If I could convince Dell to produce it—a huge if—would this be evidence enough for Tyler of the business venture Josh had been talking about? And would this be motive enough to convince him that the nephew was the murderer and to investigate him rather than the meth dealers? Or would it send him after Dell?

I had another of those disconcerting flashes, this time a clear image of Irv's hands as he fixed my gate. They were hard hands, scarred hands that had worked at manual labor all of his life. And now they would never work again. My own hands clenched around the nugget, and I felt my face get hard.

Jillian?

"I'm okay. I was just thinking of Irv. It's so wrong that this happened."

Atherton padded over and sniffed at the hankie I was clutching.

That was Irv's. He kept things in it. Rocks. Lots of rocks. There should be more.

"Yes? I thought so. But now what?" I asked Atherton. "Do I take the gold with me now? Or do I put all this back and call Tyler so he can see it for himself?"

Is this the kind of proof humans would believe?

"Maybe. It depends on the human."

What kind of human is the sheep man? Atherton asked. *Doesn't he trust you?*

That was the six-million-dollar question.

"I guess we'll find out." I got to my feet slowly. My body felt stiff and I noticed that night had begun to fall in earnest, along with the temperature. Reluctantly, I rewrapped the nugget and put it back in its hole. We'd try it Tyler's way first.

It's getting dark now.

"Yes."

I hate twilight—always have—and at that moment I was very grateful that Atherton was there with me. For the first time I admitted to myself that I was glad he could talk to me, and that I would be very sorry if anything ever happened and I lost the ability to understand him. I had come to rely on his company and common sense.

"Let's go. I think it's time for some tuna and tea and then I'll call Tyler. We may as well find out if he'll help us or if we're on our own."

A kitten is so flexible that she is almost double; the hind parts are equivalent to another kitten with which the forepart plays. She does not discover that her tail belongs to her until you tread on it.

—Henry David Thoreau

CHAPTER NINE

Darkness tumbled down fast, especially when driven by a north wind that had sharp, biting teeth. It took hold of my exposed flesh and proceeded to gnaw on it. I squinted against the pain and promised myself a pot of steaming Darjeeling tea just as soon as we got back to the house.

I was almost home when the car came at me, going far too fast for a rainy night, on the blind curve at Abby's house. I snatched up Atherton, turned my back on the lights that threatened to sear my retinas and cowered against the nearest oak, whose trunk was slightly indented due to an ancient lightning strike that had split the bark into a coffin-sized wound that almost—but not quite—accommodated me.

Gravel flew as the car lost traction and began to drift. The tree was peppered with rock and I huddled my body around Atherton, trying to protect him. Which was dumb. He would have been far more capable of escape without my so-called protection.

I grew lightheaded as I waited for death. My diaphragm refused to work. What good was breath when I was certain of being ground into the wood of the tree where I stood shivering? To the right I saw my shadow spring up, grow long, climb the tree across from where I sheltered and then disappear, run over by the old black Volvo with noisy tires that were underinflated. Thanks to the light reflecting off the white rocks of Abbey's wall, I saw who was driving the car. It wasn't anyone I knew. A stranger—and one with an odd pallor—was trespassing on our mountain.

Atherton hissed and began to struggle.

Stinky-foot man. I can smell him.

Stinky foot. The meth cooker. Now that Atherton mentioned it, I could smell something too, though it didn't remind me of feet. I squinted at the license plate as the car disappeared around the bend, taking a fair amount of flora with him. As I listened, I heard him make a sharp left and head out Twilight Lane. It dead-ended at Cemetery Road. Many outsiders made the mistake of thinking it was a shortcut to the freeway. This time of year, it was an absolute bog. He'd have done better driving into quicksand.

"One-why-ex-be-three-four-seven. One-why-ex-be-three-four-seven. One-why-ex-be-three-four-seven," I muttered over and over again, fixing the license plate number in my head. "We have to call the sheriff!"

I put the cat down and raced for my house. Tyler's birthday had come early this year. He was going to get his second meth dealer, courtesy of an overly curious me and the cat who was the only witness to Irv's murder.

As I ran, I wondered what the hell the man was doing on our hill. Could he have had something to do with Irving?

Tyler had gotten adept at understanding me and was able to take down the license plate number as well as my description of the car and driver, though my jaw was pretty clenched up by the time I got home. I think he also heard me tell him that there was something at Irv's he needed to see, but he chose to ignore that part of my message until the meth dealer was found.

I understood his priorities. Irv's place wasn't going anywhere, I assured myself a half a dozen times. Nevertheless, I felt this strange premonition, a hunch, creeping up on me like a pair of ill-fitting panties, and it made me squirm. There was only one way I could think of to get rid of my brain wedgie that was getting worse by the minute. After Atherton and I had shared some dinner and tea, I decided that maybe I should go back to Irving's—immediately—and get that nugget out of the wall. Chances were excellent that nothing would happen to it—after all, it was too wet for a forest fire to get started, and the cabin wasn't in so bad a shape that it would collapse overnight—but there was the matter of Irv's nephew roaming at large. If he knew about Irv's stash then he would probably still be looking for it. He'd especially be looking if he happened to glance out his hotel window that conveniently overlooked the sheriff's office and noticed the entire police force heading out of town. Certainly he wouldn't be sleeping yet. The inn where Wilkes was staying had a sign boasting that Mark Twain had slept there. Of course, Mark Twain seems to have slept in every haystack and flophouse in Calaveras and Tuolumne counties, so this isn't any kind of a recommendation. And I knew for a fact that the lumpy mattresses at the inn were from about Mark Twain's era. No one would linger in the sheets for a moment more than they had to.

I didn't want to go out again, but after the sheriff's Jeep and a squad car came back down the hill—the meth dealer in the cage, his car doubtlessly left in the mud pit until morning—I decided that maybe I had better make sure that Irv's gold stayed safe for the night.

I could always put it back in the morning before I brought Tyler up to see Irv's stash.

Atherton came with me again, though he was becoming quite accustomed at darkfall to curling up in a nest of pillows on the sofa while I read or, less frequently, wrote.

"Onward," I mumbled.

Upward, corrected Atherton.

He was right. It was very upward, about three paces of upward to every pace ahead. My legs were beginning to protest the walk and my jaw the cold, which had only increased in the last hour. I kept assuring myself that only hell was forever. This task would be over soon. The walk seemed endless, but eventually even the strongest mountain tires of pushing aloft, and there you get either a peak or a plateau. Ours had been the former until some ambitious lads with dynamite and dreams of gold got to working on it. Irv's family was not the first to be certain that there was *gold in them thar hills.*

There was a moon, so I didn't need the flashlight. Nor did I turn on Irv's sorry lamp when I reached the cabin. Perhaps I was showing off for Atherton; perhaps I was just giving in to paranoia and trying to stay invisible to any eyes that might be watching from the forest.

I had no trouble opening Irv's panel and fetching out the nugget and the photos. But as I was putting the board back, I heard a sound that raised those fine hairs rooted in the nape. Not a creak exactly, or a rustle. It was just a slight noise of complaint that oak trees make if you lean against them when they are bitterly cold and resentful of added burden. I'd had cause to hear that sound all too often that winter.

Unbidden, unwanted, a line from Hansel and Gretel popped into my head: *Nibble, nibble, little mouse. Who's that nibbling at my house?*

Jillian. Atherton's hair was standing up, too. His silhouette in the window looked enormous.

"I hear it." My voice was hardly louder than a sigh. "Do you see anything?"

No.

The sound repeated. It was soft but not safely distant, and it cast a dank shadow somewhere in my brain, blotting out my earlier confidence that I was doing the right thing by coming out in the dark and cold.

You know what fear tastes like, at least to me? It's like sucking on a dirty penny. If you never tried this as a child, let me fill this gap in your education. Instants after it hits your tongue, the mouth floods with coppery saliva and the sourness dribbles down the throat where it smacks the stomach. Muscles clench from your jaw to groin and you feel queasy. You get focused on the sick feeling and forget to breathe. The world starts to close in, to go brown and then black. Of course, you spit the penny out, but the taste won't go away, at least not for a long time. You'll taste it in your fillings for days.

"Do you smell anything?" I barely whispered. Fear burned up my oxygen and kept my paralyzed lungs from drawing more.

No, but the noise is out front. Atherton was facing the door now. He looked at least twice his normal size. It could have been anything out there—a deer, a raccoon, even a mountain lion—but I didn't bother suggesting this to the cat. We had to assume that it was something less benevolent.

"Come on. I'll put you out the bathroom window." I crawled silently toward the bathroom, testing each board before putting weight on it. If our observer wasn't certain that the cabin was occupied, I preferred that he remain unenlightened.

What about you? Atherton padded after me. His voice was low and oddly menacing. If he was afraid, it didn't show.

"I won't fit. You go around front and see if anyone is there. If it's safe, I'll come out."

If not, I'll go and get the others. Atherton showed initiative and I was glad he had a plan. I appreciated that tremendously, though I wished that he could fetch Tyler and not just the other strays. Whatever was out there probably required bullets rather than cat claws to discourage it.

"Okay. Let's do it."

The window opened reluctantly but without the tremendous amount of sound I feared. My heart was thudding hard enough to make my sweater twitch as I lifted Atherton and put him on the sill.

I'll hurry, he promised. And then without any hesitation he jumped into the night, disappearing immediately.

He did hurry, but by the time Atherton had crept around to the front and investigated, our visitor was gone. Atherton found no smell except for something that sounded like rubber when he described it—a smell, he said, like the latex gloves I keep under the bathroom sink. I didn't like the sound of that at all.

I also didn't know what to make of this odd event, but I didn't for one minute think that we had imagined hearing someone outside Irv's cabin. I knew that we could very well still be in danger if our observer had simply pulled back a few dozen yards beyond the range of sight or smell. I thought about calling Tyler, but what could I tell him—I'd heard a noise?

We hurried home, sticking to the middle of the road where we could not be easily ambushed, and once safely inside, we treated ourselves to more tea and tuna, and then tried to embrace the peace of mind that comes with a solid door loaded with deadbolts and chains.

Still, even with every lock in place and the house alarm turned on for the first time in three years, I couldn't shake the sick feeling of unease. Though Atherton smelled nothing definite as we hurried home, and I saw even less when I looked over my shoulder at the deeper night beneath the trees, I couldn't put an end to the belief that something malevolent had followed us down the hill and was still watching the house from the deep shadows of the trees up by the road. What it made of me and the cat visiting Irv's cabin in the dark, I couldn't say.

I believed then and now that the malevolence was called Peter Wilkes.

I didn't sleep well that night, but though I kept an ear cocked for any alien sounds, no one came scratching at the windows or tapping on the door. The deck didn't creak. The bushes didn't rustle. Whatever it was, whoever it was, it had decided to leave us alone for the time being.

The smallest feline is a masterpiece.
            —*Leonardo da Vinci*

———————

CHAPTER TEN

The phone rang around nine o'clock. I stared at it with dislike, which I was pleased to see mirrored by Atherton. The cat didn't find the ear-piercing ringtone any more appealing than I did.

Annoyance at the interruption of my first decent moment of writing in weeks, and inclination to ignore it, was soon conquered by my desire to make the noise stop before it drove another auditory nail into my head. I had forgotten to turn on the answering machine again and the damn thing would ring endlessly if the person on the other end was disinclined to take no for answer.

"Hello?" I sounded crabby, but at least my jaw was loose enough to articulate intelligently.

Perhaps surprised at my tone, the voice on the other end said formally, "This is Tyler Murphy, ma'am. Have you got a minute?"

It was nice of him to ask, though this was purely for form. When the sheriff called a person who had reported a murder and then spotted a meth dealer while walking home from the scene of the first crime, one always had time. Anyway, I was curious to hear what he had to say about Stinky foot and what the man had been doing on our hill.

His first words surprised me, though. They were an invitation to dinner for the next night, in celebration of catching the second meth dealer and making our county safer for honest citizens. And probably safer for dishonest ones too. The damned druggies didn't care whose ox they gored. We were well rid of them.

I said yes and then hung up the phone a minute later with hands that seemed to belong to someone else. Writing forgotten, I went upstairs in a daze. Atherton followed, being typically catlike, which was to say that he was curious.

Bracing myself for bad news, I looked in my closet and realized that the couture situation was as dire as I had feared. I'd lost a fair amount of weight over the last three years, and even if I was willing to take things in, everything I owned was hopelessly outdated. I took down my one cocktail frock drooping on its hanger and shuddered. My only black dress looked like it belonged at the funeral of a ninety-year-old woman and not at a restaurant where they served fruity drinks with paper umbrellas to handsome sheriffs.

"This is pathetic." Clearly it was time for a visit to Queendom Come to purchase a frivolous frock or two. Thanks to my jaw and grief I was now fashionably thin. With the right bra, I could have stylishly abundant breasts that would look nice in the latest fashions. And as for footwear—I could only shake my head at the sad collection of worn heels huddled at the back of the closet where they cowered in shame. My little piggies still had to go to market and other mundane places, but from here on they were going in new shoes. I would have to visit Golden Slippers as well—and I could get a pedicure while I was there.

"This is sad." Never mind clearing out Cal's things; it was time to throw out all the defeated sweaters and frayed pants, faded and sagging into shapeless dust sheets that made me look like a secondhand chair whose stuffing was gone.

What are you doing? Atherton asked as I began pulling things off hangers and tossing them aside.

"Getting rid of these old clothes," I said, sweeping the entire shelf of shadowy colored knits onto the floor.

Atherton came up slowly and tested the pile with his right paw.

May I have them? They would make a nice bed.

"Of course," I answered, pleased that he was showing such promising signs of domestication. "Would you like me to put them in a basket for you?"

Yes, please.

You may have noticed that I don't coo and talk baby talk to Atherton. It would be all well and good to *coochie-coo* if he didn't understand me, but since he does, I have the feeling that it would all be rather embarrassing for both of us if I treated him like a human baby.

I noticed Atherton eyeing a ribbon that had half slipped free of the wrist of one of the sweaters he had appropriated. Feeling inspired, I said, "You know, I could drag a string around for you—if you wanted—and you could hunt it."

Jewel-toned eyes looked up at me.

Thank you, Jillian, but it wouldn't be quite the same. I would know that you are dragging the string. Atherton was amused. It's like I said before. I couldn't treat this cat like a dim-witted child. Perhaps it was because of his extensive mental contact with me and Irv, but he seemed far smarter than the average animal, and learning more about me every day.

"Well, if you ever change your mind . . ."

I'll keep your offer in mind.

He was even using some of my favorite phrases now.

I forgot to put on the heater and my jaw was aching by the time bedtime rolled around. As I did every night, I went to the medicine chest looking for a night-cap. This time, before popping a pill or three, I really stopped to look at what was in there. The catalogue was fairly appalling. Lorazepam—in both the point-five and one-milligram dosages—Seconal, Valium, Vicodin. And that was just on my shelf. On Cal's shelf, carefully hidden by the aspirin and antacids and vitamins, there were stronger things, among them morphine patches that a part of me had been keeping for . . . well, a really rainy day.

After a moment I closed the door without taking any-thing out. I hadn't used them at the most horrible time, when the cancer was digesting Cal bite by painful bite and eating up my happiness and hope at the same time; there was no excuse for using them now. It was time I started living with the discomforts of daily life. Time to remember that being alive sometimes meant dealing with pain instead of running from it.

I didn't throw the morphine out, though. That would have to wait for another day when the light was bright and I was feeling strong enough to cut my safety line.

I was up bright-eyed and early the next morning, ready to shake my phantom bushy tail at the new day. For the first time in years my house felt charming. A lot of the old hopelessness had been evicted from the public rooms by new purpose, and the shades of grief were ti-died away in other less obvious places. It wasn't all gone, of course, but the memories were allotted only as much space as they deserved. The fever of despair had broken. I said to myself that the patient was on the mend and that everything would be better from here on out.

I decided to feed the cats and then maybe drag away a few of the downed limbs from the front yard. The outdoors also needed a spring cleaning. Not surprisingly, I wasn't the only soul lured out by the sun. I could hear chain saws and weed-whackers starting up all over the hill. Along with the chittering of the goldfinches, this gasoline-driven din was the true sound of spring in the mountains.

Crystal came down the hill in her bright red death machine, sliding to a stop outside my house with barely a fishtail on the loose gravel. She likes to think that her driving has panache. The rest of us tend to think of it as a reckless disregard for property and posted traffic signs. She's never hit anyone or anything, though, so we haven't complained to her.

I put down the leaf blower I had been trying to start and came up the wooden stairs, noting they needed to be stained again. Crystal rolled down her window and grinned. She had optimistically discarded her coat and was wearing only a hand-knit sweater in shades of blazing blue and violet.

"Hi, sweetie!"

"Hi, yourself," I answered. I walked over to her red Honda, crunching drifts of oak leaves underfoot. The wind had once again swept up every leaf on the hill and dumped them in my yard. "I'm glad you're here. I've been wanting to talk to you about a mission of mercy."

"What's that?" she asked, her face looking suddenly concerned. "Is someone ill?"

I shook my head.

"It's about one of Irv's cats." Actually it was about all of Irv's cats, but I didn't want to terrify her. My scare up at Irv's had made me nervous for the felines. The sooner they were safely stowed away, the better. "As you know, I've been looking after them since Irv died. Fortunately, they've had their shots, but I have no idea if they have been spayed or neutered and am not at all sure how to get them all to the vet's. I've found a home for some of them." *One of them—Atherton*. "But I'm worried about . . ." Who? Which cat did I want to foist off on Crystal? I looked down the stairs where the cats were congregating around the pie tins. It came to me suddenly. Crystal would like the small white female covered in perfectly round black and orange spots. "Tiny Bubbles. You see, she's missing her tail and I think it's putting people off. You know how shallow some people are when it comes to looks, and I'm so worried she won't find a home because she doesn't look like other kitties."

"She lost her tail! Poor kitty." I nodded solemnly, not mentioning that she had been born without a tail. I knew that Crystal's tender heart would be roused to sympathy even though she was not a cat person.

"She's a real sweetie. I'd take her in a heartbeat," I lied, "but I've already adopted Atherton, Irv's big old black tom. And he and Bubbles don't really get on." This would be news to Atherton, who seemed to like or dislike everyone equally. But Atherton was big and scary-looking so I was pretty sure that Crystal would believe me.

"You want me to take her?" Crystal asked, a bit doubtfully.

"Just for a while," I lied. I was getting really good at fibbing. "Just until she's seen the vet and we know if she needs to be spayed. You know that she has to recover indoors after surgery. And I think we need to fix the females first. What we don't need are more kittens on the hill this spring. . . ."

"No, of course not," Crystal agreed. The hill had been battling the problem of ferals for years.

"Wait here. I'll go get her. Let's see if she likes you. That's important, isn't it?"

"Well—"

I turned and hurried down the stairs. "Bubbles!" I called. Bubbles is not her cat name—she hadn't gifted me with that information yet—but she knew who I meant and looked up from her dish of crunchies.

Yes? The question was wary.

"Bubbles, there is someone here who would like to meet you. Her name is Crystal. She lives up the hill."

The cats stopped eating and looked up at the Honda.

The bird lady?

Bird lady. I ran that through my cat translator. I think they were referring to the fact that Crystal kept a small flock of peacocks. She also occasionally picked up road-kill and took it to the buzzards that lived near Eagle Lake. As I said, Crystal has a kind heart. I assured myself that she could learn to like cats as much as buzzards.

"Yes, the bird lady," I said lowering my voice. "She would like you to come live at her place. She'll give you lots of food and you'll have a warm bed to sleep in at night. And you can still come and visit me during the day if you want to."

Bubbles looked more doubtful than Crystal had.

She likes birds.

"That's because she hasn't met you yet. Look, you guys can't stay here—you know the lady across the street doesn't like cats, and she will call the catchers if you stay too long. And they are going to tear down Irv's cabin, so there will be nowhere to sleep that's out of the snow and rain." I exhaled, calming myself. I didn't mention the phantom we hadn't seen in the night. "Just try it. If you don't like living with her, you can come back."

The cats conferred among themselves, then Bubbles said: *Very well.*

I reached down slowly and picked her up. She wasn't thrilled with the intimacy, but didn't fight.

"Try and purr for Crystal. Humans like that," I muttered and then pasted on a smile.

"Here she is," I said cheerfully as I walked carefully back up the stairs. "Isn't she a doll?"

"She has orange eyes," Crystal said, surprised.

"Like citrine," I agreed. "It's very rare. Isn't she pretty? You hardly notice the poor tail is gone."

Bubbles turned and gave me a funny look.

"And she's purring. I think she likes you." I passed the cat through the window. Crystal took her reluctantly, but smiled when the cat began to purr on cue and started to knead her sweater. The claws were kept carefully sheathed.

"She really is tiny for a feline." Crystal settled the cat against her ample chest and began stroking her forehead. The purring began to sound more natural.

"Yes, and the other cats pick on her. She'll never survive out here." Lies—all lies. But for a good cause, I assured myself.

"Well, I guess I could take her . . ."

"Let me get you some food—and a litter box, though she will mainly go outside. You'll hardly notice her." I hurried into the garage and picked up one of the covered plastic paint pails—unused, of course—I had emptied most of the giant sack of cat food into. I also snagged a disposable paint tray that could be used as a litter box until Crystal got something better.

Two minutes later, I was waving good-bye to Crystal and Tiny Bubbles, who both still looked a bit bemused but accepting of the situation. I congratulated myself on a job well done. I'd just have to do that maybe a dozen more times and the cats would all have homes.

Filled with a glow that I pretended was righteous rather than smug, I put on a second thick sweater and headed into town, filled to the eyeballs with purpose and a desire for the café mocha I hadn't managed to have yet that morning. Blowing leaves could wait.

I reached town without incident and stood in the bank's parking lot at the bottom of the hill, staring up at my house perched giddily on thin stilts on the steep greening hill. I noticed then that the narcissus and camellias must have started blooming some days ago, but I had missed the first signs of spring because my gaze was turned inward, where things were still dark and there was no rebirth. Spring was trying hard to gain her dainty green feet that year, but the earth was fighting off one hell of a winter hangover and reacting sluggishly. This made me sad because all too soon she would be shoved aside by summer, the cold's fraternal and lethal twin. In the mountains, the vernal and autumnal seasons are always short, and because of that, oh so sweet. And I had missed the precious first days.

"I'll do better," I promised myself.

I took the back way into town over the wooden bridge that spans the steep-sided creek that bisects the village. It has NO DIVING signs posted at either end that should be unnecessary because even at the height of the snowmelt the creek only runs about two feet deep. Still it's there for a reason. Cities don't pay for signs unless they have to, so you know that some moron tourist actually tried swan-diving off the thing and probably wedged his head in the boulders and drowned. It was Darwinism at work.

There is another sign there that I find even more disturbing. It is mostly overgrown by berry vines, but if you look closely you can still read the faded words: NO CATS OR DOGS IN CREEK.

The only way that a cat or dog would reach the bottom of the creek from that bridge, whose railing was waist high and made of overlapping planks, would be for someone to throw them over. I told myself that sign was an addendum to the others, put up because the same idiot had tried taking his pets for a swim, but I didn't believe it. People didn't take cats on vacation. What some heartless locals did do was drown unwanted puppies and kittens. They'd tie them in a pillowcase or burlap sack and then throw them in—and they'd eventually die. But not quickly, and not until their bodies had been battered on the rocks that littered the rushing stream.

Impulsively, I dug out my pen—a leaky permanent marker that had already ruined my purse lining—and added to the sign. NO THROWING CATS OR DOGS IN CREEK.

There was a rustle overhead, and I looked up to see a small flock of crows resting on the telephone wires. They were watching with interest as I defaced public property, probably hoping I'd go away so they could fly down and see if there were any tadpoles or carrion to dine on.

"I wish you wouldn't," I said to them. "I like frogs. Why not let the pollywogs be this year and eat something else?" But they ignored me. I guess I don't speak bird. Or they didn't care what I thought about their plans for lunch on this sunny day.

I have also picnicked down by the creek, but it requires real effort for anyone without wings to get down there. There are places where the bank slopes gentle enough for two people to sit, but not until you near the fairgrounds. It's pleasantly shady under the oaks, and in late spring there are an amazing number of wildflowers down there, among them sweet peas and a spiky lavender plant my grandmother called Kiss-Me-By-The-Gate. In autumn there would be sweet Himalaya berries and feral crab apples that are excellent for canning if you can spare the blood and skin and are willing to risk a case of poison oak. And if the deer don't beat you to them, of course.

Knowing I had wasted enough time and that the stores would all be open, I capped my pen and headed for Lincoln Street. Mocha first and then clothing.

Queendom Come answered my couture prayers that morning—and at a steep discount, too. The sales rack in the back of the shotgun-style store rendered up two great dresses and a formfitting cashmere sweater in pigeon-blood red.

The dresses were both very different but shared one thing in common: while they would have been great in New York or San Francisco, they were a fashion risk for a store in our homespun town. I wondered how they had ended up here. Usually our merchants were more careful in their selections. Perhaps it was a special order that someone had rejected when they tried it on.

The first gown was a Joseph Ribkoff, a draping, black, burnt-out velvet, and possibly peeled off a flamenco dancer—probably by a handsome bullfighter lost in a moment of passion. I looked in the three-way mirror and saw a dress that outlined all my erogenous zones and lifted my breasts up into an anatomically impossible position for anyone over eighteen. It screamed sex and yet still struck me as a power frock. Only a woman who was very sure of herself would wear anything that sensually unapologetic. I took a small breath and then unzipped.

The other dress was by Save The Queen, imprinted with a phallic body-length graphic of the Eiffel Tower on lycra of antique gold and copper. Again, it was a dress for someone bold and fearless and unafraid of their sensuality. I felt that I needed both frocks. Not that I was actually having sex with anyone, or planned on having a series of hot dates with anyone in particular. It was the power and confidence the clothes exuded that attracted me. I had been lacking in both for a very long time. These garments, vested with the assurance of their designers, would help me be strong the next time I went into the world as a woman rather than a widow.

I turned back and forth on tiptoes, looking at myself from every angle.

Of course, I probably would date again—eventually. Hormones would drive me to it. Booze and pills—and memories of a lost love—were never meant to be a permanent substitute for sex. Nor did I want the sodden life of the permanently soused. Molly and Dell were all the example I needed to convince me of this. Still.

"I'll take them," I said to the new girl hovering outside the dressing room before I could change my mind. I winced a little at the total bill when it was rung up on the old black and gold register, but was determined to have something that I really wanted. It was the first time I had really wanted anything since Cal died. I looked at that as a good sign.

One of the most striking differences between a cat and a lie is that a cat has only nine lives.

—*Mark Twain*

CHAPTER ELEVEN

Tyler and I went to the 134 Threadneedle Street located at 27 on Golden Avenue. Don't ask. Someone was being clever. We dined that night in the east wing of the refurbished Victorian. The house had been built for a pair of twin sisters called Grant who despised one another but refused to live apart. Instead of either surrendering the home, they constructed a massive wall right down the middle. The two halves mirrored one another, but the west wing was done in shades of rose and the east in lavender. I'm certain that the new owner would have liked to have done extensive remodeling to make the old building more accessible, but it was designated as a historic home, which meant no structural changes. You were greeted on the porch by a hostess and then sent into one side of the house or the other through separate front doors, one done in stained glass and the other festooned with velvet drapes.

I'd eaten at 134 before, but not in a long while. Not since Cal and I celebrated our last anniversary. The house had high ceilings and enough stained glass in what used to be the front parlor windows that I couldn't help but think that I was drinking at an altar. It made me feel a bit sacrilegious, so I usually kept my back to the windows, kept my elbows off the high-top marble table and concentrated on the long-haired brunette who played jazz guitar on Friday and Saturday nights—in the east wing on Fridays, west wing on Saturdays. That night Tyler offered me a seat facing the window. I took it reluctantly and figured that if worse came to worst, I'd let Tyler wrestle with my spiritual guilt for me. I felt sure that he would be strong enough to overcome it.

But perhaps worse wouldn't come to worst, I thought optimistically. My psyche hadn't done a complete one-eighty on me, but there had been definite changes in the last few days. The impulses that had been prompting me to action—or inaction—for the last three years had all originated in my past experiences. Now, because of Tyler—and Atherton—I was doing things because I felt hopeful about the future. I was again looking forward instead of back.

Traffic surged by as we looked out the few pieces of clear glass into the tiny lot lined with crepe myrtle. Irish Camp is part of the long corridor that links the land of technology with fine skiing. People were rushing up the mountain to get in their last licks on the slope before spring melted the snow. The alley of myrtle seemed to lean over the hurrying cars, their shadows severely aslant because of the setting sun.

I caught a whiff of seared beef on the air that eddied through the door to the kitchen and my mouth began to water. My appetite had woken up and in yet another way I was remembering why it was good to be alive.

Tawny Brookes, the chef's daughter, came by to greet us and explain the specials. There were people before us, but we were head of the line. Right or wrong, the law gets good service in Irish Camp.

Tyler had never eaten there, and took his time studying the bill of fare and discussing the specials. This was a family-run business and the menu was solid rather than ambitiously exotic—their only affectation was to serve *pommes frites* with the steak, yet French fries with the hamburger. The ambience leaned heavily toward the romantic, and the wine list was more than merely serviceable. I gave it four out of five stars and hoped that Tyler would like it, too.

"I like a restaurant that has moderate pretensions and manages to live up to them," Tyler said softly when we were alone, and I found myself smiling at our similar trains of thought. But not too broadly. I knew everyone in the restaurant and he probably did too. I didn't feel like causing any more gossip than was necessary. There would be some talk about this night. My gold dress and bronze sandals would assure it.

Feeling carnivorous, we both settled on steak and ordered a pinot noir from one of our local wineries. There are several in the area. We hadn't yet caught up to Napa and Sonoma, but our modest wines were beginning to win some awards and enjoy wider distribution.

"So, tell me something about yourself that I don't know," Tyler said. His gaze was more than merely polite or curious; it was downright speculative, and I wasn't sure I cared for that.

"Like what?" I asked.

"Nothing big. Do you have a nickname?"

I thought about the advisability of answering this truthfully. You generally don't get nicknamed for your good points. "Sort of. Cal used to call me Goldilocks— because everything was always either too hot or too cold for my tastes."

"Ah." Tyler smiled and nodded.

"You?" I asked.

"No, no nicknames. But I can swear fluently in Spanish and Vietnamese."

I nodded, willing to play this game, especially since it beat talking about my work or other peculiarities. "Very useful in LA. Less so here, though. Let's see . . . well, one of the oddest things about me is that I am a tetrachromat. I have use of four color ranges instead of just the normal three available to humans. You wouldn't believe what storms look like to me."

His gaze sharpened and I could see that he was trying to calculate if this might somehow explain why I was the way I was.

"I've heard about this. It happens only in women, right?"

"Yes. I got my DNA tested when I was doing a piece for a magazine, and one of the researchers suspected that I might have this mutation. Basically it means that in addition to the blue, green and red cones in my eyes, I have an orange one as well. Supposedly I can see one hundred million hues. Maybe that's why I look at the world differently. For me, there's more to see." So much for avoiding mentioning my work or my peculiarities. I tasted the wine. "Okay, your turn. What's something *no one* up here knows about you?"

"Hm . . . Well, as a boy, I had a live dog named Tartuffe and a dead dog named Tinker."

"A dead dog?" I sounded startled.

"Tinker was my great-uncle's favorite hunting hound, and I rather liked him too. He sent Tinker to a taxidermist when he died. After my Great Uncle Liam passed on, his wife cleaned out the den and I inherited the dog."

"Did you want him?" I asked.

"Hell, no. Mom made me keep him in my bedroom and he gave me nightmares. But I couldn't throw him out either. Aunt Mara would ask after the damned thing, and I couldn't have faced her if I'd chucked Tinker out."

"I suppose you couldn't toss him then. Do you still have him?"

"Yes, but he's in storage. Tinker was the only thing my ex-wife didn't ask for in the divorce settlement. I have a certain fondness for him for that reason. Still, now that the moths have been at him, he's more than a bit off-putting and I keep him under wraps. Anyhow, it's safe to visit me at home."

I thought that rather depended on how he defined safe. "And Tartuffe?"

"Gone to the great hunting ground in the sky more than a decade ago. And not taxidermied. I've been moving around too much since then to have another pet. A live one, at any rate. I hope that will change now. It would be nice to have a dog again, an open honest creature who never sulks or lies."

I saw his eyes narrow and his lips part, and rushed into speech to forestall what I thought was coming. "Okay, that's pretty weird. I haven't any dead animals. Just live ones," I said.

Tyler leaned back.

"Maybe too weird for a first date?" he guessed. "Let's see. I also have six nieces and nephews. Three of them play the tuba. Badly. All the time. I was going to say that the other three had no sense of rhythm, but the fact is the tuba players haven't got a beat either. I'm supposed to go down to Lakewood for a concert in May but am praying for a small crime spree to keep me here."

This made me laugh ruefully. "I understand. My brother has two children—more than that I will not say. I have managed to avoid all little league games and dance recitals this year. My sister-in-law is punishing me by withholding school pictures. I could say something about her, too—but won't."

"That's probably wise. We may not care for them, but bottom line, they're still family." Tyler put his glass down. He was smiling but his gaze was still a bit fixed. He was definitely after something. "Maybe it's your one hundred million hues, but the way you react to me is interesting and different. I think you see someone or something that others don't perceive," Tyler added softly as the bread basket arrived.

"Pigments of my imagination?" I suggested, and got a small smile.

"Maybe. I definitely think that I should have you tell me something about myself. What do you think I don't know about myself and should? What do you like? What would you change?"

"How do I see you differently than others? But how would I know? I only see the world as I see the world. I have no way of making comparisons with my vision and other people's," I complained, not being shy about helping myself to a nine-grain dinner roll, but reluctant to voice any real observations about my host. The rolls were warm and plump and looked perfect on the silver-banded bread plate. Tyler looked rather perfect, too, but I left him alone. In fact, I moved carefully when I did anything that night. I had discovered why the dress had been on the sales rack. The zipper in the thing was not strictly vegetarian. It liked biting into flesh if you stretched incautiously. It was a good reminder on many levels.

"Fair enough," Tyler said. "In my experience there are three general categories of reaction that women fall into when dealing with men in uniform: vaguely guilty and therefore overly respectful, vaguely guilty and therefore belligerent, or they are attracted to the uniform—as opposed to the man in it—and the power it represents. Their seductions tend to be more like hostile takeovers because they feel powerless. But you've never had any of these common responses. I don't think you see the uniform at all. Your mind is always looking at something else. I'd like to know what that is."

I was constantly searching for ambushing felines, but I couldn't say so.

"And that's truly unique?" I stalled, and sipped my wine. I am not fond of most reds, but this was lovely on the tongue.

"Nearly, at least in my experience. The ones who react differently are too stupid to be cautious. The rest are too smart to ever get involved in the first place. Cops don't always make the best husbands, or so I'm told."

"Which am I?"

Tyler grinned at me. "Time will tell."

I nodded. "Maybe I don't react to you in the normal way because I'm not thinking of you just as the sheriff," I suggested, making something up on the fly. "We tend to know our neighbors here in Irish Camp, not just their public personas. Maybe I see you as a person who is doing a job but who has other interests as well." It sounded good, but now that I said it, I realized I hadn't actually considered Tyler as someone separate from his work. Not really. Like so many things, he had been largely lost in my preoccupation with loss, pain and fear of talking felines.

"Maybe, but if so, you see me as someone to hold at a distance. I've known stray cats that were less wary. I think this means that you're attracted to me—as a man, as opposed to a uniform—but reluctant to do anything about it. Even to be friends."

Obviously he didn't know that many stray cats. They were way warier than I am. I didn't say this, though. I didn't want to sound defensive because for once I didn't feel the need to defend myself.

"I hold everyone at a distance these days," I admitted. Then I told one of the few truths I could disclose at that point: "I've never been good with sympathy. It cuts my legs out from under me, and there was an awful lot of it around when Cal died. As you know, he lost big-time at the longevity sweepstakes a couple years back. We weren't expecting it. No one was." I was amazed at how glib I sounded. But it was that or cry, and I didn't shed tears in public—not unless I slammed my hand in the car door.

"Dawg and Tulloc speak highly of him. I understand that he was a benefactor to the town," Tyler said, doing his best not to sound sympathetic but failing. I forgave him anyway.

"He was well-loved and is sorely missed—which is wonderful. And terrible. Maybe I like you because you didn't know him and I don't have to spend my time comforting you on my loss." I was aware of the shading of bitter irony in my voice and didn't like it.

"Is this why Irv's death has hit you so hard? A second loss too close to the first?" Tyler's question was kind but direct. He seemed determined to figure me out. That was flattering, but I knew that that might get tiresome. Talking cats aside, I truly am a very reserved person.

I looked into his lovely eyes and wondered how much I wanted Tyler to know about me. A bit more perhaps than he did at that moment, but I did a quick calculation, based on my emotional state and how many people were in the restaurant, and decided not to mention that both my parents were dead and that I had the irrational feeling that everyone I loved was on some kind of endangered species list. If dead dogs were too heavy for a first date, then dead parents were too.

"Maybe. In part. Irv was a kind man, and it offends my sense of justice that his life could be snuffed out because his nephew got greedy." This was truth, but not the whole. I had a long list of half-truths that I'd told Tyler, and more than a few lies by omission. But since none of this was out-and-out lying, I didn't feel the immediate need to correct his every misapprehension.

Or mention the whole hit-by-lightning-talking-cat thing just yet. Time enough for all that, I assured myself, after we caught Irv's killer and he had gotten used to me being a bit peculiar. That I was considering telling him anything was amazing. I blamed it on the wine and the subdued lighting that reminded me of a confessional.

"You're still certain that Wilkes killed Irving," Tyler said. "Does he *look* guilty to you? Does he have a blameworthy pall that only you can see?" I didn't think he was mocking me, just trying to figure out why I was so convinced of Wilkes's guilt when Dell was a more likely candidate.

"Yes, he has a criminal hue that only I can see." I sighed. "Look, I know that superficially he's not a great suspect. There is no obvious gain that I can prove, and he isn't a drooling madman. That's frustrating for me because no one else believes what I believe. And he hasn't cooperated by doing anything suspicious, which is a shame. I mean, I wasn't expecting him to run around high-fiving the undertaker or to be wearing the mark of the Beast right out in the open, but it would be handy if he at least looked capable of violence. Then maybe you'd be more willing to consider what I'm saying. As it is, no one but me seems to notice how dead his eyes are." The last part sounded a bit pettish.

This idea seemed to amuse Tyler. "Yes, if only criminals always looked the part. And yet, though he appears to be a spineless worm, you're not giving up on him, are you?"

"Nope. I've learned to listen to that little voice in my head." *Atherton, by name.* "You just wait. Wilkes'll do something to give himself away eventually."

"Like?" This wasn't a challenge, just curiosity.

"First off, I think it odd that he's still in town. Hasn't he got a job to get back to in Fresno or Lodi or wherever the hell he's from?"

"He's apparently between jobs and wants to wrap up Irv's affairs. That's what he says. I can't argue. And for now, I'd just as soon he stayed put."

"Uh-huh. Like Irv had affairs." I sipped a bit more wine and tried not to sigh again. I wanted information about Irv's murder, but I also wanted to just enjoy my first night out in three years. The two goals lay in opposite directions. "Have you looked to see if Irv bought any property lately—anything with a mine on it?"

"No deeds of sale have been recorded for him. I haven't found any real estate people that were helping him out, either. Of course, his own property has a mine claim, but you knew that."

"It's played out," I said, pleased that Tyler was actually looking into things. That was impressive. The sheriff's department serviced the whole county, and I knew that crime hadn't taken a hiatus since Irv died. They were already stretched thin. Irv's murder had to be a terrible strain on their limited resources.

"Have your meth dealers confessed?" I asked suddenly. "To cooking meth, I mean. I know they didn't kill Irv."

Tyler raised a brow at my certainty.

"No, but they don't have to. Their fingerprints are all over everything. Also, we have one of the men on an assault charge. The second man, Pat Jaspar, actually tried to hit Dawg. The DA is delighted at this slam dunk." The first man had threatened to shoot Tyler as well, but that affair was apparently too trivial to mention. The sheriff was about as prone to hysterics as the Rock of Gibraltar. "Oh, you'll be glad to know that the shelter has already placed Jaspar's dog. He's with a rancher out on Greeley. The beast is happily digging up the backyard."

"Good! Though I was hoping to see the poor thing one more time." Just in case it happened that I could suddenly understand whatever it was he was trying to tell me. "As a matter of fact, I need to visit the shelter for a piece I'm doing on feline leukemia. Maybe I'll get the address while I'm there."

"You write freelance?" He knew the answer but was letting me do the social thing and giving me equal time to talk about my job. He was also guiding the conversation away from Wilkes. I guess he wanted to enjoy the evening, too.

I tried not to sigh again. I didn't want to be a wet blanket, but I still had questions and I knew he had some answers.

"Sometimes. I also get assignments from a couple of magazines that use me regularly. And I write the occasional cookbook." I didn't mention my fictional work for various confession-type tabloids. I didn't do those kinds of pieces often—really, only when the financial wolf was at the door. They paid well, but I hated lying about having imaginary affairs with politicians or rock stars. Unable to let it go, I brought the subject back around to Irv. "I can't help but notice that though we have discussed my theories, we haven't talked about who you think murdered Irv if it wasn't Wilkes," I said, finishing my wine. "We know my opinion. What about yours? Do you really still think it was the stinky guys?"

"Stinky guys?"

I gave myself a mental kick.

"Sorry, the meth dealers. I think of them that way because of how their camp smelled. What was that guy doing on our hill?"

"Ah. He was meeting someone. He says."

"Wilkes?" I asked.

"He didn't know who. A mysterious man in a denim coat and a knit hat."

"Wilkes has a denim coat," I pointed out.

"So do you."

"Use your imagination," I pleaded.

"Sorry. I'm the sheriff. I don't like confessing to hunches or relying on my imagination. And that's all I have. For now. So I'll keep my thoughts to myself for the time being," he said mildly, pouring out the rest of the bottle. He handled the task with grace, though his hands were large. His eyes lifted and met mine. "But you would be wrong if you thought I didn't consider everything you said and consider it well. I do believe in intuition."

He had a lot of nerve saying I was wary. He could give lessons to my strays. I wanted to kick him. But I didn't.

"Well—I'm a blonde. Maybe I don't like confessing I can think, but I still do it when necessary. On a limited basis. With certain people. When I have no choice. I never really saw myself as Nancy Drew."

"You're not that blonde. And I have a choice. I'll keep my counsel for now." Tyler drank from his own glass. The smell of the wine was delicate, a hint of early spring that rode the invisible vapor and then vanished. It was almost as appealing as Tyler's cologne.

I let the argument go. One had to choose one's battles.

"I haven't seen my stylist for a while. Usually I'm very blonde. Will you mind?" *Good Lord*, I thought. *I'm being frivolous. Hell, I'm flirting.*

"I'll keep your hair color in mind. I have nothing against blondes. They may have more fun, but it isn't because they're dumb." He would flatter, but he wasn't going to tell me that he believed Wilkes was the killer.

"Something else to keep in mind . . ." I said.

"Yes?"

"I think you need a cat for the sheriff's office. A mascot. And I have the perfect animal for the job."

"Let me guess. One of Irv's strays?"

"Yes. His name is Sleepy—for obvious reasons. And

he's had his shots so the department won't be out any- thing for vet bills." He ate like a piglet, but I figured Tyler had a good job and could afford the extra kibble.

"I see. Well, Delores, the dispatcher who volunteers on Saturday night, was mentioning that things could get lonely in the wee hours. I had thought about a dog, but . . ."

"A dog would have to be walked," I pointed out. "Un- less you unearthed Tinker, which might be a bit upset- ting to visitors. On the other hand, a cat can get by with a litter box and a bowl of crunchies. And Sleepy is very restful. Delores would love him. Everyone loves him." This was an exaggeration.

But, I'd have a snitch in the sheriff's office! This was sounding like a better idea all the time, since Tyler was determined to be closed-mouthed about the case. The cats might or might not understand what the humans were saying, but they would know who came and went from the office while Tyler was being reticent.

"Okay. Shall I come by tomorrow and pick him up?" I had expected a bit of resistance to the suggestion, but Tyler was an easier sell than Crystal. He was probably trying to make up for refusing to talk about the case.

"That would be great." I felt suddenly buoyant. Two down and less than a dozen strays to go.

"So, we've established that you're a cat person," Tyler began. I didn't think we'd established that at all, but didn't argue. Whether I liked it or not, I was stuck being a cat person. "But you like dogs, too?"

"I go both ways. I also feed the rude squirrel who throws acorns at me when the bird feeder is empty. I think I'm a sucker."

"Cats and birds? In the same yard? How do you keep the peace?"

"So far we haven't had a problem. I keep the felines pretty stuffed with kitty crunchies." I had also read the cats the riot act about not treating the bird feeder as a smorgasbord.

I noticed a dull glint under the left cuff of Tyler's shirt. I reached for his wrist but stopped short of touching him.

"What's that you're wearing?" I asked. I couldn't imagine that it was some sort of keepsake from his avaricious ex-wife, but that was—quite tellingly, I suppose—the first and only thought that occurred to me.

"It's a commemorative band," he answered at once, but I could tell that I had taken him by surprise. "My dad was in the army. When I was in grade school they encouraged kids to be patriotic and to send away for these bands. Each one is engraved with the name of a soldier that went MIA in Vietnam. When a soldier was found, his . . . guardian would be notified. My band is for a Lieutenant James Broms, Jr. Missing since August first, 1968. He was never found."

"And you still guard his memory."

"Yes. Someone besides his family should remember his sacrifice." Tyler wasn't exactly embarrassed, but I knew he wanted the subject dropped. I have enough sensitive spots of my own to ever deliberately tread on another's vulnerable places.

Our steaks arrived then, the ambrosial odor chasing all other thoughts away. I always order medium-rare. It's risky because for many chefs anything beyond rare means cremation. But my meat was sleek and glossy under its mantle of gorgonzola. I said a prayer of thanks that I had meat and not a burnt offering from an angry kitchen priest. I wouldn't have dared send it back.

We laughed some over dinner. Not belly roars, just chuckles. But our voices mingled our shared amusement and I found that I liked the intimacy. I hadn't laughed with anyone for a long while. Eventually I asked Tyler what scent he was wearing since the smell was driving me wild. It was sort of like nutmeg or cider or minced pies. I could make out a base of cinnamon and vanilla, but there was a kiss of something else as well. It reminded me of childhood autumns when my brother and I would play in the fallen leaves, running through the raked piles until they were crushed to pulp and we were wearing bits of brown and gold in our hair and sweaters, and sometimes down to our underwear if we had been rolling around. Mom would call us in at dusk and give us a cup of cinnamon-orange tea to warm our frozen hands.

"I hate saying it out loud," Tyler said. "It's called Sushi Imperiale. It's by Bois 1920."

I recognized the name. It was an expensive retro scent, which would explain the evocative qualities that called up my childhood memories.

"That's okay. I'm wearing a perfume called Wild Pansy. It makes me think of a mincing Regency fop."

Tyler smiled. "I like it, though. It smells like a florist shop." Casually he took my hand. "Shall we see if The Standpipe is offering crème brûlée tonight? That would be an excellent way to cap off this meal, and a walk would be nice."

Our luck held. The chef at The Standpipe had also made lava cake and vanilla gelato. We ordered one of each and two glasses of port and shared a sugar high.

We had a perfect evening until the moment when Tyler brought me home. He walked me to the door and then, like any other man on any other date, he gave me a good-night kiss. It took me by surprise, though I should have expected the traditional dating ritual after wearing my sex-power dress and all the hand-holding while we strolled through town.

I tried to relax, but all I knew was that my heart was beating painfully and gaining speed with every second that passed. I could feel the rhythm of my pulse in my lips. He tasted like I did, of chocolate and cream, but the flavor translated into something dangerous when it passed his mouth.

Feeling a bit concussed, like a girl receiving her first kiss, I stepped back abruptly and Tyler let me go at once. I was breathing too hard and flushed with more than one emotion. I didn't like feeling sweet and mushy inside, like one of Grandpa's chocolate cherry cordials. I only allowed myself the pleasure of feeling sappy when I watched old Audrey Hepburn movies, very late at night and in bed. Alone.

"It's okay, Jillian," Tyler said softly. "That was just a friendly kiss. No need to look at me like I was writing you a parking ticket."

Just a friendly kiss, I thought. *Tell my heart that.*

"Sorry. I'm clearly out of practice." And prone to overreact. I cleared my throat. It hurt. Everything suddenly hurt. I felt bruised inside and out and I wanted to be alone.

"It's like riding a bike," Tyler said gently. "You never really forget."

I had to remind myself that it *was* just a kiss—not Waterloo, not the *Titanic*, not Pompeii. Rome wouldn't burn because our lips had touched. I—a single woman— had kissed an attractive man goodnight. That was all. Tyler probably wasn't even seeing me as a third course of his romantic banquet. He was just being polite. At most I was just a between-meals snack coming after his first marriage and before his next girlfriend. Hell, Cal would have approved of the kiss, would have pointed out that I hadn't actually died with him, that life really should go on and part of life was attraction to the opposite sex. I'd have to have sex again eventually.

Of course, the fact that I could think about what Cal would say was the problem. He was there, a third person in all my conversations, a witness to any intimacy. That

there had been even a temporary severance from my
twilit world of grief and guilt surprised me. In some
ways, it had been like getting over the flu, and the relief
of not hurting had made me giddy and reckless.

But hard on the heels of this thought returned guilt.
I relapsed into dull unhappiness and I turned away
from Tyler's gaze, feeling suddenly concerned that this
wasn't just all about sex for him. I couldn't look at him
because I *might* see something there in his eyes—some
unwanted emotion, his heart or even his soul. Worse,
desire for some idealized woman who wasn't really me.
It wasn't a sight I wanted to risk seeing. It wasn't knowledge I wanted. I thought, with a touch of resentment:
*How on earth could anyone who had loved and lost ever
think of being intimate again?*

"I'll see you tomorrow, Jillian."

"Good night." I didn't look up and didn't wave as he
pulled away.

I waited until the sound of his Jeep had faded and
then went in through the garage, since I had forgotten
to leave the porch light on. Cal's possessions piled in the
corner by the paint locker looked dispossessed and forlorn. I looked at the dusty mound of plaques and honors
that I had taken off the walls earlier that week: Rotary,
Kiwanis, Elks, Lions, Chamber of Commerce—and
city council. If it was civic and you could join, Cal had.
Me? I wasn't so gregarious. I maybe managed to send
out Christmas cards in years ending in even numbers.
Maybe that was, in part, why these tokens of Cal's life
had bothered me enough to take them down. It was yet
another reminder that without him I was isolated, not
only by chance but by my nature.

I have to admit that my evening with Tyler had made
me feel and want things that weren't purely emotional
and that guilt couldn't entirely quell. I went upstairs,
shut myself in the bathroom, and stood in the hot

shower, soaping myself both slowly and then quickly. But I wasn't able to touch myself the way I needed. My hands did not worship. There were no eyes to gaze into, telling that I was lusted after if not adored. My release was enjoyable, but it wasn't enough. Not anymore. My body was ready to be alive again even if my heart was not. And it wanted Tyler's touch.

Bed was warm but I didn't sleep at once. The possibility of Tyler in my life in some meaningful way needed some dwelling on. Why was he attracted to me? I would like to think that to know me was to love me, but there are limits to my self-deception. I'm liked well enough but rarely loved at first sight. And even less rarely lusted after. I'm too quiet and reserved. That's why Tyler's instant attraction confused me. Some men lust with little provocation, but Tyler didn't seem one of them. Yes, I'm cute, but no Helen of Troy—not even in my gold dress. Hell's bells, I thought, I was even too long in the tooth to make a decent Nancy Drew, if my amateur crime-solving was what appealed to him. And let's not forget that I was weird, too—*wyrd* weird. Though he didn't know that for sure yet, there had to be inklings.

Still, Cal had liked me at once. And he was a good judge of character and female attractiveness. That Tyler perhaps saw the same things in me that Cal had was a good thing, wasn't it? It might mean there was some hope of a future, if I could ever find the courage to reach for it.

Finally tired of wrestling with unanswerable questions, I rolled over and sought some respite for the body, if not for the mind, which was bound to nibble at this conundrum even while I slept. That's what happens to a closet sensualist who has been on an emotionally anorexic diet. I knew the urge to binge on new feeling would be very appealing to my subconscious. That was okay in moderation and in the privacy of my bedroom.

I had to watch myself, though. I was in danger of acting like a complete ditz during my waking hours.

I closed my eyes. Then I opened my eyes. Then I rolled over. And over.

Pow. Pow. I slugged the bolster. If pillows could talk, mine would complain about the tears and bad dreams that had spilled into it these last months. Of course pillows didn't talk—at least not yet, thank God. Nevertheless, investing in new bedding seemed like a good idea. Obviously I needed something better than this lumpy old pillow.

Eventually I slept, and I dreamed uneasily that night, but no bitter and dank nightmare came up from the basement of my mind to chastise me. Cal did not appear. Perhaps because Atherton was with me and chased away the incubus who might have come to suck out my peace of mind while I was undefended.

I will never again underestimate the comfort of a warm body, however small. I do recall waking once and feeling Atherton walking the length of my torso, planting his feet carefully as he came. Concern radiated from every hair and whisker. It seemed that my dreams had disturbed him.

Jillian?

"It's okay. Just a bad dream."

Hm . . . I think I would rather be treed by hounds than have your dreams, the cat grumbled, trying to punch down my lumpy pillow and having as little success as I.

For some reason that cracked me up. Satisfied that I was no longer unhappy, Atherton curled up beside me, pressing his warm body into my jaw, and we both went back to sleep. I was glad to know that I had a guardian watching over my dreams, and no demons disturbed me that night.

How we behave towards cats here below determines our status in Heaven.

—*Robert Heinlein*

CHAPTER TWELVE

I cracked an eye at the clock. It said that it was seven, but the room was still dark. Then I recalled the weather report from three days earlier. Dawn was at hand but probably being held under duress by a swift-moving storm that could dump another half foot of snow in the high Sierras and another one or two inches of rain on us in the lower elevations. I dreaded feeling the falling barometer in my jaw, but did not let the coming event depress me into total inaction as it would have in weeks past. I was used to being drenched and I had things to do, I told myself. Like, get ready for Tyler to pick up Sleepy. That involved washing my hair and putting on a bit of makeup, a spritz of scent and my new red sweater.

I came out of the bathroom half an hour later and found the sun shining through a crack in the blinds. I went to them quickly and peeked out. The weather boffins had gotten it wrong. We were going to have a nice day after all. I could feel my mood begin to climb along with the barometer. I began to hum "Golden Slippers."

Atherton and I had boiled eggs for breakfast. Mine came with a side of mandarin oranges and his one of wheatgrass, which he sampled along with some chives out of my window-box herb garden. Or herb *jungle*. The plants had gotten overgrown, being one of the few things that thrived during my time of neglect.

I dumped the dishes in the sink—Atherton didn't care if I did the dishes immediately, which made him an ideal roommate—and then went to open the drapes. It was only then that I looked out the living room window and saw the full glory of the day that had been given to us in spite of the weatherman's predictions.

"Wow." I blinked two or three times. The horizon was full of pink, green, blue and yellow balloons. Easter balloons. Some had bunny ears and some were striped like Easter eggs, but all were the pearly color of the tiles in my Grandma Hinde's bathroom. The spheres bobbed along at about the height of my deck, and children gathered in the open parking lot of the bank to watch. I could hear laughter, and I smiled as I touched the glass. The window, thin as it was, was still a barrier between the day and me, and I wanted it gone. I felt—almost—like I could actually fly, myself.

Of course, my senses had been so dulled by winter and by the constant worry that perpetual insecurity brings that I found these bright colors to be almost painful after the season of shadows. They were from my world at the time before I had known loss. But in an odd way, the pain in my eyes felt a bit like the return of faith, and perhaps even like serenity.

Balloons. That meant March was gone and it was April now; Good Friday, in fact. To underline this point, one church bell and then another began to toll, calling the faithful to worship.

On Good Friday many people go to church to recall that Christ died for our sins so that we might have eternal life. Everyone else in town goes to Hilder-brandt's Hardware for free helium balloons to recall . . . well, I'm not sure what. Maybe that Christ rose? Or that we should be high on life because it was spring? In any event, it was tradition and made the town festive.

"If this is Good Friday, then Easter is Sunday," I said to Atherton, who had hopped up onto the sill and was watching the balloons intently. "Maybe I should ask Tyler over. I could cook a ham or lamb. . . ."

I trailed off as I thought about the last Easter dinner I had cooked—four years ago. The meal had been cata-clysmic. Too distracted by Cal—he was having a bad day and resisting taking the morphine, which made him sleepy and stupid—I had burned everything and set off the smoke alarm. The baking dish with the *au gratin* po-tatoes had gone straight into the trash. I'm not sure what happened to the supposedly tempered glass that could withstand anything an oven could throw at it, but it had turned a bright topaz yellow. Cal had actually laughed as I stood there sniffling over my blackened meal and said he was really more in the mood for ice cream anyway. Toward the end, ice cream was about all he could keep down, but in those early days it had seemed amusing.

My unhappy memory was interrupted when I saw Nolan across the street wearing a pink-and-white-checked sports coat. Of course the mayor would be there with the crowds, pressing the flesh.

You don't like that man.

"No, I don't."

I noticed with a certain amount of satisfaction that Nolan was not aging gracefully. There was a certain un-healthy pallor to his skin that apparently no one else could see. His face was lineless and tanned, thanks to a plastic surgeon in Sacramento and weekly trips to the tanning salon, and that was enough to fool others into thinking he was healthy. I felt my mouth begin to turn down at the sight of his familiar swagger. But then I deliberately looked away and concentrated on one of the few sights that always made me smile.

Irish Camp has its share of Victorian-era architectural jewels bordering our main street. Extravagance was the order of the day for those who struck it rich in the gold rush and wanted to show off to their neighbors. Most of the houses have managed to stay on the side of good taste, but there was one place—The Stenholms's—that had thrown all taste and caution to the wind and embraced some form of Italian *loco Rocco*. The house was a wedding cake in white and pink, designed by a mad Bavarian pastry chef who married a lucky gold miner. It had cherubs and swags and cornucopias of gilded fruit and flowers dripping off of every eave, wall, lintel and turret. It had Tiffany glass windows and a marble entryway, and a gilded doorway that I think of as hysterics in stone. It was an abortion of bad taste and I loved it. Today they had an arbor of pink and lavender balloons arching over the garden gate. I didn't know the owners well, but they had a cat called Revlon because of her exotic though natural eyeliner that would have done Cleopatra proud.

Thinking of Revlon reminded me that I needed to talk to Sleepy and clarify his new assignment to him. I didn't think he'd protest too much once I explained that he would be at the police station, where he could watch the inn where Wilkes was staying. I had already run this plan by Atherton, who agreed that it was a good idea. The cats were getting restless.

They had been watching Wilkes all along, of course, and I think Wilkes was enough of an animal to sense it, though he couldn't have guessed why. He knew that someone was watching; of that I was sure, because he came and went from the hotel only at night, spending his daylight hours holed up inside, or sunning himself briefly on the rooftop garden. What he did at night, I hadn't yet discovered. He hadn't been back to Irv's cabin, though, not since the meth dealer was arrested. There was always at least one feline sentry in place after the sun went down and they never reported seeing him.

The cats were getting frustrated with waiting for something to happen and so was I. I reminded myself that the mill of the gods—and police work—might grind infinitely slowly, but they ground infinitely fine. We needed to be patient while they progressed, even if I hated—*hated*—waiting.

As though hearing my impatient thoughts, Tyler called and asked if he could get Sleepy that afternoon instead of as previously planned. And could he have another cat as well? The staff had taken a vote and thought maybe Sleepy would be lonely on his own. Boy! They really didn't understand cats. But I said, yes, of course he could have two. Sleepy had a great friend called Hula Girl who liked to bathe him and generally boss him around.

"Hula Girl?" he asked.

"Wait 'til you see her walk."

What I didn't tell Tyler was that Hula had an operatic voice that would fill a large space in very short order. It had tremendous range as well, growling at a basso profundo but caterwauling beyond the reach of the highest soprano. Nor did her oddities end there. Hula Girl looked like two different animals sewn together at the waist. The front half was mostly white and short-haired. The back half was long and mainly straw-colored, but also, stuffed in at random around her belly, there were tufts of every color of fur allowed in the feline kingdom. Her wiggling gait made the hip end shimmy like a belly dancer. Marilyn Monroe hadn't used that much hip action in *Some Like It Hot*.

Hula's feminine traits ended there, though. She

gulped her food with the gusto of a full-grown wolverine, and would probably love donuts. She would do fine in an all-male sheriff's office.

I asked Tyler if everything was okay, hoping he had some hot lead about Irv's death that required immediate follow-up I could perhaps help with, but it wasn't anything so exciting keeping him away. He was needed to assist crowd control downtown, since the high school marching band had decided to give an impromptu concert in "the park." I knew what he meant. "Park" is a sort of euphemism for a bit of space that has never been developed because of what I can only call bad karma. We have a hangman's tree in town where rough justice was meted out on three occasions: the first in the autumn of 1850, and then twice more in the spring of '51. The men hanged were triple-dyed villains, murderers many times over, and deserved what they got after a fair if speedy trial of their peers, though technically no judge or formal jury was part of the prosecution. No one is truly ashamed of this historic happening. Things were different then. Justice was rougher because life was rougher.

Perhaps what bothered us was that the men were buried, uncoffined, outside the old cemetery, but no one in town knew exactly where. No markers were set up for any kin who might be grieving. No one wanted, or would allow, those men to be in any way commemorated. These days, informed opinion is that the bodies had become one with the wild blackberry patch that has grown to the size of a tennis court, and that they have more than one cedar tree mounting their bones as the roots feed on them—which is probably the most useful thing they have ever done.

But then again, maybe it wasn't. And shouldn't we at least remember their names? These men had been some mothers' sons, maybe others' fathers. Wouldn't their families have wanted to know their fate?

Anyhow, the upshot of this old tragedy is, though we are big on historic markers and commemorate every place that Mark Twain ever slept or ate or shat, there is no plaque marking the spot of these executions, and it isn't mentioned in any of the tour guides handed out at the Visitors Center. Herman's Ground isn't an eerie spot, and no one has ever seen a ghost there, but I still feel strange when I pass by it. Most of the locals avoid it too. The picnickers one sees on the sparse lawn beneath the widespread branches of the ancient oak are all tourists or defiant high schoolers bucking town tradition.

There was some talk of cutting the tree down back when Cal was on the city council, now that I think of it, but nothing came of that. The consensus was that the tree had already been injured by the hard use it was put to, and that it should be compensated, not punished further. So, money was allocated for yearly spraying and pruning, though the land wasn't zoned as a park. I'm glad they didn't kill the old oak. Nevertheless, I don't walk by Herman's Ground unless I have to, because it makes me sad.

Tyler could have sent one of the deputies to handle crowd control, but he wouldn't. I was coming to know him and believed that he had a great sense of fairness and accountability. He was not above dealing with small annoyances himself, and thereby setting a good example for his staff.

Before I could chicken out, I asked Tyler if he would like to come to Easter dinner. I know I surprised him after my deaf and dumb performance the night before, but he said yes immediately, as though sensing I was on the verge of taking the offer back. A little stunned at my temerity, I said I'd see him around two and hung up the phone.

"Well," I said to Atherton. "It looks like I'm making Easter dinner."

This is good?

"Um . . ." I looked over at my stove and glared at it. The thing was cantankerous and disinclined to hold a consistent temperature. It was the number one home-improvement headache on my to-do list. The burnt offerings of that last Easter meal weren't all my fault. I hadn't actually told the oven to go into self-clean cycle while dinner was still in it. There wasn't time to order a new one now, though. I would just have to muddle through.

"I think we'll be having ham."

What is ham? Do they live in our woods? Shall I hunt it for you? Atherton was enthusiastic. Perhaps being domestic was getting boring.

"It's pink meat—from pigs. I'll get it at the store. You might not like it, but don't worry. There will be tuna too. Or maybe shrimp."

I like shrimp. Irv gave me some once.

I made a note of this. The budget was tight but I was sure I could spring for a bit of fresh shrimp if it would make Atherton happy.

I went outside to explain their new assignments to Hula and Sleepy. Sleepy was good-natured about it. Hula made a show of listening agreeably, but the back half had its tail whipping about in annoyance. The other cats were getting first crack at the food dishes while I held them aside for a conference. Finally I put out a dish just for Sleepy and Hula. Her tail calmed, and I finally felt that I had their attention, at least enough of it to make them understand what they would be doing. They both agreed to play spy for me.

"Atherton," I asked as I came back inside, "why are you so much smarter than the other cats?"

I don't know. Irv said that he thought I was a kind of familiar.

"A familiar? Like, for a witch?"

Yes.

Witchcraft and Irv? I felt a bit bemused, but that explanation made as much sense as any. And Atherton was probably like most people. We learn what we live, and, good or bad, we pay it back to the wide world with interest that is compounded daily. He'd been spending a lot of time with me. We practiced talking a lot. It made sense that we would communicate well. It also made sense—if you accepted that he was actually talking—that he would share many of my feelings about Irv and life in general.

Irving.

I understand that much of the human experience is painful and try to have compassion for others, but I couldn't seem to forgive Wilkes, however good it might be for my soul to try. And I doubted the cats would forgive, either. At least not Atherton, who had been closest to the deceased. I wasn't sure how good the other cats' memories were. I certainly hoped that in time they would forget what had happened and move on to happier lives. No one should allow themselves to be caught by grief and entombed with the dead. Surely having new owners and homes would help them move on.

But the cats were not the only ones being educated about new things. There was also the matter of Wilkes having learned that murder pays. What was to say that he wouldn't kill again if it seemed expedient? Like if he thought there was gold on my land. Or Crystal's? Maybe I was overreacting, but as the saying goes, better safe than sorry. Somehow, some way, we needed to find some definite proof of guilt and get him out of there.

"You never think that stinky-butt man deserves forgiveness, do you?" I asked Atherton.

Not from me, Atherton replied firmly.

"Do you believe in redemption?" I persisted.

Yes. But in this case I think it will involve another death.

Smelly butt must pay for what he's done, and I do not believe that sheep man will be able to do anything to him.

I nodded and then had the stray thought: How the hell did a cat know what redemption was? The question shook me and raised all my old doubts about my sanity and the danger of his ability to talk being nothing more than a hallucination. Did I need a companion so badly that I had invested this cat with human understanding?

Jillian? What's wrong? You look pale.

"Nothing," I lied.

Are you certain?

I looked out the window. I couldn't deny that Cal's death had left a vacancy in my head and depression had moved in swiftly. And while there wasn't a lease agreement, mental squatters are hard to evict once they get entrenched. I thought I had finally rid myself of the pernicious visitor that caused so much doubt and pain. And maybe I had, but I would have to be careful that something even worse didn't move into the vacancy. I had to believe in something. Part of that plan for a new life was accepting that I could hear cats talk, and that one of them was a feline Einstein.

"I'm certain. It's just my jaw. Well, I'm off to town now. I'll be back shortly." My voice sounded a bit shaky, but Atherton didn't question me further.

As I've explained before, the road into town is a tricky one. It's all horseshoe curves and hairpin turns the entire way up and down the hill. The shortest distance between any two points is a line, but we don't believe in those in Irish Camp. We like corkscrews and convolutions if it means we don't have to quarry through solid stone.

It also makes one question whether you really, really need to go to town. Or anywhere.

The eerie half-light can play tricks with the eyes—especially mine—and that day was no exception. I was half looking for ghosts when I saw Marie Antoinette à la milkmaid at Versailles come walking toward me up the hill. This was before the guillotining, of course, because her head was still in place.

I began to giggle, and the phantom raised a hand in a casual wave. I knew it wasn't a ghostly apparition but only Crystal covered in a cloak of spun-sugar. Her hair was especially webbed with strands of pink crystals. She had told me weeks ago about being roped into volunteering at the Sierra Candy Company's cotton candy booth. It was tradition that amateurs help spin the cotton candy that was given away on Good Friday. Again, what this had to do with Easter, I didn't know, but the tradition was a lovely one, and it made the air in town smell delicious. This was also extremely messy for the volunteers, since the machine was ancient and tended to throw most of its threads up into the air to net anyone standing over it.

Crystal and I talked briefly while she did her best to stay away from the fire ants and wasps that were following her. She assured me that Tiny Bubbles was doing well. I knew that already from my feline sources, but was glad to hear that Crystal was doing well, too. I promised that we would have lunch the following week and then I let her flee for her bathtub.

I met no one else on my walk, except a family of quail who bolted for the cover of shrubbery when they heard me crunching down the road. They ran in pecking order, never breaking rank of that tiny wobbling line that ran tallest to smallest. Unfortunately, when the first bird reached shelter, it slowed down, not taking into account the welfare of the others left in the road. They were frightened and chirping, but still refused to leave their place in line. Had I been a fast-moving car, they would be dead. Cute birds. Not real bright, though.

I made it to the bank parking lot where the screeching

children had amassed, and then began following my nose. I detoured a half block back to the High Sierra Candy Kitchen where the confectionery was actually made onsite, and stopped in for some fresh caramel corn. I was probably getting contact diabetes from all the sugar in the air, but didn't care. My mouth said it had to have caramel corn or die.

I paused a moment in front of the opera house, allowing myself a moment to appreciate the oddity of the architecture. The old hall looks like a prison and a Russian Orthodox Church mated and produced offspring. Officially it is designated as being of the Romanesque Revival style, though it has variations not seen anywhere else. It's large, square, brick, tall and has an onion dome on top of a turret that shines prettily on a sunny day. An out-of-town investor—a cousin of our mayor's—had wanted to buy it and use it for a car showroom, but the public outcry put an end to that idea. We knew that new money had a way of wiping out history in our town. Our opera hall was misshapen and had lousy acoustics, but that wasn't the point. So we said no at the ballot box to the filthy lucre, even though Nolan had wanted the deal.

A troop of giggling high schoolers pushed by me as I stood smiling at the building. The kids were out for Easter break and probably on their way to the park for the concert. Seeing them made me feel wistful and a bit sad. For now they were lovely blanks, just soft contours where their adult faces would go when stress and love and loss were done carving them. Poverty, too. Few of them would ever make more than minimum wage. I silently wished them well as they rushed off to whatever urgent task called them, hoping the Divine Artist in charge of their fates would use a gentle hand on them.

I didn't do my usual cat avoidance and weave through the backstreets as I wandered town. This time I stopped to talk to every feline I could find and damn the consequences. Not that it did me any good taking this risk of being thought a loony: Whatever Wilkes was up to, he wasn't getting up to it downtown.

Wilkes might have been a no-show that day, but the birds were putting on their first real spring serenade and being watched carefully by the appreciative neighborhood cats. There was one feral cat in particular who caught my eye. He was a lean creature with a striped coat and a supple body that could go from curled up and peering at his butt with his one good eye to uncoiled and halfway up a tree faster than you could say *one-Mississippi*. The robin escaped the assault, but only barely. It took a roost about four feet up a tree and began to scold. It would be sad to see the cheery little redbreast end up as someone's snack—and far worse if there were eggs of hatchlings waiting—but I didn't reprimand the cat. Not every animal was as fortunate as Irv's cat. My cat. Whatever. I couldn't ask the animal to starve or dine off rotten food in garbage cans when something yummy and alfresco was available and practically begging to be put on the menu.

My next stop was the bowling alley. It took me by the fire museum where they had rolled out the old calliope and were pushing her for all she was worth. An ancient man with a long white beard sat atop it, playing "*Bicycle Built for Two*." I tried to pretend that the music was cheery and not minor-key creepy, but failed. Carnival music has always seemed sinister to me, and the shrill tones hurt my ears.

The bowling alley was crowded, it being a senior bowling league day, but I wanted to talk to PJ, Double Lanes' feline mascot. The cat was cozy with all the patrons. It turned out that I had to talk with Deputy Dawg's ex as well, since she was working that day. Goldie may be a preacher's niece, but she hasn't really embraced the whole forgive-and-forget concept. She referred to Dawg's latest girlfriend, a nurse from Modesto, as the *slut du jour*. I didn't argue, since I'd never met the woman, but didn't take the accusation seriously. Goldie had thrown Dawg over, but she was still being very dog-in-the-mangerish about letting anyone else near him. Once something was Goldie's it was always Goldie's, and as far as she was concerned, Dawg was obliged to live in misery and die alone pining for her.

I didn't approach the seniors at play, though I knew many of them. Most were active, healthy specimens, poster children for the benefits of calcium supplements and high doses of ginkgo biloba. But a few were not. With every decade of difference in age the teams grew frailer, until the eighty-plus group that seemed hardly more substantial than ghosts. The younger seniors laughed and cheered and high-fived. Some even bumped knuckles as they saw their grandchildren do, though more softly because of the high rate of arthritis. The older ones, like Mrs. Alcott, did not high-five, or low-five, or even pat each other on the shoulder. Any contact could lead to broken bones.

I watched Mrs. Alcott shuffle up to the yellow line and drop her child's-weight ball. I looked on in agony as it crawled away from her, willing it to reach the end of the lane, or at least roll into the gutter so she would be spared the ignominy of having one of the employees go and fetch it for her. Eventually the ball arrived at the end of the lane and knocked down one pin. She seemed very happy as she accepted her teammates' congratulations, but I couldn't endure any more. *Thou too are mortal*. I didn't want to think about it.

PJ had no news, and eventually I escaped Goldie's post-divorce vitriol and the greasy smell of French fries that was weighing on a stomach already full of sweetened popcorn. I breathed deeply of the cool air outside, attempting to cleanse my lungs and mind. The bright red banner hung over the street reminded me that there was a blues festival going on at the fairgrounds on Saturday. And I had a ticket I had bought from Gemmie, Abby's eldest daughter, when she was selling them as a school fund-raiser. The thought of going was daunting, but now that I thought of it, the fairgrounds bordered Irv's property and harbored a colony of feral cats that I should talk with, since it was possible that they had seen something.

I went up Lincoln Street and was soon pushing my way through the minicrowd in front of the courthouse where the 4-H was giving a preview of their animals destined for the County Fair. Have I mentioned my horror of being reincarnated as a dairy goat? I know it's a strange fear, but I have actually had dreams about it. The poor creatures! Their udders are so large that they walk like bowlegged sailors and practically drag their teats on the ground. Looking at them now, it was all I could do not to shudder.

I caught a glimpse of Tyler outside the courthouse, but he was with Nolan and smiling for pictures so I gave them wide berth. As I was turning away, I realized something about Nolan that I had never noticed before. The way he stood, it made him look like his loafers were on the wrong feet. The thought made me smile, and not in a kind way.

"Enough," I finally said to the lone, turkey-shaped cloud in the sky above the hardware store, and headed for home with the pitiful remains of my caramel corn. I had hams to buy and vets—and their cats—to interview. Also, I just recalled that I was supposed to bring my car in for an oil change that morning.

And I would stop at the animal shelter, too. Atherton and I would stop, I amended. He wouldn't like riding in the cat carrier, but it would give me an excuse to bring him inside when I visited the shelter. After all, what kind of irresponsible person would I be to leave an animal shut up in a car on a sunny—I checked the sky to make sure that it was still sunny—day? This would work well. He could talk to the shelter cats while I dealt with the humans.

Atherton was agreeable with my plan and sat on the desk beside me as I called Dr. Dervon to set up an interview. I already knew the horrible facts about feline leukemia but needed to have some authority figure to quote for my piece. I also rather liked Clive, the office cat. He was a bit of an aging hippie, like the doc, and never bothered me with stupid remarks about how I smell. In fact, I rarely rated more than a *Hey, Jillian*. I·have no proof that the cat or vet ever smoked wacky tobaccy, but somehow it seemed likely.

I told Atherton that I would be back soon, and headed for the garage (automotive repairs, liquor, firewood and snow supplies). I was way overdue on an oil change and was reluctant to cancel my appointment again. They do a good business there, since it is the last stop for gas, chains, and snow tires before skiers disappear behind the evergreen curtain. I was also amused by the signs leading up to the garage, put up by the owners of a seasonal fruit stand that used to operate in the parking lot but had fallen into disuse a decade ago. Once upon a time the individual placards read: SLOW. DOWN. FRUIT. STAND. AHEAD. But with two signs fallen, it now said: SLOW. FRUIT. AHEAD. I always wondered what constituted a slow fruit. One that couldn't roll? Or did it have something to do with fruit IQ? For instance, were prunes smarter than raisins?

There was a vending machine that shared space with a glass-fronted refrigerator (live bait and cold beer) in the waiting room at Gold Rush Tires and Chains. Knowing it was probably a waste of time but feeling very thirsty, I dropped in my entire supply of quarters and hit the root-beer button. As expected, the machine jeered and refused to give me either a root beer or my money back. I called it two bad names, but stopped there. I was too parched to waste my breath and limited saliva.

Denny, who ran the office, looked up from his newspaper and laughed. Above his head hung the faded picture of a naked woman. It was a 1969 *Playboy* calendar turned to December. It was always turned to December. Denny was a loyal, one-woman man.

"That machine giving you a hard time, Jillian?"

"As ever."

"It's the damnedest thing. It never does that to anyone else, you know."

"Machines hate me," I agreed, finding the situation much less amusing than he did. "Want to help me out?"

"Sure." Denny stumped over and gave the red box a solid whap. It obligingly spit out my root beer. The clunk of its arrival in the tray sounded like a bark of contempt, but I didn't complain. Denny smiled again. "You just need to know how to speak its language."

"Thanks." I picked the can up, but didn't open it. Experience said that there was a better than even chance that the thing would spray me if I didn't let it sit for a while. Machines really do hate me. It's probably because of my stance on cell phones. In this age of the Internet, word has probably gotten around.

"Denny, I've been thinking. You know what this office needs?" My tone was a shade too enthusiastic, and he eyed me a bit warily.

"Uh . . . what?"

"A cat. It hasn't been the same since Grover passed."

"Well, no. But Grover was a dog," he pointed out.

"And that was the problem. Poor Grover—once he lost his hearing, it was just a matter of time before . . ."

I didn't go on. Grover had come to a bad end when one of the car lifts in the garage had dropped on him. "But a cat would just stay here in the office and keep people company while they waited for their cars to be fixed. They've done studies, you know. Pets help lower people's blood pressure. Keeps them from being so cranky." Unless they had allergies to cat dander.

"You know, that isn't a bad thought," Denny admitted. "It would help folks while away the time. I'll talk to Ross about it."

"Good. And I even know the prefect cat. His name is—Happy." Happy really should have been called Sleepy Two. He looked like Sleepy's cousin and shared the lazy temperament. "He's a fluffy orange cat—looks like a pumpkin. He's very mellow."

"Is this one of Irv's cats?" Denny asked.

"Yes. I've found homes for most of them." That was a smallish lie. I had homes for three. Four, if you counted Atherton.

Denny returned my keys soon after, and, feeling a righteous glow at having placed another cat and tended to the well-being of the Subaru—the one machine in the world that doesn't hate me—I rushed back home.

Atherton wasn't enthused about the cat carrier I put him in—a leftover from a neighborhood yard sale that I had inherited when its previous owner abandoned it—but he understood the necessity when I explained about the shelter. I made sure to put him in the front seat where he could watch the world as we traveled. Once underway, I slipped Ian Hunter's *Rant* CD into the player. Brother Ian was a good man, and I was feeling his indignation. Of course, he was singing about socio-economic injustice in England and I was pissed off about greedy nephews who were getting away with murder, but it still felt like a meeting of the minds.

Atherton listened intently as I sang along, and I had a

moment of near-vertigo as I considered what this could mean. I could share anything with him: Shakespeare, Rossini, poetry. Of course, there was every chance that he wouldn't care about Romeo and Juliet's ill-fated love affair or the trials of the Barber of Seville. But who could resist T. S. Elliot's *Old Possum's Book of Practical Cats*? All I had to do was read it aloud.

We had a bit of bad luck on Apple Road. I got stuck behind one of the many turkey trucks headed for the ranch where they raise free-range fowl. The options, once trapped on the two-lane tarmac, are limited. There is no place to pull over and no place to safely pass. Cars have tried it, with disastrous results. Last year we had a truck overturn and it was a blood fest. Panicked juvenile turkeys went racing to their deaths on the freeway that runs parallel to Apple Road. They committed mass suicide by motor home and tour bus, and hundreds of turkey dinners were lost just before Thanksgiving. The road was covered in turkey slaw that had to be scraped up with snowplows, and there were white feathers ghosting around for months. The collisions hadn't done much for the vehicles, either. The truck driver was unhurt but badly shaken, and soon retired from the turkey-hauling business.

It was difficult, but I bided my time and crawled along at six miles per hour until I reached Ranch Road where the vet's office was. It wasn't the most painful of ways to pass the time. Daffodils were blazing on the hillside and the first lupines had leapt out of the ground overnight and burst into glowing purples and whites that almost hurt the eye with their vivid hues.

Dr. Dervon was kind and very eager to cooperate on a story about the perils of feline leukemia. For those of you who don't know, it's an incurable viral disease that affects 2 to 3 percent of all cats. The rate goes up in cats that are ill, very young, or living in stressful situations. The disease can cause cancer, blood disorders, spontaneous miscarriages, and a host of immune deficiency disorders that sound a lot like AIDS. The only way to avoid infection is never to let your cat interact with infected felines, since it can be transmitted through saliva or mucus. There is a vaccine that is fairly effective but not foolproof. What I didn't know was that there were some treatments for the disease that could add a couple of years to an infected animal's life. I wrote them down carefully—Immuno Regulin, Interferon Alpha, Staph Protein A and Acemannan. I had to leave my readers with some hope if their beloved pets turned up infected.

I managed a quick word with Clive while Dr. Dervon looked Atherton over and pronounced him healthy. Atherton tolerated the contact but didn't enjoy it. He had come a long way, though, in just a few days. A week ago, he might well have bitten the vet for taking such liberties.

The next stop was the animal shelter. I had high hopes of getting some news there. Cats came in from all over the county and there was a good chance that this clearinghouse for feline gossip would have some news about Wilkes's activities.

"What a handsome kitty," Caitlin Brown said, stuffing her fingers through the carrier's bars.

Jillian, what does she want? She won't touch me, will she? She smells of dog. Atherton was offended.

"You'll have to forgive him. He's a bit reserved. Too dignified to ask for chin scratches, and I'm afraid that Dr. Dervon rather ruffled his feathers during the exam."

"Poor kitty." Caitlin pulled her fingers out of the carrier. I shifted so that she had to turn away from the carrier to face me. I opened my notepad and began explaining what I was writing about. I started with the question about the worrying rise of the disease among cats being brought to Animal Control.

It didn't surprise me that Arthur, the shelter's only permanent resident, sidled up to the carrier and began a low-voiced conversation with Atherton. I wanted desperately to eavesdrop, but they kept their voices down. I thought I heard Atherton ask if Arthur liked living at the shelter, but his reply was lost under Caitlin's recitation of dismal statistics. All I could do was nod and scribble and trust that Atherton would remember to ask about news of Wilkes.

As I had half-expected, there were no new reports of Wilkes's doings among the shelter cats. They knew of him and the meth dealers but had no news. A bit discouraged, I asked Atherton if he wanted to go with me to the grocery store, though it would mean waiting in the car while I shopped. Feeling more at home in the Subaru now, he agreed to come with me to the lower Bag-N-Sav. It wasn't fun for Atherton, but I felt better about being out in the wide world with the cat riding shotgun.

I thought that shopping might be stressful but found that planning a dinner was much like riding a bike. You wobbled a bit and took things slowly, but everything did come back rather quickly. After all, at one time I had been an enthusiastic amateur chef.

Conscious of Atherton out in the heating car, I trolled along as quickly as possible, hooking in only what I absolutely needed. Even at that, the grocery bill still came to ninety-eight dollars, since the refrigerator was down to cultures of botulism and a decade-old jar of pickles. Shaking my head and wondering if I couldn't just serve chili—on sale, two for $1.35—and dinner rolls, I rolled my cart out to the car and stowed the groceries in back.

I saw Atherton's nose twitch, and knew he was

smelling the steamed shrimp. That made me feel better about the money spent. Two bucks' worth of shrimp would send him to heaven. If only I could find nirvana so easily.

Tyler picked up Hula and Sleepy that afternoon but couldn't stay for a cup of tea; he had been asked by Father Browne to attend evening services at Saint Patrick's, built at the very apex of Bellemont Street where it could overlook the town's sinners and admonish them with its white spire that thrust upward like the very finger of God. Tyler explained that there had been some trouble at the church with pranksters letting air out of parishioners' tires, and no threats of the evildoers getting extra hell-time had put an end to the nonsense. That made the priest suspect that the culprits were rival Methodists whose place of worship was right down the street. In the interest of continuing interfaith peace and harmony, Tyler was planning on sitting in the parking lot and making sure that the Catholics' tires remained unmolested.

Disappointed that he couldn't stay for a cup of tea and a visit, after Tyler left for church I asked the cats to put the word out to the neighborhood that I wanted to know who was messing with the cars at Saint Patrick's. And to please make note of what kind of clothing they were wearing, not just how they smelled. It wasn't that I felt especially obliged to defend the Catholics' automobiles from malefactors of any religion, but I didn't see any need for Tyler to be spending his time waiting around a parking lot to catch a petty vandal when the cats could do it for him. There had to be more benefits to this talking to cats thing.

Ignorant people think it is the noise which fighting cats make that is so aggravating, but it ain't so; it is the sickening grammar that they use.

—*Mark Twain*

_____

CHAPTER THIRTEEN

Saturday dawned bright and warm. It took courage, but I decided that I would zip myself into some jeans and a halter top and go to the blues festival. I would eat a tri-tip steak sandwich, maybe have a beer, and talk to the feral cats who lived at the fairgrounds, since they were about the only cats I hadn't talked to yet.

In my investigative fervor, I completely forgot why Cal and I stopped attending this annual event.

The day did not begin auspiciously, and I should have taken note of the signs and portents. When I stepped outside I noticed the gutters along the garage's southern face were growing a bumper crop of miner's lettuce and vetch. I'd cleaned them out already three times that winter, but there were always more oak leaves to fill them. Oak leaves are supposed to be hostile to other plants but, just like the ivy the deer aren't supposed to eat—ha! Those giant vermin would eat poison oak when nothing else is available!—plenty of weeds seemed to do just fine in the oak's acid mulch. The shingles were also a lovely shade of spring green, which meant that the moss had come back and was busy devouring the asphalt shingles that kept the rain off my head.

Annoyed, I turned to look at Abby's wall, which was now a shaggy green monster seething with various species of hard-shelled moss-eating bugs that gave it an eerie kind of shimmer and made the green fur seem to crawl. I was certain that if I stared long enough I would actually see her moss spitting spores onto my roof. And Abby absolutely refused to consider spraying it with weed-killer.

As I knelt to pick up a broken branch that was blocking the communal drain, I noticed a stealthy shifting in the leaves in her gutter. I thought at first there might be a mouse or lizard foraging in the dead foliage, but as I watched, a baby cyclone spun to life at the edge of the street, rearing up quickly on dead, brown, leafy legs. It whirled drunkenly toward my front stairs, growing more golden as it picked up drifts of pollen and other street detritus. It gibbered in a dry, scraping voice. The little tornado was a valiant and quite scary effort, reaching almost human size, a whirling Golem of leaves and twigs that reached for me with its many arms, chasing me as I backed away down the stairs. I clamped my lips tightly together, refusing to scream though I was suddenly terrified.

Fortunately, the dust devil wasn't strong enough to survive my stairs. The baby twister collapsed on the top step, twitched twice and then died in a small explosion, leaving a fresh pile of debris on my front deck. I had always wondered how the large piles of kindling and moss came to land at my front door. Now I knew: They shambled there with the help of the wind. It was dust devils that sometimes came scratching at my door in the dead of night.

The notion suddenly creeped me out. It was too close to having a poltergeist haunting me.

Feeling nervy and restless, I decided to walk to the fairgrounds. It's a bit of a hike and involves taking one's life in one's hands when inching along the cliff face on Stockyard Road where there are no bike lanes or sidewalks, but it is better than trying to find parking at the fairgrounds when a major event is happening. As is the case everywhere in Irish Camp, parking is at a premium on event days.

Torrence Smith was taking tickets at the gate. He is a retired cowboy, almost ninety, bowlegged and toothless, and what people used to call simple—meaning that some rooms in his brain have been left unfinished, and those he lived in were all rather dusty and unkempt. Certainly the cloudy blue of his unfocused eyes proclaimed his age and announced his mental bulbs had dimmed. Still, he seemed happy enough in his work, and I was amused to watch him labor at his slow pace even though—or perhaps because—it annoyed the out-of-towners in line ahead of me.

That's one of the problems with tourists, I thought smugly. They just don't know how to slow down and get along in a town where very few people wear a watch, preferring to rely on the clock at the top of the courthouse—though it was notorious for getting stuck at the ten o'clock hour—or the tolling of the church bells (Saint Patrick's for the Catholics, and about three minutes later the bells at Mount Zion for the Protestants) to tell them the hour.

My amusement with the outsiders didn't last long. It never does. Amusing tourists become annoying tourists after only minutes. I think it's their cell phones. Why do people go to concerts and then spend the whole time yammering to people they didn't like enough to invite to the event? You know, I liked it better in the days when families kept their freaks locked up in the attics at home. Really. It was better for society as a whole.

I know that sounds weird coming from me, the queen of freaks, but I stand by this assertion. The Victorians weren't wrong about everything. There is no need to pack up your oddballs and take them to other people's cities and towns and turn them loose on the unsuspecting public—especially when you are at something billed as a family event. If you have two heads and bad manners, keep them both at home.

Before I begin my tirade in earnest, let me say that the music at the festival was fabulous—Shane Dwight, Cafe R&B, The Mofo Party Band. All awesome from what I heard. The weather was perfect, the venue fine. It was just all the rude out-of-towners who came for the festival that ruined it for us townsfolk and the other normal people.

Of course there were the rude and drunk attendees. This happens at any and all public events, but usually not in such numbers as I saw that day. One female in black leather chaps and a tube top was staggering drunk by ten A.M., and just before eleven attempted to strangle herself in front of the main stage where the MoFo Party Band was warming up. Since she had already thrown up near my feet and spattered my sandals with half-digested beer and churros, I thought her friends should let her get on with the job without interfering. I thought it an interesting experiment for the other drunks to watch: Can you actually kill yourself that way, or would you stop throttling when you ran out of air? But her companions seemed to like her more than I did, and they took steps to save her. It required three people to pry her hands off her own neck but—darn it—they persisted until she passed out and they could cart her away.

I saw another drunk pitch down face-first on the lawn a few minutes later and have to be dragged away by the medics, who seemed reluctant to touch her. It was a relief because every fifteen seconds or so she'd scream out, "This shit don't stink!" And it was scaring the ferals, who were trying to enjoy a snack at the dumpster near the BBQ RIBS AND TATERS trailer.

The rest of the drunks were men—usually with cigars, toilet breath and T-shirts from Harley shops in Modesto and Stockton (the new murder capitol of California, I heard someone say; thirty-seven homicides so far this year, one man bragged). The amusing part was that few of these men actually rode motorcycles. The genuine gentlemen of the road were far better dressed and mannered. These same biker-pretenders were also covered in tattoos. *What's wrong with that?* you ask. You will argue that some tattoos are absolute works of art, and I agree. You probably have lovely flowers and butterflies and cute animals riding mascot on your shoulder, or maybe the small of your back. But these men's markings were mainly words and pictures of violence. The women went more for forms of sexual degradation. I believe that these were markings and mutilations meant to offend rather than entertain, and they succeeded—at least with me and probably with their mothers. Words have power, and symbols carry meaning. Swastikas, death's-heads, phrases like "Kill them all and let God sort them out," "cunt" and "slut" are meant to provoke strong visceral reactions. These were disturbing labels to see on human bodies, frightening even, but no one else in the crowd seemed to mind or even notice, perhaps because violence and bad manners truly have become the coin of the realm where most people trade. The thought of trying to ever go back and live in that society makes me shudder. If I could build a wall around our town, I would. We would all be safer and happier if we could keep the barbarians on the other side of the gate, allow them in only when they offered a needed good or service.

A man in motorcycle boots and a tattoo that said PIG-STICKER trod on me. He didn't apologize, and I didn't try and make him once I got a look at the tattoo. I at first assumed that pig-sticker was some reference of disdain toward law enforcement, but then I got a good look at the illustration, which made his bestial sexual preferences exceedingly clear. At that point, all I wanted was away from these people, and quickly. So I started moving through the crowd, looking for signs of the feral cats who had abandoned the Dumpster near the screaming drunk.

The smell of cigars and marijuana grew more intense. I began to feel dizzy but also stubborn about completing my self-appointed mission. I would not flee in the face of these monsters. I would stay and talk to the cats, damn it; I didn't care how many smelly, sweaty, tattooed drunks I had to push through. So, I pressed on in spite of my growing light-headedness.

It was freaky—all of it—for a small-town girl who avoids crowds. But it got worse the further I went into the fairgrounds. I was Alice down the rabbit hole. I'd expected some psychological friction while attending this event. Four years is a long time to avoid crowds, and there would have been assimilation problems even with the well-heeled crowd at the opera, but this was far worse than anything I anticipated. It seemed to me that in the last half of a decade, society had devolved into something hateful and dangerous that respected nothing, not even itself.

Oddly though, the mental aspects of contact with the multitude turned out to be the least of my woes. The thing that pushed me to the borderline of hysterics was the presence of these physical freaks who had invaded our town and seemed to be pulled to me like metal filings to a magnet. For instance: the lady beside me at Shane Dwight's dance party. She wore one open-toed shoe and one sneaker. The open-toed shoe showed off her toes—which were mixed up. The big toe was in the middle, the little piggie where the big toe should be. The nails were a thick yellow like sheep horn and twisted out into claws. And she wore a ruby class ring on the big toe. I can't tell you how wrong that looked. God only knows what was in her sneaker. Maybe a cloven hoof. I tried not to stare, but didn't want to make eye contact with her because she kept chanting fuck-you-fuck-you-fuck-you and making small stabbing gestures with her hand.

And then there was this woman at the dance party with the fattest ass in the world. Think of the biggest you've ever seen and then double it. Normally, this would have moved me to pity and concern for her health, but she wasn't just a butt—she was an asshole. Her idea of dancing was to bend over and bounce her behind off people, and laugh when they toppled over or shrank away in disgust. Being laid out by a stranger's ass would have been horrible enough, but she was wearing short shorts that were just gobbled by her flesh until gone. In thirty seconds it was like she was in a G-string. And then nothing but dreadlocks of pubic hair and a tattoo on one cheek that said SLIPPERY WHEN WET. And she was absolutely slick with sweat. She touched me once. Ewww. I pulled a sharp pencil out of my fanny pack and prepared to defend myself as I scrambled for safety over the folding chairs at the front of the stage. The three people on the end row seats behind me also fled from her—and who could blame them? That crack could swallow someone's head! Sorry, that was rude. But really, beyond a certain size and age (and species) you just don't need to be rubbing your butt on strangers. I really hoped Atherton wouldn't say anything about my smell when I got home. I knew I would have to shower immediately or risk offending him.

In my haste to escape the Butt that Ate the World, I collided with another person. At least, I think it was a person. It might have been a demon come up from hell for the day to do a little recruiting. Unable to help myself, I actually ran away from the man who had done something that looked like Trapunto to his face. On a quilt, the raised embroidery would have been lovely, but in flesh? He had his eyelids pulled back so far that they didn't close completely when he blinked. He had also filed his teeth to sharp points. The thought of the pain involved in filing those teeth made me want to vomit. His skin also had a horrible pallor reminiscent of jaundice. I am certain that this man was carrying some terrible disease.

I saw another boy so full of facial piercings that he actually jingled like a Christmas sleigh when he walked. He, too, looked pale and unwell, and his eyes were as empty as those I'd imagined in the dust devil.

Now I'll be really despicable, and you can know the very worst about me and hate me if you must. Someone had the bright idea of bringing in a busload of blind people to the show—an excellent notion, and one which our town has always supported: We are absolutely handicap accessible and make sure all our musical events are friendly to persons with physical challenges. But this group came with only one seeing guide, and the noise level made spoken instruction impossible. So they had to form a conga line of the blind about thirty people long. Each show and at every stage, they gave them front row seats. Why? They were blind! The noise in these small venues is the same—that is to say, deafening—front or back. Why inconvenience the whole crowd who settled in early by making them move at each performance— folding chairs, blankets, coolers, umbrellas—when there were plenty of seats at the back? But the powers that be did it anyway. And thus the poor group stumbled through the increasingly intoxicated crowd, turning ankles—both their own and those of the people they trod on. The guide was oblivious: a case of the deaf leading the sightless, perhaps. Only a severe hearing impairment could have kept the guide from noticing all the rude comments and threats from the crowd. It was obvious that many of the blind visitors heard what was being said, and were troubled, but they were at the mercy of their stupid leader and could only stumble on and hope that human goodwill would prevail. I was afraid that it might not, and seriously considered calling Tyler. But what could I say that would sound reasonable? There were security guards around and no one had actually done anything violent.

For the final touch of madness at this event, proof that the way to hell is indeed paved with good intentions, the organizers had learning-disabled children there picking up trash in an effort to keep the fairgrounds clean. A nice thought, supposing one thinks ear-damaging music, drugs, booze and public fornication is wholesome entertainment for impressionable minds. As I have said, public service for all citizens is a sound idea in theory, but these kids had their instructions to keep the fairgrounds clean drummed into their brains, and being unable to improvise or adjust to unexpected situations, they tried to take away food and drinks before people were done eating them—and then cried and wailed if there was a fuss. Sheesh. After a couple close calls with these crying kids, the cats had fled entirely.

Exhausted, I fled too. I tried following the ferals down to the creek, calling out questions, but all they said in answer to my questions was: *Food man is dead! Food man is dead!* I finally lost a sandal heel on the muddy bank overgrown with kiss-me-by-the-gate. No great loss. It was the shoe the stupid drunk had thrown up on;

I was tossing the footwear anyway as soon as I got home. Still, it made walking a difficult affair.

The fairground cats didn't seem to know anything much, I assured myself as I limped toward home, avoiding the broken glass of discarded beer bottles at the side of the road, tossed by the disdainful visiting litterbugs. And, I added sternly when I heard myself sniff, I should be saying prayers of gratitude that the only thing I had wrong with me was the ability to hear cats talk. I could have ended up a drunken jerk with facial embroidery and mutilated teeth who clearly had massive self-esteem issues and probably a failing liver.

Feeling grumpy and cheated out of a tri-tip sandwich, I stopped off at Pop's BBQ and Mexican Food, and ordered a sandwich with extra chipotle sauce.

I had barely planted my butt on the duct-taped upholstery of a back booth before a fresh assault on my nerves began. I made an effort to be nice since she was one of our own and probably new on the job, but realized I was suffering from something very close to what I call irritable book syndrome. Realizing that my nerves were overloaded from the festival and that I might actually crack if I stayed much longer, I shouted to Dotty Brighton to please make my order to go.

For those of you who aren't writers and don't understand what I mean, irritable book syndrome is the state you achieve when a book is coming to you like a core dump from beyond, and your muse won't shut up long enough for you to get through a meal without scribbling rough paragraphs on your napkin or the palm of your hand. And then, when your fingers and brain are on fire and you are ready to start typing what will be the masterpiece of the century, the phone begins ringing—and it's people you thought you'd trained not to call during the day unless they needed an immediate kidney transplant. Or, worse, it's computerized voices that want you to switch to MCI, shop the no-tax sale at some department store, or offer you a supposedly free vacation in Cabo San Lucas so you can learn about real estate possibilities. *Congratulations! You've been selected to receive a year's subscription to* Urine Donors Daily—*just press 2 now! Do you need to speak to a representative about financing?—Press 8 now! Would you like to disconnect this call? Stay on the line for our next available representative.*

And then neighbors drop in to visit—though they never have before—and even when you stare pointedly at your watch and tell them you are really busy, they just won't shut up and go away. They invite themselves to lunch.

Good Lord! I love living in a small town where we know each other, except when I'm wrapped up in my own thoughts and trying to bring order to the chaos in my brain. Which is a lot of the time. Then it just makes me feel guilty for wanting to be left alone. I sometimes wish it was possible to get a meal, a haircut, and grocery shop without everyone you know wanting to chat, because no matter what they are saying—"Look! I've cut my throat and I'm bleeding to death." Or, "My daughter just gave birth to Bigfoot's baby." Or "My sister, the crack whore, is out on probation"—it just isn't as compelling as what's in my head. And it offends and hurts them when I fail to listen to the details and make the correct response.

Of course, this time it wasn't a book that had my attention, it was a crime. But the same kinds of feelings were coursing through me and I wanted desperately to be left alone so I could brood.

Fortified with an appetizer of stale chips and salsa, I began mulling over everything I knew and suspected about Irv's murder. I was deep in thought, doing total eye aversion with everyone, hands over the sides of my face, scribbling on my napkin with my mercifully clean pencil that hadn't ended up in someone's butt. Basically, all body language saying I was busy and to leave me alone—and the stupid waitress wouldn't go away. Becky, her tag said. She was new and eager. *Here's an extra fork for salad. Not having any salad? Well, then, more salsa? Oh, you have plenty! Let me wipe that table. Your order is to go? More salsa, then? Perhaps a Coke? Dessert? More of that salsa you didn't want five minutes ago? Well, how about some chips to go with the salsa you don't want?* I finally turned to ask her point-blank to please give me a few minutes alone. It was after one o'clock by then, and the place was empty. They didn't need the table for someone else, so this wasn't an unreasonable request. I guess my face scared her because she backed up and quit smiling. I felt like I had just kicked a kitten, but didn't apologize in case it encouraged her to come back to try being friendly again.

Dotty, Pop's widow, came over with my order then, all bagged and ready to go. She is better at reading body language than Becky is, and having seen me in this state before, she didn't detain me with small talk. I paid the bill, left a tip, and hurried for the door with the re-grouped Becky still at my heels. No, I didn't need extra forks or salsa to go, but thank for asking.

I all but ran home. My hands were shaking as I unlocked the front door of my house. I began to think that I should put myself back in quarantine for the duration of the investigation, but knew that wasn't reasonable. Maybe Sherlock Holmes could solve crimes from his armchair, but I wasn't that good. And, little though I liked it, some part of me had woken back up and, if I didn't get away from the computer occasionally, someone would eventually find me dead, wrists slit, covered in cobwebs and the screen filled with gibberish:

ALL WORK AND NO PLAY MAKES JILLIAN A DULL GIRL.
ALL WORK AND NO PLAY MAKES JILLIAN A DULL GIRL.

ALL WORK AND NO PLAY MAKES JILLIAN A DULL GIRL.
ALL WORK AND NO PLAY MAKES JILLIAN A DULL GIRL.
ALL WORK AND NO PLAY MAKES JILLIAN A DULL GIRL.
ALL WORK AND NO PLAY MAKES JILLIAN A DULL GIRL.
ALL WORK AND NO PLAY MAKES JILLIAN A DULL GI

Of course, that might happen anyway if I didn't get a grip on myself. I couldn't let normal human contact make me so crazy. I had to be able to deal with chatty waitresses and hot dog vendors and clerks at the grocery store. If I couldn't, I would end up in a trailer in the middle of the Nevada desert, a hundred miles from the next human being.

Atherton was waiting for me in the kitchen. He didn't say anything as I dropped the sandwich on the counter and rushed for the shower, and I didn't volunteer anything except, "People touched me and I have to go wash." I knew he would understand that. He didn't care for stranger-stink on his body, either.

After I was scrubbed and my clothes were flung in the washing machine, Atherton and I sat down for some lunch. He liked the tri-tip, but not the soda, which made him sneeze when he sniffed at the can. He told me that he couldn't taste anything except vague bitterness anyway, and I recalled that cats don't have the ability to experience sweet flavors. What a loss—life without dessert.

Finally able to relax, I found myself telling him about the festival and confessing to him about my frustration with the lack of physical evidence that Wilkes had killed Irv. Atherton was likewise frustrated but suggested optimistically that perhaps Tyler would bring news with him when he came to Easter dinner. I let this idea calm me further. Tyler had resources and know-how that I didn't.

Cheered with the possibility of information to come and the soothing and sympathetic company, I asked Atherton if he would like to dye Easter eggs with me. As usual, he agreed to try something new, and climbed into to my herb box to watch me as I boiled eggs in pots of water with onion skins, carrot tops and beets. This is a slower way of dying eggs, since the eggs must sit for a lot longer than they do in commercial food dyes, but the colors are pretty and the veggies infuse the egg whites with a subtle but pleasant flavor. Atherton was especially intrigued with the green eggs, so I set one aside, telling him that would be for his Easter breakfast. I don't think he cared particularly about Easter, but he could tell that this ritual was making me feel better, so he went along with it.

He was less interested in watching me make a lemon meringue pie, except for the part with the rolling pin whose ancient squeaks attracted him, though not for very long. The sunny window was a nice place to nap, so he stayed in the kitchen while I made lemon curd and whipped egg whites into frothy peaks, occasionally cracking an eye and surveying the messy activity with sleepy approval.

That napping cat, without saying a word, made me feel much better. Soon I forgot about the dust devil and the violent freaks at the fair that I assured myself were neither kin nor kind.

The clever cat eats cheese and breathes down rat holes with baited breath.

—*W. C. Fields*

CHAPTER FOURTEEN

Tyler isn't the fashionably self-indulgent type who would show up late just to make a grand entrance and prove how important he is. Nor is he self-destructive. What he has in abundance is an old-fashioned social lubricant: good manners. In our neck of the woods the pleases and thank-yous keep society running smoothly. Though things have changed in other parts of the world, in our town, a bottle of wine or flowers is still an appropriate gift to bring to a dinner party. Tyler played it safe and arrived on time with both.

"How do you like your wine?" I asked. I felt excitement shoot up my body, starting with my semisensible but very fashionable two-inch heels and ending at my deep-conditioned hair.

"In a glass will do," he said smiling. "I didn't know the menu and figured we'd end up bending a few rules no matter what I brought."

I put the tulips in water and the wine on the counter. I didn't want to drink anything cold that would make my jaw lock and have me sounding like Yosemite Sam.

Tyler hung up his jacket on the wrought-iron tree by the door and we pretended to get comfortable in the living room. Maybe Tyler really was comfortable; I had too much nervous energy. Atherton sensed this and watched us carefully from the top of the wing-backed chair near the fireplace.

It seemed a good time to find out something about Tyler's musical likes and dislikes. As the first litmus test, I put on Tom Waits's *Closing Time* and skipped to the second track, "I Hope That I Don't Fall in Love With You." Waits's music is poetry and spins some strong spells with its lyrics. He's quirky and classic and that out-of-tune piano is both bluesy and dreamy. Not everyone likes him, though. Like the goat cheese appetizers I had on the coffee table, he's an acquired taste.

"Ah, so you're a fan of Mr. Waits? Makes sense." I didn't ask him to explain this comment. It sounded complimentary, and I let myself enjoy it without analysis. I had already done too much thinking—brooding—that morning, and it had tied my stomach in knots. It was time to begin taking things in at different level, where the emotions were a bit less bright and blinding. It would probably freak Tyler out if I started to sniffle over the last time Cal and I had done everything. It had been years now; he should be safe from such displays.

Of course, it was natural that I had thought a bit about Cal and the Easters we'd had together. Most were very happy; and if I had stopped there, it would have been fine. But I hadn't kept my thoughts to sweet reminiscences of jelly beans and Easter parades we'd marched in. I thought about the one where he'd been too ill to attend. And then I had actually started thinking about the future, a life where I had other jelly beans and parades with someone else—and kisses like the one Tyler and I shared—and that scared the hell out of me and made me feel disloyal.

Sound crazy? It is. You can't build a life on loving the dead to the exclusion of all others. Nevertheless, we sometimes do it, because the known loss is better than the unknown. When we love, especially for the first time, we're giddy and unheeding. We dive headfirst into deep emotional waters and swim without fear because love has given us all the tools we need—and that's wonderful until someone or something cuts your air hose and you discover just how far you've come from safety. Assuming you make it back to shore, your next invitation to take the plunge is going to cause some consternation no matter who you are. Frankly, I'm still not sure if it's more brave or foolish to consider wading out again. I mean, who in their right mind would ever love more than once?

But then, my Memory Lane has some bad speed bumps that other people don't have, so I tend to stay on the evenly-paved expressway where things are smooth and impersonal. This morning's detour to Easters Past had been a mistake.

I considered explaining all these thoughts to Tyler, but I decided that there was no need. First off, it was early days yet. No one was tossing around the L word. And anyway, he was also a survivor of the deep, cruel seas of loss and life's rocky roads of abandonment. That his marriage ended in divorce rather than death didn't mean he wasn't as cautious as I was about trying something again. He would be taking things slowly, too. Or so I told myself.

Still, a part of me despised myself for this fear and hesitation. Fear is the enemy of love. It is the enemy of all happy emotions. It makes us cowards. But I cannot deny that fear exists for a reason. It warns us of danger, and I had not forgotten this detail. I was weaker than I used to be—that was fact. While Cal lived I could always borrow from his determination. It's how I survived my parents'

deaths. I was reminded of his steel will whenever I
looked at the ring around my finger. And later I had
found that I could—for a while—borrow the strength
to face what was, and still is, an impossible thing. But
after the unthinkable actually happened and I was really
alone, my golden talisman didn't work so well. I was often frightened and felt that I lived in a universe that was
no longer friendly.

But, as the saying goes, sometimes the only way out is
through. I couldn't stay where I was, and going back
wasn't an option. I decided it was time to tell Tyler a
bit—just the tiniest amount—about what had happened
to me last autumn and to see how he reacted to my story
while we were only knee-deep in emotional tidewater.

"I was hit by lightning last October . . . on Halloween,"
I said, getting up to open the wine. I felt the need of a
bracer. Also, I wanted to check on the ham. I wasn't trust-
ing that ornery-tempered stove with an expensive piece
of meat. Murphy's Law applies to ovens, too.

I felt Tyler's gaze settle on me. Atherton's as well. It
was hard to know which was more surprised.

"I take it that you don't mean that metaphorically.
You didn't have some emotional epiphany like Paul on
the road to Damascus." Tyler joined me in the kitchen,
taking the corkscrew from my hand to open the wine. I
watched him deal efficiently with the cork and realized
how much I missed this ritual of opening a bottle of
wine and then sharing a home-cooked meal.

"Nope, I mean that literally. I even saw it coming.
The world changed color right before the bolt struck,
and I knew something bad was about to happen. The
warning wasn't a help, though, since there was no way to
avoid it. Lightning actually has a color. For me," I added
hurriedly. "I know other people don't see it as anything
but light, but I guess because of all those extra hues
the orange cone in my eye gives me, I did see it—and

believe me, it isn't a color you find even in the largest box of crayons. If I had to describe it . . . I'd call it neon bile. It should have flash-fried me, too, but for some reason it didn't. I got tossed backward about five feet into a tree and blacked out for a moment, but was fine otherwise. No burns. In fact, when I came round a couple moments later I got right up and started walking home. I was feeling fine except for"—*that outraged orange cat jabbering at me all the way to my door*—"the ringing in my ears. And the lockjaw. I guess my muscles must have spasmed. I couldn't open my mouth for a week. And I still have problems when it's cold or stormy, or anytime there is a rapid atmospheric change. I guess, though I didn't die, it also altered the way I look at the world. Having something like that happen out of the blue . . . well, it made me feel unsafe—put on some endangered species list. It's paranoid, but you start thinking that even nature has it in for you. I was already a bit of a recluse, anyway, and my sounding like a cartoon character every time it gets cold just made me worse. Weird, huh?"

"More than weird. You were damned lucky." Tyler's voice was mild enough, but there was buried feeling in it. "There could have been all kinds of terrible consequences. I knew a fireman who got hit by lightning down in LA. He was way up in a canyon when this storm moved in. It cooked his brain. There was nothing his buddies could do except call for a rescue helicopter. He was only one degree away from being a root vegetable when he arrived at the hospital."

"Poor guy. I know it can be bad. The only other person I know who survived a hit was Irving. I think it made him a bit weird, too." I left the topic for the time being. Turning from Tyler's concerned stare, I opened the oven door a crack and, when no fireball whooshed out at me, I bent down and peered at the ham and scalloped potatoes. The merlot and brown sugar glaze looked perfect and the potatoes had a lovely brown crust. A few more minutes and it would be ready. I muttered, "You just have to control yourself ten minutes more."

"What?" Tyler asked.

"Not you. I talk to the stove sometimes," I explained. "It's old and cranky and has to be coaxed along. If you don't say the magic word and plead sufficiently, it spits fireballs at you. I had it actually blow the door open when I tried to bake Christmas cookies last year. The repairman said it was a bunch of bad propane, but this thing has been trouble from the day we moved in. I've been considering having a shaman in to see if he can drive out the evil spirit that must live in its metal guts."

"I am all for the power of prayer, but I think maybe I better have a look at thing later and we'll save the shaman as a last resort," Tyler said, his brow knitting. "It probably isn't calibrated right. There is a difference between settings for gas and propane. Don't use it again until I have a look."

"Is there a difference?" I asked, pleased. "Makes sense. Oh, that reminds me, there is something I've been meaning to show you." I'd suddenly recalled Irv's nugget stashed away with the clove and nutmeg. I closed the oven door and accepted a glass of wine. Tyler must have looked in the cupboard while my back was turned and fetched the goblets. He was making himself at home and I didn't mind. I am not territorial about the kitchen.

"What is it? A leaky faucet?" he asked. "I'm good at plumbing things. Not so great with electrical." I could smell his aftershave and still really liked it, but tried not to be obvious about my sniffing.

"It's something of Irv's." I opened the spice cupboard and took out an empty baking powder tin where I had been keeping Irv's nugget wrapped in some cheesecloth.

I showed the gold lump to Tyler and told him how I had gotten it, though I was a bit hazy about when. The last thing I showed him were the pictures I had taken from Irv's hole in the wall.

"You think this came from one of the old mine shafts on Irv's property?" Tyler asked, turning the uneven lump over in his palm.

"No, you get ore out of mines. Irv had more what you would call coyote holes. Those are shafts that go down twenty or thirty feet until you hit bedrock. That's where the gold is because it's heavier than the other kinds of stone and accumulates at the bottom," I said, simplifying. "But lumps like this are usually found in stream beds. The thing is, like you, most people are kind of hazy about the difference between the mining and panning parts of the operation, and Irv's nephew might well have seen this—or other nuggets Irv had—and come to the same conclusion about them coming from a mine or some kind of a dry dig on the property."

"And this is why you believe that Wilkes killed Irv? Because he doesn't know the difference between nuggets from a stream and ore from a mine?" Tyler didn't seem impressed with the thumb-size nugget. I decided it was a good thing he didn't suffer from gold fever, but I couldn't quite comprehend how one could hold that much gold and not be a little excited.

"It's a lot prettier when it's shined up," I said. "And, yes, I think Wilkes killed Irv for some played-out coyote hole that won't yield up anything because it was picked clean decades ago. Look at the hanky. He had more nuggets in here. A lot more."

Tyler had a faraway look on his face.

"What?" I asked. "You're thinking something."

"I'm just thinking that it might be interesting to inform Wilkes about this fact. Just to see if the disappointment runs deep."

"And I would love to be there to see it." This wasn't a subtle hint.

"I'm sure." Tyler sipped his wine but made no promises about catering to my vengeful whims. I took the nugget and put the pretty lump back in the tin. Tyler didn't suggest I hand it over to Wilkes. He picked up the two photographs I had taken from Irv's hidey-hole.

"I can't tell what's in this pan. It might be nuggets but it might not."

"No, I can't tell for sure, either," I admitted. "The pictures are bad. But why would Irv shoot film of plain old dirt and rocks? And look, he only exposed two frames on this roll before he took it in for developing. Something in these photos is significant—or was to him. Otherwise, he'd have waited until he used the whole roll. Irv wasn't profligate."

"It's damned suggestive," Tyler admitted. "I'll keep these, okay? Maybe we can blow them up and get a better look at what's in them."

"Sure." I appreciated that he'd asked. We both knew that he didn't have to.

The timer gave a soft chime and I reached for the pot holders beside the stove. I lifted the small pot of baby artichokes and carried them to the sink, where I poured off the garlic water. I had found that a clove of garlic and a drizzle of olive oil made even the toughest 'choke soft and tasty. I had hesitated briefly over making my creamy salsa dip, since it has pepper fangs and claws and isn't to everyone's taste. But Tyler had stood up well both to garlic and gorgonzola cheese—not to mention really bad coffee at Don's place—so I figured he could handle it. Or would fake it like a good macho man and do his panting later when I wasn't looking.

"That smells delicious," Tyler said. "I never seem to find time for cooking these days. This is a real treat."

"For me, too. It's been a long time since I did anything

other than survival cooking." Like, since Cal got really sick. And I had missed it. I nodded at the pot holders beside the oven and said, "Would you turn the oven off? Give it a twenty count, and if there's no fireball rushing at you then pull out the ham, okay?"

"Sure. Do you want me to give it a last basting?"

"If you're feeling brave. The glaze is over there." I jerked my head at the counter by the window.

We prepared the last of the meal together, working as though we had done it a dozen times before.

The feast was a success. It's hard to go wrong with traditional foods. We ate through the courses in the breakfast nook rather than the dining room. The small wooden table and chairs were less comfortable physically but much safer emotionally.

We talked easily as we noshed our way through the well-dressed ham and spicy sides and then through small slices of lemon meringue pie. Atherton kept his distance while we dined, but I knew he was watching and listening to everything I said.

It turned out Tyler was an Ian Hunter fan; he also liked Sourdough Slim, the yodeling cowboy. Of course, everyone likes Sourdough in these parts. Not liking the king of cowboy accordion players is cause for a denial of residency in this county. It might even be a hangin' offense.

The conversation turned serious only once. Tyler mentioned having lunch with Nolan the next week and I warned him that it might be best if he kept our friendship quiet for the time being. "Nolan didn't like Cal, and therefore he doesn't like me."

"He didn't like Cal?" Tyler sounded surprised. I didn't blame him. Everyone liked Cal, and to go on hating him after he was dead was downright mean-spirited.

"He and Nolan locked heads when they were on the city council." I shrugged. "You know Nolan. If grudge-holding were an Olympic event, he'd be a gold medalist.

Don't expect him to be thrilled when he hears that we're involved."

"Nolan can be officious, but even he wouldn't dare bring this subject up. My private life is private." Tyler sounded confident.

I shook my head at his naïveté but said no more. Some things a person just had to learn on their own.

And there were some things a person didn't have to learn on their own! The cats had found out the identity of the Catholic car molesters. I told Tyler that rumor had it that it was the Wilson twins who had been getting up to mischief with the parishioners' automobiles. The twins always smelled vaguely of Vicks VapoRub.

"The little devils. I'll look into it tonight. I should be going anyway," Tyler finally admitted as the sun began to set, turning the living room windows to sheets of fiery glass. I knew that he was taking the six to two A.M. shift and needed to stop by his apartment to change into his uniform before he went to the station. "But let me help you with the dishes first."

"Don't bother. I'll do them in the morning."

"You're certain? It was always a rule in our house that the one who cooked didn't have to clean."

I smiled. "I like that rule. But I don't ask first-time guests to risk dishpan hands. The china has to be hand-washed, so it isn't a quick job." Also, Atherton was probably going to want to sample the leftovers clinging to the baking dishes, and I wasn't sure if this would offend Tyler's sensibilities. After all, his dead dog probably didn't have a lot of disgusting eating habits.

"Next time, then." Tyler leaned over and kissed me good night. After what had happened last time, I was prepared to be overwhelmed, but he kept it casual and brief. I wasn't deceived by this show of restraint. I was certain that mentally he had me stripped naked and spread-eagled, hopefully on a bed because I am not big on sex on hard furniture or in the great outdoors, and I had a sneaking suspicion that his thoughts often became manifest. Still, though his eyes were intent and his breathing a bit rough, he didn't push, and I gave him high marks for patience. His actions said: *See, I can wait until we're old enough to join AARP if that's what it takes. Hell, I can wait until we're drawing social security. I dare you to show that much self-control when you want something.*

"What are you thinking?" Tyler asked, his lips grazing my ear when I didn't immediately pull away.

"I'm wondering if I should keep you at tongue's distance," I said without opening my eyes. I could feel the rails on the back of the chair pressing into my spine. "It seems wisest. This . . . this dating thing is a hurdle for both of us. Though I have to admit that my hurdle is probably a bit higher than yours."

"And you're thinking it's a bad idea to just jump at the opportunity and see what happens?"

"Yeah, but I'm also having a hard time coming up with anything I'd like better." I could almost hear my grandmother scolding me for this admission—no woman but a fallen one could want a man that much. And none but an immoral idiot would admit this out loud.

"No need to rush. I can be as patient as you like," he said, telling me I had read his thoughts accurately. "Will I go down in your estimation if I admit that I find hurdles, even high ones, often surrender to coercion, and that I'd like to try some coercion with you? Only the nicest type, of course."

"I guess that remains to be seen," I answered. "Does coercion involve foreplay?" The chill that had been constant since Cal died was being driven back by Tyler's heat. I had been freezing to death, but suddenly there was lifesaving fire. Beautiful fire. Potentially dangerous fire. But backing away was difficult, though my mind said to beware. It would be even harder to back away if I actually gave in and let myself have Tyler.

"Foreplay? Always." Teeth grazed my neck and he made a soft sound. "Not to hurry you, since I've been bragging about my self-control, but have you decided anything about tongues and distances?" he asked. Tyler sounded amused, but something else as well. I didn't open my eyes to check his expression. In spite of his warmth, his breath on the side of my neck was giving me delicious goose bumps, and I wanted to feel, not see, what was happening between us.

"Decision? Just that I'm feeling reckless today." I turned my head, took a deep breath and made the first jump. I must have cleared the hurdle. The fall into the kiss was a headfirst, high-momentum freefall into brain-melting lust, but I had no fear as I did it. Sensing this, Tyler also threw caution to the wind and let himself plummet. The chair toppled backward as I stood up. We ignored the clatter as we swayed toward the living room, arms locked around one another.

Tyler's erection was a bit disconcerting when I leaned into him and found it there between us. I shouldn't have been surprised. Kiss, erection—they did tend to go together. I had just been enjoying a temporary amnesia that allowed me to forget that we were not innocents, and that kissing could and often did lead to actual sex.

"Do you have time for this?" I asked.

His laugh was soft. We sank to our knees on the living room carpet. That was good. I didn't want to go to the bedroom or anyplace that would remind me of Cal.

"Are you kidding? I'll find budget for Farland's overtime."

I let him lower me to the floor. The rest I'm not going to talk about.

* * *

The room was almost dark as he smoothed the hair back from my face and separated our bodies. I hoped my mascara hadn't run. It usually did when I perspired. At least I'd had the forethought to wear attractive panties. Not that there was much time for Tyler to see them.

"I've asked myself a hundred times what it is about you that I find so damned attractive," Tyler said. "And I still don't have an answer. In the end it probably doesn't matter. Some things just are what they are."

"It's my winning personality." I tried to keep it light. To either side lay my own Charybdis and Scylla: guilt at betraying Cal with another man, and fear of getting hurt again if I dared care for Tyler. I didn't want to slip off the narrow path where things felt momentarily safe and pleasurable.

"No. I don't think so." He tugged gently on my hair.

"My scalloped potatoes, then?" I suggested.

"No—nor your ass. Though that is world-class." I think I actually blushed. What are you supposed to say to a comment like that?

"I'm at a loss then," I said.

"I'm not."

And he was right. So what if he didn't know why he liked me, and I didn't know why I liked him? We could enjoy it without any deeper understanding. I rolled to face him. Our second time making love was more leisurely.

I discovered some things about Tyler that evening, among them that the three middle fingers of his right hand were marred by horizontal scars, a fleshly reminder that knives—especially when carried by twelve-year-olds hopped up on crack—can cut deeply.

The physical scars were the least of it, of course. He had lost much of the feeling in the tips, and had finally given up playing the fiddle because, though he might be willing to be second-rate, he wouldn't settle for third, and that was all he would ever be now.

Not sure what to say to this sad revelation made, I think, because it was dark, I finally suggested, "Perhaps you could follow your nephews' example and take up the tuba. I don't think a sensitive touch is required."

"God, no. There are too many of them in the family already," he answered, and then laughed. He reached up and turned on an end-table lamp. I could tell that confidences were over for the evening. The grin he wore when he turned back improved his looks at least five percent. That was about all the room there was for improvement, at least in my eyes. Tyler was growing steadily more attractive.

"I'm sorry I have to leave. The budget only has so much discretionary funds, and Farland will be wanting dinner," he said, finally glancing at his watch. His tone was chagrined.

"It's okay." And it was. Now that the hormonal shock wave had passed, I desperately needed some time alone to gather my scattered thoughts. And also to check on what I suspected was going to be a case of rug-burn.

"I'd like to take you to brunch tomorrow at the bed and breakfast in Knight's Crossing."

I was impressed. The only place to get brunch on a Monday was also the best place in the county—and priced accordingly. I considered making a token protest, but decided to go on being reckless.

"I'd love to have brunch with you," I said, smoothing my clothes back into place. We hadn't taken the time to undress completely and now I was grateful for it. Getting dressed is always a bit awkward after that first time, especially when someone is leaving immediately. Socks or panties or earrings—something always gets left behind.

"Good. I'll see you at nine tomorrow—rain or shine."

Tyler gave me a swift kiss as he finished buckling his belt and then he was gone, locking the front door behind him.

It took a moment for the last eddies of his cologne to disappear. I inhaled hard, enjoying each breath until they were gone.

"What the hell have I done?" I asked the stilling air.

Atherton had been a gentleman and excused himself when things turned passionate, and I found that I didn't like talking to myself even when my questions were potentially embarrassing. I could feel shame and guilt still hovering nearby, tugging at the thin leashes of compassion and reason that held them back. They were looking for an opening into my addled head where they could break in and feast at will on the conflicts there. But I had enough junk in my head weakening me already, so I refused to give them any opportunity to enter by dwelling on the fact that I'd had just had sex—protected sex, thank God—with a man that I barely knew, and that we had been in such a fever-sweat to get at each other that we hadn't bothered taking our clothes off. And now he was gone, and though I knew about the scars on his hand, I didn't know about other scars on his psyche . . . or even if he had hair on his chest. Or anywhere else.

Of course, on the bright side, I'd just had sex with a man I barely knew and we had been in such a fever-sweat to get at each other that we hadn't bothered taking our clothes off. Surely this was some kind of progress—at least movement from one ring of hell to another.

Suddenly I was ravenous.

"Atherton," I called, rubbing at my abraded backside, "would you like to try some ham and scalloped potatoes?"

I wish I could write as mysterious as a cat.
—*Edgar Allan Poe*

CHAPTER FIFTEEN

After Tyler left and I'd had my second dinner, I wandered the house, turning lights on and off, straightening chairs that didn't need adjusting, and generally feeling restless. I passed the refrigerator as I paced through the kitchen and noticed the school pictures of my niece and nephew—a year out of date, but at least I finally had them up.

Cal and I never had children. It wasn't even an option for us, and we'd had no regrets about this, not even at the end. And I had none now, because I knew I wasn't fit to have the molding of a child. What chance would the kid have with no dad and a mom who heard cats talking to her? No, it was best we'd never had any children. Still, there were days when I felt very alone, and that time was eddying by me and I had no way to mark its passage. Unlike my neighbors, I celebrated no graduations or birthdays or anniversaries except the one marking Cal's death, and that I would just as soon not remember.

Feeling a bit melancholic, I wandered into Cal's office, a room that I was half-heartedly converting into a spare bedroom—for whom, I couldn't say. I didn't want anyone to visit me. The job was taking forever because the cartons seemed intolerably heavy as I carried them from closet to desk, where I still expected to find Cal at work. It was probably the weight of history, the past—mine and Cal's—refusing to pass quietly into the long night of storage that led to the Salvation Army and then total oblivion.

I was standing on the median of the highway of life. Cal's memory was in one lane and Tyler in another, and I was balancing on a barbed wire fence between them.

"I need a sign, Cal. Tell me what you would do." I spoke to an empty room and, of course, no one answered.

Being at loose ends and wanting to keep the encroaching depression at bay, I opened another box and began going through the papers. This one was boring: copies of old tax returns. But in the bottom I found a treasure. It was a photocopy of the first story that Cal ever published. It was called "The Kiss."

Cal and I are—were—what you would call omnivorous readers. And we were the same in our writing. We did it all except novels, and I would have done those if there was better money in it. Cal's tastes were even more eclectic than mine, and one of the things he loved was romantic comedy. "The Kiss" was his first, and I thought best, attempt. The magazine he had sold it to had agreed with me and published it in their Valentine's Day issue six years ago.

I laughed softly as I pulled the yellowed pages from the box.

What is that? Atherton asked. He had followed me around silently, a sympathetic shadow as I paced the house.

"A story. Shall I read it to you?" I asked impulsively. "It's very good. My late husband wrote it."

Yes, please. Atherton hopped up on the desk and made himself comfortable among the piles and boxes. I've noticed that cats have a natural capacity for looking at-home almost anywhere.

"Okay. It's called 'The Kiss' and it's loosely based on his childhood when he was growing up in a huge city called Los Angeles." I pulled out Cal's old beanbag chair, now sadly deflated, and propped myself up against the wall.

I began reading aloud. My voice spoke the words, but my ears heard Cal talking in his familiar gentle voice. My heart began to ease.

"The Kiss"

My name is Steve Merriman and I'm eleven years old. I go to Darby Avenue Elementary School where I'm in the sixth grade. Today, March 11th, 1969, after school, I have to kiss a girl.

Now, you may be asking yourself how a guy can get himself in such a pickle that he's got to kiss a girl. In the movies I've seen and heard about, it happens all the time. It usually happens because of a confusing but funny string of events, and afterward the boy and girl are happy about it. The reason I have to kiss a girl is simple, and I'm not happy about it at all.

It all began today during recess. The sixth-grade guys were playing dodgeball on a sea of black asphalt the teachers call the playground. I haven't mentioned yet that I live in Los Angeles, in the San Fernando Valley, and that the only grass at my school grows out in front of the principal's office. You get in trouble if you step on that grass. So, instead of playing on grass, we have to play on black asphalt painted all over with lines to make boundaries for games like two square, four square, kick ball, tetherball, and my favorite game, *dodgeball. The playground also has hopscotch squares painted on it, but only girls play hopscotch, and when they do they like to draw their own squares with chalk they take from the classroom. The sea of asphalt, painted lines, and chalk lines stretch for miles in all directions—at least it seems that way, right up to the bungalows the principal keeps moving onto the playground to handle the new kids that show up every week. It's funny to think that as the school grows the playground shrinks.*

Another thing worth mentioning about the playground is that in the 110-plus degree heat of summer, you can see waves of heat being pumped out of the asphalt, making the school buildings, monkey bars, and surrounding houses shimmy like they're doing the hula. The asphalt becomes so hot that it melts the patches laid down over the cracks in winter, making pools of hot, sticky tar that'll sure ruin a new pair of Keds in a hurry. Take my word for it.

Anyway, I was about to tell you how this kissing thing got started. Like I already mentioned, I'm in the sixth grade, am what's called an upperclassman, but what I haven't mentioned is that I'm the biggest kid in the sixth grade and that all the other guys in school look up to me as their leader. Being a leader can be tough, and one good way to keep being a leader is to win at dodgeball. It was looking like my team was going to win again today, and I was slinging the ball really hard to make sure that's what happened, when something else happened instead.

It all began with a try at splitting Jimmy Pazooli's lip with a shot to the chops. My red rubber menace had some heat on it. Jimmy was a wisecracker, and it was time to remind him why it was best to direct his wisecrackery toward kids other than yours truly. I launched the ball using my catapult-sling technique—borrowed, with some important improvements, from a stupid game called cricket—and to my satisfaction saw that my aim was dead-on. Unfortunately, Jimmy was looking straight at me. He was prepared, and he was squirrely—and by that I mean quick. As the red sphere of death went whistling toward his kisser, he managed to drop to all fours. He was in time to have his hair parted by the passing shock wave and to avoid more serious damage. Maureen Keller wasn't so lucky. She was glancing my way, and therefore must have clearly seen the dreaded orb speeding toward her face, but she was not prepared and was definitely not squirrely. Her reaction to the ball could best be described as tortoise-y.

What happened next, happened quick. Only later was I able to replay it in my mind in slow motion to fully appreciate the magnitude of the disaster. The rubber ball hit Maureen high on the head, just above the left eye. The speed behind it made the ball seem to deflate on impact, turning it into a wide sheet of rubber that slapped down and wrapped itself around her head and ears like a mask. The mask then flew from her face as the ball's energy was converted into a sharp backward snap of Maureen's head, followed by her body when her head could go no farther. She went down like a felled tree, and would have received even more abuse from the asphalt if she hadn't been lucky enough to fall backward into the arms of Katie Wilcox, who fell on Cathy Spenser, and so on. A line of girls went down like dominos, receiving little harm beyond black asphalt smudges on their dresses and butts. Except Maureen. After the shock wore off, which also happened pretty quick, she started to wail.

I ran fast to Maureen's side, not just to help, but to shut her up, and here's why. As I already mentioned, I'm the biggest kid in the school, and in response to past accidents, I had already been warned by Principal Drake to take it easy with the smaller kids. Based on many past conversations, I knew the principal would believe me when I told him that hitting Maureen was an accident, but what about my intended target, Jimmy? Principal Drake was no dummy, and I had no interest in finding out whether rumors of a spanking machine hidden in a back office were true.

"Maureen, I'm really sorry," I solemnly offered. "Are you okay?" I slipped on my earnestly concerned face.

By this time, the domino girls were beginning to set themselves upright and take notice of the stains on their clothes. It was obvious that things were about to go from bad to worse when their voices joined in a piercing chorus of whining.

"My dress," said Cathy Spenser. "You completely ruined my Sunday dress!"

Her dress was pretty badly smeared, owing to the fact that Cathy had been at the back of the conga line and most likely bounced and slid the most when she hit the ground. Of course, my first thought was to point out that it served her right for playing dress-up for school. Fortunately, this probable troublemaker stayed buried in my mouth as additional voices sang out.

"Oh, I think you broke my backside, you stupid idiot!" Wendy Barns accused. Wendy Barns had a huge backside, which I doubt could be broken by a fall from an airplane. "You big jerk, you hurt Maureen!" Paula Sinclair bellowed, punching me in the shoulder—didn't hurt. And then came the real killer. "I'm telling!" Katie Wilcox threatened, hands on hips and turning to seek out the recess lady.

Holy smoke, I thought. I had to do something and quick. Having no time to think, I blurted out the first thing that came to mind, hoping to buy time.

"Maureen, I'm really, really sorry." This time I doubled the "really" part to show that I meant it. "I didn't try to hit you. It was an accident. Please don't tell!" I added in short bursts. Getting no response, I decided to go for broke. *"I'll do anything to make it up to you. Anything—just name it!"* I pleaded.

I really didn't expect this last-gasp effort to work, the previous concerned look and apologies having done no good. So, I was surprised when I heard Maureen stop crying. I guess the domino girls were surprised too, since the threats and attacks stopped and all eyes turned to Maureen—except Katie's, of course, which were instead turned my way, along with a look that said, *"Now you're going to get it, you big creep!"* Katie is just that kind of girl.

Maureen looked up from her lap. Although her eyes still pooled with tears, they were no longer filled with pain and anger. Instead, they hinted at confusion and a touch of curiosity in response to my offer. I wasn't sure that I didn't prefer the pain and anger. She brushed her hair out of the way and I could clearly see an ugly red bruise forming over a large portion of her face. She seemed to be mulling over her options, her eyes staring straight through me; then I guess she made up her mind, since she broke her stare and dropped her gaze back to her lap.

"You can kiss me," she offered timidly.

I blinked hard, then swallowed harder.

"What did you just say?" I asked, sure that I'd heard what she said but equally sure that I couldn't have actually heard what she just said.

"You can kiss me," she repeated, this time with confidence, returning her gaze to my eyes. I noticed that all confusion was now gone from her face, replaced by a look of stubborn determination. I found myself missing the confused curiosity.

At first, I didn't know what to say. After some thought, I still didn't know what to say. Being this close to her, what she'd just said, and the creepy look she kept giving me, all combined to make me feel antsy. It didn't help that the other girls started whispering and giggling, *then turning their heads back and forth between the two of us like picnickers watching an egg toss and hoping for someone to get yolk on their face.*

"If you really, really mean it, that you'll do anything, then today after school you can meet me behind the bungalows and kiss me," she said, restating her terms in greater detail and keeping me pinned on the tines of a wicked glare. I had to admit that it was pretty clever, throwing that repeated "really" thing back in my face.

Sometimes it's tough being a leader. For one thing, you need to know when to try new things and when to pass. Like the time John Patterson offered me a shiny, ripe, black olive picked fresh from the tree in his front yard. I didn't know that olives straight off the tree taste worse than dog poop. It just seemed like John was a little too eager to offer me a treat, being my brother Andrew's best friend and all. So I passed. After seeing Ricky Sayer's reaction when he finally gave in and chomped that shiny, black olive between his molars, I'd say I dodged a bullet that day. The only good part was that Mrs. Patterson saw Ricky gagging in her front yard and asked John what he had done. She boxed his ears good when he told her, and then took Ricky and me into her house for a cookie and a glass of milk. I still don't think this made it worth doing—Ricky didn't look like he was really enjoying that cookie a whole lot. And his tongue was black for a week. Anyway, I always say that you should never let a guy see you cry and never, ever let him see you puke—at least not if you want to be a leader.

"If that's what you want, then fine," I said flatly. "I'll meet you behind the bungalows right after school."

I remained crouching beside Maureen, returning her glare. Then I realized what I'd just said. I felt my stomach begin to cramp up and sweat begin to form on my forehead. I thought I was going to heave but we continued to glare at each other instead. I was sure that this stare-down would soon end with me passing out in front of everyone from the terror I felt punching me in the gut. Then Maureen up and ended it for me.

"Fine," she said, smiling and bouncing to her feet as if nothing had happened. She then turned and walked away across the playground, the rest of the girls following like a gaggle of geese, but looking back over their shoulders to blow me kisses.

What had just happened? Was she faking it? Did I really just say what I know I'd just said? Did I just get conned?

I was very confused and feeling very shaky. What a guy needs at a time like this is his friends to stand by him, to tell him everything is okay, and most important of all, help him figure out how to get out of the mess he'd just gotten himself into. Apparently sensing my need, the guys gathered around me and a raucous discussion was soon underway.

"Geez," my best friend Stanley Becker said to open things. "I mean, just geez." Admittedly, this was not the most brilliant contribution, but his statement did manage to convey a proper degree of concern and certainly summarized my thoughts. Most of the guys showed that Stanley spoke for them too by nodding, patting me on the back, and then bursting into laughter.

I was still stunned by what had just happened and by the fact that Maureen wanted to kiss me, especially after I'd hit her in the face with a scorcher. I knew she liked me but, as Stanley would say, geez! I think I first impressed Maureen by not getting involved when others started calling her Murine—that being the name of drops parents put in their eyes the day after bridge night, or just about any other night they stay up late and the kids are sent to the back rooms of the house. I mean, I agree that Maureen is a funny-sounding name, but I didn't see it as a big put-down getting tagged with the brand name of an eyedrop. After all, it isn't like they were calling her More Butt, or The Marine. Now, those are names you can have some fun with.

Anyway, after the others saw that I wasn't laughing, they seemed to get bored and laid off. I think Maureen saw that I was the reason they stopped, and that may be the reason she wanted to give me something now. To say thanks. But a kiss? Why not a Matchbox car or a neat marble she found on the way to school? Anything but a kiss.

"Steve, you can't do it," said Jimmy Satz, looking at me like I had just been condemned to the gas chamber. I returned a look that showed that I fully agreed, but threw my hands out to show that I didn't know how to avoid it, not wanting to be a welcher. I did the mime act because I couldn't speak yet. Jimmy acknowledged my dilemma with a nod, then got an excited look on his face and blurted, "Maybe you can kiss her but be wearing wax lips. I got a pair last Halloween."

It seemed to me that Jimmy was onto something with this advice. After all, using wax lips to kiss a girl made sense the way that a drop drill makes sense. Drop drills are something teachers make us practice once a week just in case the Reds decide to drop the big one on us. They involve dropping onto all fours, crawling under your desk, and throwing your arms over your head to protect yourself—and doing it all as quick as possible. And the teachers always holler at the kids about keeping their backs to the windows so flying glass doesn't get poked into their faces and eyes. Now, I view drop drills as a good thing; after all, if the Reds are in such a hurry to bomb my school, then I want to be ready for them. But I've always wondered how good a wooden desk could really be at protecting you from an explosion strong enough to knock all the windows out in your school. Heck, the Pattersons, who live three houses down from us, built a concrete and cinder block bomb shelter in their side yard to protect them from the big one. What chance did I have hunched under a flimsy, wooden desk? And besides, wouldn't there be other bad stuff going on if the commies did try to bomb our school? It seems to me that handing out guns might be a better way to protect ourselves from attack than learning how to climb under our desks fast. Anyway, the point is that I was willing to hear Jimmy out, but with what my dad calls reservations.

"Okay, Jimmy, I like your idea," I responded.

"Aw nuts," Jimmy interrupted before I had time to urge him on. "I think I ate my wax lips last week," he explained. I was crushed by the news. After a short exchange, round-table fashion, I found that no one else had a pair of wax lips and that this was the only plan that made any kind of sense that anyone could think of to avoid kissing Maureen. I hung my head in defeat and despair.

"You're gonna get cooties," said Henry Barnes, staring up at me with eyes that always looked too big for his head but now looked like they might pop right out. Henry is a second-grader, so technically he shouldn't speak directly to me. Instead, he should have given his two cents to someone in the third grade, maybe fourth, to be considered and then forwarded if it made sense. However, realizing that this breach of command structure probably had more to do with concern for my well-being than a need to challenge tradition, I decided not to give him a wedgie on the spot.

By the way, a wedgie is what happens when someone, usually someone a lot bigger and stronger than you, reaches down the back of your pants, grabs your BVDs, and gives them a yank. Depending on the seriousness of the reason for the wedgie, it can be used as a mild reminder or a major reprimand, actually lifting the target clean off his feet or even tearing the underwear if *they're an old, favorite, heavily worn pair. Depending on the hygiene of the guy getting a wedgie, the wedgie can cause a monster skid mark in the underwear that Mom can't even get out with Boraxo.*

One final note: It's worth mentioning that no one ever gives a girl a wedgie. I think this is either because no one wants to put their hand down there since they're afraid of what they might find, or because girl's panties don't work like guy's underwear so that you couldn't give a girl a wedgie even if you wanted to.

"There's no such thing as cooties, numbnuts," said Randy Smith in reply. Randy was the member of our group who was always coming up with neat new expressions he heard from his two older brothers, Hiram and Lenny. I had heard the numbnuts one before, and although I knew what nuts were and what could make them numb, I still wasn't sure what accusing a kid of having been kicked in the "family jewels"—another of Randy's expressions—had to do with anything.

In any case, Randy had in a roundabout way supplied support for my own feeling that cooties were like Santa Claus: fun to believe in but a bunch of malarkey. That word is a favorite of my dad's.

"He's right," I stated confidently. "There's no such thing as cooties." And with that, I turned away further discussion of the topic . . . only to be brought up short by my second best friend, Billy Moony.

"They do have The Siff," Billy announced.

All eyes turned his way. I knew I needed to regain control of the conversation fast.

"The Siff," I said in disgust. "What's that supposed to be?"

Billy seemed hurt by my response, but had obviously come prepared to defend his beliefs.

"It's something girls get on their lip from the toilet seat," he replied confidently.

"How do you get something on your lip from a toilet seat?" I asked.

Billy looked a little uncomfortable about my challenge, but then he explained.

"My oldest brother told me he got The Siff from either being with a girl or the toilet seat," he began. I accepted this as fact, but still felt like he had fallen short of a full explanation. Apparently Billy was only beginning to outline a string of well-thought-out facts because he soon continued. "He told me that being with a girl means kissing and stuff. So, he could have gotten The Siff off a girl's lip. Since girls don't kiss girls, that means that girls can only get The Siff from a toilet seat."

It took a while to mull this over, but in the end I couldn't argue with the facts as he'd laid them out. Besides, Billy always gets better grades in everything than I do. Also, I could tell when Billy was lying, and this time, he wasn't lying.

"So, how can you tell if a girl has The Siff?" I asked. "I mean, what does it look like?"

"I'm not sure, but it's supposed to itch and I think it doesn't smell very good," Billy responded, throwing up his hands to show that the well was now dry.

"So, all you gotta do is watch to see if she scratches a lot and pull back quick if she smells funny," Johnny Westbrook offered.

"That's no help," Alex Bateman replied. "All girls smell funny."

With this, an argument broke out. I lost track of what anyone was saying, but in the end was told that no one had seen Maureen scratching at her face and I should turn tail and run if I found out she smells worse than Eddie Randle's older sister's bedroom—a place Eddie and I sneak into to use her makeup to make realistic war wounds on our G.I. Joes.

It still didn't make sense that a girl could get

something on her lip from a toilet seat, but then I re-membered the time in fourth grade when Jimmy Bolton was thrown into the girl's bathroom. Jimmy is the smallest guy in our class and I guess it was just his bad luck to be walking past Mike O'Reilly the day Mike failed his math test. Mike hung out with a bunch of the bad boys in his sixth-grade class, and seeing Jimmy walk by, they decided to work out some of their anger by grab-bing him and chucking him into the john. Jimmy stayed in there a long time, at least long enough for the catcalls to end and the sixth graders to get bored and wander off. After he came out he seemed confused. I asked him what happened and that's when he told me: There are no uri-nals in the girl's restroom. Since they have to use the toi-let for everything, it seems to make sense that they are doing some strange stuff in there. Thus, whatever they're doing may result in lip-to-toilet contact.

At this point in the debate the bell rang, putting an end to both recess and further discussion. Although I felt that more information could only help, I was also pretty glad to stop talking and head back to class, disappointed that it took so little time to learn all that my pals knew about both kissing and girls. So, I joined the stream of kids marching back to their classrooms. Sitting down at my desk, I was without a plan and running out of time. But at least I would be running out of time slowly, since this would prove to be the longest afternoon of my life.

The hands on the clock across the room slowed to a snail's pace. School clocks don't have second hands, prob-ably to keep kids in predicaments like mine from simply watching the them go round while attempting to psy-chically speed them up—like Dr. Strange in that comic book. Time was definitely crawling.

Mrs. Hanson began the afternoon with spelling. I hate spelling, probably because I can't spell. To hear Dad talk about it, I would guess I inherited it from him.

Of course, my favorite part of any school day is when Mrs. Hanson reads to us from a book. We're currently doing Charlotte's Web, *which is kind of a girl's book, but pretty good anyway. It's about a talented, loving spider and a pig. I was excited to make it to the ending when we got to hear about Charlotte, the spider, and Wilbur, the pig, going off together to live happily ever after. Unfortunately, I was going to have to wait two more days, for Friday to arrive, before hearing the next installment of the story. In the meantime, I had to endure spelling along with waiting for the school day to end.*

I was glaring up at the clock, trying to psychically will it back to its normal speed, when Mrs. Hanson called on me.

"Stephen?" she asked, and from the tone of her voice I could tell that she already knew I hadn't been paying attention.

"Sorry, Mrs. Hanson," I replied. "I wasn't paying attention and didn't hear the question," I confessed.

Possibly due to the hangdog expression I was wearing, but more probably due to the fact that she had already caught word of my plans for this afternoon, Mrs. Hanson decided to take pity on me rather than read me the riot act.

"That's alright, Stephen," she replied, flashing me a really convincing concerned look of her own. Mrs. Hanson could sometimes be unexpectedly kind. "It's obvious that you have important things on your mind. So, we'll move ahead to Joey Beckman," she continued, finding a new victim to drag from his daydreams into her dreary world of words.

Of course, being left out of the spelling and vocabulary milieu—which proves that I've paid enough attention to pick up some pretty big words along the way—also left me to stew in my own juices. And boy, did I stew. As I came to terms first with the fact that

I was indeed going to be kissing a girl in a little under an hour, I then found that I needed to consider just how to go about it. I mean, I didn't want to come off like a complete ignoramus in front of Maureen and who knew how many other kids. As I started considering the finer points of kissing—whether and where I should touch her, how long to kiss her, whether to wet my lips first, and if so how wet, and if not, what to do if our lips stuck together—I felt my intestines seize up, and I wondered if I would need to emerge from my comfy classroom exile to beg permission to run to the bathroom.

Uncoiling my legs from around the legs of my chair, I was preparing for a potential dash when I noticed first that I'd had my legs tightly coiled around the legs of my chair, and second that my heart was racing like a stallion running the Kentucky Derby. (Dad's phrase again.)

I tried to steady my heart, but the more I tried I realized I just wasn't going to pull it off. I would never have admitted this to another guy, but had to admit it to myself—I was excited. I was curious about what it would be like to kiss Maureen. I was scared that I might not do it right. I had short fantasies of sweeping Maureen into my arms like in the movies and then leaving her yearning after me as I went off to war. I wondered if she'd taste good, like candy, or bad, like liver. In the end, I wondered if she'd like it or hit me in the face after I was done.

I was pondering all of these thoughts, and many, many more, when all thought was suspended by the sound of the bell tolling the end of the school day. I could have sworn I heard the class share a collective intake of breath, but realized it was probably just me gasping for air. I noticed that this day had not ended with the typical excited talk of kids waiting to be dismissed, and looked around to find all eyes turned my way, even Mrs. Hanson's.

"Class dismissed," Mrs. Hanson announced, sounding

like the voice of doom. I rose from my seat on legs of rubber, and was glad to feel a hand slip under my arm to steady me. I turned to find Jimmy at my side. He guided me like a blind man out of the room and back onto the playground where this whole stupid mess had begun.

Once more on dry ground, I soon found my land legs and started to walk. I rounded the corner of bungalow 12B to find what looked like the people on either side of a street waiting for a parade to pass. What boys weren't already following me lined one side of the alley between the bungalows leading to the far corner of the school grounds. The girls were all on the other side. I was expecting cheers and confetti to start flying any time. But as I walked through the crowd, instead of cheers, I heard nervous laughter and whispered words; instead of confetti I saw anxious looks of concern and disbelief. I guess the kids who had stopped by to see the show were surprised that the lead hadn't decided to take a powder.

Assuming that Maureen was most likely already waiting for me, I led my posse to the farthest bungalow on campus, 13A, intending to continue behind it to meet my fate.

"No," a voice announced to accompany an outthrust hand. "Only Steve may pass." It was Margaret, of course, Maureen's right-hand girl.

Margaret Slizbury was large, smelled bad, and had the beginnings of a mustache. She was the kind of large that's just short of fat. She wore thick, black, plastic-rimmed glasses and had black, frizzy hair that came down to her shoulders, making her look like the sphinx. And she was strong. We found out how strong she was the day she got tired of being teased by Freddy Shultz and decided to throw him down and sit on him until his face turned purple. I figured I could take her, but it would hurt.

Turning back to my buddies, I indicated that they

should stay behind rather than rushing Margaret and pinning her down while the rest of us passed. I wanted to avoid any unnecessary violence; there'd already been enough of that, and besides, I didn't think that an audience would help with what needed to get done.

Taking a deep breath, I put one foot in front of the other and ended up walking around the bungalow into the secluded alleyway formed by the building I'd rounded and a large oleander bush growing along the fence marking the edge of the school grounds. Someone once told me that oleander is poisonous, which made me wonder why you could find it growing at every school I'd ever visited. Looking up, I spotted Maureen about ten paces ahead, midway down the alley. I cleared my throat and she twirled to face me.

The dress she wore, I only just noticed, was white and had little flowers on it. Although stained in several places with black smudges, especially in the back, it was pretty. She wore short white socks, with a decorative fringe on top, which were folded down to make them even shorter. These socks rode within a pair of nicely polished black, patent-leather shoes in which I felt I should be able to see my own reflection. Her golden hair was pulled back away from her face and gathered in one of those springy hair things. The left half of her face was covered by a barely visible purple stain that looked like a birthmark. It was where I'd hit her. When I saw this, the fascination I felt in examining her gave way to shame, and I felt my own face turning red.

I walked forward to get closer and she shyly looked down at her feet as I approached. I stopped in front of her, and she looked back up with a smile that made me smile in return.

"Hi, Stephen," she said, using the formal version of my name like she was one of my teachers.

"Hi, Maureen," I replied.

"I didn't think you were going to show," she said, cocking an eyebrow to show her curiosity.

"Neither did I," I found myself confessing.

I was surprised that she seemed so calm, considering the situation. Then, as she walked over to toy with an oleander blossom, she explained.

"You don't have to worry, Stephen," she began. "I'm not actually going to make you kiss me."

"You're not?" I asked, a little shocked. I was also shocked that it was actually possible to feel both relief and disappointment at the same time.

"No," she said smiling back at me. "That's why I decided to meet you alone. We only need to wait a few minutes, then walk back out and tell the others whatever we want them to believe."

Wow, this girl's mind had a seriously devious streak running through it. It's like I told Billy Sayer after he got back from a route I sent him on to catch a long bomb behind a parked car for a touchdown: Sometimes you've got to be tricky to get what you want. Maureen was apparently quite tricky. Her stock had just jumped several points in my books.

"Yeah, you're right," I answered. "That's a really clever idea," I had to admit aloud.

Maureen's smile broadened as she walked back to stand next to me.

"Although I should make you pay for putting this ugly purple splotch on my face," she said. "Maybe pin you down and give you an Indian rope burn. Isn't that the standard price for such an offense?"

"Yeah, that would be about right," I admitted as we shared a laugh. I couldn't believe how quickly a person's world could change. A few moments ago, I had been afraid I was going to puke, and even more afraid of this girl standing beside me. Now I felt great and was really beginning to like her a lot.

"Well, that's probably enough time," Maureen said, beginning to walk to the corner of the bungalow. "Let's go show our faces and tell our tales," she concluded.

"Maureen," I said, stepping up to her as she stopped, then forgetting what I was going to say. "Thanks," I offered as the obvious choice, then added something a little closer to what I was really feeling. "You know, you're alright."

This last statement seemed to please Maureen, since it brought a huge smile to her face. I liked that smile a lot, and I wanted more.

"Maureen," I began, then simply decided to go for broke one more time.

What happened next happened even quicker than the dodgeball fiasco, but in this case I knew that what was happening was something I'd replay many times in slow motion for the rest of my life. I grabbed Maureen by the shoulders and pulled her to me, surprised at how light she was in comparison to any of the guys. She seemed a little shocked and scared, but I didn't have long to check on her expression as my face moved quickly toward hers. I was pleased that I had the intuition to turn my head sideways to avoid a nose collision. Then our lips were touching. I continued to press my lips against hers and was at first concerned by the rigidity of her response, but then felt her relax as both our lips parted slightly to more fully experience the contact. Her lips felt good, and she sure didn't taste like liver. Of course, she didn't taste like candy, either. She tasted different, but really, really good.

I have no idea how long we remained with our lips together. At first I thought that I wanted the kiss to last forever, and then I started to feel self-conscious. I began to wonder if I should be moving my lips, or my head, or squeezing her tighter. Guessing that I had probably reached the point at which the spell had been broken, and finally understanding what that meant, I gently pushed Maureen away, causing our lips to part. I then felt the muscles of my face tense in preparation for getting hit, but Maureen didn't seem to be paying any attention to me. Her eyes were still closed and she was rocking slightly on her heels. Her tongue poked out of her mouth to lick her lips, like she was getting a tasty bit of sauce off her mouth after spaghetti night. Then she opened her eyes and smiled real hard. I felt her grab my hand and was afraid I was in for another lip-lock, but instead she simply squeezed it twice before turning to run around the corner of the bungalow. She never said a word and didn't even look back. Just like that, it was over.

My name is Steve Merriman and I'm eleven years old. Today, after school, I kissed a girl. They say that being a leader is hard, but being a follower is even harder. I don't know much about that, but I do know that I plan on doing a lot more kissing in the future. It isn't always easy, but it needs to be done.

Jillian, why are you crying? Atherton was at my side, a paw resting gently on my arm. Without thinking, I reached out and stroked his head. He let me do this, perhaps even enjoyed it though I could feel his concern for my sudden shift in mood.

I reread the last paragraph to myself.

"Am I crying?" I finally asked, finding this odd because I was also smiling. I touched my lips, still tender from Tyler's last kiss. "I . . . This is hard to explain. I think it's because my husband just told me that it's okay to get on with my life. He's saying it's all right if I see Tyler."

And you want to do this, don't you? You like the sheep man.

"Yes, I think I do."

If Atherton had been human, he would have nodded. I think he was dubious but he wanted me to be happy.

Will you tell Tyler about me? That I talk to you?

I hesitated, taking time to wipe my cheeks dry while I considered this question. It was a tough one. I was still suffering from regret for not being open and honest with Cal at a time when he needed me, for shying away from the pain that honesty about his chances of survival could bring. And hadn't I decided that the pain of regret was worse than confronting the truth, however hard? Yet being completely honest in this situation . . .

"I don't know," I finally said. And that was the truth. I wanted to, but I didn't know if I would. It would be asking a lot from a very young relationship, especially when Tyler was such a logical, unfanciful man. The best I could do was promise: "I will never do anything that would hurt you or the other cats."

And we would never hurt you, Jillian.

When I play with my cat, who knows if I am not a pastime for her more than she is to me?
                                    —*Michel de Montaigne, Essays, 1580*

CHAPTER SIXTEEN

In most places, the Stanislaus River runs rather fast and is not especially scenic, but right near Knight's Crossing it slows down and widens out into something that looks like it should be feeding the Mississippi. You know what I mean? It's the sort of stream you see in the South, perhaps in Arkansas—snags of deadfall, giant old trees with limbs trailing in the peaceful water. While Tyler got his hat from the car I sat on a broad stone and stared at the pastoral scene with sleepy eyes. Letting breakfast digest at a leisurely pace, I didn't attempt to think about anything in particular, except that I liked Tyler's after-shave and it was nice to hold hands with someone again, even it was under the breakfast table.

There were the occasional golden leaves floating by—like faerie boats—and you could see the young fish darting about in the clear lazy water that lapped in the shallows. Pale blue butterflies lined the grassy banks that rolled down to the stream, and small birds bathed in the miniature pond whose banks were woven of tree roots. I don't know what plant was growing at the bottom of the river, covering it like a carpet, but it looked like a vast garden of thyme swaying to unheard music. I wouldn't have been at all surprised to see a mermaid swim by.

"Ready?" Tyler asked. I looked up at him and was a bit amused and dismayed to see the orange paper in his hand. They had them at the visitors desk in the lobby. All our hotels and parks have displays of such pamphlets and flyers. We like to make things very easy for the tourists. "It looks like they have a lot of interesting things out here," Tyler said enthusiastically.

"Lots," I agreed.

Tyler read out loud. The pamphlet from visitors center said that people fished for salmon here and I could believe it. Salmon fishing has always seemed rather peaceful to me, especially when Tyler read about it in his slow deep voice. They also had some interesting stories about the ruins of the old mill destroyed in a flood—a haunted place, if the pamphlet was to be believed—and the old covered bridge we had just crossed. According to the flyer, its three hundred and thirty foot length is the longest west of the Mississippi. I believe that. In spite of Tyler's large hand, all I could think about was how the old planks might give way under me, dropping me onto the giant boulders far below, cracking my leg bones and maybe my spine. I made the walk across because Tyler wanted to, but I was fighting vertigo—and rebelling eggs Benedict—the whole time.

We didn't talk much that morning. Perhaps neither of us knew what to say about what had happened the night before. But on the far side of the bridge, I broke the silence and suggested that we take the long way around back to the parking lot. It wasn't scenic, but it would aid my digestion. It was also where the ferals hung out. I didn't try and question them with Tyler there, but I felt that I needed to check up on them and see that they had enough food. They all seemed fit, but I was both delighted and sad to see the new generation of kittens. They were so darling—and so damned if they weren't trapped and given a chance to bond with humans while they were young.

We strolled slowly, our eyes mostly looking upward, not wanting to miss the osprey nests in the cedars at the edge of the pond, but we frequently got distracted by the amazing display of wildflowers encroaching on the trail—Chinese houses, fairy lanterns, twining lilies, and I think all eighty-one varieties of California lupine. There was also a truly lush paradise of poison oak that the deer had been eating in spite of it being poisonous. The whole morning was so beautiful and our path so exquisite that I came away feeling truly blissful and with a feeling that all would be well. It had to be, on a day that perfect.

Possibly it affected Tyler differently, since the scenery was somewhat foreign after his years in the concrete jungles of LA. I noticed that he seemed more energized than meditative. In fact, he sometimes seemed downright distracted, his brow occasionally furrowed. I thought maybe it was the lack of sleep and all the coffee he'd had at breakfast. But I saw him smile as he looked at the lake and the sky, with its solitary eagle-shaped cloud, and knew he was present enough to appreciate at least some of the wild beauty.

"You really like it here? I mean, in Irish Camp?" I asked. "It isn't too . . . slow for you? There's not much to do except watch the flowers bloom and chase big fish in slow creeks."

Tyler looked down at me. "How could I not like it? The Sierras in early April. I had no idea it was so damned beautiful. I've got to get my family up here for a visit. My sister would love it."

His family Here. I was a bit startled, but then thought, well, why not? They were probably nice people.

"We'll have to hike in Yosemite. Another couple weeks and the flowers will be at their peak. That is a sight that shouldn't be missed," I said. This took a bit of courage, suggesting that we would still want to hike together two weeks from now. I was proud of myself for being so brave.

Tyler turned his smile on me. He settled an arm over my shoulders. I had the feeling that public displays of affection were as difficult for him as they were for me, not because of any puritanical streak, but because he was a private man and didn't necessarily want to share our very new relationship with the wider world. Still, a part of me wanted to reach beneath his shirt and touch everything I hadn't gotten to see the night before—and to hell with anyone who might be looking. I had gotten past the shame and guilt of being intimate with anyone but Cal. The rest of the town held no terror for me.

"I'd love that. Is the park open on Tuesdays? That's my day off. If the weather is nice, we could go then."

"I think so. I can check." I leaned my cheek against him. He was wearing my favorite aftershave, and I let myself breathe deeply. I felt a light kiss on the top of my head and he tucked a strand of hair behind my ear.

"Thanks," he said. I think he meant this for many things.

Tyler was back on duty at noon, so we bypassed the walking tour of the mill and headed back for his Jeep. He is too disciplined a driver for us to hold hands while he was behind the wheel, but he made no objection to the hand I rested on his leg just above his knee. There was a homey peace about the ride back.

I tried to work after Tyler dropped me at home, but I didn't have much luck. I finally gave up attempting to write an outline for my piece on feline leukemia and went to make a pot of tea. The barometer was falling again and I wasn't feeling inspired. Instead I sat on the sofa, sipping Darjeeling and doodling on my notepad, hoping that my scribbling would give me some clever new insights that would lift this sad story of feline casualties above the mundane warnings and into something that would provoke people into action.

What are you doing? Atherton asked, watching my pen wiggle back and forth as I sketched the limbs of an oak tree. I've noticed that scratching sounds intrigue him, especially if he can't see what's making the noise.

"I'm drawing," I said. "Making a picture of a word."

Why?

"Because I don't want to write about death yet."

Oh.

"Would you like me to draw you?" I asked impulsively.

Atherton thought about this.

Yes, he finally said.

"Okay, just sit still for a moment." I turned to a clean page and began drawing. The picture wasn't as good as one done by a trained artist. In fact, it was a bit cartoonish, but I thought it a fair enough likeness.

"There," I said finally, turning the pad so he could see it. "What do you think?"

Atherton stepped closer, walking gently down the back of the sofa. He sniffed the drawing, recoiling a bit at the scent of the wet ink. He raised his left paw as if to touch the picture but then put it back down.

The color is almost right, I think. But it doesn't smell like me. And I am not flat.

"No, you're not," I agreed, amused. "But if I showed this to another human, they would know it was you. Even without the right smell."

Humans don't have very good senses, do they?

"No, we don't have much sense at all," I said, thinking

of Tyler and how I was mooning over him instead of working. I turned the sketchpad back. "Let me draw something else."

I added a mouse to the picture. It wasn't as good as my drawing of Atherton, since I had no model, but any human would have known what it was.

I turned the pad back toward Atherton. "There. What's this?"

You're trying to draw a mouse, aren't you? he said kindly. *The face is good, but the back legs are wrong.*

"Oh." I squinted at my picture. "I'll take your word on that. You've probably seen more mice than I have."

Probably. But your pictures are very nice. If you can learn how to draw smells, I am sure all the cats will like them.

Draw smells. I didn't think that would be happening anytime soon, though the idea was interesting. How would I go about this? Rub quills on the subjects' body before I drew them? Dip my nibs in their urine? No, me producing art for cats probably wasn't going to happen. I didn't say this, though. It seemed a bit unfair that Atherton had to do most of the accommodating in our relationship.

The sun slipped behind a cloud around two o'clock and this time didn't reappear. I tried to get comfortable and sipped more tea, but it wasn't working. Something was nibbling away at the back of my brain and I couldn't concentrate.

A part of me wasn't surprised when I heard a knock on the door and it turned out to be Josh. I had been expecting a visit from someone in Dell's camp for a couple of days. Josh, surrounded by an invisible cloud of stale cigarette scents, inched his way into the foyer and at my invitation took a seat on edge of the spool-backed bench on the wall behind the door. Hands twitching, he said he had been up to visit Irv's cabin and was stopping in to see if I needed any help. What he had been doing at Irv's cabin wasn't something he volunteered, and I didn't ask.

Thinking swiftly, I mentioned that I needed to mend a broken spindle on my brass headboard, and did he think that a chemical weld—basically a two-part epoxy for metal—would do the job? We discussed the merits of different brands of epoxies—by the way, Josh recommends J-B Weld—and then, when the subject was exhausted, I just flat out said that I knew about Irv and the gold and asked if that was why he had been up to the cabin.

Josh was surprised, but also looked relieved to be able to speak freely.

"I thought maybe he'd talked to you about it. Maybe asked you to keep his stash? He was real fond of you, Jillian."

"And I of him." This was a bit of revisionist history, but all in a good cause. "He didn't give me his gold, though."

"I can see that you liked him, what with you takin' in Irv's cats. No one else was willin'. Especially not that useless nephew. That one's mean through and through."

I nodded, hoping he would feel the need to fill the silence with something useful. Nature and Josh seemed to abhor a vacuum.

"Irv never did tell us where he found that gold. I was thinking it was maybe down one of those coyote holes his dad dug way back," Josh said eventually.

I didn't blink, but wanted to. So, Irv hadn't told his closest friends about where he found the gold. And if Josh could be misled—perhaps deliberately—into thinking that Irv had been working the old shafts, maybe the nephew had been, too. In fact, the more I thought about it, the more it made sense. Of course Irv lied about where he'd found the gold. These people were his friends, but gold was gold.

"I told the sheriff that I thought Wilkes killed Irv for his gold," I said softly. "But . . ."

"He doesn't believe you?" Josh sounded surprised.

"I think he believes me, but we haven't got any proof. It's all circumstantial evidence and Tyler can't take that to the DA."

"I'm sorry to hear that," Josh said, and I believe he meant it. "That bastard's gonna walk free and get the gold, too. It makes me mad enough to spit." To spit, but not to kill. Not mad enough to go to the police with his suspicions. He would leave that to me.

Well, fair enough.

"I don't think he'll go free. No, I don't think that at all." My voice sounded definite, so definite that I shocked myself.

"You think God'll put a hurt on him for killin' his uncle?" Josh was again taken aback.

I hesitated. I didn't think it was God who was going to get Wilkes; not directly. But someone or something was. Finally I said: "I think that what goes around comes around. No one gets away scot-free forever." I looked up at the top of the stairs where Atherton crouched. He was watching with unblinking eyes. The god of retribution would have just such a stare. I spoke again, this time talking to Atherton. "No, Wilkes is going to have to face the consequences of what he's done. Maybe not today or tomorrow. But eventually. Too many of us know. One way or another, he'll be punished."

Josh nodded, clearly hoping I was right.

What greater gift than the love of a cat?
                                    —Charles Dickens

————————

CHAPTER SEVENTEEN

I hate the basement of my house. It's dank in the winter and smells like bad breath in the summer. However, it's a great place for wine and storing daffodil bulbs. It was a bit late in the season but I decided to go ahead and plant the three-year-old King Alfred and Pheasant's Eye Narcissus I'd been storing and see what happened. Perhaps, like me, they were ready for rebirth and would seize the chance to live again.

I brought the bulbs upstairs but the world got dark before I was done sorting them into baskets. I looked out the window, feeling glum and unexpectedly a bit nervous. I thought suddenly about that poem by Robert Frost. You know, the one about the world ending in fire or ice? I didn't know which would be our fate, but felt pessimistically that we humans would probably have a hand in our destruction. Unless we got KO'd by a meteor from outer space first, of course. There are some scientists who believe this could happen.

What's wrong? Atherton asked, jumping onto the sill. The first fat drops of rain were splatting across the window and making the privet's limbs bow low and then spring back upright. Atherton's tail twitched, and I saw a ripple of unease travel across his skin. His dark coat appeared to creep toward his tail.

"I . . ." There was a weird light shimmering in the air, and the sky was swiftly covering up with sour clouds the color of old bruises. There were no silver linings there, just rancid things. Dangerous things. And they were starting to fall to the ground disguised as raindrops. I knew this storm, this dangerous thing whose color could not be found in any crayon box.

A pain stabbed behind my eyes and I exhaled slowly, trying not to jar my head. After a moment it passed, but I stayed by the window, staring out in reluctant fascination. The sky looked awful, like it had last Halloween. When I was hit by lightning. On that day there had also been sickly, leech-shaped clouds that hovered close to the earth and sucked the color out of the plants and dirt and even the air. Death's vampire had returned to Irish Camp, and was taking a long drink from our hill and draining the world of hope and perhaps life. It would drain me, too, if it got the chance.

"Fuck you," I muttered. I wasn't planning on giving the vampire any opportunity to get at me again.

Jillian? What are you thinking about? Do you see something?

I made myself release the dish towel I had been wringing in my hands. I forced my panting breath to slow.

"I'm tired of being afraid of storms," I said to Atherton, unwilling to admit to the whole vampire-cloud thing and how very afraid I was underneath my bravado. "Maybe it's stupid, but I feel like I need to hide. Now. Just because . . . because of the lightning. It feels like death. Or insanity." And I did want to hide. Because of my growing fear of the unnatural storm, the urge was illogically strong.

That seems wise, Jillian. I don't care for the smell of the air. It's bad—very bad. You must stay under cover.

Yes, I knew that hiding from the storm was the wise if undignified course. I knew that I should back away from the window, run for the stairs that led to the basement because something was coming, something was—

Before I could move, a feline scream of outrage and terror filled my head. The voice, perhaps audible but perhaps not, was desperate and impelled me to action. Sudden fear for Irv's cats—my cats—was a snake springing with fangs extended right at my heart, and it squeezed out all other emotion, even my terror of the storm. I had no more time to be afraid of the congealing clouds that looked like curdled egg or the frightening smell of ozone growing in the air; I could only hope that lightning wouldn't strike the same person twice, even if that person was stupid enough to go out in it.

"It's Day-O!" I cried, recognizing the cat's voice as I fumbled with the deadbolt on the front door. At last I popped the stubborn latch and Atherton and I raced out into the breaking storm, leaving the door open behind us. Ahead, I heard more feline screams and knew in my heart that the cats had finally decided to corner Wilkes— and he was fighting back. They were being hurt, perhaps badly.

A fiery lash whipped across the churning, yellowed sky, tearing the air the moment I stepped foot on the bare ground. The rain stopped, though, as if it preferred to watch from overhead until we knew what the outcome of this deadly confrontation would be. Lightning chased me up the hill.

"Hurry!" I gasped, but there was no need. Atherton is faster uphill than I am and had already pulled in front. I tried to keep up, but the air on the hillside had been replaced with something yellow and vile that had no oxygen. The vampire was closing in.

I didn't try to avoid the poison oak that day. I kept an eye out for holes that could break my ankle and brambles too thick to force my way through, but most of my attention was focused on our destination. We were heading for Irv's property. But not the cabin. The screaming was coming from somewhere to the southeast. Where Irv's old mine was. I knew—knew with the certainty of one guided by a higher power—that it was Wilkes out there, and that the damned idiot had actually been trying to work Irv's old shafts.

True hatred, the kind that wells up from the gut and soul, is pure and hot as molten gold. But more singeing even than hate is the fear of losing a loved one. And it can give us the strength to do and face things we never would otherwise. I refused to even consider that one of the cats might die.

Have you ever been in a fistfight? I hadn't until that day. As a girlie-girl I didn't spend my school-yard recesses brawling in the playground. I'd never boxed or wrestled. I wasn't adequately prepared for a physical confrontation. However, I did recall some advice given by a vice cop who came to talk to our gym class in high school on the subject of rape. He said you had to realize that if you decided to fight an attacker you were going to get hurt, and you couldn't let the sudden pain or shock deter you. I hardened my resolve. I would face whatever Wilkes threw at me.

A part of me wished desperately that Tyler was there. He would know what to do and wouldn't be afraid.

We broke through the manzanita and I saw Wilkes swing his shovel at Day-O. The world telescoped, like the lens of a camera that zoomed too quickly. For a moment I felt invisible, powerless, a ghost who could watch but not intervene. All I could do was emit a thin, almost silent scream.

Wilkes's head jerked in my direction. Day-O ducked

the swing, but the edge of the shovel caught him on the hip. Wilkes brought the shovel up again, but Dodge and Inky were on his back, claws tearing deeply. Wilkes reached over his shoulder and grabbed Dodge, ripping him off and flinging him against a tree. I heard the man snarl: a sound far uglier, more animalistic and more terrifying than any the cats were making. He seemed no longer human.

My body, acting of its own volition in spite of the obvious danger, kept moving at the cats' attacker. I had no weapons, not even claws, but I charged at Wilkes, also screaming like an animal and probably looking like one.

Lightning hit the ground in front of me, a battle-axe of light that for a moment was as solid as a wall. I swear I felt it singe my hair as I passed through it, jumping over the sudden crack where it clove the leaf-strewn earth.

Then Wilkes was there, raising his arms to swing. His shovel was aimed at my head.

No, if he had ever been a man, he was no longer. What faced me was some sort of demon, a half-bull whose misshapen head was outthrust, lips curled back from its teeth, murderous eyes completely insane and merciless.

I whirled away as he swiped at me with the shovel. I landed wrong, turning an ankle. I tried to jump away but he caught me from behind and jerked me like a rag doll, or like a terrier trying to snap a rat's neck. He stank, and his hands were appallingly strong. His nails were stained red—with soil, I assured myself, not cat blood. I watched as the clawed hand on my right arm let go of my flesh and clapped itself over my mouth, trying to stifle my screaming. He crushed my lips against my teeth and I tasted blood. Already hurt, I bit down hard into his hand, not caring what damage I did to my mouth.

Another cat hit him on the back, and then yet another.

We both staggered. He didn't let go, though, just moved his bloodied hand down to my neck. I tucked my chin down before he found my throat, and lashed backward at his shin. My sneakers did little damage, but we were on stony, unstable ground; shale slid under his boot and we both fell down the embankment. I saw cats go flying in all directions and prayed they escaped our crushing weight.

Had he landed on top of me, I wouldn't be around to tell the tale. The upthrust rocks we ended upon were sharp, and he was heavy enough to break my bones on them. But Wilkes was undermost as we toppled, and his cruel grip slipped from my throat at the moment of impact. More importantly, he dropped his shovel.

I heaved to the side immediately, rolling, twisting—anything to get away before he grabbed me again. Brambles clawed at me as I rolled, but I grasped their thorny lifeline and pulled myself to my feet.

Jillian, run!

I wanted to—believe me—but I wouldn't, simply couldn't, leave my cats to face this monster alone. They wouldn't leave, so neither would I.

I threw myself at the shovel, but didn't quite make it. Wilkes's hand closed on the handle. Then Day-O, Dodge and Inky landed on Wilkes again. Then Peaches and Holly and Blaze. I have never seen such ferocity in an animal attack. Lions of the Serengeti couldn't have matched it.

Lead him this way, Jillian! It was Atherton again. *Hurry!*

I looked toward his voice and he was perched on some ruined lumber that looked like a fallen scaffold. Not questioning his judgment, I abandoned the struggle for the shovel and scrambled over the rocky outcrop toward Atherton. As I got closer, I could see that what I had mistaken for a miniature gallows was actually the shattered frame of an old windlass. You found these over wells and coyote holes. Both were very dangerous.

I heard Wilkes and smelled him. He was right behind me. No longer trying to pull off the cats, he came on, intent now upon nothing except seeing me dead. Panic bade me hurry, but my limbs seemed unable to do my mind's bidding. I felt his hand on my bruised shoulder, and its brutal clasp was as agonizing as a branding iron pressed into my flesh. Darkness swam around me.

I fell again in the carpet of stabbing needles, and Wilkes kicked me, a blow to the ribs that would have been worse if I hadn't already been rolling away from his foot.

Don't freeze! I told myself. *Don't let pain deter you or you're dead.*

I fetched up against an oak, hard enough to knock my breath away. Wilkes staggered to my head and raised his foot again, prepared this time to stomp down with all his weight. The sole of his waffle-stomper was caked with red earth and pine needles, but it would crush my skull anyway and leave bloody footprints like those on Irv's floor. Only, this time no one would see them.

Atherton leapt at Wilkes's face, and I swear that I saw him rip off the man's eyelids and tear out his eyes. For a moment I saw Wilkes's gooey sockets, and then they were gone, drowned in a veil of blood and other ichors. His clawing hands reached for Atherton.

I knew in that instant that Atherton and the others would defend me to the end, even if it meant their deaths. I absolutely would not allow that. I had to stop this son of a bitch.

The rest happened very quickly. My painful last roll away from his crashing boot sent me into his legs, and simultaneously Wilkes screamed in rage as he toppled over. He staggered sideways, helped by a feeble kick from me, with an enraged cat still on his skull and five others on his back, shredding his clothing and flesh until bone showed through the bloodied layers. Then he was tottering at the edge of the sinkhole that had once been an old mine and possibly some unlucky miner's grave. He stepped hard onto the rusted hog wire that covered the opening, and I heard something snap.

I screamed a warning—at the cats, not Wilkes. At the last possible moment, Atherton and the other cats leapt away from Wilkes's falling body, landed, claws digging for traction on the slippery pine-needle carpet. Then Wilkes was gone. In front of me was only the empty spot where the monster had been.

After a moment there was a thud, a horrid, solid sound that was at once wet and crunchy. There was no more screaming, not from him and not from the panting cats. There was nothing. No moaning. No cursing. No noise of any kind. Even the wind was silenced. Wilkes was dead.

I knew of his death even before I rolled onto my knees and looked over the edge. His body was at the bottom of a coyote hole, one that had possibly killed other men, swallowing them without a trace and leaving only ghosts. Where Wilkes's soul had gone was anybody's guess. Not to Heaven; of that I am sure. But Hell-bound or earth-bound for his sins, it made no difference. And in that moment I just didn't care.

I fell over on my side and took several agonized breaths, letting my mind reconnect all the neural junctions that panic had severed. All at once I felt every cut and bruise and sprain.

Jillian, it isn't safe. Come away from the edge. I barely recognized Atherton's voice, but I obeyed it instinctively. It was all I could do to regain my knees and crawl a few feet away from the crumbling rim of the shaft. My ribs were a fiery agony and I could hardly endure the pain of drawing mouthfuls of needed air.

Overhead, the indifferent clouds looked down. They shed no tears. They threw no more lightning. Death's vampire had fed.

I didn't weep. I hadn't enough breath, and that bastard Wilkes didn't deserve it.

Be careless in your dress if you will, but keep a tidy soul.
—Mark Twain

CHAPTER EIGHTEEN

Eventually my lungs managed to draw air without pain. The world ceased pulsating and color returned to the earth, relieving my monochromatic horror. I sat up slowly. Mind and body were both beginning to function again, albeit under protest.

My first thought was that *Murderus-lopithecus* was dead—really, truly, actually dead—and though I should report it, I probably couldn't walk into the sheriff's office and claim to have just discovered the body while out on a walk. Leaving aside the little matter of the likelihood of someone who is highly allergic to poison oak casually taking a stroll through a noxious bower on a stormy day, or that I probably looked like I had just lost a fight with a wolverine, there was no way to hide the fact that there were claw and teeth marks—mine and the cats'—on Wilkes's face and body.

My second thought was that I could get rid of the DNA evidence under my own fingernails by scraping the skin out and using some bleach, and perhaps I might even be able to round up the cats and get them clean;

but even if I could reach the body, it wasn't as if I could put all the skin and blood back again. They might not be able to prove Irv's cats had been the ones to attack Wilkes, but the suspicion would certainly fall on them and the other strays. And society was not kind to animals who took human life—even if the animals were agents of justice.

"Shit."

I extricated myself from the clumps of musty-smelling mountain misery and limped over to a boulder beside the remains of the broken windlass that had once sat astride the coyote hole, both to think and because I found that my knees were still too weak to carry me much farther. I rubbed at my arms and legs, trying to brush off the sudden cold and fatigue that was creeping up them. But all I did was rub the pain of my scrapes and bruises deeper into the muscles. Around me, the wind whispered nervously and the trees shivered.

A small curl of steam rose up from the shaft, looking like a miniature ghost twisting helplessly in the skittish wind. Warm body, cold hole. This was a natural phenomenon. Still, I felt the tiny hairs at the back of my neck lift as I was reminded of the dust devil that had staggered to my door before dying on the stairs. Some of our natural phenomena were damned unnatural-looking and . . . well, I didn't want to be haunted by this vicious man in any way. I inched backward, avoiding the vapor.

Day-O appeared at my feet. His hair was standing on end and I could see blood on his mouth. I bent slowly, running my hands down his body, assuring myself that there were no bones broken; Wilkes had been swinging that shovel with lethal force. Wilkes's blood smudged my hands. I was repulsed, but relieved that none of the gore was Day-O's.

"Good kitty. Brave kitty," I said absently. My voice

was calm but my thoughts were beginning to race as I weighed the various options.

Day-O tolerated my touch for a moment and then dashed away. His eyes were wide and frightened, and he seemed confused by what had happened. I figured mine were probably the same. What the hell was I going to do?

My first review of circumstances said that the situation wasn't good. Being a law-abiding citizen, my instinct was to phone the authorities and report what had happened. But even after a second calculation, I could see that if I went public and told some version of the truth of what had happened—really any version—Tyler would have to arrest me. Certainly he would if the DA decided to prosecute. Not for murder, most likely, but perhaps involuntary manslaughter. If that came to pass and the case went to trial, would twelve honest men and true understand what had happened to Wilkes? Maybe. But the whole he-was-attacked-by-cats thing sounded awfully suspicious when my own obsession regarding Irv's murder was so much easier to understand. Would they not think I had simply taken it upon myself to get revenge? I had said some slightly incriminating things to Josh. And Tyler. Really, most everyone I had talked to in the last week knew that I suspected Wilkes.

The thought of facing Tyler made me shudder, and conjured up the tears I hadn't been able to find for Wilkes. I swiped at my face with my sleeve, not wanting that murderer's blood on my face.

Tyler might well think I was making it all up, or was crazy. It indeed sounded crazy to say that my cats attacked Wilkes, first to avenge Irv and then to save me. He might believe that I had flung Atherton at him myself. He'd likely call it self-defense; after all, Wilkes had had a shovel and I was clearly hurt. But a jury might not agree. After all, it was Wilkes who was dead. And again, either way it would draw attention to the cats. Dogs who attacked people were put down. I couldn't imagine a stray cat would get any better treatment—not when they got a look at Wilkes's face. Wounds on his arms could have been inflicted by the cats in self-defense. The rest, though . . .

"Damn." I knew then that, more than anything, I wanted to be with Tyler—if not for always then for as long as possible. I was skating on perilously thin ice and didn't know which way it would break if I stuck the pickax of hard truth into it.

On the other hand, I also knew that lies abrade the soul. They were grit that wore out even the most loving of relationships. Did I want to begin our time together with a huge lie?

No.

And yet, a lie seemed marginally better than falling through the ice and back into the cold place I had been living before Tyler pushed himself into my life. A part of me wanted to tell Tyler the truth, to confess everything and let the chips fall where they may, because without trust, without faith that he would understand, that he would believe me, there was no hope of love ever growing between us. You can't love what you can't trust.

But I could too easily picture Tyler before me, standing tall in his uniform, badge gleaming on his chest. One moment he was wearing the uniform and in the next the uniform was wearing him. First he was my lover; then he was The Law. Which Tyler would I be dealing with if I confessed? Would it be the man I had made love with, or the sheriff of Irish Camp who had sworn to uphold the rules and regulation of the land?

It would be Tyler, I decided, my lover who heard me out. I was ninety-nine percent sure that it would be the man and not the office that I dealt with, and he would be appalled and enraged, especially if I went to him now, as a victim, covered in mud and blood and bruises and said that Wilkes had attacked me. Those were good odds. You could take them to Vegas and stand to make a fortune.

But would I have good fortune with this? How well did I really know Tyler? I wasn't a child, or even an innocent who should be protected from the consequences of her actions. And to ask for Tyler's complicity in hiding Wilkes's death, or at least in covering up certain facts, was to shift the burden of my guilt onto him. Even if he could absolve my spiritual culpability—and that was unlikely, because I knew precisely what part I had played in this debacle—had I the right to ask? I had known all along that the cats' frustration was growing as the days passed and we failed to make any progress toward collecting proof that would meet the human standards of guilt. They had seemed driven, almost possessed, indulging in some very unnatural behavior. I had suspected all along that they would kill Wilkes if they could, and I hadn't stopped them—hadn't even warned them away. I had even thought about killing Wilkes, myself. In that respect, I was guilty of having a hand in planning Wilkes's death. In law, that is called premeditation, and I wouldn't buy my future peace of mind, or even my freedom, at Tyler's expense. That wasn't what a loving person would do. Tyler might be willing to shelter me—to lie for me—but I knew it would be at a great psychic cost to himself. I couldn't ask this of him, and he couldn't volunteer to do it without first being forced into knowledge about me that he'd rather not have. There were no take-backs in this situation, no stuffing the genie back in the bottle after it got out.

And I was fairly certain that he wouldn't protect the cats no matter what he did for me. After all, if I didn't kill Wilkes then someone else had. I think he would feel that someone or something had to be blamed in order to reassure himself that the public was safe. How could he responsibly believe that this had been a onetime aberration and that the cats would never hurt anyone again?

He couldn't. It was beyond him. It was beyond anyone who didn't know these animals as I did, to know that they were no threat now that Wilkes was dead and their compulsion toward vengeance was fulfilled.

So, I decided to split a few hairs and indulge a rationalization of two. I would trust—believe with my whole heart—that Tyler would protect me if I asked him to. But I would hold my silence on this matter to spare him worry and pain and professional conflict. It was an act of mercy, a belief in his goodness and his protective instincts, without any proof. That sounds crazy, but then I think we have already established that I am not entirely sane. And this is no more foolish than believing that cats can talk to me, is it?

And anyway, I finally decided, I was not ruining my life, or the cats', because Wilkes had been too stupid to realize that he wouldn't gain anything by killing his uncle for a played-out gold mine. No way. He had tried to kill me; I had fought back and now he was dead instead. That was justice.

So, for the second time in my life, I was going to break the law in a big way. I resolved that even if asked point-blank, I would not tell the truth, the whole truth, or any fraction of the truth. Nothing that endangered me or the cats or put Tyler in a difficult moral situation. It would be hard, but I would hold fast to this resolve.

Completely clear-headed, though still cold all the way to my soul, I fetched the shovel with which Wilkes had tried to kill me and threw it down the hole, that gaping wound in the earth that had not—and would not—heal in my lifetime. I closed my ears and ignored how the spade didn't hit stone but something softer that absorbed the blow.

I pushed my hair out of my eyes and looked tactically at the terrain we had fought over; it was time to start thinking like a general and not a foot soldier. The land was ringed almost all the way around by brambles and stony ground punctured with the spearlike trunks of cypress trees and bull pines. The cypresses weren't natives, but that hadn't stopped them from setting down deep roots like the rest of us immigrants; they'd be here until the Last Trumpet called. If I dragged some of the brambles across the one gap, it was doubtful that anything but birds would find their way into this place, even if someone brought in equipment to pull down Irv's cabin. That was good. Nevertheless, I decided to obscure things a bit further.

Atherton came back as I began dropping armloads of pine needles down over the corpse. It was unlikely that anyone would see Wilkes down there, even with a powerful flashlight, but I thought I'd make doubly sure that there was nothing to see should someone happen to be wandering around with a spotlight. I was careful in my work, skimming only the top layers of needles and making certain I left no obvious signs of trespass and tampering. Some of the needle thatch was roughed up in places, but there were tufts of cat hair lying about, which should tell a convincing if misleading tale of some feline having a showdown with a raccoon or coyote. It happened in these hills more often than people liked to believe. That would also explain any traces of blood.

Atherton jumped up on a stone slab and watched intently. He seemed to understand what I was doing. His fur was still standing on end and matted with gore in places, but he was calming down. The eyes that watched me were as wise as Solomon's, and they approved of my work.

"Atherton, how old are you?" I asked, suddenly curious. Who was this animal? Surely not just some stray cat.

He looked at me, either calculating or still genuinely disturbed enough to need to time to process the question.

"How many winters have you seen?" I asked, pulling back a step as a living blanket of ants came boiling out of the ground. I backed off a few steps, giving them room to organize. These ants had a nasty bite, and I didn't need any more body damage to hide or explain.

Many. How many I couldn't say for certain.

The vet had said that he thought Atherton was seven or eight but couldn't tell for sure.

"More than seven?" I asked.

Yes, many more than seven.

Many more.

"Did you have a . . . person before Irv?"

Yes, but she wasn't as kind as food man. She was . . . what you call crazy. I left when she died. I was free until the day that food man started hearing our voices. Then I belonged to him.

Atherton's answer made me sad and also a bit uneasy. It was the phrasing. *I was free until the day that food man started hearing our voices. Then I belonged to him.* It sounded like involuntary servitude. I didn't want him to feel that way about me.

"I guess that makes you a senior cat," I said.

I had heard of some cats living until twenty or so, but most only made it to about fifteen, and cats in the wild had even shorter lives. It was stupid to complain about biological destiny when the universe wasn't going to re-order itself to suit me, but I didn't want to lose anyone else. I had had enough of bad things: death, depression, hallucination, now murder. Still, what would mourning the inevitable avail me? I knew full well that it was like arguing about how many traumatized angels could dance on the head of a pin.

Don't worry, Atherton said kindly. His fur was now back in place and his eyes were relaxed. *Isn't it said that cats have nine lives? I'll be with you for a long time to come.*

I prayed it would be so.

"Was anyone hurt?" Anyone other than Wilkes, I meant.

Not badly. We are bruised and limping, but we live.

"Good. That's good." I put a hand against my ribs, trying to quiet the pain. "Could you go and tell the others that it would be best if they slept in the garage tonight? The side door is open. I want . . . It would be best—safest—if they remained out of sight for the next little while. Just in case the neighbors heard something and called Animal Control. We don't want anyone getting nabbed." Not with blood on them. I was being paranoid, but even small towns knew about DNA testing. "I'll bring out towels and food as soon as I get home."

And you want us hidden in case the sheep man comes to ask questions because Smelly butt is gone.

Atherton had a point. Tyler would probably be around once the inn noticed Wilkes was missing. Not because he suspected me of anything, but because I was the one who'd insisted that Wilkes killed his uncle, and would want to know about any suspicious behavior.

I took a long, slow breath and thought things through again. Should I begin this lie? Once started, it would take on a life of its own. I reminded myself that Tyler was a compassionate man, a committed one who still wore a cuff acquired in childhood to honor a soldier who never came home from Viet Nam. But there was no denying that such devotion to what he thought was right could work both ways. I trusted him ninety-nine percent, but that still left a single percent of doubt. Might he put together reports of animal fights and Wilkes vanishing and begin to wonder if they were related? He knew there was a played-out mine somewhere on the property and it wasn't too big a stretch to think that Wilkes might go looking for it.

I exhaled a long, loud breath. Until I had gotten involved with Tyler, I hadn't realized that there were so many gradations of the truth, and that I would spend so much of my time selecting which shade of gray I wanted to live in.

"Yes. Tyler is a friend but . . ." He was my friend, not the cats'. At least not in the way that I was their friend, their protector.

I understand. Atherton turned and walked away. He wasn't limping, but I could tell his muscles were strained. He'd left bloody paw prints on the rock. *We are grateful, Jillian. Not everyone wants us.*

His words hurt. Because they were true. No one wanted the strays, the castoffs. They were, to many people, just living garbage.

"You saved my life, Atherton. I think it's a push. Anyway, I want you. Others will too, I promise." And they would, if I had to bribe or blackmail them into it. We were having no more strays on our hill. By next winter, every cat would have a home.

I went back to the shaft. The hog wire that had covered it was buckled on the left and almost rusted through everywhere else. It wouldn't hold an adult's weight but would probably catch any child or dog that was unlucky enough to wander this way. I couldn't imagine anyone coming up here, but later I would need to find a better grating. Just in case. For now this would have to do. I bent down slowly, favoring my ribs, and pulled it back into place. Then I scattered more pine needles and downed limbs on top. I was sodden and cold but didn't stop until things looked pretty much as they had before our fight. The returning rain would also help wash away the red splotches on the rocks and Atherton's damning footprints.

Jillian? a distant voice called. *I hear a car on the road.*

"Coming." It was probably nothing, but I hurried as best I could.

Ants robed in angry orange were already busy crawling over the needles and down into the mineshaft. The drizzle didn't seem to bother them. I also saw the first of the yellowjackets arrive. Rain would not deter these aerial scavengers, either. There is another local name for these wasps: meat-bees. As a child I watched them strip a dead sparrow of its flesh in under an hour. Wilkes was bigger than a bird, but every obscuring bite was welcome. I had seen enough dead animals to know that blowflies would also come soon to lay their maggots in the corpse. They were always hungry and worked swiftly.

My stomach rolled over as I thought about the animal kingdom dining on Wilkes only yards from my neighbors, but a voice that could only have been mine said: "*Bon appetit.* And be swift about it."

I went home and looked after the cats. They assured me again as I wiped them down with a wet washcloth that they weren't badly hurt. It took almost the last of my strength to pour out food and water and to drag out all the linens in the cupboard for their bedding. Some of the cats were uncomfortable being indoors, but none protested when I explained that it was to keep them safe. I also left the door ajar so that they would know they were not prisoners.

I finally showered, taking inventory of my own hurts. I put antibiotic cream on my various scratches and bandaged the worst ones. The bruises would have to heal on their own; I wasn't going to a doctor.

Unable to put it off any longer, I dialed the sheriff's office. I knew Tyler was on duty and hoped that I could speak to him directly because, in spite of the shower, my jaw was locked tight and snapped painfully every time I forced it open.

A volunteer dispatcher answered. I didn't recognize his mellow baritone voice and worked especially hard to speak clearly. I managed, but felt like I was forcing open a pair of rusty scissors every time I spoke.

There was a rasping noise as he laid the phone against his shoulder and called to Tyler. I thought I heard him say, "It's your girlfriend."

Was I the girlfriend? Did people know about us already? I almost groaned. The garden path to carnal knowledge is rarely straight and narrow in a small town. And the woods of emotion are thick and obscuring, and there are plenty of side paths on which to go astray—paths that didn't lead to happily-ever-after even if they might be exciting. I wondered which path we were on and how many spectators and Peeping Toms were lurking in the shrubbery.

"Who was that?" I asked Tyler when he came on. I sounded pretty normal. For me. "He has a nice voice."

"Oscar Levoi. He's a retired policeman from Modesto who is helping out three days a week."

"That's great," I said, and it was. The sheriff's office couldn't run without volunteers.

"What's up?" Tyler asked. "Your jaw sounds a bit tight. Is the rain bothering you?"

It was raining now, a hard cleansing rain. I closed my eyes and picked a shade of gray that was very close to black. I promised that I wouldn't live in this darkness for long and that my only lies to Tyler from that day forward would be to protect him and the cats from what I had done to Wilkes.

"A bit. One of the cats got caught in a tree. Maybe a coyote treed it. There's quite a bit of fur about. Anyway, he started howling like blue bloody murder when it began to rain." I heard myself lie smoothly, not so much as hesitating as the word *murder* crossed my lips. "I got him out eventually but I'm kind of scratched up and have picked up a vile case of poison oak on my legs and face." It made me oddly happy that the last part was probably true. I was already beginning to itch. "I'm going to lay low for a couple of days, just until my face heals and I won't scare the neighbors."

"Poor Jillian. Those cats have been a burden and a half. You have a heart of gold to bother with them. Do you need me to bring you anything?" Tyler asked with his usual ready sympathy.

"Nope. I have chicken soup in the cupboard, baking soda for baths, and calamine lotion. I am set for a couple days in solitary. And maybe I'll finally get some work done. I've been lollygagging." I actually had stronger things than calamine lotion and baking soda, but didn't feel the need to go into why I required them. Vicodin or morphine for poison oak was a bit extreme.

"Are you sure you don't want me to stop by? I could come around nine tonight. I have to go to the hospital first. Three drunks got into a peeing contest down at The Mule. For round two they got up on the roof and tried to pee on the hardware store across the street."

"That old tin roof?" I was involuntarily distracted from my own problems. The Mule's tin roof had the steepest pitch I'd ever seen on a building. It was practically a church spire.

"Yes, and they promptly fell off. Onto Dell, who was refereeing. In front of a bunch of tourists from the Modesto Baptist Church. With their pants unzipped. All four of them are on their way to the hospital. Dell has a broken leg. The others are concussed, and two need stitches."

"Oh, for pity's sake!" I said, and then almost laughed. I sounded just like my mother whenever she found me in dirty clothes. Which was rather often when I was young.

"Unfortunately, there were no fatalities." Tyler's voice was dry.

"Think of the paperwork you've avoided by having them live," I said lightly. "I imagine that a corpse—let alone four—would be cause for a lot of red tape." I couldn't believe that I'd said that. I had gone from tempting Fate to taunting her.

"I think, in the long run, they'll cause me more work alive than dead." I heard Levoi laugh in the background, and then say something. Tyler snorted. "Anyhow, I can come by after I go by the hospital and look in on you."

"I hope I'm asleep by then. Antihistamines knock me out." This wasn't a lie either. Especially when you took them with Vicodin. "I'd just as soon sleep through the worst of this, anyway. I hate looking like a leprous tomato, and refuse to let anyone see me. Especially you."

"I don't blame you, though I doubt you look all that awful, even with a rash." I snorted, and he chuckled. "So, I'll call you tomorrow and see how you're doing. Maybe ply you with donuts and coffee." It probably wasn't wise to see Tyler until I had completely healed, since many of my bruises were clear hand or boot prints. I'd have to invent some excuse to put him off in the morning, but this promise of future contact made me feel better. This was going to be a long, lonely night. I needed to believe that better days were coming.

"Maybe, if the swelling has gone down. Good night, Tyler. Be safe—and stay away from falling drunks," I added, glad that he was at the office with someone else listening in. It meant that we had to keep things brief and superficial.

"Good night. And call if you need anything. I'm serious, Jillian. You're not alone anymore."

"I will," I said. But I wouldn't. Not until the marks of Cain had faded from my body. My mind was made up.

No matter the invitation from him, I would never ask Tyler to share the burden of what the cats and I had done to Wilkes. This was a good man, a kind one, and he would never be asked to compromise his standards, to obfuscate, to lie. "Good night."

I put the phone down. Atherton was there and I petted him gently. We were both too bruised for much physical contact.

I carry a snakebite kit in the car, purchased when Cal and I were fresh from the city and didn't know that such kits are usually ineffective and mostly unneeded in our part of town. Thriftiness wouldn't let me throw it out, but I was vaguely annoyed by my old city-girl naiveté every time I saw it peeping out from under the car blanket and snow shovel—neither of these items ever being needed, either, since I didn't go out in bad weather. But along with a scalpel, the kit also had cortisone cream. I hoped it was still effective. My ankles already felt like they were on fire, and the rash was spreading toward my knees. I was going to need something for the itching but wouldn't take the stronger drugs until I absolutely had to, because I didn't want to fall asleep and maybe get trapped in bad dreams. There *would* be dreams, of that I was certain. I was going to have a long, painful night.

Still, throbbing skin, bruised ribs and nightmares were far better than having my head caved in by Wilkes's boot and my body dumped down a coyote hole like his now was. Far, far better. I would cope.

"Atherton? Have you ever watched TV?"

What is tee-vee?

Appropriately, I showed him the wonders of *Nature* and the endangered snow leopards of the Himalayas.

Cats, as a class, have never completely got over the snootiness caused by the fact that in Ancient Egypt they were worshipped as gods.

—P. G. Wodehouse

CHAPTER NINETEEN

The day after Wilkes's death, Atherton had news. Mac-Duff, Annabelle Winslow's manx who lived on Green Street, had finally caught a glimpse of Wilkes on Friday night, as the murderer had been forced to park on Green Street when the inn's lot was full. He'd staggered toward the inn just before dawn carrying some kind of large pan and a lot of angry dejection that had led him to try and kick MacDuff, who'd unwisely gotten too close. It was Irv's gold pan he was carrying, I was betting. And he'd probably finally gotten a lesson in the difference between panning for gold nuggets and flakes, and in mining for ore or carrying on a dry dig. Of course, while this was interesting to know, and I was grateful for MacDuff for passing the info along, it was too late now to be of much use. Still, at least I now knew where Wilkes had been and what he'd been doing all the days and nights I couldn't find him in town.

It was four days before I saw Tyler again, and when I did it was in his office. Tyler was welcoming but a bit distant at first, perhaps because we weren't alone, or perhaps I had been putting him off with what might have seemed flimsy excuses and he was feeling a bit wary. Our favorite volunteer, retired officer Levoi, was there as well. I was surprised to find that he was a redhead.

I had taken the precaution of bringing in a . . . not a bribe; let's call it a distraction. A culinary sleight of hand that I had made before and which garnered a great deal of praise. It had taken the better part of the morning and emptying my spice cupboard, but I had managed to whip up my favorite show-off dessert, Pêche de Vigne. I had to sacrifice the last of the brandied peaches that Crystal had given me for Christmas, but it was worth it. Sliced thin, covered in chocolate ganache and then drenched in dark chocolate, the brandied peaches gave the dish a piquancy and sophistication that fresh peaches did not have. As distractions went, it was a pretty good one. Levoi went into immediate bliss and left Tyler and me alone to talk.

"We got word this morning about Wilkes being questioned in a homicide in Oklahoma," Tyler said, when Levoi had retreated to his desk out front with the dish of chocolates. I exhaled, bracing myself for the conversation I knew we had to have. But first Tyler would tell me about this homicide. There was about as much chance of this story having a happy ending as there was in a Sam Peckinpah movie. After all, Wilkes hadn't stayed in Okalahoma, gracing one of their jails.

Tyler went on: "His late girlfriend was killed in a hit-and-run. Actually a hit-and-hit-and-hit-and-run. Somebody ran her body over with a car three times. That has to be deliberate. Even Mister Magoo isn't that blind. There wasn't enough evidence to charge Wilkes, but the police there are pretty sure he's guilty. It turns out that he has a long history of violence against women."

I nodded. This didn't surprise me. Once a smelly-butt man, always a smelly-butt man. It was a comfort to know that he would never do anything cruel again.

"It sounds like something that cowardly weasel would do," I said, when it became apparent that I should comment. I knew my face was red, but maybe Tyler would put it down to the poison oak. "I'm very glad he's gone. He gave me the creeps."

"So you think that he really is gone?" Tyler's gaze was steady.

"Yes, he's gone. I hear that he skipped out on his bill at the inn—didn't even bother to pack his stuff." Atherton had heard this from Beaumont, the hotel's resident cat. I had also heard it from Crystal, who had a friend who worked at the establishment.

Tyler nodded, his expression as somber as I had ever seen it. "It seems that he was using Irv's gold panning supplies. We found them in his room. We also found the poker that killed Irv in his car. It was wrapped in a blanket in the trunk. I don't think there can be any innocent explanation for this." He paused. "It looks like you were right. The man is a murderer."

"I can't think of any innocent explanation for the poker," I agreed as I looked over at the window where Hula Girl was watching the birds. I probably didn't need to mention to Tyler that cats tend to be avian epicures, and that he should keep her indoors until nesting season was over. I tried to think of something else appropriate to say but my mind was nearly blank. I couldn't think of much of anything that wasn't some form of a lie, and I was getting tired of telling them. "Maybe Wilkes had an accident. The rivers are running fast with snowmelt this time of year. Or a mountain lion might have gotten him. It's wild country out here. Anything could happen."

"Maybe. That would explain his failing to pack up his

gear or take his car when he left." Tyler was still watching me. I could feel his gaze, and that day the weight of his regard was burdensome.

"Relax, Tyler," I said, managing a smile. "I promise that I didn't kill him for Irv's long-lost gold mine, so you don't have to worry about your love life becoming a conflict of interest on this case."

"That's good." Tyler nodded again. I can't say that he appeared relieved, but the shoulder seemed to relax a bit. He knows I'm a bad liar and was certain that I was telling the truth, however limited the selection. This shouldn't have surprised me. If anyone knew about shades of gray, it was a small-town sheriff. "I'm sure that if you ever killed anyone it would be in self-defense," he added.

This statement shook me a bit, and it was all I could do not to reach for my ribs where the print of Wilkes's boot was still visible, but I think I managed to keep my poker face in place.

"Or to protect someone else. Especially if they were defenseless." I thought I needed to make this point. "I could never stand by and watch someone smaller or more vulnerable being hurt."

Hula Girl jumped up onto the desk and regarded me with wide eyes. She couldn't understand Tyler's words, but mine were plain enough and she was feeling alarmed.

"I don't suppose you could. And that's as it should be." Tyler said slowly. "It's the job of the strong to protect the weak." He waited a moment for me to say something, but when I didn't his voice became brisk. "So, I've put out an APB on Wilkes and have told Dawg and Farland to keep an eye out on the country roads, just in case he's been hurt. If his body fell in the river, it will probably wash up downstream eventually, dead or alive."

"Probably. Though there is some hard water this time of year and lots of rocks where a body might get hung up. The water will go down eventually, but there are a lot of scavengers out there. He might never be found."

"I suppose it would be better if we didn't find him alive," Tyler said thoughtfully. "I like things tidy, but a murder trial would cost the county a lot of money."

I nodded. Tyler nodded, too. We shared a long look and I knew that we'd never discuss this again. Unless I brought the matter up. In that moment I thought of Cal and honesty. And regret.

"Levoi," Tyler called suddenly. "Bring back that chocolate. It's not nice to bogart the candy my woman made me."

"I wasn't bogarting," Levoi promised, but his voice was sticky with peach and chocolate, and almost half the truffles were gone.

I did laugh then, though it hurt my ribs. I hadn't heard anyone use the term *bogart* since smoking a joint behind the gym my freshman year at the Sadie Hawkins dance. I also didn't mind Tyler calling me his woman. It suggested that we had a future after all.

Suddenly, I knew what I needed to do.

"Never mind those. They'll just make you fat," I said. "Let me fix you some lunch. There's something I've been wanting to tell you anyway."

A strange expression flitted across his face. It looked a lot like relief. Maybe I had been acting more oddly than I realized. I hadn't meant to worry Tyler.

"Let me get my coat," he said.

Are you going to tell him about us? Hula Girl asked when Tyler's back was turned.

"Yes."

I smiled at Tyler as he escorted me to the office door and opened it for me. The bells clanged loudly.

"Tyler, have you ever heard of a horse whisperer?" I asked as the door closed behind us.

Whenever the cat of the house is black, the lasses of lovers will have no lack.

—*Folk Saying*

CHAPTER TWENTY

The phone began ringing two days after Wilkes's disappearance became generally known, which is to say that it was reported in the newspaper. It was my neighbors calling in with requests for cats—companion cats, playmate cats, mousers for barns and stables and basements. I knew right away that I had Crystal to thank for this. She had probably sat everyone down for a little one-on-one over tea and told them about Irv's strays and the missing nephew who would never help with his uncle's pets and then browbeat them into admitting that the cats were a neighborhood problem that Cal's widow "shouldn't have to deal with alone." And, as they always had done before, the neighbors came through. I think they were even glad to finally have a way to aid and comfort Cal's reclusive widow.

I live with some of the best people in the world.

Tyler was oddly accepting of my story about the talking cats. It turns out that he had a cousin who married a Sioux in South Dakota who actually is a horse whisperer. He said that he also knew I had some strong affinity with the animals after our run-in with the mountain lion. His only comment was that he was relieved that I spoke to the cats in English and didn't meow at them.

Crystal's birthday was coming up that next week, and she would be having a party just as she did every year. Many of her parties are fun because she doesn't mark the usual holidays. She has drummings at the solstices and equinoxes. She celebrates the butterflies' return from San Juan Capistrano, and every year on Ground Hog Day she has a bonfire and we all eat potatoes and corn on the cob roasted in the embers. Most fun of all, every June thirtieth she has an End of the Ice Age skinny-dipping and scotch-tasting party at the family's hot springs in Nevada City. I've attended most of these events, but Crystal knows that I don't usually do birthday parties anymore. I've always felt that when one has reached an age where you are lighting enough candles to set the frosting on fire it is probably time to stop playing with matches and accept the inevitable with some dignity. Also, nobody looks good in a party hat. If you think that you do, well . . . you're wrong.

Nevertheless, Crystal was having a party and she would expect me to be present at it. And it wouldn't be entirely horrible. There would be a piñata and some kind of stupid hats that would make my elderly and more stately neighbors look silly. Last year the theme was pirates, the year before tiaras, and the year before that cowboy hats—and everyone wore them. Gender did not get one excused from donning the party regalia. This year, the invitations had had a vaguely tropical feel, so I was hoping for maybe something simple like a flower to tuck behind our ears, but it was far more likely that we would be made to wearing Balinese headdresses or something with rubber fish.

"I think I'll ask Tyler to come this year. It'll be his

trial by fire," I said to Atherton, with a grin that wasn't very nice. "It would be good to expose him to some of Irish Camp's older traditions. Anyway, we can't keep things quiet too much longer. Everyone on the hill probably already knows that we're dating."

Sheep man will like this. Tiny Bubbles says the cats are coming too. Bird lady is making us our own piñata with catnip.

"Crystal would. She's very thoughtful," I added, thinking that I would not only bring Crystal her birthday present—a bootleg recording of Elvis Presley at a rehearsal session in Atlanta—but that I would denude the hillside of every daffodil and narcissus and take Crystal the largest, yellowest bouquet the town had ever seen. It would be a thank-you gift from the cats and me. Without her, we wouldn't have had as happy an ending.

Still smiling, I went to the phone to call Tyler.

EPILOGUE

So that's my story. Believe it or not as you choose.

If I am not yet completely happy in my secret life with cats, at least I am hopeful that someday I'll be used to it. In fact, I know that I prefer having the gift than not.

It isn't too surprising that Tyler eventually asked for a demonstration of Atherton's skills. Reluctant, but willing to make the effort, I sat Atherton down and asked him to tell me some office gossip from Hula and Sleepy. Atherton had glanced once at Tyler and then said: *meow*.

"Atherton?" I had asked aloud, and also silently. He never said *meow*. "Come on, Atherton."

But the cat had just looked at me and meowed again.

"What's wrong?" Tyler asked.

"He's not talking." This alarmed me. I suddenly wondered if all my bitching had finally been heard by the gods and if they had taken my gift away. Just when I was getting really upset at the idea Atherton grinned at me.

Got you, Jillian!

"What's he doing? What's that noise?" Tyler demanded.

"The cat's laughing," I said, feeling very relieved. "Felines have a strange sense of humor."

"Oh." Tyler thought about it. "That's weird, isn't it? I've never heard a cat make a noise like that."

I hugged him and then turned and scratched a still chuckling Atherton under the chin.

So . . . I survived each day after Cal died, but I didn't know why. Now I do. As it says in Ecclesiastes there is a time to weep and a time to laugh; a time to mourn and a time to dance. The wheel has turned and the season of grief has passed. I am Lazarus resurrected from an emotional grave. Like Lazarus, I suspect I will always be aware of the grave, but still I say, let the dance of life go on. I am certain that Cal wants me to be happy in this new existence, however strange it may be. Certainly, if he were here and I were gone, I would want the same for him.

I also know that he and Tyler would have liked each other. They are two of a kind, and I am fortunate beyond all reason to have had two such wonderful men in my life. Who says there isn't a God?

I am not the only one embarked on a new life. All of Irv's cats have first-rate homes now. Atherton stays with me and seems happy, so my home is good, too.

Tyler has set me an excellent example of how to deal with my human family, and I think that maybe this summer I'll ask my niece and nephew to visit. It would be a fine thing to get to know them, since they and my brother are probably all the blood kin I'll ever have. Besides, I'll have a cat and a sheriff to entertain them if they get bored gold panning with their eccentric aunt.

And I *will* be panning this summer. What Irv could find once I can find again, and I think that Irv would like it if I did. He'd have used the money from the gold to help stray cats, and so will I.

So, this is the end of the story and we must part company. Be well, gentle reader. Visit the Gold Country if you can—just stay away from the lightning, you hear? And be kind to the feral cats you find in the campgrounds and parks. *Hoc facite in meam commemorationem*—Do this in Irv's memory.

Author's Note

Dear Reader:

Gentlemen of seventeenth-century France had a social code that, roughly translated, went something like *"Inflict no pain, put everyone at ease and make them feel at home."* I try as an author to adopt this code and do nothing painful to my readers. Characters are another matter of course. They—and I—must suffer a bit or there isn't much of a story.

However, the pain of this book ended up hitting a bit closer to home than I ever planned or wanted. Last November, on the Tuesday after Thanksgiving, I had just finished spell-checking chapter five of this story and started dinner when I got word that my husband had had a heart attack. Suddenly, there I was, smelling turkey-curry soup burn on the stove while shouting questions over the phone to an EMT on a rescue helicopter, and facing the real possibility that I might be widowed before I could reach the hospital and say good-bye to my husband of twenty-eight years. Fortunately, all turned out well—a million thanks to the EMTs who were with my husband at the gym when the attack happened, and to the top-flight surgical team at Doctors Hospital in Modesto.

Still, I had a hard time coming back to this book, whose story about a widow was a little too near my own situation. Finishing it was an act of faith; all would be well for Jillian, and for me, too. Say some prayers for us, won't you? We could use them.

Every book must have a point of view. In this case, it's the less usual first person, the most intimate POV. It is sometimes fun to turn the world on its ear, to make people see things in a different way—hence the first-person narrative and the talking cat, Atherton.

There is a lot of me in this story, but I have never been hit by lightning. I do talk to cats. All the time. Atherton is one of them. We met at the Tuolumne County animal shelter and struck up an instant friendship. I went daily to visit, but all too soon he was adopted by a discerning family and I haven't seen him since. He has stayed with me in spirit, though, and I find myself watching for him from the corner of my eye when I am writing. He's my imaginary friend.

My own cat is aware of this spirit intruder, and she is at times both indignant and jealous. Sound too humanistic for an animal? I think not. As proof of this very human reaction, I offer the fact that it is only since I began writing about Atherton that Snowy has taken to slipping behind my desk and turning off the power strip that feeds electricity to my computer monitor. It's petty revenge—a very human thing to do, and she does it because she knows it annoys me.

Unlike Atherton and my own beloved kitty, Irish Camp is a made-up place, a romanticized composite of several gold-rush towns with a few extra things thrown in for good measure. There is no Viper's Hill and no Three-Legged Mule Saloon, and though we have many wonderful music festivals, none are held on the Saturday before Easter. If you would like to know more about the music scene visit www.fireonthemountain.com.

Likewise, the people in this story are also fictitious creations, and exist only in my imagination, though all of my real neighbors are as wonderful and kind as any I could imagine. The cats, however, are all quite genuine. You can visit them at the Tuolumne County Humane Society at 10040 Victoria Way in Jamestown, CA. Perhaps I'll see you there one day. I go every week so they can whisper in my ears while I gaze into the yellow, green and blue eyes that are windows into the feline soul.

By the way, they have some great dogs at the shelter, too. Alsfo and Branco and Sandy—and everyone—are all good dogs and are looking for loving homes. They send slobbery kisses your way. If you would like to see any of our cats or dogs, please visit us online at http://www.petfinder.com/shelters/CA71.html.

"The Kiss" appears courtesy of the author, Brian Jackson, and I am very grateful that he has allowed me to use it here.

Happy Reading, and you can always write to me at melaniejaxn@hotmail.com or PO Box 574 Sonora, CA 95370-0574, or visit my Web site www.melaniejackson.com.

If you would like to visit Atherton, he keeps a blog at My Space. The URL is www.myspace.com/athertoncat

Be well, my dears, and hug your loved ones—on two legs and four.

Melanie

✂

☐ **YES!**

Sign me up for the Love Spell Book Club and send my FREE BOOKS! If I choose to stay in the club, I will pay only $8.50* each month, a savings of $6.48!

NAME: _____

ADDRESS: _____

TELEPHONE: _____

EMAIL: _____

☐ I want to pay by credit card.

☐ VISA   ☐ MasterCard   ☐ DISCOVER

ACCOUNT #: _____

EXPIRATION DATE: _____

SIGNATURE: _____

Mail this page along with $2.00 shipping and handling to:
Love Spell Book Club
PO Box 6640
Wayne, PA 19087
Or fax (must include credit card information) to:
610-995-9274
You can also sign up online at **www.dorchesterpub.com**.

*Plus $2.00 for shipping. Offer open to residents of the U.S. and Canada only. Canadian residents please call 1-800-481-9191 for pricing information.

If under 18, a parent or guardian must sign. Terms, prices and conditions subject to change. Subscription subject to acceptance. Dorchester Publishing reserves the right to reject any order or cancel any subscription.